Spirit Born

SPIRIT BORN

To Alison

Good luck ♡

NICOLA HODGES

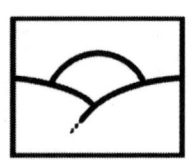

MORNING MIST
Poole
Dorset
BH16 6FH

Copyright © Nicola Hodges 2025

The right of Nicola Hodges to be identified as the author of this work has been asserted by him in accordance with the Copyright, Designs and Patents act 1988.

All the characters in this book are fictitious and any resemblance to actual persons is purely coincidental. Places are either of the author's imagination or are used fictitiously.

A CIP catalogue record for this book is available from the British Library

ISBN 9781068714870

Printed in Great Britain by
Biddles Books Limited, King's Lynn, Norfolk

Prologue

I was eighteen years old when I was reborn, thrust into an unfamiliar world and embroiled in a conflict whose origins eluded me. Even when the dust had settled, I still struggled to understand what was the truth and what had been the artful fabrications spun by a corrupted narcissist.

The Spirit Borns were aware of the acute threat Beau posed. He had been a stain on our eccentric faction for years, the proverbial bogeyman that had haunted every one of our stories, his malevolent energy casting a continual sense of unease amongst us.

Despite our best efforts, he had always remained one step ahead, a master of deception who lurked around every corner and disguised himself in the murky depths of each twisted shadow.

The hopes for an end to our war with him had rested on my shoulders for some time, relying solely on my fledgling skills as a Spirit Born. Yet internally, I was fighting an unforgiving battle within myself, trying to repel the malevolence living quietly inside me, a formidable demon that I found impossible to exorcise. It was like a tinder box waiting for a single spark to ignite an inferno, and my boundary between control and chaos seemed to blur more and more each day.

As I slowly came to my senses, my eyes stung with tears, and the acrid taste of ash filled my mouth, a tangible reminder of the destruction around me. While I had proven myself a potential asset to the bizarre band of individuals I had fought alongside against The Ungrounded, all that remained in front of me was the bitter taste of defeat, lingering in the air like a palpable presence.

My bloodshot eyes reflected the desolation I felt inside. Each ambitious dream I had nurtured had crumbled into dust, replaced by a profound sense of loss. It was hard to believe that our confrontation would spiral so disastrously out of control or that the price we would have to pay would be so steep, exacting a heavy toll on both sides.

As my vision grew sharper, the smoke billowing from the sprawling property ahead stretched towards me, its coarse tendrils attacking my nose and lungs. The once-clear night sky was now obscured by a dense cloud of black, and the oppressive heat made my skin prickle with discomfort.

As I surveyed the scene, the gravity of the devastation I had wrought upon those I loved registered. Not only had I become everything I despised about Beau, chasing the monster until I became one myself, but I had also failed the war heroes and healers trapped inside Red Rock's towering walls. The sandstone masonry glowed orange and red as flames licked in and out of every blown-out window, painting the night sky with an eerie glow.

In my ambitious fantasies, I had envisioned myself as the fearless leader of The Spirit Borns, the vanguard in our battle to maintain the fragile balance between the living and the dead.

However, my rise to that position had come at a steep price. I was the one person able to defend those I loved, but instead, virtually swaggering with pride, I had led the wolves to their door.

I closed my eyes, muttering in a delirious mantra. "Please, please, please," I whispered. "You can't be gone. You must have made it out."

But as I lay on the dampened grass, feeling the dew soak through my clothes and cool my skin, a howling emptiness resonated from my gut, telling me they were gone.

The daylight had yielded to the darkness, turning the sky into an inky canvas on which the fire could paint its destruction. Its voracious appetite devoured everything in its path, its thunderous roar like a freight train.

As I struggled to expel the smoke from my lungs in hacking throes, I had no desire to escape the flames. My sole impulse was to find my family, no matter how futile or suicidal the endeavour seemed.

I tightened my jaw, my teeth grinding as I growled to myself, forcing my body and mind past its physical limitations. "Move, Harper Reynolds-Woodbury. *Move.*"

I rolled onto all fours, a groan escaping my lips as what remained of my sandy curls fell around my face in bloodied clumps, but it wasn't being half-scalped that hurt.

As the adrenaline in my bloodstream dwindled, every movement sent pain radiating from the ravine-like gash in my thigh, leaving me reeling with nausea as my jeans became sticky with claret.

I tore a strip from my T-shirt and bit my lip to stifle my screams. As I wrapped it around the wound and tied it in place, the property's adjoining structures set alight, and the bare bones of the house were revealed, sticking up out of the flames like disjointed limbs trying to claw their way free of the inferno.

The once bright masonry succumbed to an ominous hue, rendering it unrecognisable. The intricate stone carvings of the aces of hearts, diamonds, clubs, and spades that had lined the gutters like curious gargoyles came tumbling down like children's building blocks, fracturing into jagged pieces at my feet.

A sharp crack cut through the cacophony of sounds as the final shards of the roof gave way. The floors collapsed under the weight like dominoes, one onto another, projecting fragments of burning rubble skywards. Against the backdrop of billowing smoke, the fiery debris glimmered like a swarm of fireflies, creating a breathtaking yet haunting effect.

I gritted my teeth, suppressing the pain and forcing myself onward. I had already lost one of my loved ones to Beau's lunacy, and I couldn't bear the thought of losing any others due to my own.

Feeling soil clogging my nails, I plunged my fingers deep into the lawn. Clenching my trembling hands, slick with blood, around fistfuls of grass, I dragged myself forward, clawing and thrashing like a dying animal as toxic fumes swirled around me.

As I reached the driveway encircling the house, my crawl slowed, and each agonising push felt like a herculean task. The world around me seemed to ripple and distort as I shook my head, struggling to fight off the encroaching unconsciousness.

Physically, I couldn't edge any closer to the flames, but I couldn't summon the strength to turn back, either. I had devoured the last of the adrenaline that had been fuelling my body, pushing through the ordeal, leaving me depleted and suffering in its absence.

Every jarring stab of pain was a reminder of the limitations my injuries had imposed on me as my muscles seized, feeling like iron against my bones.

As I lay dying, I turned onto my back, my anguished cries carrying the names of my loved ones into the boundless sky. Tears cascaded down my face, washing away the soot on my cheeks as my voice grew hoarse. My ash-mottled eyelashes fluttered weakly as my mind fought against my battered body, willing it to survive.

In the distance, the comforting wail of sirens echoed through the valley. However, we were in the middle of nowhere, and the grim reality set in that no rescuer would arrive in time to save me, the house, or those dear to me.

But as I faded in and out of awareness, I found myself grasping onto the sound of a voice, its fraught and anxious tone barely discernible amidst the chaos of the blaze and my own ragged coughing.

The billowing smoke enveloped my surroundings, making it difficult to see through the haze. My raw, stinging eyes strained to make out any signs of life amidst the chaotic scene, but the twisted remains of the house stood unchanged, with no one miraculously emerging from the debris. And with the emergency services miles away, nobody had yet come to my aid.

However, I still heard it, the voice growing progressively louder, calling my name.

"This is it," I slurred, my words barely coherent. "It's all over. I'm going home."

The battles I fought, both triumphant and tragic, had led me to the inevitable embrace of death. It was as if it beckoned me back to the beginning of my journey, to a time of innocence and purity when the mistakes I would later make had not yet wrought their trail of utter destruction.

Through the haze of smoke, a figure emerged, her tiny body convulsing with violent coughs as she stumbled closer. Standing over me, her muscles taut with tension, she swiftly threw her jacket over her head, seeking refuge from the relentless advance of the flames.

Despite the heat, her complexion was as pale as the flakes of ash that peppered her ebony hair like snow. Her trembling voice called my name as her unblinking eyes danced across my body. Her gaze lingered on each injury before settling on the telltale charring on my limbs that she had seen firsthand once before.

Her hazel eyes narrowed, blazing with palpable fury. Her jaw tightened, and the veins in her neck stood out like cords, visibly pulsing with each frenzied beat of her heart.

She stood frozen, her hands trembling as she brought them to her mouth, her chest heaving. "Christ, he... he did this to you?" she asked, her voice wavering between shock and rage.

An explosion erupted deep within the bowels of the property, the shockwave rippling through the earth and stunning her into action. She grabbed my ankles, throwing all the weight her diminutive frame granted her into tugging me to safety.

I struggled against her grip like a rabid animal, clawing desperately at her hands. "No, Lola!" I shouted. "They're in there!"

Prologue

Once we reached a safe enough distance where the flames no longer posed an immediate threat, Lola carefully lowered my legs to the ground. She kneeled, pulled my head onto her lap, and gently rocked me, providing a soothing rhythm that helped counteract the devastation surrounding us.

Her face was a portrait of empathy as her fingers delicately traced a path along the contours of my face, gently brushing away the tears cascading down my cheeks with her thumbs.

Lola's gaze held mine with a gentle intensity. "I know, honey. And I'm so sorry," she soothed. "But Red Rock's boundary's been broken, and the house's foundations will be wrecked. We need to get out of here."

"But they're still inside."

Lola gestured towards the ruins of Red Rock. "Look at this place," she said. "They can't be. Deep down, you know that."

"But... ambulances are coming," I argued, my voice hoarse and unconvincing.

"Yes, but the *police* will be on their way as well, and what would we tell them?" Lola reasoned, her eyes widening. "We can't be here when they arrive."

My bottom lip trembled as the weight of Lola's words sank in. "I can't just leave them," I said.

"I promise we'll come back, but right now, we need to get you to a hospital," she said, concern etched onto her face as her eyes twitched towards the bloodied dressing on my thigh. "Your leg, how bad is it?"

I bit my lip, my entire body tensing in anticipation of the pain as Lola gently pulled the makeshift bandage free. The jagged six-inch-long cut had soaked my jeans, turning them a vivid shade of crimson that infused the smoky air with the sickeningly sweet smell of arterial blood.

Lola recoiled, swallowing hard as her eyes widened. The concern on her face mounted, teetering on the brink of panic. "There's so much blood," she said. "How long has it been like this?"

Her words sounded muffled and indistinct as if I were submerged underwater. The world around me took on a surreal quality, with colours and sounds blending together in a disorienting kaleidoscope.

Lola tore off her studded belt and used it as a makeshift tourniquet. As she wrapped it tightly above the wound to stem the flow of blood, she noticed my eyes shifting in and out of focus, alternating between moments of clarity and haziness.

Her voice grew louder as she tapped my cheeks roughly, her face inches from mine. "Harper, stay with me!" she yelled. "Come on. Let's get you up, okay? We need to leave."

I howled as Lola dragged me to my feet, wrapping my arm over her shoulder and gripping my waist to stabilise me. Pulling her phone from her back pocket, her fingers trembled as she dialled.

Lola spoke into her phone, her voice clipped with panic. "I've got her, but it's bad. I don't know how she's even alive right now..." she stammered. "No, she was alone. He's still out there... Yes, hospital...now."

As Lola finished the call, my vision swirled, mimicking the smoke encircling us. My head slumped backwards as my body folded into Lola's like a marionette abandoned by its puppeteer and freed from its strings.

Lola begged me to stay awake, her voice low and urgent, as if she was trying to keep me tethered to life. As her pleas faded into the distance, I wanted to fight it, but it was like trying to hold back the tide. The darkness crept in, tugging at the edges of my awareness, eroding the boundaries of the world around me until they gave way.

There was only peace in the sweet relief of unconsciousness, a blissful nothingness that was a welcome respite to the pain and sorrow as Lola's voice faded into a whisper. "Just hold on."

Chapter One

The locals say our family is cursed, and every morning, their words seem to hold true.

Standing at my kitchen sink, I tried to ignore the gooseflesh mottling my skin as I absentmindedly brushed zesty-smelling suds from my dishes. I tried to force the eerie whisperings of the unseen voices I had heard that morning into the darkest corners of my subconscious, locking them into a Pandora's box that I had never dared open.

Every morning had been the same for as long as I could remember, the voices lingering like a dark stain that refused to budge. I would wake in sheets clinging to my body like a second skin with their dampness as the indistinct voices came from everywhere and nowhere all at once, like an unseen force that was beyond my control.

My chest would tighten, and cold beads of sweat would trickle down my temples as the voices whispered incomprehensibly through the ether, making it impossible to concentrate on anything else.

I often questioned whether they were echoes from my past, memories I had buried deep within me that I hadn't been able to confront or didn't want to remember.

But as time passed, the possibility that the voices were a figment of my imagination faded away, and fear took hold of me. I started to doubt my own sanity, wondering if the prolonged isolation that the war had brought me had caused my psyche to fracture and that my grip on reality was slipping. However, if it was the latter, my mind had been in peril for some time.

I had always managed to keep their existence a secret and lie convincingly enough to myself about their origins, blaming an overactive imagination. Still, it was something was always niggling at the back of my mind, especially with the stories that encircled our family home at Red Rock Manor, in which some of its earlier inhabitants had lost their minds and committed unspeakable atrocities.

Every morning, it was all too easy to get swept up by a sea of negative thoughts. No matter the season, the little gamekeeper's cottage I called home at the edge of the property line was always cast in Red Rock's overbearing shadow, the enveloping darkness blanketing the mossy cobbles and thatched roof in a continual shroud of mist.

Out of the window, Red Rock stood tall and imposing on the brow of a gentle slope like a stone giant. The weathered exterior bore witness to the centuries that had passed since its creation as its eye-like windows cast their calculating gaze over the land, staring directly at me, lacing my spine with ice.

Despite having grown up there, I had always looked at the house as an intimidating place, somewhere that felt more like an entity than a building, with a personality as unique and enigmatic as the ancient ground it was anchored to.

As I locked eyes with the giant, I plunged my hands back into the soothing warmth of the water, the remaining dishes and cutlery concealed by a blanket of frothy suds.

An abrupt pounding at the door jolted me from my trance. The rusting hinges rattled metallically in protest, vibrating through the thick wood. In the slick water, my hand slipped, and immediately, something sharp pierced my skin.

As I raised my hands, the suds turned crimson as a knife splashed into the water. Blood rippled through the water like spilt ink until my entire sink was tainted.

The sickly odour of blood, combined with the scent of the dish soap, turned my stomach as I grabbed a dishcloth and wrapped it around the cut on my palm.

My sister's voice rang from the other side of the door, her tone sharp and insistent. "Harper? Are you alive in there?"

"Coming," I called.

I combed my uninjured fingers through my sandy hair and answered the door.

Sophia entered with an almost statuesque poise, exuding an air of confidence as her eyes sparkled with a radiance that lit up the room and lent an air of magic to the atmosphere. The brisk autumn wind rushed in with her, carrying with it the rich smell of the earth as crisping leaves tumbled onto my welcome mat.

Chapter One

Her designer heels struck a rhythmic beat against the stone floor as she strode towards me, arms outstretched, beckoning me into her loving embrace.

Her unparalleled elegance never failed to leave me self-consciously retreating into myself in her presence. Despite being over a decade my senior, her appearance was timeless, her supple skin seeming to glow from within. Her shimmering platinum hair fell in waves like liquid gold around her bust, starkly contrasting her lips, always carefully painted in the only shade of lipstick she ever wore, a vivid pillar-box red. Even with the chaos of Hitler's war confining us to the safety of the grounds and never receiving visitors, she was never seen without a full face of makeup.

"Harper, darling, where were you?" she asked, her brows knitting together. "You missed breakfast. *Again.*"

"I know, I'm sorry. I guess I just lost track of time," I said, shrugging as I avoided Sophia's keen gaze.

Sophia cocked her head, her brows raised as she crossed her arms. "You're a terrible liar, Harper," she said, a hint of amusement in her voice. "Come on, out with it. Are you finding it tough being here? There's no shame in coming home if you are. I mean, there's nothing here for you."

Whilst I could never confess it to my family, my damp little cottage provided a buffer from the voices clamouring for my attention every morning.

For some reason, at Red Rock, they were louder, angrier. The fear of the inevitable discovery of my secret was what fuelled the move. However, I had another excuse for shunning the grandiose house for the crumbling shack that sat in its shadow.

Glancing downwards, I shrugged. "Yes, there is. It's where my parents lived."

"The only parent you've ever known lives at Red Rock," Sophia said stiffly.

"You know what I mean. My birth parents."

"They lived here for a week at most," Sophia scoffed, rolling her vivid blue eyes. "And no one even knew they were squatting down here."

Moving into the gamekeeper's cottage hadn't been a whimsical decision. It had been a place I had always felt drawn to. My birth parents had briefly lived in it before I was born.

I had hoped that living there would help me unearth the truth behind their disappearance or discover what tragedy had resulted in me being abandoned on Red Rock's doorstep without so much as a note. But in the past year that I had lived under its thatched roof, I hadn't learned anything of significance.

The only information I knew about my parents and my birth were the stories my family had told me.

I was found before the light had stretched across the neatly manicured lawns, swaddled in bloodied rags like some gorily wrapped gift by our beloved housekeeper Annabelle as she ventured outside to fetch the morning paper.

She wrapped me in freshly washed linens and clutched me to her breast, gazing down at me with a mixture of wonder and concern as my new family grouped around her.

Sophia joined my new father, brother William, and his best friend Alfie as they threw jackets over their nightwear and tentatively ventured outside, eager to find any clue where I'd come from.

The sky was painted in a seamless masterpiece of colour as the first light of dawn fell over Red Rock. Their breath created misty clouds around them as every rustle of leaves and every minute sound made them stop and listen intently.

On the grass, intermingled with the morning dew that sparkled atop the sea of green like a million tiny diamonds, was a subtle but clear trail of blood on the gravel path that split Red Rock's gardens in two and led towards the gamekeeper's cottage.

When they reached the damp building, as Sophia fought back the bile threatening to overflow her throat, they found piles of blood-soaked rags by the front door. It had been left ajar, with just enough space for the wind to whistle eerily through the narrow opening. The sound echoed into the house, creating a haunting melody that rose and fell with every gust.

The cottage had looked cold and utterly devoid of life, the air thick with the musty scent of neglect. Still, they continued inside. The silence was only punctuated by the creaking of the narrow staircase beneath them as they apprehensively followed the spots of blood staining the floor to the small bedroom upstairs.

Whilst the metallic odour of blood permeated the air, my adoptive family never found its source despite searching with an almost police-like diligence. Nothing was out of place, yet the overbearing scent of death hung in the air like an unspoken secret.

Chapter One

Despite the ground being sodden by rain the night before, not a single footprint could be found. Consequently, with no sign of my parents, speculation about their disappearance was rife at Red Rock in the days that followed.

Each family member had their own theory, ranging from the outlandish to the downright macabre, and the lack of concrete evidence fuelled their imaginations. My new father, however, remained neutral, an impartial observer who refused to be swayed by gossip or suspicion. His only focus was the welfare of his unexpected new daughter.

My adoptive father, Peter Reynolds-Woodbury, knew from the charities that he and his late wife supported that the outlook for children under the care of the authorities was bleak, so he decided to raise me as a Reynolds-Woodbury, or an "RW" as we affectionately called ourselves, and should anyone ask, I had arrived via one of my father's foundations.

As the days turned into weeks, my father's unwavering commitment to his parental role had a positive impact on my family. The wild speculation gave way to a sense of calm and rationality as they worked together to support the development of the newest Reynolds-Woodbury daughter.

That was back when he still had control of himself and his mind. Before the malevolent force at the heart of Red Rock had sunk its teeth into him, twisting him into a shadow of his former self and forcing him into the wheelchair that he'd not left for over a decade.

I raised my hand, shaking my head. "It doesn't matter. This house is the only connection I have to them."

Noticing the bloodstained towel wrapped around my palm, Sophia's eyes widened, a look of sisterly concern softening her features further as she reached towards me. "What happened?"

Even when concerned, Sophia's words carried a seductive purr, making listening to anything she said enthralling.

I drew my hand back, holding it in the other as I forced a smile onto my face and a joking tone into my voice. "It's nothing. If anything, I blame you. My hand slipped when you knocked on the door."

"Shall we have Annie take a look at it?" Sophia asked.

I shook my head. "She's busy enough with the house. Honestly, it's fine. A bandage will do, I don't even really feel it anyway."

"Then do you think you'll be up for some target practice today?" Sophia asked, with a clear tone of enthusiasm in her voice. "I've already set us up on the lawn; we're ready to go."

My face tightened, my jaw rigid as I winced. "Do we need to?"

Sophia chewed her lip and nodded as an almost childlike look of apprehension washed over her. "It was a bad night."

Out of fear of the house's retaliation, my family and I never spoke openly about our blatant fear of Red Rock. Once dawn had broken, the house seemed to smile down on us again, helping us to nervously laugh off the unsettling noises we'd heard during the night, like fingernails clawing on wood and footsteps pacing empty halls.

In dealing with our anxieties surrounding the malevolence festering at Red Rock's heart, we found that one of the most effective coping mechanisms was target practice on our lawns. Despite my father and brother William's decorated military service, Sophia's rifle skills were unmatched in the house, a fact that William and his best friend Alfie had always found infuriating.

However, rather than a source of competition, for me, the hobby was a source of calm and empowerment that I couldn't recreate elsewhere.

When everything around us seemed chaotic and uncertain, it served as a much-needed oasis of control. It had become the perfect antidote to soothe our wracked nerves after what we only ever described as a "bad night", and for some reason, there had been far more bad nights than good in recent months.

As a result, Sophia had been clinging to our hobby like a life raft in stormy seas. With the losses she had already suffered, her heartbreak followed her like a shadow, and I could never refuse her.

Red Rock's name alone was enough to evoke a sense of dread that lingered in the minds of anyone who knew its history. It was a place where the past and present coexisted in a delicate balance, creating an unsettling atmosphere that blurred the lines between reality and myth.

The house was nestled in a tranquil valley, surrounded by towering trees and an ocean of emerald fields. However, the serene facade belied a grim history that could still be felt in the air.

A notorious battle had taken place here during the English Civil War, leaving a trail of death and destruction in its wake. Even now, centuries later, every dark corner of the house seemed to whisper the memories of the conflict, like a living, breathing museum, pressing onto anyone who entered the fragility of life.

Chapter One

The fighting had been so ferocious, so bloody, that the ground and stones beneath the land had forever been stained crimson with the blood of the fallen.

The battlefield was desecrated when these rocks were quarried for their distinctive colouring to construct the early manor's foundations. In older sections of the cellar, the ghastly red stones could still be seen, a lasting testament to the land's gruesome history.

Whenever we suffered a heavy downpour, the cellar would inevitably flood, and the stones would appear to bleed, with small rivulets seeping out of every vivid crevice.

The resulting pools of claret-coloured water would linger for days after a storm, staining our shoes and clothing if we ventured below ground for a bottle of wine.

Moreover, it was where the idea of the curse was formed. After violating the battlefield and disturbing the war graves of countless soldiers, the Reynolds-Woodbury family endured loss after loss as all its children suffered and died under Red Rock's roof. The only survivors were those shipped off to relatives or boarding schools until adulthood.

With the gamekeeper's cottage at our backs, Sophia looped her arm in mine. I finally felt the sun on my face as we walked the gravel path to Red Rock that split the lush gardens in two, feeling its towering sandstone walls beckoning me forward. As we walked, the melodious chirping of birds blended seamlessly with the blessings of nature.

The first crisping leaves of Autumn crunched beneath our feet as summer relinquished its assault of fresh bloom and gave way to a diversity of vibrant oranges and fiery reds.

It was a season that signalled change, a time for renewal and rebirth. The autumnal landscape seemed to mirror my inner state, shedding the feeling of stagnation I felt and making way for the new. It represented a shift away from the monotony of the war raging in Europe and a chance to embrace a new perspective on life and see the world through a different lens.

It felt as if life couldn't continue until Hitler's madness had been quashed as we lived in a perpetual state of uncertainty. However, news on the war's progress was scarce, especially in our quiet corner of the Kent countryside.

Adding to the tension was my father's explosive anxiety. The mere mentioning of the war, or anything he and William had encountered whilst serving overseas, was enough to trigger an outburst. Even discussing Red

Rock's history set off bouts of wild hysteria, so both were considered topics to avoid at all costs.

To keep him docile, we refrained from listening to the radio, opting for the gentle hum of the phonograph or Sophia and Alfie's talents at the piano. Despite our best efforts to ignore it, my father's mysterious illness was a constant presence in our lives, never discussed but always feared, like the house itself come nightfall.

Our family's experience during the war was one of relatively good fortune compared to many others. Officer's positions afforded William and my father a degree of safety from the dangers on the battlefield. Unfortunately, that wasn't enough to save them from both being injured during the invasion of Normandy, after which they had both been forced home indefinitely.

Meanwhile, Alfie's chronic asthma had rendered him unfit for military service and barred him from serving his country, a fact he had struggled to come to terms with ever since. But it meant that our family was among the fortunate few who had survived the war relatively unscathed.

Sophia's fiancé Nick, however, had not been so lucky, and we'd not heard from him for years. As she continually twirled the diamond engagement ring sparkling from her finger, it was clear that Sophia's troubled mind often wandered to where he was. But she never aired her fears to anyone, as though she believed confessing them aloud would make them real and that her silence would keep him safe.

Chapter Two

As we neared Red Rock, I felt its inherent magnetism, as though I'd been tethered to the structure itself.

The grounds surrounding the house hosted a symphony of vibrant wildflowers, from the richest purples to the softest pastels. Sculptures and topiary designs dotted around the estate were refined and spoke to the family's love of the arts.

The house had been in the family for centuries. Each generation had left its mark on it, adding a wing, tower or other attribute that showcased their individuality and prosperity. As a result, the house had continually grown, like it was a living beast of granite and marble with a distinct character and personality of its own.

With a radiant smile, Sophia eagerly pulled my body into hers as the wind tumbled through the strands of hair framing her face. "You'd have been so proud of me this morning. I brought up last night's events at breakfast."

I arched one brow as I shifted my gaze towards Sophia, my voice laced with scepticism. "Really? Is that...wise with father?" I asked carefully.

"It was before Annie had gotten him up and dressed for the day. But..." Sophia paused, raising one finger and ushering silence. "Hold on."

Her demeanour shifted, slipping into a revered silence as we passed The Garden of The Eight, the sweet fragrance of its white lilies permeating the air. My heart raced in tandem with our quickened steps as we bowed our heads, lowering our gaze to our feet. The lilies' delicate petals nodded as if acknowledging our appearance as the sound of rippling water whispered faintly on the breeze.

At the end of the rear lawn was a meticulously designed statue garden of angelic children, surrounding a fountain bordered by stone benches and lily bushes. The sunlight played off the water's surface, pure and pristine.

Visually, it was stunning, a perfect example of the gothic artistry that Red Rock was renowned for, but anyone who knew the house's history knew of the grief that The Garden of The Eight had been born of. The tears that had been shed and the sorrow that had been felt were all embodied within the garden's tranquil beauty.

It was created by a devoted Reynolds-Woodbury mother blessed with eight children. It was a rare time when the house was vibrant with life as its occupants successfully fought back the darkness that had taken root within Red Rock's walls. However, this happiness was not something the house would abide for long.

When the Spanish flu broke out in 1918 and ravaged the world, it saw the opportunity to regain control as the disease crept inside the house and prowled the halls, mercilessly picking off the children one by one.

Their mother, inconsolable with grief, couldn't bear the thought of never seeing her children again. Taking matters into her own hands, she commissioned a gifted sculptor to create a tribute to her children that would stand the test of time.

With each child that passed, a statue was created that matched their exact likeness. Each was as unique as their personalities, with every feature and detail meticulously captured.

Determined to keep their memory alive, it gave the grieving mother comfort to be able to look out over the grounds and see her children at play, frozen in time. She never imagined that little by little, the garden would continue to grow until the house fell silent and lifeless.

Although the mother survived the outbreak, staying in the statues' constant company gradually chipped away at the woman's resolve. As weeks turned into months, she slipped further into a state of madness. Tormented by the lifeless statues of her children, she was left vulnerable to Red Rock's sinister forces, and she became another one of its victims.

The garden was another area to which we respectfully gave a wide berth. We had been the only Reynolds-Woodbury children to survive into adulthood under Red Rock's roof for centuries, and at every opportunity, the house seemed keen to remind us of that.

Unfortunately, the gravel path to and from the gamekeeper's cottage ran parallel to The Garden of The Eight, making it unavoidable.

As the sound of the babbling fountain faded into the distance behind us, an unbridled burst of a child's laughter briefly pierced through the rustling leaves. The laughter was like a call to the birds, who responded with a chorus of eerie song, their haunting melodies blending with the child's glee.

Chapter Two

The high-pitched tone carried far and wide, resonating with my surroundings and filling the air with a sense of innocence. I could feel the voice as much as I could hear it, like a physical force reverberating through my body. It was as though I had stumbled upon something beyond my understanding or that carried a message I wasn't supposed to hear.

The fine hair on my arms stood erect, tickling my shirt sleeves as my body grew tense and my heart raced in anticipation.

My grip on Sophia's arm tightened, my nails digging into her skin as my eyes widened. "Did you hear that?"

"Hear what?" Sophia asked, her eyes narrowing as she shook her head. "You're not trying to scare me, are you? I get enough of that from the boys."

Sophia caught her bottom lip between her teeth; the creases on her face and the subtle twitching of her fingers spoke volumes about her concerns.

Her makeup was thicker than usual, obscuring the dark under-eye shadows and pallid complexion that indicated a restless night.

Despite her efforts to appear composed, her sluggish movements, punctuated by repeated yawns, betrayed the depths of her exhaustion. She needed comfort, someone to listen to her fears rather than add to them. As I offered a sympathetic smile, the tension in her face eased.

"Nothing, it was just the wind," I smiled and jostled her arm. "Go on. You were telling me about your morning."

"Right. Well, before Father came down for breakfast, I brought up Red Rock with William and Alfie."

"I can't imagine that went well," I said dubiously, my brows raised.

Sophia nudged me in the ribs playfully. "I thought you'd be there to back me up. But they just want to bury their heads in the sand."

"Sorry, Soph," I smiled apologetically. "You're not the only one struggling to sleep right now."

An expression of empathy fell over Sophia's face, softening her features. "You too? Then come home. Don't be..."

"I promise you, it's nothing to do with the cottage," I interrupted, meeting her gaze. "It's just...bad dreams."

"Then we've got to find you an alarm or something, so you stop missing breakfast. It's the only time we can get any of it out in the open whilst it's fresh in our minds."

"Are you sure that's the best idea, with..." I drifted off, casting a wary gaze towards the house.

"We can't ignore it much longer. You don't understand how bad it's getting come nightfall."

True to her word, Sophia had collected all the guns, ammunition and targets we used during our practice sessions and arranged them on a bench that overlooked the front lawn.

I pinned our dog-eared bull's eye to a sturdy wooden board, its frayed edges attesting how often we had hit the mark. On either side, an assortment of empty glass bottles stood tall, their vibrant hues shining brilliantly in the sunlight and reflecting vivid rainbows of colour on the grass.

Sophia's emerald silk dress rippled against her body like the surface of a stream as she loaded a cartridge into the rifle and shells into the double-barrelled shotgun, her movements smooth and precise.

She exuded femininity on the outside, but inside, she was a tomboy, eager to play with "boy's" toys with her male peers.

Despite this, she excelled in these activities, displaying a fierce determination to prove that gender should not restrict one's abilities or passions, a determination she instilled in me at a young age.

It had been Sophia who had assumed responsibility for teaching me how to handle firearms, urging me that if Britain were ever invaded, it'd be everyone's responsibility to defend it, regardless of gender. I often thought she was born in the wrong era and that the 1940s didn't deserve her. But I could see she was struggling.

Over time, I'd grown astute at listening to our family's problems, lending an empathic ear to whoever needed one, or acting as a mediator when my siblings needed their heads banging together.

Sophia stood tall and steadied her feet, the heels of her sandals slowly sinking into the grass as she raised her rifle and took aim. She stared down the barrel of the gun and fired three rounds in quick succession into the target.

Each shot that echoed across the lawn was a cathartic release, and for a moment, everything else fell silent as the tension slowly melted away from her body. Her face remained stoic as she handed me the gun, the frustration of the morning offloaded onto the bullseye.

Sophia let out a frustrated sigh. "It didn't matter anyway," she said, her words tinged with bitterness. "As soon as I opened my mouth, Alfie shut me down and wouldn't let me speak. Maybe he's tired of controlling the library, so he wants to try his hand at controlling us?"

Chapter Two

I blew a short puff of air through my nose, shaking my head. "That isn't it, and you know it," I said softly. "Managing the library has helped Alfie regain some resemblance of control in his life. Don't try to take that away from him just because you had an argument."

Feeling the weight of the weapon in my hand, I loaded a cartridge and fired. My grouping was spread far wider than Sophia's, though it never bothered me. I'd already made my peace with being unable to challenge her exceptional skills with a rifle. I had yet to find that one talent that made me unique.

I returned the gun to Sophia, the metal barrel tinkling metallically against the diamond of her engagement ring. "The world is in chaos, and there's nothing he can do," I said. "Father and William returned home heroes, so he feels almost...emasculated."

Sophia's eyes narrowed teasingly; her vivid blue eyes sparkling. "Don't make excuses for him. He can do no wrong in your eyes, can he?"

"I know he can be difficult," I shrugged. "But he's gentle when he wants to be."

Sophia fired her rounds, shattering three of the bottles in a haze of broken glass.

"Hmm, so you keep saying," Sophia said, arching one brow. "But you're the only person that ever sees that side of him anymore, and even that's occurring less frequently."

My jaw tightened as I took hold of the gun, my fingers clutching the cool metal so tightly that my knuckles blanched white.

Alfie's behaviour towards me was precarious at best, and the affection he'd once shown privately but regularly had been waning. I squeezed off a round and felt the recoil kick back into my shoulder.

My aim was off, completely missing the bull's eye and grazing the board's edge. Usually, I was a better shot, but Sophia's comment had lingered in my mind, unsettling me and shifting my focus.

I sighed, glaring at my ailing marksmanship. "I don't get it. Alfie will be considerate one day; the next, he'll avoid me entirely."

I fired my remaining rounds at two empty wine bottles, sending explosions of ruby-coloured glass splintering across the lawn. Whilst I smiled satisfactorily at their destruction, it did little to soothe the inner turmoil raging inside of me.

Sophia cocked her head, a considerate smile pinching her cheeks. "Is it that bad?" she asked softly. "Last week, you looked so close cosied up by the fire? I thought he was going to finally make a move."

Alfie and I had stayed up talking long after everyone else had drifted off to bed. He rarely shared anything significant about himself during the rare occasions he showed me any attention. Still, he always listened intently, his piercing blue eyes, the exact shade of one of my own, fixed on me.

After we exhausted the subjects of our recent literary journeys, he listened to my aspirations about my future after the war ended. However, the topic always brought a strange, anguished look to his face, and his eyes seemed to lose focus in a way I couldn't understand.

The following day, however, Alfie had retreated into himself. He reverted to his cold, unreachable persona as if he felt remorseful for letting his guard down.

I often felt like he was fighting a relentless battle within himself, struggling to reconcile his desire for emotional connection with his deep-seated fear of being hurt.

As much as I tried to understand, I couldn't help feeling that his primal instinct was to distance himself from me as much as possible. It was as if he considered it some kind of sin to want me. The continual change in his demeanour left me questioning whether I was somehow to blame for the inexplicable tide of his emotions.

Sophia rested a hand on my shoulder, her voice as soft and soothing as warm honey. "He's just...troubled," she said. "It's not that he doesn't have feelings for you. I just don't think he knows what to do with them."

"Or maybe he's incapable of them altogether," I huffed.

Sophia's grip on my shoulders remained as she forced her gaze on me. "Come now, it's not that bad. He used to be such a joker when he was young. I still see it sometimes."

Despite Alfie's stern demeanour, the brighter part of his personality would, on rare occasions, peer through his veil of severity like sunlight peering through a cloudy sky. It was as if he was guarding the hidden depths within himself, though nobody could fathom why.

"But why won't he let *me* see it?" I asked.

"Darling, I've no idea," Sophia shrugged, a compassionate smile tugging at the corners of her lips.

"Could it have been losing his parents so young?"

"Maybe? But after he got over it, he was still...Alfie," Sophia said.

Chapter Two

I chewed my lip as my eyes, one green, one blue, remained pinned on Sophia. "Then what happened?"

"Not long after you arrived with us, the weight of the world seemed to have collapsed onto his shoulders, and over the years, that weight has just buried him."

My eyes narrowed confusedly. "What are you saying?"

A smile inched across her face, making her eyes sparkle brilliantly. "I'm saying, grab a spade, darling."

"Or maybe a dump truck," I said, chuckling.

A refreshing breeze caressed my face, bringing with it swollen raindrops that infused the air with the rich smell of the earth. Unprepared for wet weather, we quickly packed the rifle and shotgun and headed inside.

Target practice usually unwound me, but Sophia's words had only left me feeling hollow. I was growing tired of disenchantment, and the unanswered questions surrounding Alfie's behaviour had begun to grate on my nerves.

I had never intended to surrender my heart to the charm of his complicated persona, but my body and soul were inexplicably drawn to him like the proverbial moth to a flame.

Despite my efforts to resist, my senses would come alive whenever Alfie was around, and my heart would pound like a drumbeat, reverberating through my entire body. The all-consuming feeling was raw and untamed, almost like an inexperienced animal opening its jaws and howling for its mate.

He was an enigma, a man of few words who always seemed lost in his thoughts. However, the profound emotion in his eyes spoke volumes, as if he carried the wisdom of an old soul within his youthful frame, weathering many storms.

He was a puzzle I was adamant I would solve. I longed to peel back the layers and uncover the secrets hidden beneath his stoic facade, praying he would one day see me as I saw him, flawed yet gifted with an inner beauty that transcended his imperfections.

The sky was a canvas of transitioning hues; the serene blue that had dominated the sky had shifted to a heavy grey. Black storm clouds crowded the horizon, casting Red Rock into obscure shadows. The air was heavy with the smell of rain, and as the three-storey sandstone building sat waiting for us, I could feel the energy in the atmosphere building. A distant roll of thunder slowly rumbled in the distance, like an ancient beast had awoken in the sky.

Flanked by black marble pillars, the front door, with its brass doorknob rusted into place through lack of use, was wide open, like a dark monster with gaping jaws waiting for its next meal.

As I approached the house, the fading shadow of its windowless turret rising from the third floor loomed over me, stretching across the gravel driveway like a bony finger. I shuddered, rubbing the gooseflesh that mottled my arms. It never failed to send a chill through me whenever I saw it.

The large windows surrounding it like curious onlookers almost mocked the peculiar extension that craved light, taunting its desire.

Red Rock was full of unique and bizarre additions, most of which were merely conversational pieces that could be brought up and shown off at dinner parties.

For instance, the aces adorning the rooftop in place of traditional gargoyles were one Reynolds-Woodbury son's final act of defiance to the father who had left him the house but abhorred his womanising and gambling habits.

However, many features were profoundly macabre. Things we hoped were mere fabrications or exaggerations of the truth, and others we wished could be scrubbed from our history books and disassociated from the family altogether.

Red Rock's imposing turret and its baffling lack of windows prominently looming over the house's west wing was one such place.

It had been designed that way intentionally for a Reynolds-Woodbury daughter in the 1850s. Her chronic epilepsy left her with debilitating migraines, during which any light triggered bouts of untreatable pain.

It was initially intended to be a place in which she could take refuge from her symptoms, but as the years progressed, her condition only deteriorated. She spent more and more time in the turret until it eventually became her prison. Her only human interaction became when food and water were pushed through the door once daily as she begged for release, for light, for a *reason*.

Otherwise, she was ignored in the filthy, dark room, the sound of her screams muffled by the thick stone walls. She was far enough away from the inhabited areas of the house that her conceited family no longer felt obligated to nurse her condition nor suffer the disgrace of leaving her up

Chapter Two

there to rot in her own filth. Forgotten and alone, she and the ominous turret became a symbol of the shame and arrogance that had left a dark stain on our family name for decades.

It was a place my family and I had never ventured near or into, and the rusted hinges of the locked door had seized in place. Whenever the sun dipped below the horizon, muffled screams and the screeching of fingernails against the door could often be heard as a pervasive, musty smell seeped through the wood and permeated the hall.

Even Annabelle, who took such pride in keeping Red Rock in order, avoided that part of the house. She had let the decay take over like a creeping disease, allowing the dust in the hall leading up to the turret to settle thick and heavy.

Sophia and I entered the foyer before an almost unnatural downpour of rain descended upon Red Rock. The sound of it beating against the windows as I slammed the door shut behind us was deafening, creating a rhythmic melody against the windowpanes.

We wrung the water from our hair and clothes, creating little puddles on the polished marble floor that reflected the soft ambience of the crystal chandeliers overhead.

Sophia looked lost in thought, her brow furrowed as she checked her appearance in the gilded mirror that spanned one wall of the foyer. Her eyes betrayed her mood, taking on a darker hue that hinted at the thoughts preoccupying her mind. Her delicate fingers twisted her engagement ring, its elegant diamond sparkling in the light.

Meeting Sophia's gaze in the mirror, I smiled, pointing my thumb down the hall. "Are you coming to the library?"

Sophia chewed her lip, toying with the damp strands of her hair. "No, I'm going to... I've got to..." she trailed off, her voice faltering as her gaze fixed on a distant spot.

Knowing she couldn't finish her sentence or even say his name aloud, I spoke for her, my voice soft and understanding, like I was speaking to a child. "Write Nick?"

Nodding sharply, she steeled herself and tried to hide her pain with a gentle smile. She wandered upstairs to find a quiet corner of the house where she could be alone with her thoughts and offload the burden of her emotions onto the page. It was another release she desperately needed that helped make sense of the chaos inside her.

I wholeheartedly believed it would've been healthier for her to accept his loss and let him go, but she refused to accept the harsh reality of the situation. Every time the subject was breached, she became irrationally hostile. Despite all the evidence pointing to the contrary, she clung to hope that Nick would still return.

It left Sophia trapped in a world of her own making, unable to see the truth staring her in the face as false hope slowly eroded away at her from within.

William and Alfie's coddling didn't help. They clearly struggled with accepting Nick's passing, too. Still, their indulgence of Sophia's delusion was only delaying the inevitable, prolonging her grief as well as their own.

Nick, William, and Alfie had been friends since school and often found themselves acting as the couple's mediator for the arguments most couples endure in their infancy.

Despite being together for several years, very much in love, the relationship fell apart after an argument that seemed insurmountable.

The root cause was Nick's lack of support for Sophia's acting career. He thought she was too intelligent to limit herself to merely walking the boards performing other people's work. He implored her to develop her immense talent as an artist instead, and as a result, arguments about her life choices became frequent.

Finally, when she'd been cast as the lead in a major production, she hoped Nick would realise that acting was her passion. She left him a ticket at the gate on opening night, but he never showed, and to Sophia, that was unforgivable.

Only when war broke out eight months later, and the pair faced being parted permanently, was their flame rekindled. The night before he, William and my father left for Europe, Nick proposed.

Wherever she was in the house, Sophia's eyes habitually drifted to the mailbox, eagerly awaiting the postman's arrival. Despite her unwavering hope and enthusiasm, I'd never seen him personally, and our mailbox only ever contained the morning paper.

Seeing Sophia's continual irresolution was difficult to bear, leaving me wishing that that dreaded telegram would arrive despite knowing the heartache it would bring. It would allow Sophia and the boys to finally grieve and, eventually, heal from the uncertainty that had been haunting them. Because watching Sophia reappear each afternoon, puffy eyed,

Chapter Two

with her tears leaving clear streaks on her delicately powdered face, just killed me.

I headed to the library, trying to ignore the countless eyes that glared down at me from their frames, each portrait more imposing than the last. Paintings of revered Reynolds-Woodbury descendants filled every alcove of the long corridors, their stern gazes boring down on me.

Some of them appeared so overbearing that come nightfall, I could feel their critical eyes following my every step, analysing my every move, as if they knew I wasn't of their blood.

The ground floor boasted several expansive rooms, but the library was its centrepiece, the crowning jewel of Red Rock.

In the centre of the house, it was a vast space, lit by ornate chandeliers overhead that sparkled brilliantly, even as the storm cast its shadow over the house. A horseshoe-shaped balcony that could be accessed by twin baroque spiral staircases added to its grandeur.

My father's robust, leather-topped desk, polished to perfection, occupied the bay window in the centre of the room, giving him a commanding view of the room and ample light to read.

However, we weren't entirely sure whether he understood what was in front of him anymore or was just going through the motions.

The floor was burnished wood, with earthy antiquarian carpets that added a touch of warmth to the room. Every wall was lined with towering bookshelves stretching from floor to ceiling, stuffed with leather-bound books from every corner of the globe.

It was a treasure trove of knowledge and adventure, filling the atmosphere with the scent of old paper, leather and ink. A large marble fireplace offered heat, but the size of the space meant that the library never felt warm. The few armchairs grouped around the fire were so well used that the fabric on their arms had worn bare, yet they were often fought over.

Despite its frigid temperatures, especially in winter, it was where we spent most of our time. Determined to defy the boredom that our seclusion had brought us, we turned to books as a means of escape, hunting down a new favourite novel or revisiting an old one.

It was a place I adored, not just because it was where I could exercise my brain, immersing myself into the fantastical lives and worlds of the characters in my favourite books, but because it was where I could usually find Alfie.

My stomach twisted into knots as I wiped my palms, slick with sweat, onto my tailored trousers and pushed open the door to the library. I was greeted by the familiar fragrance of old books and charred wood burning in the fireplace.

I paused and surveyed the room, half praying that Alfie noticed my arrival and the other half hoping I'd slip in undetected. My heart was always torn between conflicting emotions, leaving me unsure of its true desires.

My father sat behind his desk, his wheelchair tucked beneath as he stared vacantly at the wrinkled newspaper spread out in front of him, his eyes unfocused and distant. William tucked the blanket covering his legs tighter to his body and sipped his bitter-smelling coffee.

He always remained close to our father, able to intervene should he suffer one of his breakdowns. William was always far better equipped than the rest of us in those situations. Perhaps it was due to the traumas of war they had shared, but he always knew exactly what to do.

A warm smile lit up my face as I leaned over him, planting a kiss on his temple, my voice soft with affection. "Hey, Dad."

My father's frail frame remained hunched over his desk, his hands trembling slightly. He made no response or greeting, almost as if he didn't see me there. The room was silent, save for his laboured breathing.

William's auburn eyes twinkled as he smiled towards me, his face a picture of brotherly love. "Good afternoon, sis," he said, checking his watch.

"Don't you start, too," I said, rolling my eyes.

He raised his hand, his smile growing further. "Did I say anything?"

My brother was the exact opposite of his best friend, Alfie. He was a funny, chatty character. Someone who always radiated the same warmth and kindness as Sophia.

"How is he today?" I asked, my brows raised inquisitively as I affectionately brushed my father's hair from his eyes.

William responded with a shrug, his smile fading as he sighed. "Just the same," he said. "Silent...confused. There's just nothing there anymore. Like his spark has burnt out."

My father's decline had become more prominent in recent years, and little remained of the man we treasured. What had started with bouts of amnesia and agitation had grown into something more sinister, something that consumed more of him each day. It was as if Red Rock was feeding off his misery, leaving an empty husk behind.

Chapter Two

When I was a child, he had stood as a towering pillar of strength for our family, but he had since withered away to a frail shadow of his former self, lacking the vigour and vitality that once defined him.

His vibrant eyes that had once radiated with an unyielding confidence had sunken, lost within the dark shadows of his face. He looked like a man thirty years his senior, his face etched with deep wrinkles. The transformation had been so drastic that he was virtually unrecognisable to the man he had been.

I leaned closer, my tone barely above a whisper. "And how's the other one?" I asked. "Where's Alfie hiding today?"

William's eyes sparkled with mischief as he raised his voice to an intentionally embarrassing level. "Oh, Alfie? You're looking for *Alfie?*"

I waved my hands frantically, my brow furrowed as I hushed him. "No, I'm not. Shut up!" I hissed through clenched teeth.

"But you just said you were looking for him," William continued, his tone laced with amusement, relishing my discomfort as his lips curled into a devilish grin.

A rush of heat flooded my cheeks, betraying my embarrassment as I stumbled over my words. "No, I'm not looking for...I just..."

"It's okay; I got you, little sister." William leant against the desk, casually crossing one foot over the other as he pointed upwards. "He's right upstairs, putting away some books. In fact, he's probably heard our entire conversation."

My gaze fixed on William, seething with irritation, even as I kept my expression stoic.

On the balcony level, a sudden clamour shattered the awkward silence as books fell to the balcony floor above, reverberating through the metal framework of the platform.

Alfie cursed under his breath; his frustration was palpable as a book hurtled over the railing towards me. I quickly stepped to the side, my instincts taking over as I reached out to catch it.

My quick reflexes refused to abandon me as the leather-bound book toppled into my arms. I felt the weight of it as it splayed open in my hands, revealing its ageing pages. I closed the cover and ran my fingers over the embossed gold lettering on the spine.

Alfie's face appeared over the balcony railing, his fingers gripping the brass framework tightly as if afraid to let go. His brows drew together as an inherent look of concern fell over him. His piercing blue eyes, which mirrored one of my own, seemed to bore into my soul.

My lips curled into a shy smile as I half shrugged. "It's okay, I'm a good catch."

The corners of William's lips twitched as he stifled his laughter and innocently brought his coffee cup to his lips. "I'm sure there's a compliment there somewhere, Alfie."

The lighting sparkling overhead made the intricate gold leaf print on its spine stand out vividly, and as I read it, I couldn't stop the playful frown forming on my face. "Really, Alfie? Bronte?"

"It...it wasn't mine," Alfie stuttered, his voice a low purr. The highlights of his elegantly styled auburn hair glistened angelically under the light of the chandeliers.

He smoothed down the ruffles in his comfortable navy suit and tie as his eyes fell to the floor.

"I remember using the same excuse to Dad in my teenage years," William added, a hint of amusement in his voice. "Though they weren't exactly for the same type of books."

Alfie thudded down the spiral staircase towards me, his steps heavy with frustration as he held out his hand, waiting for the book. "It was *Sophia's*," he said, his voice sharp. "If everyone had the common courtesy to replace their books, I wouldn't have to do it for them."

"Oh, don't deny it," William teased. "You love playing librarian."

As my skin prickled with anticipation, I handed the Bronte title to Alfie. His fingers grazed mine, sending a jolt of electricity coursing through my body that challenged the building storm outside. His gaze lingered on mine for a moment too long, and the corners of his lips twitched as if he were suppressing a smile.

Without another word, he spun on his heels, his gait stiff and his back rigid as he disappeared back up the stairs and busied himself rearranging books.

William offered a sympathetic smile and shrugged. "Sorry, sis. I gave it my best effort."

I narrowed my eyes playfully, my tone light. "I hate you."

The irresistible aroma of roast chicken and potatoes filled the dining room at dinner that evening. However, Alfie's mood soured the pleasant ambience, casting a pall over the table as his mind wandered elsewhere.

Chapter Two

His stormy eyes were cast down, avoiding my gaze and concentrating solely on his food as he cleared his plate as quickly as possible. The mechanical scraping of his silverware against the china plates echoed through the room, adding an unsettling note to the meticulously set table.

With Sophia still absent, writing to Nick, conversation at the table felt forced without her to guide it, and the silence felt oppressive.

We tried to fill the void of her absence and gloss over Alfie's mood with trivial nonsense about the weather and the changing seasons, but the words fell flat. Every topic failed to fill the uncomfortable silence, as the flickering glow of the candelabras on the table failed to thaw the icy atmosphere.

As soon as he'd finished his meal, Alfie excused himself, ignoring our devoted housekeeper Annabelle's offer of his favourite dessert.

Sophia returned after dinner and joined us in the sitting room for brandies, her finger stained with ink, an unconvincing smile betrayed her genuine emotions. Her satin pyjamas clung provocatively to her curves, accentuating her toned physique. Even emotionally exhausted, her magnetic allure was as undeniable as her fighting spirit. As she sank into the sofa armchair opposite me, her perfume infused the air with the scent of jasmine and vanilla.

As darkness fell, Red Rock's mood shifted. It was a feeling we all sensed and knew well, like a subtle change in the atmosphere or the disconcerting sensation of being watched in an empty room.

The air prickled with static as the storm outside persisted, filling the air with an energy that left us all on edge, glancing up from our books or sewing and meeting each other's flickering eyes in unsettled silence.

Torrents of rain quenched the earth and created a continual drum roll against the windowpanes. Vivid lightning strikes split the sky, momentarily bathing the room in white light that illuminated every detail.

The angular shadows of furniture stretched across the walls, creating a play of light and dark that was both beautiful and ominous, flickering like ghostly apparitions.

The accompanying growl of thunder that followed shook the house to its foundations.

As the wind howled like a pack of wolves, rattling the windows in their frames, I knew that below ground, Red Rock would be bleeding.

Sophia rose to her feet, the light fabric of her dressing gown rustling as she pulled it tighter around her body as if to ward off the chill creeping through the room. "I'm just going to grab my slippers," she said.

"You want me to go with you?" I offered, setting my book down beside me.

Sophia chuckled nervously, though her tone was as apprehensive as her face as she tried to mask her unease. "I'm sure I'll be fine."

I forced a smile, but I couldn't help but curse her careless choice of words. You could never be sure of anything at Red Rock. The house was notorious for its unpredictable nature, and it continually punished overconfidence in new and unexpected ways.

Sophia tentatively ducked her head out of the room and glanced up and down the intimidatingly dark corridor. Shaking the nerves from her hands, she took a deep breath, mustering the courage to step into the shadows.

Though her head was held high as her rose-coloured ensemble billowed behind her, the brisk pitter-pattering of her bare feet, virtually jogging towards the stairs, betrayed the palpable fear radiating from her.

I rubbed the chill from my arms and wriggled into the plush warmth of my armchair by the fire. Opening my book with one hand, I swirled my glass of brandy with the other, releasing its rich fumes into the air. I grimaced slightly as I savoured the decadent flavour, warming me from the inside out.

Alfie sat on a nearby sofa, leaning into the armrest. The waves of his hair fell into his eyes as his head bowed over a book. As if drawn by a gravitational pull, my eyes flickered involuntarily in his direction.

His oceanic eyes met mine, holding my gaze in a silent exchange. I felt that familiar tightening in my chest, my heart drumming faster, as the tiniest hint of a smile played on the corners of his lips.

This was how our time together usually began, with a hungry look that made me feel like the only person in the room. He glanced at the empty seat on the sofa beside him, then back to me in a silent invitation to join him before Sophia returned and monopolised my time.

His gaze lingered on me as he chewed his lip, the air prickling with a palpable longing that we had both felt for years, a longing that he rarely acknowledged.

The stillness of Red Rock's foreboding halls was suddenly shattered as a jarring scream echoed through the entire building. It rang in my ears like a bell, long and shrill, vibrating through my body.

As my body grew tense, my brandy glass slipped from my hand, shattering into a thousand pieces, its shards glinting dangerously within the glossy pool of caramel at my feet.

Chapter Two

I sat upright, my back painfully straight as I gripped the arms of my chair, my nails embedded into the soft material. My eyes darted towards Annabelle and the boys.

Their saucer-like eyes stared wildly back at me, their chests heaving as the ear-splitting sound continued, saturating the frigid air with an intensity that made my eardrums ache. A flash of lightning highlighted the contours of our apprehensive faces like the flash of a camera, immortalising our fear for all eternity.

My voice was a breathy whisper, barely audible over the sounds of the raging storm. "Sophia,"

Chapter Three

I set my bare feet on the floor, crunching the glass into sparkling crumbs that resembled shattered diamonds. I could feel the tiny fragments digging into my skin, but I didn't feel the pain as I darted into the hall without hesitation.

My heart hammered in my ears as I hurled myself up the stairs, every step leaving tiny spots of blood mottling the plush carpet as if marking my path for William and Alfie, following closely behind, their heavy steps echoing against the walls.

As we reached the top of the stairs, the screaming stopped. A sudden, haunting stillness fell over the house, broken only by our drumming feet and laboured breaths. As we neared Sophia's bedroom, muffled sobbing could be heard through the closed door, starkly contrasting the screams that had shaken the air.

I burst into Sophia's spacious bedroom, my eyes darting around the space. Decorated in a feminine palette of dusky pink, with plush velvet drapes framing the windows and balcony, the room was lit only by the crackling fireplace that infused the air with the smell of charred wood and cast flickering shadows against the walls.

Sophia stood with her back pressed against the wall, her shoulders raised as her arms wrapped around her body in a self-soothing gesture. Her face was drained of all colour, and her breathing was shallow and unsteady. Her delicate body visibly jolted at my sudden entry as her wide eyes fixed on mine.

She hurled herself into my embrace, knocking me off balance as she locked her arms around my neck, her entire body quivering.

A sharp gasp escaped her lips as she buried her face in my hair. "Thank God."

I eased out of her arms and held her at arm's length, searching her eyes. "Soph, are you okay?"

Chapter Three

Thick veins of mascara ran from her bloodshot eyes as she pointed a perfectly manicured finger shakily towards the fireplace, her voice barely audible as she spoke. "I... I heard something."

Alfie lingered in the doorway, his eyes narrowing as he crossed his arms across his chest, his eyes carefully assessing every flickering shadow.

William pulled Sophia and me into his arms. "What happened?" he asked.

"I heard it again," she said, her bottom lip trembling. "By the fire."

William cast a wary glance at Alfie, still standing at the door. Peeling myself from Sophia's embrace, I met Alfie's stone-cold eyes, his face an unreadable mask, as I switched on the overhead lights.

The room flooded with an almost unnatural amount of light, but nothing was out of place, nothing unusual. The only sound coming from the hearth was from the popping embers of a dying fire. Despite the room's stillness, a palpable sense of tension lingered in the air like smoke.

I tried to think logically, proposing a simple explanation to placate Sophia's fears. I approached the fireplace and prodded its contents with a poker, releasing sparks that vanished into the chimney.

Red Rock was notorious for its strange noises; the storm only worsened things. The wind was howling through the halls, rattling the windows and doors, adding to the unease that permeated the air.

I took a deep breath, trying to force a confident and reassuring tone into my voice. "It's just the fire."

Sophia raised her hands, facing her palms towards me. Her voice became more despairing as she shook her head vehemently. "No. I know what you'll say, but it wasn't the storm or wind, either. I heard crying by the fire."

Alfie crossed the room and peered through the gap in the curtains as rain lashed the windowpanes. "There's nobody else here," he interjected. "The storm's just playing tricks on you."

Sophia's eyes met mine, wide with almost childlike desperation, as she gripped my hand so tightly that her nails left tiny crescents in my skin. "*Please*, it's not the storm," she insisted. "I've heard it before, but it was so loud this time that I couldn't escape it."

William sighed, rubbing the growing tiredness from his eyes. "Soph, you're not a little kid anymore." He turned to me, arching one brow. "When we were little, Sophia constantly claimed she heard a ghost in her room."

Despite disbelieving my own words, I chuckled. "There's no such thing as ghosts." But these were the lies we told ourselves to help us sleep better at night, the lies that painted Red Rock as a home of magnificence rather than malevolence.

"Don't tell me you've forgotten what it's like here, Harper. You *moved* so you wouldn't have to deal with it anymore." She pointed a trembling finger at Alfie and William. "And you two. Don't lie and say you haven't seen or heard things."

Alfie, William and I stole furtive glances with one another, trying to gauge each other's thoughts. Seeing the bold and tenacious Sophia so vulnerable was unnerving, but there was little I could do or say to comfort her.

The suffocating feeling of being trapped in the house left us feeling like the walls were closing in on us, confined in a prison of our own design. We'd all experienced strange occurrences in or around the house; we just rarely acknowledged them, leaving them buried deep within ourselves. But our silent pact of denial was becoming intolerable, and I could sense things hurtling towards a tipping point as the weight of the house's secrets became too heavy a burden for us to bear.

We'd all made a solemn vow never to give the house what it coveted most, the fear of its inhabitants, but whatever had happened at the fire had pushed Sophia to her limits.

Sophia smoothed down her pyjamas and wiped the tears from her eyes, trying to regain her composure. "You can't live in a house like this and not believe at least *some* of the stories."

My brows drew together as I glanced around the room, taking in the antique furniture and pastel upholstery. "But there aren't any stories from this room. At least none I've heard."

"There's one," Sophia answered slowly, her eyes darting to the walls as a look of uncertainty crossed her face. "But not here. I won't tell it here."

With a bone-chilling grip, Sophia's icy fingers closed around mine as she tugged me into the hall. We scampered back to the security of the drawing room in silence, with the boys following a few paces behind, our eyes darting to every twisting shadow.

Only when we re-entered the drawing room did we start to relax, our rigid shoulders relaxing and tense expressions fading. The air was infused with the comforting scents of home, a heady mixture of the crackling fire and the sweet fragrance of molten wax from the burning candles.

Chapter Three

Annabelle soothed my father as he mumbled unintelligibly. She met Sophia's gaze, her face steeped in motherly concern. "What was it, Soph?"

William and Alfie headed for the drink cabinet in tandem. As Alfie pulled a crisp handkerchief from his pocket and soaked it in alcohol, William poured Sophia a generous glass of brandy, the amber liquid shimmering in the firelight. Her delicate hands shook gently as she gratefully accepted it, cradling it with both hands like one would a steaming mug of hot chocolate on a cold winter's night.

As I settled onto the sofa beside Sophia, Alfie knelt at my feet. He held the handkerchief out as he curled his fingers towards him. My brows knitted together as I peered at him confusedly.

"Your feet," he said, his voice monotonous as he glanced at the drops of blood camouflaged in the rich colours of the antiquarian rug. His gaze then settled on me as he arched one brow. "You're bleeding all over the carpet."

Sophia set her drink down, her eyes widening in concern. "Darling, you're hurt?"

I raised my hand, shaking my head. "It's nothing."

Alfie brought the handkerchief to my skin. "This might hurt a little."

As Alfie pulled my feet into his lap, my stomach twisted in anticipation of his touch. I felt no pain from the glass, no sting of the alcohol; I only felt the softness and warmth of his fingers.

He went to work delicately, his movements slow and measured as his brow furrowed in concentration. He cleaned the crumbs of glass from my skin and swept away the blood as if each touch was infused with a tenderness that transcended the situation.

As he neared the end of his task and wiped the last streak of blood from my heel, he drew a deep breath and squeezed his eyes closed, creating a moment of quiet intimacy that felt almost sacred.

"Darling, how did this happen?" Sophia asked.

I closed my eyes and pulled my bottom lip between my teeth as I savoured the moment. Throughout my entire life, Alfie had only ever touched me on purpose a handful of times. He accepted warmth and affection from the rest of my family, but he never touched me. The warmth of his fingers seeping into my body felt intoxicating as the rest of the room fell into shadow, the voices muted into a distant hum. My attention only shifted when Sophia gripped my arm, jolting me back into reality. "Darling? Does it hurt?"

"Hmm?" I mumbled. "Sorry, what?"

"Does it hurt?" Sophia repeated.

"It's fine," I said. "I can't even..."

"Feel it *much*, can you?" Alfie said pointedly, his eyes meeting mine intensely as his grip on my foot tightened. "The foot doesn't have many nerve endings, I'm sure it just feels like a scratch, right?"

My brows drew together curiously as I slowly nodded. "Right."

"You poor thing," Annabelle said. "I cleared up the rest of the glass whilst you were upstairs, but just be careful. Will she need anything from the first aid kit, Alfie?"

"No, she'll be fine," he said. "We should be able to successfully avoid amputation."

"Good. So, tell me then," Annabelle said. "What happened?"

"I heard the crying again, but nobody believed me," Sophia answered.

Alfie stuffed the bloodied handkerchief into his pocket and rose to his feet. The sudden booming of his voice filled the room, startling me. "Because ghosts don't exist!" he snapped, his tone emphatic. "They're simply the product of an overactive imagination."

"I thought we agreed not to talk about it?" I said cautiously, my eyes scanning the walls as if the house was listening.

"That was before things started getting worse," Sophia answered, her tone grave. "The noises...things being moved. Explain that, Alfred."

I raised my brows and shifted my gaze downwards, sensing the tension in the air. Alfie vehemently hated his full name, so we rarely used it, which only signalled the level of Sophia's frustration.

But what intrigued me more was Alfie's passion for ending the conversation about ghosts. His jaw tightened, the veins in his neck bulging as his face flushed in a way I'd never seen before, starkly contrasting his usually collected demeanour.

Sophia nodded upwards as she took a sip of her brandy. "We all know what happened up there."

"I don't," I said, stirring.

"Nothing happened," Alfie sighed, rolling his eyes. "It's a story we were told to keep us in our beds at night, nothing more."

"They're buried on the grounds, Alfie, all four of them!" Sophia snapped, throwing up her hand. "So clearly, it's not just a story."

"Respectfully, Alfie..." I said carefully. "...if whoever is involved is buried here, there must be some truth behind it. So, let's hear it."

Chapter Three

Alfie stomped towards a sofa by the window and picked up his book. "Fine," he huffed. "I just wanted to save you from jumping at shadows for the next week."

Annabelle packed away her sewing and approached my father's wheelchair. "I'll take your father to bed then. Spooky stories on a night like this will only upset him."

His eyes were vacant as he left the room, the soft squeaking of the wheels growing fainter until all we were left with were the sounds of the storm.

Outside, dark, broiling clouds had engulfed Red Rock. The wind was whipping along the sides of the house with such ferocity that it created an eerie drone that rose and fell with each gust, accompanying the ominous groans of the old house.

As a growl of thunder shook the windows, the electricity struggled, plunging us into darkness before flickering back on as if nothing had happened. The tops of trees swayed back and forth, their branches flailing helplessly like lifeless limbs.

The weather provided an idyllic ambience for retelling spine-tingling ghost stories by firelight. Still, Sophia's demeanour made her unease clear. Her eyes shifted around the room with a bird-like trepidation as William handed me a brandy and joined Sophia and me. I accepted my glass gratefully, savouring a deep breath of its rich, amber scent before the warmth of the liquid spread through me, helping to settle my rattled nerves.

Sophia took a deep breath, her tone low but confident, always the perfect storyteller. "Early last century, a Lord lived here with his vibrant and tenacious bride entirely devoted to him and together, they renovated Red Rock. Their joy knew no bounds when they received news they were expecting, and they completed their refurbishments with a stunning nursery on the top floor, staffed by a team of nannies. The atmosphere in the house was electric as they eagerly anticipated the new baby." Sophia paused, holding one finger in the air. *"But,* while the pregnancy went to plan, the birth did not. As the Lord paced the halls, anxiously awaiting news, the pained screams of his wife echoing through the house turned his blood cold."

Sophia stared at the fire, warming her hands, as a shock of lightning splintered through the sky like a branch of pure energy. The roar of thunder that followed was deafening.

"After hours of waiting, the door to the birthing room creaked open, and a sliver of light stretched into the hall as the Lord wrung his hands, expecting to meet his child. But the only things leaving the room were buckets of blood-soaked sheets, whisked away by tearful nurses."

I unconsciously clasped my hand to my mouth, my voice low. "She died?"

"No," Sophia shook her head.

"The baby died?"

"*Worse.*"

From his spot by the window, Alfie looked up from his book and cleared his throat, raising one eyebrow teasingly as his lips curled into a wry smile. "Harper, perhaps consider that a story *worse* than a mother and/or child dying in childbirth *may* not be a story you'd appreciate hearing."

Ignoring him, Sophia continued. "Unable to wait any more, the Lord tentatively entered the birthing room. As his wife's bleeding continued, her skin turned grey as she begged the doctor to save the baby's life over her own. Unable to watch her suffer, the Lord averted his bloodshot eyes, his fist clenched to his mouth. But then he heard it. The first cry of his baby."

I sighed, my shoulders slumping with relief as Sophia continued, forgetting Alfie's warning that worse would come.

"As the baby, Harry, was cleaned up, the Lord turned to his wife, gravely concerned. He held vigil by her side until she grew stronger, splitting his time between his newborn and his fragile wife. Gradually, the colour returned to her cheeks, but when a thorough examination was completed, they discovered that the traumatic birth had left the Lady barren."

I took a large swig of brandy, its spices mingling with the scent of the fire, without tearing an eye from Sophia.

"The Lord and Lady had dreamt of a large family and of filling Red Rock with children's laughter, so whilst it was devastating news, having nearly lost them both, the Lord felt grateful. And when his wife's health returned, they entered a period of true happiness."

Alfie's eyes peered over his book, fixing on mine. "But we all know what happens to kids at Red Rock," he smirked, nodding towards The Garden of the Children.

"Alfie, show some respect," Sophia warned, a fierce frown darkening her soft features.

"Then who's buried outside?" I pressed. "And who's crying by your fire?"

Chapter Three

"Around four months later, the Lord awoke to a sickening howl coming from the nursery," Sophia continued. "And immediately, he recognised the voice as his wife's."

The tempest outside seemed to have an eerie sense of empathy with the gravity of Sophia's story. The wind intensified with newfound vigour, matching the shrill, mournful tone of the Lady's wailing, like an echo of her pain. The floorboards groaned as a deafening crash of thunder rolled overhead, reverberating over the house like a drumbeat.

"The baby died?" I said, part question, part comment, as a dejected look fell over me.

"Cot death," Sophia said, bowing her head, eyes closed.

"One down, three to go," Alfie muttered.

"Alfie!" Sophia screeched, glaring at him and tutting before she returned her attention to the story. "Now, death stirs up different emotions in different people, but in some, their grief consumes them, and they're never the same. The Lord was at a loss as to how to help his wife. He worked through his grief by keeping busy and found a new purpose by supporting charitable causes and volunteering in local orphanages. But he'd return home to his wife every day exactly where he'd left her, unwashed, in her nightwear, with meals left untouched. Eventually, he sought professional help. They medicated her and began counselling, but both had no effect," Sophia said, shaking her head. "But after being around children in need of a home, the Lord considered that perhaps his wife needed a child to feel complete and wondered whether she'd accept an abandoned baby as her own. However, when he suggested it, she flew into a violent frenzy. She attacked him before smashing a mirror and cutting her wrists with its shards."

"She killed herself?" I frowned.

"No, her husband bound her wounds and fetched a doctor. But he knew she'd turned a corner, where the allure of joining her baby was stronger than her will to live. Knowing he could no longer keep her safe, he came to the difficult decision to have her institutionalised. Now, these were ghastly places for the average patient back then." Sophia frowned, shaking her head. "But the Lady was far from the average patient. Her husband sent her to the best place money could afford, a quiet seaside retreat where she could receive treatment in peace and dignity."

"Did she get better?" I asked.

"She was there a long time, sometimes responding to treatment and others succumbing to bouts of depression. But whilst her husband visited regularly, the Lady often refused to see him." Sophia shrugged. "Eventually, the Lord grew lonely, missing the warmth his wife had once provided him, but around a year later, he'd taken on several new servants, including a pretty young housemaid named Penny, who reminded him very much of his wife in her younger years."

My frown grew as my jaw fell slack, my voice a pre-emptive whine. "Oh, he *didn't?*"

"He did," Alfie smirked cockily as his eyes flashed up from his book.

"Late one evening, the Lord heard a commotion in the kitchen and found one of his stable hands with Penny, hoisting her skirts upwards as she begged him to stop. Without a second thought, the Lord threw a quick and effective punch at the boy and threw him out of the house," Sophia said. "He sat Penny down with a stiff drink, but what was only intended to be support for his staff turned into more. He was adamant he'd remain faithful. However, the more his troubled wife pushed him away, the more appealing the idea of taking a lover became. And as Penny and the Lord spent more time together, attraction turned into love."

"His poor wife," I muttered.

"The "poor wife" who attacked him and refused to see him?" William argued, using exaggerated air quotes. "Poor Lord, more like."

"Fair point."

"Penny knew the condition of the Lord's marriage but sympathised with him, and an intense affair was born," Sophia continued. "But their fledgling love was interrupted."

"The wife found out?" I asked, leaning forward in anticipation.

"No, by an unplanned pregnancy that left the Lord in an impossible situation," Sophia said. "He wanted to have his wife well again, but in the darkest parts of his mind, he considered the fact that he'd never have another chance at fatherhood. To Penny's surprise, he was elated by the news that another baby would grace Red Rock's halls, and he wracked his brain for a solution where he could keep his wife whilst keeping the lovechild he'd conceived in her absence."

"The term, "having your cake and eating it" comes to mind," Alfie commented, his eyes9 catching mine.

"Indeed. Before he confessed his adultery, he approached his lover with a solution," Sophia said. "Penny knew she could never provide the baby

Chapter Three

as good a life as the Lord and Lady, and wanting the best for the child, she agreed that if the Lady was willing, she'd let them adopt the baby and return to her parents."

"Could a child that was the product of an affair really help her though?" I said, my tone doubtful.

Alfie's eyes locked with mine as he winked at me, making my head spin. He'd never been so obviously flirtatious before. "Finally, someone's thinking sensibly," he said.

"He'd braced himself for his wife's reaction but was taken aback by her enthusiasm. She was, as expected, disappointed by his infidelity, but she was compassionate in ways he'd not felt from her in years," Sophia said. "As Penny's due date arrived, the Lady's long-awaited discharge letter was signed. Together, the couple finally made the long trip home to prepare for the baby's arrival. Fearing the pressure the baby would put on his unstable wife, the Lord begged her to hire new nannies, but she refused, wanting to care for it alone."

"After what had happened to Harry, maybe she just didn't trust anyone." I shrugged as my sympathy swelled for her.

"The birth went according to plan, and a boy, Robert, arrived. Penny spent a few hours with him and remained at Red Rock until she'd regained enough strength to leave. For a fleeting moment, the Lord felt that everything was going to plan, imagining a future of possibilities, watching his boy grow under his wife's watchful eyes," Sophia smiled. "But in the Lady's mind, trouble was brewing. Rather than seeing an innocent baby in need of a home, she saw only the product of the affair as jealousy coursed through her veins."

Sophia's words rose in intensity, each one building on the last, drawing me deeper into the tale until I could hear the cries of the Lord's sons echoing down the halls and see the sweeping skirts of Penny and the Lady in the room.

"On Penny's last night, she was packing her things when the Lady attacked her, viciously scratching her face whilst laughing maniacally."

"Did she kill her?" I gasped.

"No. But Penny was injured badly enough that despite her innate fear of the woman she'd wronged, she had to stay longer to recover," Sophia said. "But fearing the Lady's wrath, Penny started seriously doubting her decision to hand her baby over to such a lunatic, but the Lord assured her that once she left, the memories of the affair would fade, and baby Robert would be safe."

"Lovely Lord there," Alfie grunted. "Knock her up, take her child, and throw her out."

"Either listen quietly or leave," Sophia snapped, returning her focus to the story. "Penny's last night in the house arrived, and she headed upstairs to say goodbye to Robert. However, she found his nursery cold and empty."

A strike of lightning flooded the house, spreading into every dark corner of the room. Sophia temporarily halted the story as we braced ourselves for the accompanying clap of thunder. For a split second, all was quiet, as if the room was holding its breath, until the rumble of thunder rolled over us and gently tinkled the chandeliers.

Sophia's eyes skimmed the room like a cautious feline. It was as if the spirits themselves were responding to her storytelling, begging her to stop before the finale was reached.

"Penny searched frantically, terror washing over her. Finally, she heard Robert burst into loud cries on the floor above, followed by a maniacal cackle. When Robert's crying suddenly stopped, Penny's fear intensified as she ran as fast as she could, her heeled boots clicking loudly against the floor. Click, click, click."

Sophia stomped her feet on the floor as I gripped the arm of my chair, my nails embedded in the soft fabric.

"Finally, she reached one of the bedrooms, *my* bedroom. She found the Lady chuckling and rocking on her heels over the fireplace, the orange flames lighting up her contorted face. Even though she feared the Lady's psychosis, she thought only of the missing baby. Penny begged her to hand Robert over, but the Lady didn't answer. She giggled, seemingly unaware of Penny's presence as she hypnotically stared into the flames. Penny grabbed her shoulders, shaking her."

Sophia twisted her hands into claws before her, jerking them back and forth, imitating Penny's gestures. "Penny begged the Lady for forgiveness, for mercy, but she just laughed."

Another flash of lightning illuminated the room as a subtle change in pressure fell over the room as if an unknown presence had just entered.

Sophia's light and airy tone disappeared, replaced by something deeper, almost as if she was speaking from an entirely different part of herself, somewhere darker and more subdued. Her words carried a purring quality as she spoke, drawing the listener in with their intensity and power.

Chapter Three

"Penny glanced downwards, paralysed by fear as her blood ran cold." Sophia leant towards the fire, gesturing with her hands towards the flames. "Protruding from the hearth, she noticed a small flash of colour—a half-charred corner of a light...blue...blanket."

"No," I breathed, my jaw dropping as I cupped my mouth with my hands, my eyes impossibly wide. "How could she?"

"She was completely mad. She'd feigned her progress for the simple reason of returning home to enact her revenge. Penny was inconsolable, burning her hands to the bone trying to pull Robert's remains from the fire, but it was too late," Sophia said, shaking her bowed head, strands of her glistening hair falling delicately in front of her face. "Guilt and grief washed over Penny. A breeze rolled in from the balcony, toying with the curtains, as she spotted its open doors. As the Lady continued to laugh in the background, Penny calmly walked onto the balcony, spread her arms, and jumped."

I stared into my glass, hiding the slow tear rolling down my cheek from the incredulous Alfie. "What did the Lord do? He must have sought justice?"

"A full investigation was launched, and the Lady's mental state was reassessed. They discovered she'd not been taking her medication, and that fact alone kept her from the gallows. But the enquiry demanded that the Lady be institutionalised for the rest of her life. Then Penny and Robert were laid to rest with baby Harry as a family on the grounds. The Lord's final act of insubordination in his marriage."

"So, what happened to him?" I asked.

"Once his wife had been carted off to the asylum, he divorced her and never saw her again."

"She deserved far worse," I said sharply, my words laced with anger as I sipped my brandy to fight the gooseflesh mottling my skin.

"It depends how you look at it. The Lady was once a kind, loving woman, and had she not suffered losing her baby, she likely would have remained that way. Or..." Sophia shrugged nonchalantly. "...did the Lady always harbour a darkness that would've always been exposed one way or another? Perhaps she was just another one of Red Rock's victims herself?"

"What happened to them both?" I asked. "The Lord and Lady?"

"The Lord never took another wife or lover. His business empire grew, but nothing was enough to fill the immense hole the tragedy had left. He drank heavily and died young, at which point Red Rock was passed to his cousin. As per his final request, the Lord was buried alongside Penny and his sons, becoming in death, the family that never was in life."

"And the wife?" I asked, my jaw tightening.

"Nobody knows," Sophia shrugged. "Some say she committed suicide; others say she was killed by another patient. I don't think anyone really cared which."

"Then the crying in your room must be Penny, surely," I said.

"That would be my guess, but some have suggested it's the remorseful spirit of the Lady, trapped between worlds, tormented for her sins," William said, distorting his voice into a ghostly tone as he wiggled his fingers in front of his face.

"Unlikely," Sophia scoffed. "That witch went straight to hell when she died. I'm sure it's Penny. And the baby we hear crying..."

"There's a *baby*?" I said, my brows rising.

Alfie snapped his book shut and strode towards us, slicing his hand through the air. "There's no crying! Not from women, babies or anything else. It's an old house full of stories, but they're just that, *stories*."

Ignoring Alfie's outburst, Sophia met my gaze and answered. "We don't hear it often, but sometimes we hear a baby crying or cooing at night."

"If you thought Penny's sobbing is eerie..." William shuddered. "...wait until you hear the baby."

"All houses with long histories like ours are bound to have some skeletons in their closets—in Red Rock's case, literally," Alfie said. But as for ghosts? They *don't* exist."

Alfie crouched in front of my seat, leaning towards me to enforce his point. The subtle scent of his aftershave enveloped me, igniting warmth in my cheeks as his stormy eyes locked onto mine.

He rested his hand on my knee and gave it a gentle squeeze. The warmth of his fingers sent a shiver of excitement running down my spine, but I was confused.

He'd intentionally touched me twice in a short space of time. I didn't understand what it was about the story that had potentially broken down one of his barriers and whether they would pop back up again come daybreak.

His words were spoken with clarity, driving his point home with conviction as a rare smile creased his face. "Draw up your own conclusions as you will, Harper, but any story originating from Red Rock should be

Chapter Three

met with scepticism," he said. "There's a big difference between the creaks of an old house and hearing some vengeful spectre."

Sophia rested a hand on his shoulder, shaking her head. "Darling, I love you, but you couldn't be more wrong. Are you forgetting how terrified you were of the house when you first moved in? It took you months to sleep alone."

"I was a child who'd just lost his parents," Alfie said dismissively. "But gathering around the fire telling ghost stories won't help you keep your wits about you. And with that guidance, I wish you all goodnight."

Alfie stood tall and squared his shoulders, acknowledging Sophia and William with a polite nod. My eyes waited expectantly for a departing gesture, but I didn't get one; I never got one. It always sent a bitter sting of disappointment through me, a feeling I'd grown all too familiar with. No matter how I tried to numb the pain, it persisted, a constant ache in my heart that refused to fade.

His eyes merely found mine. He stared intensely for a moment, his eyes brimming with a strange sadness that appeared punctuated by regret.

His gaze dropped to the floor, and he swept out of the room, his pace resolute as it faded into the distance. It felt like he was taking a piece of me with him that I didn't realise I had given away.

William, Sophia and I sat in an uncomfortable silence for a moment, lost in our thoughts as we listened to the symphony of the storm.

Sophia shivered, her teeth chattering softly as a yawn escaped her lips. "Harper, darling, don't go home in this weather. Please stay," she said, cupping my hand in her own. "I'll lend you some nightwear, and you can take your old room next to mine."

"After that story, I think I'd rather take my chances with the storm," I chuckled.

"You'll catch your death. It's getting late, and you'll only be back here for breakfast in the morning anyway."

William drained the remaining dregs of brandy from his glass, his lips curling into a heartfelt smile. "She's not taking no for an answer, sweetheart. Besides, she'll only make me walk you home if you don't."

I chewed my lower lip, my gaze twitching towards the magnificent spectacle of nature erupting around us. As much as I craved the comfort and familiarity of my own bed, far from Red Rock's clutches, I didn't relish the thought of trudging through the storm back to my cottage or the leaky roof that awaited me there.

As I considered my options, Sophia seemed to notice my gradual surrender. She flashed a reassuring grin as she took my arm and dragged me upstairs, her stride too determined for me to draw back from.

When we entered Sophia's bedroom, a cold tingle ran through me as my eyes were drawn to the dancing flames in the fireplace. I couldn't help but flinch at every pop of burning wood. Sophia crossed the room, trying to shake off the palpable anxiety permeating the air as her bare feet padded softly against the hardwood floor.

With a graceful flourish, she flung open the doors to her ornately carved wardrobe, a grand sentry standing tall in one corner of the room. The scent of supple leather and delicate fabrics wafted into the room, mingling with the acrid tang of fear hanging heavy in the air.

Items of clothing rustled, and hangers rattled as Sophia's fingers danced over each garment. She finally produced a set of rich purple pyjamas and handed them to me. "If you need anything, I'm only next door."

"Likewise," I nodded.

Sophia prodded my stomach playfully, her tone light as a suggestive smile inched across her face. "*Or*, if you feel brave enough, Alfie's just around the corner."

"I don't think I'll ever feel brave enough," I sighed, chuckling as I shook my head. "He barely looked at me tonight."

"You're kidding," she frowned. "I know it was a stressful evening, but all the time you're busy trying to stop yourself from staring at him, William and I watch *him*. He was constantly stealing glances at you. I'm telling you, there's something there. I wouldn't encourage you if there wasn't; the last thing I want is to see you hurt."

I slipped into Sophia's pyjamas, feeling the luxurious kiss of the silk caressing my skin. Standing in front of the mirror, I tilted my head, taking in my reflection as my insecurities glared back.

I envisioned the woman I might be if I could muster even a fraction of Sophia's prowess and capture some of the confidence and poise that seemed to come so easily to her.

In my mind's eye, I conjured an alternate version of myself, one self-assured and bold. A girl who could take on the world with the same unwavering tenacity my older sister embodied. A girl who could walk into a room and command its attention.

Chapter Three

I imagined myself as a girl who was unapologetically herself, someone who radiated unparalleled confidence in everything she did. Someone who was undaunted in her fight for what was right, taking no prisoners.

However, my dreamlike reverie was shattered by the sound of heavy footsteps approaching my room, jolting me back into reality. Their distinct pattern, brisk and measured as they echoed down the hallway, had the severe sort of pace that belonged to Alfie.

I took a deep breath, trying to quell the heavy drumming in my chest as I self-consciously ran my tongue over my teeth and raked my fingers through my sandy curls. The footsteps, punctuated by a distinctive clicking sound, slowed. My palm was slick with sweat as I wrapped it around the doorknob and swung open the door.

The soft glow of the bedside lamp spilt into the hall, throwing my distorted shadow onto the wall. I peered into the darkness, trying to discern any movement, but saw only the empty halls staring back at me. My skin prickled with the unnerving feeling of being watched as the stillness only served to amplify the sense of dread creeping up my spine.

My eyes narrowed as I angled my ear to the hall, straining to hear any sound that might indicate that someone was lurking nearby. But all I heard was the sound of my own breathing, ragged and uneven, and the howling drone of the wind.

I wondered whether Alfie had lost his nerve and returned to his room, but if that was the case, I would have heard him. Footsteps in Red Rock tended to echo loudly and disappear gradually, yet the ones I'd heard stopped abruptly the second I opened the door, leaving me questioning whether I'd heard them at all.

The electricity flickered, creating a disturbing energy that caused the hairs on my arms to stand on end. My breath collected in pale clouds around me as a sudden drop in temperature crept under my skin and settled in my bones. I wrapped my arms around myself, rubbing warmth into my limbs.

This was how the inexplicable things always began, a series of anomalies that were each more intimidating than the last: the sounds, the cold, the fluctuations in power, and the strange shift in energy that I could feel in the atmosphere as if it was pulsing through me. My heart raced faster, drumming a heavy beat in my ears as I wished I'd paid attention to Alfie's warnings about retelling ghost stories late at night.

Spirit Born

As my body grew rigid, I slammed the door shut and edged backwards, my eyes never leaving its ageing wood. I kept walking backwards until my heels hit the cold metal of the bedframe and pulled the covers to my chin as if they could offer some protection from the darkness.

Fearful of being swallowed by the shadows, I left my bedside lamp on and squeezed my eyes closed, praying for sleep to pull me under swiftly. Outside, the bare branches from the shivering trees lashed the windowpanes incessantly, their skeletal fingers scratching at the glass as if trying to claw their way inside.

Chapter Four

I awoke with a start as a cool breeze brushed against my face, bringing me out of a deep sleep.

The inky blackness outside told me that dawn was still a long way off, but the storm had finally burnt itself out, leaving only the remnants of its fury behind.

Rain beat lazily against the windows as the wind subsided to a low drone. However, with the details of Sophia's story still lingering in my mind like a dense fog, I could not shake the vivid images her words had conjured up. A decent night's sleep felt out of the question.

As I rubbed my eyes, I caught movement in the corner of the dimly lit room. A figure loitered in the shadows, towering over me and breathing heavily.

As my body jarred upright, I recognised his long limbs and the contours of his face, but he was the last person I expected to be in my room. He had never stepped foot in it before.

"Alfie?" I frowned. "What's wrong?"

"Nothing. I was just...worried," Alfie said, his tone soft and considerate, the one he saved for the rare occasions we were alone. "I was grabbing a drink when I heard you talking in your sleep, but once I saw you stirring, I had no clue what to say."

One corner of my lip pulled upwards teasingly. "So, you just hovered in the corner?"

"It felt like the right thing to do," he chuckled, his voice purring like a tomcat. "On a stormy night...after a ghost story."

"It's okay," I smiled. "You know I hate this house at night. Sometimes I feel like it's...talking to me."

He approached the bed and perched at my feet, his eyes sparkling even in the soft lighting. The lamp provided just enough light to highlight his features. "I think Red Rock talks to us all in a way. Even me," he confessed.

I can't believe Sophia still sleeps there, knowing what happened. Then again, it's probably just a story."

"Oh, it happened," Alfie nodded.

"But you said..."

"I know what I said," he interrupted. "I just didn't want Sophia scaring you out of your wits."

He paused, looking down and fidgeting with his buttons, betraying a nervousness that he couldn't hide. I adored this side of him, the gentle, slightly awkward Alfie. In my heart, I knew that was who he was meant to be, not the surly librarian, but I had no idea why he seemed so determined to resist his true nature.

"Since you moved out, I feel like we hardly talk anymore," he said.

I always felt guarded whenever Alfie's attentiveness resurfaced. I knew it wouldn't be long until he shut me out again, but his affection was like a potent drug.

The worst part was that I was fully aware of the pattern. I knew it was only short-lived, but whenever Alfie turned his attention to me, I felt myself falling under his spell again. It was a vicious cycle of disenchantment and addiction that I couldn't break free from.

"I'm here every day. We have plenty of opportunities to talk," I shrugged. "But honestly, I'm surprised. It's been a while since you last were interested in me."

His voice was a whisper as he answered. "I'm always interested in you."

I braved the distance between us, reaching for his hand. "Then did I do something wrong?"

Alfie's shoulders tensed as he recoiled, slipping his hand from beneath mine. His smile, however, remained unchanged as his eyes fixed on mine, revealing a mixture of emotions I couldn't decipher. "You could never do anything wrong, Harper. I just... can't," he whispered.

"Why do you do this?" I asked. "Why do you shut me out?"

His gaze was intense and probing, searching my eyes as if trying to read my thoughts. "I could ask you the same."

A frown blossomed across my face, and his voice was understanding as he continued.

"There are things you don't tell me, aren't there? Things you don't tell anyone."

"I...no," I stammered.

Chapter Four

He let out a long sigh, clipped with the faintest hint of sympathy. "I know you're not ready yet," he said. "Just know that when you are, you'll find no harsh words or judgement from me."

I pulled my bottom lip through my teeth, my heart pounding harder every minute, forcing courage through my veins as I peered through my lashes. "I'll tell you mine if you tell me yours."

"That's not how our relationship works," he smiled, nodding once as he drifted towards the door. "You'll do amazing things one day, Harper Reynolds-Woodbury. You'll set the world on fire."

He lingered at the door, his fingertips gripping the frame as if anchoring himself to the spot, unwilling to leave.

"Alfie, would you stay with me?" I asked, trying to hide the hopeful tremor in my voice. "Just until I fall asleep?"

He closed his eyes and swallowed heavily as if weighing his options. After a moment, he nodded. "Of course."

He returned to the bed, leaning against the headboard and crossing his feet atop the bedding. The warmth of his body enveloped me, radiating through the layers of sheets and blankets as I nestled beside him. His breathing caught in his chest as he leaned over me and softly kissed my hair.

"Goodnight, Harper," he whispered.

Tentatively, I rested my head on his shoulder and held my breath, waiting for a rejection that never came. Whilst his every muscle grew knotted and rigid, he didn't push me away, and the fluctuating beat of his heart provided the melody for the hope that had been bolstered within me.

Each feeling and question came hard and fast, one after another until I felt buried by their weight.

Had the pattern of Alfie's moods finally been broken? Did he know more about my secrets than he was letting on to my family? And above all, were his moods just a facade to hide something deeper?

But as the events of the traumatic evening took their toll, I could feel exhaustion creeping in. My eyelids grew heavy as my consciousness faded, like a flame on the verge of flickering out.

In its place, a cosy darkness enveloped me, soothing the fraying edges of my restless mind and leaving nothing but peace and comfort.

I woke with a start by the voices jolting me from my dreams, angrier than ever. A cacophony of noise filled my head, seeming to come at me from all directions, assaulting my senses.

It was as if they were trapped in an intense argument, layering over one another until their message was lost, whispering secrets that were too terrible for mortal ears. I'd forgotten how intense they were within Red Rock's walls.

As my body sparkled with sweat under the morning sun, I clutched my hands to my ears and squeezed my eyes closed until the voices faded. I glanced around the room, but Alfie was nowhere to be seen.

Feeling overwhelmed and in need of clarity, I made my excuses to Annabelle and returned to my cottage before anyone else ventured downstairs.

I spent the day absent-minded and unfocused. My mind felt enveloped in a dense fog, making it difficult to focus on anything for more than a few moments. The hours slipped by unnoticed, leaving me feeling disconnected from the world around me.

It wasn't until the sun began to slip towards the horizon that I emerged from my thoughts. Realising I'd been gone all day and expecting Sophia's concerned knock at any minute, I drifted back to Red Rock for dinner with the family.

The sky was awash with shades of orange and pink, casting a warm glow on the landscape that had been ravaged the night before. Broken branches and leaves littered the ground as the scent of damp earth drifted on the breeze. But despite the chaos, there was an inherent sense of beauty in how the fading light played across the debris, highlighting the intricate veins that ran through each leaf.

As soon as I entered the dining room, Alfie crept into eyeshot behind me as if he'd sensed my arrival. His hair caught the last of the sun's rays, giving him an almost celestial halo. His vivid eyes fixed on mine, and the warmth in his expression made it clear he was still the compassionate Alfie I adored.

He crossed the space between us in a few swift steps and stood silently for a moment, almost as if his body had moved faster than the cogs of his mind. "You were gone all day," he said, a hint of timidity in his voice.

"I had some things to do," I shrugged.

"You're a terrible liar, Harper Reynolds-Woodbury," he smirked.

I blushed, biting my lip. "Well, it was a long night."

"True."

Chapter Four

I remained silent as Alfie edged closer, his gaze holding mine as a thick fog of desire overwhelmed my senses. My body tensed, my muscles feeling like iron against my bones.

He cocked his head, slowly looking me up and down. "You look deep in thought there," he said. "...penny for your thoughts?"

"Trust me. You don't want to know what I'm thinking."

"What if I do, Harper," he said, reaching forward and gently tapping my temple. "What if I want to know everything that happens in there before it's too late?"

I felt unable to breathe, unable to speak, and drunk on his heady aroma, the same aroma that had clung to my clothing that morning. Hearing Annabelle approaching to serve dinner, our conversation was cut short. Not that I knew what to say in reply anyway.

Half of Alfie's mouth curved upwards as he headed to his seat. As I released the breath I'd been holding and felt the air in my lungs again, he paused and glanced over his shoulder. "I missed you today," he whispered softly. "Please don't disappear like that again. Not yet."

Despite the longing tone in his words that replayed in my mind on a loop, Alfie turned quiet over dinner. As Annie cleared our plates, he announced that he'd be tending to the library rather than joining us in the drawing room.

However, the evening grew tedious without Alfie's company or the opportunity to admire him from afar. My heavy eyelids were a continual reminder of the lasting fatigue from the previous night, and craving the comfort of my bed, I said my goodbyes earlier than usual.

As I headed into the hall, I was met with the dulcet tones of the piano echoing from the ballroom. Assuming Alfie had taken a break from his books to indulge in his musical passion, I felt re-energised.

I'd always envied his talent for communicating through music. He conveyed sentiment with a mere change of tone or pace, letting the arrangement divulge the secrets of his heart for him, laying his innermost feelings bare.

Thankfully, not everywhere in Red Rock was so heavily steeped in misery. The ballroom my father had built for his late wife was one such place, born out of the celebration of love rather than the mourning of loss.

Like Sophia and Alfie, Eleanor Reynolds-Woodbury was a talented musician. She believed music had the power to heal troubled emotions and lighten sorrow.

As cancer devoured her body, one of her dying wishes was to know that Red Rock would forever be filled with music, leaving a legacy of hope and joy. Painted in her favourite colour, pale yellow, with rich gold trim, the windows ran from the floor to the ceiling, flooding the space with an almost heavenly amount of light.

Although its origin was positive, it was rarely used. Despite the bright decor, the room stayed a solemn place, evoking memories of the mother and wife my family had lost. It was almost as if the space had taken on a life of its own, a silent and ghostly presence that lingered in the background of our daily lives.

Not wanting to disrupt his piece, I drifted towards the ballroom's closed door, tucked my hair behind my ear, and listened. I didn't recognise the melody, but the sad, almost haunting tone reverberated down the halls and shuddered through me. Each note lingered in the air long after it was played, weaving a tale of longing and heartbreak.

Wrapping my fingers around the brass handle, I pulled the door slightly ajar. A gust of frigid air swept out of the room, flurrying my hair and cooling my skin.

A shiver ran through my bones, leaving me feeling encased in ice. The disconcerting feeling that I didn't belong there blew through me like a hurricane, like I was an intruder in a place that didn't want me, as the house stretched its limbs and awoke.

Desperately seeking Alfie's reassurance, I wrenched the door open, its hinges groaning loudly in protest as if warning me not to enter. The music abruptly stopped, and a heavy silence descended, broken only by my shallow breathing.

The room was in darkness, its beauty sheathed in black. A thin sliver of light bled from the hall as my eyes adjusted to the shadows, but the room was empty.

I stood rooted to the spot, my brows furrowing as I tried to rationalise what I'd heard. I tentatively forced my feet forward as my eyes flickered around the room, every detail seared into my memory as my movements echoed loudly. The polished wooden floor stretched before me, reflecting the faint light of the moon that filtered through the windows. The grand piano sat on a slight platform, its black lacquered surface gleaming.

As my breathing grew ragged, a delicate crackling sound reached my ears, reminiscent of the muted sound of a burning fire.

Chapter Four

On the windowpanes, a veneer of ice crept across the glass until the entire surface had been blanketed in elegant, crystallised patterns that shimmered in the moonlight, both mesmerising and unnerving.

Pale clouds collected around my face as I marvelled at the astonishing speed with which the ice was glazing the windows, each moment bringing new swirls to the featherlight designs.

Suddenly, a hand gripped my shoulder as I let out a startled yelp and spun around.

"Did nobody ever tell you it's rude to linger in doorways?" Alfie said, his tone light, smiling comfortingly.

"I'm not...How did...?" I stuttered. "I heard you playing the piano."

"I've been in the library all evening," he shrugged.

"Then Soph..."

"I just passed her," he interrupted. "She's dozed off in the sitting room."

With Alfie at my heels, I ventured further into the ballroom and turned on the lights. Our steps were deafening as they cut through the eerie silence.

"Harper, what's...?"

"Shh," I snapped, waving my hand. "I heard something."

"Christ, not you, too. Sophia probably put a record on."

"You just said she was asleep," I replied sharply, wrapping my arms around myself. "I heard the piano. Someone was here."

Alfie flicked off the lights and wrapped an arm around my shoulders, tugging me out of the room and slamming the door behind us. "You didn't hear anything. And it'd be wise not to tell the others about this," he said, his tone shifting from flirtatious to authoritative as I glanced back to the ballroom door. "You're jumping at shadows. Look, it's late. Why don't I walk you home?"

I frowned at him, looking him up and down. He'd never once walked me home. On the rare occasions that I needed company, William always accompanied me.

Alfie's vehemence to do so made me immediately suspicious. "Why are you trying to get rid of me?"

"I'm not. I just..." Alfie stuttered.

"Let go of me, Alfie," I snapped, trying to unsuccessfully squirm out of his grasp.

As we passed the sitting room, my outburst roused Sophia. She stretched her limbs and stared concernedly. "Darling, what's wrong?"

Alfie's breath warm in my ear as he huffed loudly and released me. He rolled his eyes and stormed towards the drink cabinet, his heavy pace betraying his frustration as Sophia sat me on the sofa and rubbed my shoulders.

"I heard the piano," I said. "But when I opened the door, nobody was there."

William looked up from his book, and Annabelle paused her sewing, mid-stitch, but both avoided my gaze.

Sophia broke the uneasy silence in a barely audible whisper as her eyes glistened in the firelight. "It's mother."

"See?" Alfie snapped, crossing his arms as his eyes bore into mine, the resentment within them palpable. "Didn't I tell you to keep quiet?"

Sophia frowned viciously, pulling me closer. "It's not Harper's fault. Mother's obviously trying to communicate."

"Sophia, *please*," Alfie sighed, pinching the bridge of his nose.

"That room was made for her," she continued. "I know we agreed not to discuss it, but for whatever reason, things are happening more frequently. You can't deny it, Alfie. I've heard you in your room at night, telling them to leave you and Harper alone."

I turned to Alfie, frowning, but his focus was solely on Sophia, his eyes seething. "You're *eavesdropping*?"

"I'm not trying to pull you into the fray, Alfie. I'm just saying that we're all being affected," Sophia said. "The footsteps, the crying, and now the piano? Something's changing at Red Rock, and I want to find out why."

Sophia's face was resolute as she spun on her heels and stormed down the hall. I sat, fiddling with my sleeves, unsure whether I should follow. Seeming to sense my discomfort, William handed me a brandy with a sympathetic smile as the heavy silence in the room felt as oppressive as the house.

I hadn't realised the extent of my alarm until I was handed the glass. As its rich spices wafted towards me, my hands visibly shook, creating a miniature amber maelstrom.

After a few minutes, Sophia reappeared, sweat glistening from her forehead. One hand pulled the cobwebs entwined in her hair free whilst the other held her slippers and a large wooden board to her chest, its edges splintered.

Her bare feet left claret-coloured footsteps on the floor, leaving a vivid path that trailed through the house to where she stood. She'd clearly been

Chapter Four

in the cellar, which, by the amount of reddish water collecting around her feet, was still waterlogged from the storm. She had a dogged look of determination on her face as if driven by a sense of purpose.

Alfie noticed the board, and his eyes widened as he shook his head vehemently, his jaw clenched. "No. Absolutely not."

Sophia patted down her clothing, releasing a small cloud of dust. After coughing the remnants from her lungs, her eyes fixed on Alfie. "It's the only way."

"What is?" I frowned.

Sophia brushed away most of the dust and cobwebs clinging to the board and carefully turned it over. Intricately carved numbers and letters were etched into its surface. They were so detailed that they seemed to come alive in Sophia's hands as if they had been waiting for her touch.

However, one edge of the board had been stained an ominous red where it had been resting on the cellar floor.

Finally, Sophia spoke, her voice low and respectful. "It's called a Ouija board. For centuries, they've been used in séances to commune with the dead," she said. "But supposedly, you never know who'll come through. You could ask to speak with your dead relatives and end up with a murderer or a demon."

"And let's be honest, with this house, it would likely be the latter," Alfie said sternly.

A strange look had fallen over William's face. His jaw tightened as his eyes widened, meeting Annabelle's with an intensity I didn't understand. "Annabelle, will you take our father to bed," he said, his voice a demand rather than a request. "*Now*, please."

"Of...course," Annabelle said, frowning curiously as she piled her sewing away.

Annabelle guided our father's wheelchair out of the room, but as he passed Sophia, his eyes widened with a spark of recognition as he noticed the board.

The vacant look on his face vanished, transforming into one of intense focus and fear that distorted his features. With a sudden surge of energy, he leant over the arm of his chair and lunged towards Sophia, his chest heaving with the effort as his eyes remained fixed on the board as if nothing else in the world mattered.

His trembling jaw betrayed the intensity of the emotions raging within him as he grabbed Sophia's clothing, stretching out his fingers to snatch the board from her, tugging her off balance.

"Please... don't," he mumbled, his voice as frail as his body.

Sophia regained her balance and looked at him with a mixture of concern and bewilderment. "It's alright," she soothed.

As Annabelle continued pushing his wheelchair from the room, equally as disturbed at his outburst, Sophia peeled his fingers from her arm individually, his nails leaving angry scratches on her skin.

"You... can't," he stuttered.

William knelt beside his chair, nodding to emphasise his point. "Calm down, Father. We're just looking at it," he said. Let her go. Look, you're hurting her."

His grip finally loosened enough for Sophia to wrench her arm free. Despite the continual reassurances that Annabelle whispered into his ears, we heard our father's pleas echoing through the halls for several minutes before they descended into heart-wrenching sobs.

"What was that about?" I asked.

Sophia spluttered, rubbing the marks left on her arm. "I've no idea."

We turned to William as he approached the window, staying silent and staring at his feet. "That wasn't a flashback, was it, William?" Sophia asked. "What was it?"

He sighed, turning back into the room. "The board is his," he said. "Soph, you were too young to understand, but after our mother died, he thought he felt her presence in the house. He'd smell her perfume, find her favourite whiskey glass left out, or find her sewing box a mess. So, he had the board specially made to contact her."

"Did it work?" Sophia asked.

"Father hired a psychic to hold a séance, and I sneaked downstairs after he'd put us to bed to watch," William said, swirling his brandy and staring into the glass. "I was expecting some hocus-pocus nonsense, but the psychic knew things. Minute details about their marriage and things mother said before she'd died. Once father was confident of her abilities, they used the board." William took a deep breath. "The planchette moved violently back and forth, but it wasn't Mother they were talking to. Whatever was said terrified them both, and when the lights started flickering and the chandeliers started swinging, I ran. Father never spoke about it. I just assumed he'd destroyed it. Where on earth did you find it?"

Chapter Four

"I spotted it while storing my old paintings," Sophia shrugged. "Maybe he thought we'd need it again?"

"You saw his reaction," Alfie said, pacing back and forth in front of the fireplace. "You can't seriously be considering this?"

"Red Rock is affecting everyone," Sophia said. "It's just that nobody discusses it."

"It feels like all we've done lately has been discussing it," Alfie muttered.

"Well, maybe it isn't each other we should be talking to," I shrugged.

Sophia glanced at the clock. "It's too late to start now," she said. "We'll have Father put to bed early tomorrow and do it then."

"But tomorrow's Harper's birthday," Alfie nagged.

I'd completely forgotten it. Days at Red Rock seemed to bleed into one, like the stones that made up its foundations. It was as if time stood still there, each day a replica of the one before, indistinguishable from the last, lasting an eternity and disappearing in the blink of an eye all at once.

"We can still do it tomorrow; it could be exciting," I said, smiling nervously. "Do we need to prepare anything beforehand?"

"The planchette's missing, so we'll need a glass and maybe some candles to set the mood," Sophia said. "We can do it in the ballroom. We might have better luck reaching Mother in a place she loved."

As I headed home, I felt buoyant, not because of my birthday or Alfie's consistent attentiveness but because of the upcoming séance.

Finally, we were breaking away from our mundane routine and embarking on something unexpected, something that had the potential to offer the answers we craved about Red Rock's tenacious prior tenants.

Despite the echoes of my father's anxiety that lingered in my mind, I couldn't suppress my inquisitive thirst for knowledge. The thought of uncovering the house's mysteries was exhilarating.

A voice called from behind. "Harper!"

I turned to see Alfie jogging towards me, the gravel crunching beneath his feet as a benevolent smile warmed his face.

"I wanted to apologise for being so short with you earlier," he said. He pulled his pocket watch from his jacket pocket and showed me its face. It was just after midnight. "And I wanted to be the first to wish you a happy eighteenth birthday."

"Uh, thanks," I smiled, unconsciously chewing my lip.

His tone lowered, and his eyes became intense as they locked onto mine. "I have a gift for you—one I'd rather give privately. Mrs Reynolds-Woodbury left it to me on the promise that I'd give it to someone important."

As my mouth turned bone dry, I swallowed hard, trying to dislodge the lump that had formed in my throat. I'd always known how to react to each of Alfie's distinct personalities. However, as this new one emerged, one that touched me and offered habitual affection, I had no clue how to handle myself.

He pulled a large blue felted box from behind his back and slowly opened the lid. Inside was nestled a white gold necklace adorned with diamonds, emeralds and sapphires that sparkled like stars, even in the night's shadows. It was a masterpiece of artistry and elegance, an exquisite combination of luxury and beauty.

A series of diamonds shone from the chain, each one dazzling in its own right. They built in size until they met the centrepiece, a teardrop-shaped sapphire encased in a halo of rich emeralds.

My jaw slackened as I blinked repeatedly and tentatively reached forward, my fingers trembling, almost afraid to touch the necklace and disturb its breathtaking design.

"It's a necklace, Harper, not a bomb," Alfie teased, grinning.

"I know this piece," I frowned. "Mrs Reynolds-Woodbury wore it in all her portraits. It's one of the few pieces she didn't donate to charity when she died. But why are you giving it to me?"

"Firstly, isn't that what you do on birthdays? Give gifts?" he said. "Secondly, I'm keeping my promise to Eleanor. And the fact the sapphires and emeralds match *both* of your eye colours is a bonus."

Before I could form a sentence, he stepped forward. I felt the warmth of his body as he effortlessly slipped his hand around my back and pulled me towards him.

"Wear it for me tomorrow, and I'll know. I'll know I'm yours," he whispered. "I'll always be yours."

As my body surrendered to his touch, sending a shiver of anticipation down my spine, he cupped my face, his thumb grazing my jawline. His cobalt eyes closed as he pressed his lips to mine, exploring them gently as the sweet taste of brandy lingered in his mouth.

The softness of the kiss was at odds with the strength of his embrace, and the memory of it lingered like a promise of what was yet to come. As

Chapter Four

quickly as it had begun, it was over, leaving me swaying with the weight of my own desire as my chest heaved breathlessly.

"Happy Birthday, Harper," he purred.

Chapter Five

With a sudden jolt, I flung my bedding into a tangled heap on top of myself as I sat bolt upright in my bed. My chest tightened as my eyes snapped open and darted around the room. I could feel my jaw clenching so hard that my teeth ached.

The voices were getting louder, closer, their indistinct whispers echoing through the air like a sinister chorus.

I strained to hear their message, but it was like trying to decipher a code. Amidst all the garbled speech, my name was the only thing that came through. It cut through the static like a knife, hissing through the ether like a paranormal serpent.

Just as suddenly as they had started, they faded, leaving an unnerving silence in their wake that was only interrupted by the rapid pounding of my heart as it pumped adrenaline through my system.

Before I could gather my thoughts, a persistent knock thumped on my door, pulling me back into the present. "Harper?" Sophia hollered. "If you don't answer, I'm coming in after you."

"Coming," I groaned, thudding downstairs and opening the door.

Sophia stood rubbing her hand, a teasing pout curling her lips. "Finally, I was getting splinters," she said, pulling me into her arms. "Happy birthday, darling."

"Thank you," I said, yawning.

"Late night?" she smirked.

"No, just still not sleeping well."

"Alfie trouble?"

"Actually, no," I answered, a slow grin spreading across my face as Sophia followed me upstairs.

"Ooh, why the coy smile?" Sophia asked, her eyes twinkling with curiosity.

Chapter Five

I picked up the box containing the necklace from my nightstand and carefully opened it. Its jewels caught the light and projected a kaleidoscope of rainbow prisms onto the ceiling.

"He gave me this," I said.

Sophia's fingers delicately traced the intricate patterns of the jewels, her lips pressed together in a fond expression. As I watched her, I couldn't help but wonder when she had last seen the precious necklace, perhaps during the last Christmas she spent with her mother.

"Oh, I hoped he would," Sophia beamed. She sniffed and regained her composure, hiding her emotions behind a struggling smile. "Now I understand the need for a lie-in after your little witching hour walk with Alfie, but everyone's waiting."

I rolled my eyes, a smile twisting my mouth. "It was hardly the witching hour."

"Don't lie," Sophia grinned, prodding my stomach teasingly. "I was drawing my curtains when I spotted you two walking the property line at three a.m."

I spun towards Sophia, my expression shifting into a frown as I pulled a white, navy-trimmed A-line dress from my wardrobe and clutched it to my chest. It was the one outfit I saved for special occasions.

The soft texture of the fabric between my fingers did nothing to soothe the anxiety that had taken root in my stomach. I pulled my lip between my teeth, biting down until the taste of copper blossomed across my tongue like an unfurling petal.

"We walked the gravel path; we were nowhere near the boundary lines," I said. "And after Alfie gave me the necklace, he left. I was in bed by twelve thirty at the latest."

Sophia continued softly teasing me, dissuaded by the ashen sheen that had washed my face. "Well, it was someone who looked *awfully* like you."

"Soph, I'm telling you; it wasn't me," I snapped, my voice rising. "He just kissed me and left."

Sophia's reaction was instant. Her eyes widened like a child on Christmas morning as her hands braced my arms with a grip so firm that it almost bruised. "You *kissed?*" she said, virtually bouncing with excitement. "What was it like?"

"It was...incredible," I said.

I squeezed my eyes closed and shook my head in an attempt to clear my mind of the lingering memories of the kiss. Instead, I focused only on the other woman's identity. "But who was he with afterwards?"

"It's Alfie we're talking about here. He's hardly got that many secrets," Sophia commented dryly, resting a hand on her hip. "Before the war, he had loads of friends; maybe one paid a visit?"

My frown deepened. "At three a.m.?"

I sank into the softness of my bed, burying my face in a pillow and inhaling the lingering vanilla scent of my perfume. Sophia sat beside me, teasing my dishevelled curls out of my face, tucking strands of gold behind my ears with a sense of care that only a sister could provide. "If you're that worried, ask him," she said, shrugging. But you've waited for this for so long. Don't hunt for reasons to tear it apart already."

With a groan, I wrenched myself up and drifted to my dressing table, dragging my feet as my muscles ached from another restless night.

I stared at my reflection and the dark shadows beneath my eyes. My stomach was in knots as I tried to expel the image of Alfie with another woman from my mind.

Despite Sophia's reassurance, I couldn't shake my persistent feelings of inadequacy and self-doubt. The nagging suspicion that I would never measure up to Alfie's expectations crept through my thoughts like a tangled vine. That feeling of unworthiness bore down on my chest like a heavy stone, making each breath harder than the last.

Sophia appeared behind me, gently working a brush through my hair as her voice softened. "He has funny ways of showing it, but he adores you," she said. "Take it from someone who's known him his whole life."

I wanted to crawl back into bed and stay there, but with my family eagerly waiting to start my birthday celebrations, that wasn't possible.

I'd always assumed that Alfie and I understood each other, both feeling trapped and longing to become something more than we were. However, if someone else was in the picture, it would have explained his indifference and the discernible shifts in his mood.

I touched up my appearance and, with Sophia's help, wrestled my hair into something resembling style. Then, as Sophia waited downstairs for me to change, I put on my dress and Alfie's priceless necklace.

Every gem sparkled brilliantly in the daylight, reflecting and refracting the light in a vibrant display that made it look like I was surrounded by a host of twinkling stars.

Chapter Five

Alfie's words from the previous night replayed in my mind on a loop, like a broken record. The velvety tones of his voice spoke directly to my soul, etched permanently into my memory in a continual reminder of his emotions, each word vivid and clear.

"*Wear it tomorrow, and I'll know,*" he had said. "*I'll know I'm yours.*"

That voice helped me temporarily push my suspicions surrounding the other woman into the darkest recesses of my mind. After a brief wobble in the heels that I only wore once or twice a year, I found my feet and tentatively walked downstairs.

Sophia smiled, flashing her perfect teeth. "Darling, you look beautiful."

As we headed outside, she slipped her arm through mine, the sun's warmth enveloping us in amber light and painting slender shadows across the lawn. The sky was a pristine canvas of azure-blue, its vast expanse of colour extending to the horizon, unblemished by clouds. The air was sweet with the perfume of blooming flowers, and birds provided a symphony of nature's music, chirping their morning chorus.

If I had known then that it would have been my last day at Red Rock, I'd have taken the time to appreciate it more, immersing myself fully and savouring every moment. I'd have traced every contour of the house, tiptoeing through the shadows of the four aces and admiring the way the sun bounced off the weathered texture of the rock, encapsulating every detail to create lasting memories.

I'd have stopped to smell every flower, letting its scent invigorate my senses and awaken my soul while admiring the intricate details on each petal. I'd have stilled my mind, quieted the constant hum of my body and listened to every sound, leaves crunching beneath my feet, the ambient undertones of the wildlife that called Red Rock home, and the gentle whisper of the breeze through my hair.

"What's the plan for today?" I asked. "Are we really doing the whole Ouija board thing?"

"Why?" Sophia frowned. "Do you not want to?"

"No, I do," I nodded. "But after father's reaction, I doubt the boys will."

Sophia leaned towards me, speaking in a hushed tone as if she were sharing a secret or was concerned about being overheard. "Father isn't exactly stable these days," she said. "But it's *your* birthday. The boys will do whatever you choose. And if we could just talk to our mother again..." She drifted off, her expression turning wistful.

"But if she didn't come through last time, what makes you think she will this time?"

"If she doesn't, she must be in a better place," Sophia shrugged. "But I know it's not her scaring me half to death in my room at night, and something needs to be done about them."

I unconsciously flinched; my face twisted into a look of apprehension. "Is contacting Penny or the Lady the best idea?" What if we end up making things worse?"

"It can't get much worse, can it? As much as Alfie wants to pretend nothing's wrong, I can't," Sophia said.

My lips pursed thoughtfully. "Does Alfie really...talk to them too?"

"Oh yeah," Sophia nodded, brows raised. "I've heard him begging to be left alone and to "let her stay", whatever that means. But he claims he's just talking in his sleep whenever I ask him about it."

As we neared the house, my compassion for Sophia swelled. Knowing Red Rock's history only served to heighten the eeriness of its seemingly luxurious facade during daylight hours. It was like a poisoned apple, its fresh and tempting exterior concealing the danger and decay within.

I'd found somewhere on the grounds to retreat to, even if I were still haunted by incomprehensible voices every morning. But Sophia and the rest of my family were still trapped there, unable to escape the malevolent presence that seemed to grow stronger each night, feasting on their fear.

If conducting a seance to uncover the house's secrets eased Sophia's concerns, I'd support her, regardless of our father's protests. If it meant putting an end to the terror that had been holding us all hostage, I would rally beside her, irrespective of the risks or consequences.

The thick marble columns framing Red Rock's front door gleamed in the sunlight as I passed through them into the foyer. The space had been transformed into a wonderland of colours, with red and blue streamers crisscrossing the ceiling in a carefully colour-coordinated pattern.

Matching balloons were pinned to each rung of the staircase as dozens more littered the floor, bouncing cheerfully at my family's feet. An artistic hand-painted sign by Sophia had been hung from the ceiling, the bold lettering seeming to jump off the paper.

My family stood clustered beneath the sign, their faces bright and animated as they yelled happy birthday wishes. As the screech of party horns vibrated through the air, I could feel my cheeks growing warm. I

Chapter Five

smiled shyly, grinding the toe of my shoe into the floor. A sea of balloons crowded around my feet as if welcoming me to the party.

"Ta-da!" Sophia exclaimed, an infectious grin lighting up her face as she gestured towards the display with a graceful sweep of her hand.

I felt Alfie's presence before he even touched me. It was as if the air itself had shifted, and a subtle energy pulsed through the room that only I could feel.

He leant closer, the warmth of his breath lingering on my skin. Looking me up and down, his thumb brushed against the hem of my dress. As I held my breath, my heart pounding faster, the overhead lights flickered, though with the sunlight streaming into the house, no one else noticed.

"You're perfect, no matter what you wear," he whispered. His breath was like a summer breeze on my ear.

He stepped back, and his unwavering eyes locked onto mine for what felt like an eternity as the rest of the room fell into shadow. His stoic mask seemed to be slipping as the corners of his lips twitched upwards in a subtle smile that, for once, he didn't attempt to suppress. It revealed a hint of vulnerability to his features, as if he were finally shedding the weight he'd been struggling under for years.

A loud bang disrupted the moment and brought me back to my senses as Sophia uncorked a bottle of champagne. She shrieked as its rich foam overflowed onto the floor, infusing the air with its fruity notes. She passed us each a glass, and after a brief toast, Sophia eagerly hauled me towards a side table overflowing with gifts, each artfully arranged and wrapped.

Amidst the turmoil of the war, my family and I had no choice but to resort to the custom of making or repurposing gifts for special occasions.

We took pride in creating unique gifts from within the confines of Red Rock's grounds rather than buying something mass-produced if indeed it had been safe enough for us to leave Red Rock to do so.

Annabelle had spent hours hand-sewing delicate handkerchiefs with my initials embroidered above our family's insignia.

William, always the connoisseur, had rummaged through the dusty bottles in our wine cellar and found a bottle of eighteen-year-old Scotch. He presented the whisky with a flourish, the amber liquid sloshing around the bottle as his eyes twinkled.

Sophia gifted me some diamond earrings and matching hair grips, hoping to rein in my unruly fringe with a touch of glamour.

Spirit Born

Alfie edged forward when the gift table had been reduced to a disordered mess of crumpled wrapping paper and ribbons. His eyes occasionally shifted to the floor as he steadied his breathing and gingerly approached me, holding a wrapped package so tightly that it was almost like he was guarding it.

My family gathered around us, their eyes brimming with anticipation. The air was thick with the buzz of hushed whispering as if everyone were holding their breath. Watching how they bit their lips and grinned, it was clear that I wasn't the only one waiting for what felt like a lifetime for Alfie to stop denying me.

I've always believed that new love is the closest thing to magic in this world. It carries a certain energy, a rare spark, which promises future happiness and touches every soul nearby. In the late autumn sun at Red Rock, hope for a new beginning was alive, bursting with vivid colours and sounds. The world seemed to open before me, filled with endless possibilities and opportunities.

As Alfie presented me with the gift, I narrowed my eyes, a smirk lifting one cheek. "You've already given me your gift," I said.

"That was mostly from Mrs RW. This one's just from me," he winked, his blue eyes shimmering like a tropical sea. "I've noticed you reading and re-reading this over the years. You understand its rarity and have always taken such great care with it. Therefore, it's a fitting gift, seeing how extraordinary and utterly priceless you are yourself."

Hearing Alfie's words, I already knew what was inside. It was a rare first-edition, pre-publication presentation of Lewis Carroll's "Through the Looking Glass and What Alice Found There," signed by the author in his signature purple ink and an even rarer signature of the original Alice.

Alice Hargreaves, formerly Alice Lidell, was the inspiration behind the Alice in Wonderland novels. Despite the books being written for her, Hargreaves refused to sign a single book in her lifetime. However, with the help of monetary compensation, she was eventually convinced at an advanced age to sign one thousand copies.

It was one of the books Alfie had strictly enforced never to be removed from the library. Therefore, in my younger years, I'd often bravely walk the halls alone at night to curl up in my favourite armchair in the library and read into the early hours, getting lost in the story. As the first light of dawn crept over the horizon, I would carefully slide the book back into its designated place on the shelf and run back to my room.

Chapter Five

I carefully peeled the paper away and turned the book over in my hands, gently tracing the gilded lettering on the spine. My voice was barely a whisper as I met Alfie's gaze, squeezing the book to my chest. "Thank you, Alfie."

Sophia beckoned us all outside to the picnic area on the rear patio, surrounded by an oasis of vibrant flowers and greenery. Without a cloud in the sky, the weather created a picturesque backdrop for an outdoor celebration.

All my favourite dishes had been lovingly created, each one an explosion of flavour and colour, presented on crisp lace doilies. An expertly iced cake made by Annie's loving hands stood as the centrepiece, complete with eighteen candles that danced in the gentle breeze. I closed my eyes, inhaled deeply, and blew as I brought a childlike wish into the forefront of my mind.

I wished for endless time with Alfie and my beloved family. But as I opened my eyes, one candle remained stubbornly lit, defying the breath in my lungs. I pursed my lips with a frustrated scowl and blew the last flame out with unnecessary force.

We spent the afternoon relaxed and carefree, indulging in the feast Sophia and Annie had prepared while regaling each other with embarrassing stories.

The sun eventually crept towards the horizon, transforming the sky into a mesmerising palette of vivid oranges and pinks as finger-like shadows stretched across the lawn towards the house. As we cleared the remnants of the food littering the tables and moved our party indoors, a feeling of contentment washed over us. The flowing alcohol and the joy of being together made us forget our worries, and our fear of disturbing the malevolent house's slumber became nothing more than an afterthought.

After Annabelle retired for the evening, taking my father with her, we cracked open another bottle of whisky. The rich liquid glowed in the light of the fire, its heady scent invigorating my senses. The ice cubes clinking in our glasses added gentle percussion to the music playing on the phonograph as we grew progressively louder and giddier.

Alfie was never far from my side, occasionally pulling me to his side or skimming his hand over my shoulder. His every touch evoked waves of relentless butterflies within me as sparks of electricity ran unimpeded through my veins. It was like we were trapped in our own little bubble of happiness, and for a few fleeting moments, everything was perfect.

If only I knew I'd never see another sunset at Red Rock again, I would have savoured the transition of colours, from warm amber to soft pink and finally to a tranquil black.

I would have marvelled at the stars sparkling in the darkness, their brilliance as captivating and hypnotic as the diamonds that adorned my neck.

More importantly, had I foreseen it would be the last time I'd see Annie or my father again, I'd have done things differently. I would never have nonchalantly waved them off to bed. I'd have held them both close and cherished the warmth of their bodies against mine, never letting them go.

I'd have studied every line and contour on their faces, immortalising each feature in my mind. The twinkle that still fought to be seen in my father's faded eyes, the softness of his trembling hands, the curve of Annabelle's smile and the fruity scent of her perfume would all have been committed to memory.

If only I could have turned back the hands of time to cherish those precious moments that I had naively taken for granted. But how could I have known what was coming? How could I have imagined that my world would soon crumble around me and that every memory of Red Rock and my family would haunt me with their bittersweetness?

Chapter Six

In a break in the conversation, Sophia smacked her hands onto her thighs, her speech slurred as she cast her gaze around the room. "So, are we going to do it?"

I coughed, the sharp tang of whisky spurting from my nose. "What?"

"The *board*," she smirked. "But good to know where your head is at. Right, Alfie?"

Alfie's cheeks flushed a vibrant pink as he shrank onto the sofa beside William. As they both remained silent, deliberately avoiding our gaze, I stood, wobbling slightly as I picked up my glass, a look of determination on my face.

I could count on one hand the number of times in my life I'd been drunk, and my eighteenth birthday had quickly become one of them.

If I hadn't been so inebriated, I might have looked as apprehensive as the boys did, but the alcohol had given me a false, almost dangerous confidence.

I raised my chin, grinning. "Let's do it."

"I don't know, Harper," Alfie winced. "Are you sure?"

"It's *my* birthday," I replied in an almost childish tone. "And I vote yes."

"I second that vote," Sophia said, raising her hand. "And Harper gets two as it's her birthday. So, boys, that means you're outnumbered."

Sophia stood, her balance equally as unsteady as she took my arm and pulled me into the corridor, grabbing the half-empty whisky bottle from a side table.

Alfie and William quietly followed behind, their faces washed with an apprehension that was the polar opposite of the giggling erupting from Sophia and me that echoed through the halls.

Our glasses clinked against the heavy whisky bottle as we stumbled towards the ballroom. We grabbed a few candles and the board we'd stashed behind a hallway cabinet and threw open the double doors.

Every hair on my arm rose as an arctic breeze escaped the room, but in my inebriated state, I paid no attention to the eerie similarities it bore to the night before.

As I rubbed warmth into my arms, Alfie undid the buttons of his jacket. "Are you cold?" he asked.

I smiled at his attentiveness. "I'll be fine."

The only sound in the darkened room was the echoing of our footsteps. As Sophia set down the board, we slipped off our heels and sat on the polished floor, our dresses pooling gracefully around us. William and Alfie hovered above, their backs rigid as their arms folded and their brows furrowed.

I looked at Sophia inquisitively. "Do you know what you're doing?"

"Sort of," she shrugged. "I once played this creepy voodoo witch from New Orleans, so I have a rough idea."

Sophia positioned the candles in the circle around the board, borrowing William's matches to light them one by one, bathing the circle in a comforting glow.

With the shadows beaten back by the candlelight, William and Alfie's apprehension seemed to ease. Their shoulders relaxed, and their restless eyes settled.

Sophia reached for her glass to drain its contents. "We just need a glass."

"Oh no, you don't," William warned, in an almost parental tone as he pulled the glass out of reach. "You've had way too much already. You, too, Harper."

Sophia pouted sulkily before glancing around the room and pointing into the shadows. "There!"

I followed Sophia's finger to a chunky whisky glass atop the empty glasses' cabinet in the corner. William turned it over and examined the initials carved into the dusty glass.

"E.A.R.W," William said confusedly. "It's our mother's."

"But it's usually kept in the drawing room," Alfie said. "We all know not to move it. It upsets your father."

"It wasn't there yesterday," I said, shrugging.

"Then maybe we can ask her," Sophia said. "If it's here, maybe she wanted us to use it?"

Alfie shook his head as he edged towards the door. "We can't. I'll grab one from the kitchen," he offered. "It'll take two minutes."

Chapter Six

"No, it's here for a reason," Sophia said, her voice growing sharp with insistence.

"Perhaps it'll help us contact her if we use something that belonged to her."

"Sophia, if it gets broken, I swear..." William said, his eyes severe as he handed her the glass.

"We won't break it," Sophia interrupted, carefully setting the glass on the board.

William and Alfie reluctantly sat. I could feel the warmth of Alfie's body radiating from beside me, his body tense.

"Now, everyone places a finger on the glass," Sophia said. "Then we'll ask questions."

"What kind of questions?" William asked.

"I'll show you," Sophia answered. "But nothing too complicated."

"Why?" Alfie asked.

There was a brief pause, but as Sophia drew a breath, I cut her off as the answer somehow flooded my mind. "Energy," I blurted out. "It consumes energy for spirits to communicate."

Alfie's frown was immediate as he turned sharply towards me, his eyes narrowing. "How do you know that?"

"I don't know," I shrugged. "I just...know."

A heavy silence descended upon the room as we all placed a finger on the upturned glass. The candles cast flickering shadows across our faces as the floorboards groaned beneath us.

The group's collective breath seemed to still as the weight of the moment set in. All eyes were fixed upon the glass as we waited for Sophia to begin.

"Spirits of Red Rock, are you there?" Sophia asked.

"Nope," William sniggered. "Harper and Sophia drank them all."

A smirk curved around my lips as I stifled laughter. Alfie's face, however, remained a picture of stoic unease, his brows permanently drawn together.

"Stop it. You need to take it seriously," Sophia said, her brows raised.

Like nails on a chalkboard, a piercing screech rang out from the centre of the circle and reverberated through the room as the glass slowly moved a few inches. The sound sent a chill through me, leaving my skin riddled with goosebumps.

My eyes shot around the circle. "Who did that?"

"Stop trying to be funny, Soph," Alfie muttered.

"I didn't do anything, I swear," Sophia said, vehemently shaking her head as she collected herself and refocused on the glass. "Is anyone there?"

The glass moved further, shuddering over the rough grain of the board towards the edge stained red by the cellar. The glass ground to a halt over the word "yes," written in large, Gothic letters.

"Keep going, Soph," William nodded, his eyes widening. "It's working."

"Spirits, what is your message," Sophia said.

Another draught blew through the circle, flurrying my hair and leaving the candles struggling to stay alight as the glass picked up speed, stopping briefly over a series of letters.

We read collectively, following the movement of the glass with rapt attention. "H..."

The glass continued to the following letter and the next. "A... R"

My stomach churned, and beads of sweat collected on my brow as my name was slowly spelt out. When the glass reached the letter "E", I snatched my hand from the glass, holding it in the other as if it had burned my fingers.

"Darling, put your hand back," Sophia said. "Maybe it's someone from your blood family. It is your birthday, after all."

My eyes shot around the circle as my mouth set into a thin line. "If one of you is..."

"We wouldn't do that," Sophia interrupted. "Come on, we're here for answers."

Cautiously, I placed my finger back on the glass. Before Sophia opened her mouth, it moved again. The unnerving scraping filled the room as the glass jolted back and forth, repeating my name over and over.

William chuckled nervously. "Like Soph said, it's probably your relatives."

The glass picked up speed, so much so that our fingers struggled to keep up as it spelt out the word "Stop."

"We should listen," Alfie said, his tone firm. "We don't need any more nightmares."

"Not yet, we're getting somewhere," Sophia demanded, focusing on the board. "Do you mean we should stop living here?"

The glass slowed as if to emphasise its point as it relayed its message. "They are watching."

"Who?" Sophia's voice trembled.

Chapter Six

The glass moved again as if possessed. My pulse raced as my mind grew foggy with questions that came thick and fast, one after another, too fast to process.

No matter how far I physically got from the house, the voices always found me. But if they really were ghosts or echoes of the dead, what did they want with us, and why was my name specifically mentioned?

It was as if the answers were just beyond my grasp, and the ambiguity of the board's responses only added to my confusion. Sophia clearly shared my frustration, her body tense as her jaw tightened.

"Who's watching us?" Sophia said, her voice growing louder.

The board answered, "Evil."

"Do you mean the Lady?" Sophia asked. "Is she still here?"

The glass indicated "no" before moving erratically and spelling gibberish as we looked on in stunned silence, our faces ashen as our mouths fell agape.

"Someone else should try," Sophia huffed, turning to me expectantly.

I swallowed and cleared my throat as my eyes danced around the room. "Spirits...?"

As soon as I opened my mouth, the candles burned stronger, radiating heat towards us. The smell of molten wax infused the air as their flames rose several inches higher as if fed by gas.

"Who's watching us?" I demanded. "Are they in my cottage?"

"Here," the board read. "Everywhere."

"Who are you? Did you live here?" I asked.

The board slid towards "no".

"Then who are we speaking to?"

"A friend," the board spelt as the glass's movements slowed. "Help."

"Who needs help?" I asked.

"Harper," the board said.

"Why?" I asked. "Is someone trying to hurt me?"

In one sudden jolt, the glass shot towards "yes".

A slow metallic creak emanated from overhead. When I glanced upwards, the heavy chains suspending the chandeliers began to move. They ominously swung back and forth with increasing intensity, each movement wider and more erratic than the last, as if some unseen force was toying with them.

William squeezed his eyes closed, trying not to look at them, no doubt reimagining the séance that had terrified him as a boy.

"Who wants to hurt me?" I demanded.

Slowly and deliberately, the glass screeched across the board, spelling the word "Beau".

Alfie's voice rose above the sound of the glass. "Enough!" he yelled, his eyes suddenly filled with a panic that seemed to soak into every inch of him, leaving his hands shaking. "We have to stop this *now!*"

"Just a little longer," Sophia muttered, her voice monotonous, almost lifeless.

Her gaze was fixed on an unseen point across the circle as she stared vacantly. The bright sparkle in her vivacious eyes was replaced with a distant glaze as her lower lip quivered, making her lipstick appear even more vivid against her suddenly pallid complexion.

I tried to snap her out of her reverie by waving a hand in front of her face, but she made no reaction.

"He...sees...you," the board continued.

"Who, Beau?" I asked. "Who is he?"

"Too late. Too dangerous," the board read. "I'm coming for her."

Alfie's eyes met mine, wide with desperation. "Harper, look what this is doing to Sophia," he pleaded. "You won't find the answers you seek here, only nightmares."

As I searched his face, my eyes narrowed confusedly at the word "you" instead of "we". We were all equally curious about uncovering Red Rock's secrets, so I couldn't help but wonder why he had singled me out.

William nodded. "Alfie's right, we have to stop."

"Alright," I said, turning to Sophia. "Soph, how do we end the séance safely?"

"Just a little longer, keep the connection," she murmured. Her lashes fluttered as her eyes rolled backwards, revealing the whites of her eyes.

The chandeliers continued to move, swinging like a violent pendulum as the chains groaned in protest and the crystal droplets tinkled against one another. The windows crackled as a thick frost crept across their surfaces like a living organism.

I shivered, the temperature dropping rapidly as if a premature winter had penetrated the walls. Yet the whisky glass was growing warmer to the touch as it spun endlessly around the board in dizzying circles that seemed to mirror my confusion.

We suddenly felt very alone, dabbling in things we didn't understand as the house towered over us and laughed. I turned to Alfie for guidance, but

Chapter Six

before he could respond, a resounding crack vibrated through the air as the sturdy whisky glass shuddered beneath our fingertips.

A thick fracture spread across the glass, snaking up one side, over its base, then down the other, before it shattered into a thousand tiny fragments.

The tiny shards of glass flew in every direction, glimmering menacingly in the candlelight as we scrambled to shield our faces.

William instinctively dragged Sophia towards him, wrapping his arms around her head as she stared mindlessly at the board. Alfie mirrored William's reaction, pulling me into his arms. His chest heaved beneath my cheek as his warm scent engulfed me, overwhelming my senses.

As the last shards of glass hit the floor, gently clinking against the wood, a sudden burst of wind swept through the room. It billowed through my hair and blew out the candles, plunging us into darkness.

The silence was only interrupted by our laboured breathing until Sophia burst into gut-wrenching sobs that shattered the eerie stillness. Her cries echoed around the room as if she was releasing all the pent-up emotion that the rest of us struggled to contain.

"Harper?" Sophia sobbed.

"Soph, what happened to you?" I asked, my voice waving. Are you alright?"

William's hands shook violently as he frantically tried to light a match, his fingers slick with sweat. Fleeting sparks of light momentarily illuminated his tense face like a camera flash before the match fizzled out, and the darkness reclaimed him.

I fumbled in the dark, trying to reach across the circle to Sophia. As her fingers clenched around my forearm, squeezing tightly, loud footsteps echoed throughout the ballroom.

The sharp clicking sound started right beside us. Their swift, almost angry pace cut through the air like a knife before disappearing through the open door and down the hall. Alfie's strange reaction was immediate. His breath caught in his throat as his entire body became painfully tense, his knotted muscles twitching.

"Will, light the damn match," Alfie snapped.

"I'm trying," William said, tossing another spent match.

"Harper, where are you?" Sophia whimpered.

I squeezed Sophia's hand, her fingers as cold as ice. "I'm right here, Soph. I'm squeezing your hand."

As William managed to light a candle, casting a dim halo of gold around the circle, Sophia's hand gave way under my touch as if it had evaporated into the ether.

Through the faint light, I noticed her sitting opposite me, far out of reach. With her knees drawn to her chest, she rocked back and forth as her bare feet clenched tightly. William knelt beside her, carefully plucking glass from her hair. Only Alfie was within reaching distance of me.

My eyes scanned the circle accusingly. "Who touched me?" I asked. "Just now, who was gripping my arm?"

"Kinda busy over here," William said, gesturing to the candle and Sophia.

Alfie shook his head as his face blanched a sickly pale.

"Look, guys," William said. "We can clean this up in the morning. Let's just get the hell out of here."

We knew there would be inevitable arguments about who was to blame for the destruction of the precious glass. Still, for the time being, we were relieved that the chaotic seance had ended with only a few minor scratches. Despite suffering the vast majority of them, with the adrenaline pumping through my veins, I felt no pain.

We fled into the hall, and despite slamming the ballroom door behind us, we kept looking over our shoulders, our gaze restlessly searching the shadows. The tightness in my chest eased with each step we took towards safety, but it was only upon reaching the drawing room that I felt like I could regain my composure and breathe again.

William poured us each a generous glass of brandy, the chunky crystal decanter clattering loudly against the glasses as his hands trembled. As the sweet scent of the brandy infused the air, I sat Sophia down and shrouded her in a blanket, wrapping my arms around her and rubbing warmth into her body.

Alfie busied himself, wetting one of the handkerchiefs Annie had made with vodka before reappearing at my side. "This might sting a little," he warned, his eyes narrowing.

I caught his gaze, a hint of a smile playing on my lips. "Where have I heard that before?"

"Well, if you will keep getting yourself injured," he said, gently dabbing the scratches peppering one side of my face as William handed out drinks.

Chapter Six

Sophia noticed the blood marring our family crest on the handkerchief. "Darling, are you hurt?" She sniffed heavily, her eyes wide and staring as mascara streaked down her face.

"It's nothing," I said. "I was more worried about you. What happened? You were out of it."

"I guess I blacked out," Sophia shrugged.

Alfie sighed, pocketing the bloodied handkerchief. "All done," he said, squeezing my shoulder. "It's been a long night. I think I should walk Harper home."

Alfie offered his arm, and I stood. I affectionately brushed Sophia's face with my hand and tucked a stray strand of hair behind her ear. Despite the blanket and the roaring fire beside her, she was still shivering, her skin icy.

Her face was ashen as she grabbed Alfie's arm, tears welling in her eyes. "I'm so sorry," she said, shaking her head. "You were right, Alfie. We never should have done this. But what happened in there? Shouldn't we talk about it?"

"We will, but not now," Alfie said. "I think we all need a good night's sleep first."

"Like that's possible," William scoffed.

I took Alfie's arm, and we progressed into the hall in stunned silence, passing the tired decorations littering the floor. The once vibrant streamers and balloons now hung limply from the ceiling, their colours fading. The smell of leftover food mixed with the scent of alcohol hung in the air, adding to the already chaotic atmosphere.

As we neared the foyer, Alfie's posture straightened, and his grip on my arm tightened, pulling me so close to his side that I could feel the warmth of his breath on my skin.

A sudden chill ran down my spine, making the tiny hairs on the back of my neck stand on end, tickling the fabric of my dress as I felt aware of a presence behind us. With the rigidity of Alfie's body, I knew he felt it, too.

Gradually, the distinct tapping of women's heels reappeared, echoing behind us. I shuddered as the chilling memory of the footsteps pacing the halls during the storm and after the séance pushed into the forefront of my mind.

Despite my growing fear, I mustered the courage to glance backwards, only to find an empty hallway stretching out behind me.

Alfie's grip tightened further, and he squeezed his eyes closed as he quickened his pace. "No, no, no," he whispered. "Please, not now. Not yet."

My voice grew more insistent as I glanced over my shoulder. "Alfie, what is it?"

He pulled my face forward. "Don't look at her, Harper," he warned. "She might leave."

"Who?"

Behind us, a woman cleared her throat, causing us both to stop in our tracks as the footsteps slowed and came to a stop.

The woman's voice was confident and authoritative, leaving no room for argument. "It's time to go, Alfie," she said.

As I spun around, I caught sight of a woman, not otherworldly in nature but of flesh and blood, standing halfway down the hall, towering over us both.

The light cast a warm glow on the woman's athletic physique, her sculpted muscles accentuated by the light playing over the curves and contours of her body. The almost painfully tight bun pulling her auburn hair from her face highlighted the sharp angles and points of her porcelain face.

Her pointed stilettos protruding from the bottom of her black wide-legged trousers were a testament to her impeccable fashion sense, exuding a perfect blend of sophistication and modernity. She tucked her hands into the pockets of her black trench coat as I looked her up and down. Her face was impassive, betraying no emotion as if her eyes pierced straight through me.

A painful lump formed in my throat at the realisation that she must have been the woman Sophia had seen Alfie with. I struggled to stem the flow of furious tears that welled up in my eyes, blurring my vision and making it hard to escape the feeling that my world had shifted on its axis.

I turned to Alfie, my eyes blazing with visceral rage as he stared at the woman, unblinking, mouth agape. His chest heaved convulsively as his eyes, unable to meet mine, shifted to the floor, his shame evident in his body language as his shoulders crumpled forward.

"It's time to go," the woman repeated, her voice emotionless.

"I heard you the first time, Kay!" Alfie snapped.

I glared at Alfie as my cheeks grew warm. "Go where?" I said, my words laced with venom.

Infuriated by his silence, I felt my blood boiling like molten lava, my nails leaving tiny crescent shapes in my clenched fists. Desperate to elicit a

Chapter Six

response, any response, I prodded his shoulder roughly, knocking him off balance. "So?" I said through gritted teeth. "Where are you going?"

Kay glanced up and down the hall, her eyes constantly flitting back and forth. "She needs to keep quiet," she warned. "The others will hear."

I narrowed my eyes at Kay, my voice a growl. "This is *my* house. I'll do as I please," I said, turning back to Alfie. "So, all this time, you've been with her?"

"It's not like that," Alfie mumbled, avoiding my eyes, and staring at the floor.

"Then explain," I said, crossing my arms. "Going anywhere nice, are you?"

"I'm not going anywhere," Alfie whispered.

In all the years I'd known him, Alfie was a man of few words and even fewer emotions. Therefore, when his eyes finally met mine, swelling with tears while his bottom lip trembled, the sudden display of unexpected vulnerability caught me off guard. As I watched him struggle to hold back tears, I couldn't help but feel a sense of empathy as the tension in the air continued to mount.

"You are, Harper," he said.

Chapter Seven

My response was both immediate and visceral. My pulse quickened as my eyes narrowed at Alfie, brimming with a malicious intent that could rival the devil himself.

His betrayal cut deep and raw, like a wound that refused to heal. I didn't let it show; instead, I buried it under layer after layer of seething anger.

At that moment, I was a force to be reckoned with, a blaze of emotion that threatened to torch everything in its path.

"I'm not leaving you in my family home with her," I said, my jaw tightening further with each word.

"Please, Harper," Alfie said. "I swear it's not..."

Cutting him off, Kay's voice grew more insistent as she glanced at her watch. "We don't have time for this."

"Please, Kay. Just let me explain it to her."

I wrenched my hand out of Alife's reach. "I don't want to hear it!"

I stormed towards the front door, my bare feet pitter-pattering against the polished marble as my clenched fists swung at my sides. Alfie's fingers encircled my wrist.

As Kay's heels clicked loudly behind, trailing our every step, Alfie pulled me back towards him sharply. Gripping my shoulders, he shook me. "Harper, listen to me. It's not what you think."

"We have to go *now*," Kay demanded. "Alfie, you were warned this could happen. You've only yourself to blame for cutting your years short."

The look of wide-eyed panic on Alfie's ashen face as he pleaded with Kay seemed disproportionate to the situation. It was more than a simple case of infidelity. An underlying sense of danger seemed to permeate everything.

"Just give us some time," Alfie said, his voice wavering as his hands trembled.

Kay shook her head. "We don't *have* time. I'll explain everything to her once you're both safe."

Chapter Seven

"But Harper's tenacious; she won't listen to you. I'm begging you." Alfie released me and grabbed Kay's arm, pleading. "She'll believe me."

Kay glanced down at Alfie's hand as if his touch had offended her. She wrenched her arm from his grasp and smoothed out the wrinkles in her clothing. "It doesn't matter," she dismissed, sparing a glance in my direction. "They never believe anyone until they've returned."

As they argued back and forth, ignoring my presence, I felt like a silent, unwitting observer of the intense argument unfolding before me. Alfie begged for time, his face flushed with emotion, while Kay remained resolute in her refusal to budge.

Exhausted by their pointless squabbling, I felt my patience wearing thin. The argument seemed to go in circles, with neither side making any sense, nor reaching a conclusion.

Even during times of crisis, I had always been known for my ability to remain composed, but on this occasion, something inside me snapped.

I drew a sharp breath and clenched my fists. "What the *hell* is going on?" I yelled.

My outburst caught Alfie off guard, capturing his attention as he frowned at me with an expression of surprise and concern. Meanwhile, Kay continued checking the hall, biting her lip as if she knew she wasn't supposed to be there.

"We can't do this here if she won't simmer down," Kay said, her eyes fixed on Alfie's. "Library?"

Alfie nodded sharply, grabbing my elbow, and manhandling me towards the library. I stumbled, trying to keep up with his pace as Kay followed. She quietly closed the doors behind us and leaned against them, sighing with an unmistakable air of relief.

Alfie threw another log on the dying fire, sending a spray of red sparks up the chimney as an amber glow highlighted the gilded lettering on the books' spines. The smell of charred wood infused the air as he sat me on the sofa, folding my hands into his as he crouched before me.

Kay headed to the liquor cabinet, displaying a level of familiarity with my family home that made me feel violated. It was as if an intruder had trespassed into my private sanctuary. Offering me a brandy, she smiled.

Accepting the drink, I glanced once at the amber liquid and once at Kay's face before flicking my wrist and launching the glass's contents towards her.

With cat-like reflexes, she stepped aside, following the liquid's trajectory with her eyes and nimbly avoiding the splashes that landed on the carpet beside her. I watched in frustration as the liquid slowly seeped into the carpet's fibres, staining it with its amber hue.

Half of Kay's mouth curled into a smile. "Oh, you'll fit right in. We're going to have to work on your aim, though, kid."

"Told you she was tenacious," Alfie smirked.

"It's always the quiet ones," Kay said, her gaze softening. "Look, Harper, I'm not here to hurt you or take Alfie away—who *adores you*, just saying. But that only makes this harder."

I frowned. "Makes what harder?"

"Leaving."

"Kay's only here to take care of you," Alfie said.

"I'm a big girl. I'm pretty sure I can take care of myself."

"Not where we're going," Kay said, brows raised as she drifted towards the window and perched on it's ledge.

Alfie's tone was still pleading, his eyes desolate. "Kay, she just needs time to understand. To be told properly. Not like this."

"You've left me no choice," Kay snapped as she peered through the curtains. "Thanks to your stupidity, there's no time. He could be on his way here right now."

Alfie drew a shaky breath and interweaved his fingers with mine, his face pensive. "Harper, there are things you don't know about where you are."

"About Red Rock?" I said.

"Not specifically Red Rock. Well, I suppose so, in a way," Alfie stuttered. "But it's... it's more about you."

Kay rolled her eyes, huffing. "Jesus, we'll be here all night at this rate." She planted her glass on my father's desk and strutted towards me, her jacket flapping behind her like a raven's wings.

She locked her hands across her chest, and her focus conveyed a sense of impatience as she towered over me. "How's the war going, Harper?"

"What's that got to do with anything?" I asked.

"Kay, stop," Alfie pleaded. "She should hear it from me."

Kay continued, dissuaded. "It's been going on a while, right? Almost like it's all that you've known?"

I glared at her unflinchingly, my face emotionless. "Wars are always too long."

Chapter Seven

"True, but you've heard nothing about its progress, have you?"

"Discussing it upsets my father," I said.

Kay nodded, pursing her lips. "Fair point. Okay, supplies, then? What about those? Do you shop in the village?"

I shrugged. "That's Annabelle's business. We never leave Red Rock because it's not safe."

"So, if nobody ever leaves, which is strange in itself, you must receive deliveries?"

As my eyes narrowed, I opened my mouth but didn't have an answer. Our every need and desire had been fulfilled before we even needed to ask. I'd never even seen the postal worker delivering our morning paper.

"If you never leave and have never seen any deliverymen, how is your pantry always full?" Kay said. "And the shells for target practice, you never run out, do you?"

I fixed my gaze on Alfie, my voice sharp. "Alfie, what's this all about?"

"Now, I want you to think about this carefully," Kay continued. "Other than your family, Annabelle, and now me, you've never met another soul your entire life, have you? You've never once left Red Rock. Don't you find that odd?"

"It's...the war," I stammered. "People aren't going out."

Kay arched one brow. "People still go out in wartime, Harper. Otherwise, the entire country would grind to a standstill. Not to mention, World War Two didn't last eighteen years."

"Kay, *enough*," Alfie said through gritted teeth.

Kay stared at me intently, seemingly oblivious to Alfie's pleas. "And your perfectly preserved sister, how old is she?"

I shook my head. "I... I don't..."

"She's not aged a day since you've known her, has she?" Kay sighed, her tone softening. "I'm asking you these things because the war ended long ago."

My eyes shifted between Alfie and Kay. "So, we can leave?"

"This is where it gets hard," Kay said, a hint of empathy in her voice. "Alfie and your family can never leave Red Rock, but you can. It's why I'm here."

My brows knitted together as a dubious smile twisted my mouth. "Why? Are they under house arrest? What did they do wrong?"

85

Alfie squeezed my hands as the tumultuous storm gathering in the depths of his eyes met mine. His harrowed expression was marked by lines of emotion etched so deeply that they looked like rivulets on a landscape.

"You're not where or when you think you are," he whispered. "You *died*, Harper. We all have. We're the spirits grounded to Red Rock."

My lips slowly twisted into an awkward smile as I struggled to suppress the laughter that erupted from within me in staggered bursts.

I scanned the room, waiting for my family to burst from their hiding places, holding their sides in fits of hysterics, but nothing happened. "That's the best birthday joke you could drum up. That I'm...sorry, *we're* the ghosts?"

Alfie's tone was unnervingly flat, his face stoic, as if I'd told some horrendously offensive joke. "It's not funny, Harper."

I drew my hands from Alfie's and slapped them on my knees. "Well, Kay, whoever you are, I'd like to say it was nice meeting you, but I'd be lying."

I stood, patting down my dress, only to feel Alfie's hands on my shoulders, forcing me back into my seat.

"If you don't listen, she'll take you anyway, and we'll be robbed of a proper goodbye. If you ever had any feelings for me, *please* listen," Alfie said. "Think about it. The never-ending war, the isolation, the fact that we haven't aged. Not to mention, you've never been sick a day in your life, and you don't really feel pain, do you? None of it makes sense unless you entertain the possibility that we're telling the truth."

My fingers traced the jagged scratches on my cheek. I hadn't felt them after the séance, and I didn't feel them now. As I lowered my hand, smudges of blood shone glossily on my fingertips, yet still, I felt numb.

"I have a high pain threshold," I said dismissively. "Look, I've had enough of this for one night. I just want to go home."

Kay shook her head. "You can't. You need to come back with me."

"I'm not going anywhere with you," I frowned, inching across the sofa, trying to gain some distance. "I even don't know you."

"But I know *you*," Kay said, raising her brows.

"What has Alfie told told...?"

"How are the voices, Harper?" Kay interrupted flatly. "They're getting worse, aren't they? They're getting stronger the older you get, the closer you get to leaving."

Chapter Seven

The presence of the voices was a closely guarded secret, buried beneath layer after layer of shame and fear that had held me captive for years. Yet, somehow, Kay knew. Her piercing gaze left me feeling exposed and vulnerable, but a tiny part of me, a part I wasn't yet ready to confront, felt like a weight had been lifted.

My cheeks burned as I avoided Alfie's eyes. "What voices?"

"Don't feel embarrassed, I told Alfie years ago."

My words came in fragmented bursts. "But...how?"

"Try and understand," Kay said, each word slow and deliberate as if speaking to a child. "This isn't your life, but your afterlife."

"That's impossible," I frowned. "I grew up here."

"You died shortly after your birth in the spring of 1945. But the afterlife has rules. One is that infants who die under the age of five can grow into adulthood in the afterlife so that every soul has a chance of developing a real personality," Kay said. "Once you reach adulthood, you stop ageing. Alfie and your family lived normal lives and died as adults during the war. It's how they're eighteen years your senior but only look a few years older. The afterlife has layers of differing times, but as you all died in the same year, you've been fortunate enough to remain a family."

"So, *if* you're telling the truth..." I said, my eyes narrowing. "...who brought me to Red Rock?"

She nodded once sharply. "I did. You've been my responsibility ever since. I brought your spiritual body here, where you could be brought up in a loving home. Your parents took your physical body with them to be buried."

"Are you...dead too?" I said, grimacing.

Kay tilted her head, her auburn eyes glancing upward thoughtfully. "I'm something...in between. We're called Handlers, and I'm yours."

I pinched the bridge of my nose. "Do my family know?"

"Just Alfie. He's your Guardian, someone The Handlers entrust with the truth to ensure our assets are kept safe. Alfie's what we call an Informed Grounded spirit, someone who's aware of their death and the afterlife. The rest of your family are Uninformed Groundeds," Kay said. "They have no memory of the last few months of their lives. When a person dies, it's like their slate gets rubbed clean. The fight to survive is over, and people are less challenging in nature.

That's why you've not been concerned about the ongoing war or have tried to leave your grounding. You're at peace. This is where you belong."

"Kay suspects your father may have been ungrounded briefly at some point. That's what's affected his mind," Alfie said. "He wasn't like this when you were younger, but we've no way of knowing for certain."

I shrugged. "Can't you just ask?"

"It's against the rules," Alfie said, shaking his head.

"Rules?"

Kay took a swig of her brandy. "They're in place so the afterlife stays peaceful and doesn't interfere with the living. They'll never remember it, but the dead choose their grounding the moment they die, as long as it's a place where they've lived, died, or were born in," she said. "Most of the rules are simple. For instance, don't harm the living. But another key rule is never to inform another spirit about their death. And once you're grounded, you can never leave, though the vast majority never want to anyway. Whether Informed or Uninformed, their spirit will feel tethered to their grounding. And everything you ever need is always available. It's why the pantry's always full; Sophia has her art supplies, and you have everything you need for target practice."

Watching me absorb the information, Alfie handed me his brandy. Despite the queasiness in my stomach, I was grateful for the numbness its warmth provided.

I pursed my lips, endeavouring to keep my tone steady. "Why can't we leave?"

"Your grounding is an integral part of your identity. Without it, even for a moment, you'll lose touch with who you are. You'll lose your personality, memories, and everything that defines you." Kay's tone lowered. "You'd become an *Ungrounded,* and the process is irreversible. It's where aggressive, dangerous spirits come from."

Alfie squeezed my knee, a proud smile glowing on his face. "Which is where you come in," he said tentatively. "You belong to a group of gifted individuals called The Spirit Borns. They enforce the laws of the afterlife and hunt down The Ungrounded."

"Only Spirit Borns have the ability to pass on The Ungrounded and other rule breaking spirits to The Infinite, a paranormal prison of sorts," Kay said. "We have the power to grant you life, *real* life, if you devote it to maintaining peace in the afterlife."

Alfie's voice was a gentle purr, in tranquil contrast to Kay's severity. "Life's fleeting, Harper. It's the afterlife that's eternal. It must be protected."

Chapter Seven

I squeezed my eyes closed, the room spinning as my mind tried to keep up with the barrage of questions that came one after another. "What happened to everyone? How did they die? Did we win the war"?

"Yes, The Allies won," Kay said. "But William and your father weren't just injured in Normandy; they died there in the summer of 1944."

Alfie bowed his head. "Two months later, Sophia was serving as a nurse on a warship when it was sunk by a torpedo. She drowned helping men into lifeboats."

"But she never mentioned that part of her life," I frowned.

"It's only when you become an Informed Grounded that you remember everything," Alfie said. "She'd only been serving a month or so when she died. It was all very new, so she won't remember it. She will if she ever becomes an informed."

I swept away the tears sparkling on my lashes as I imagined Sophia floating gracefully in the water. I could almost feel the chill of the water on my skin. "She must have been terrified," I whispered. "What happened to you and Annabelle?"

"When I entered the afterlife, Kay was waiting for me on the gravel path. She told me everything," Alfie smiled. "And that I'd be your Guardian until she returned."

Kay cocked her head, smirking as her brows raised. "I didn't tell you to fall in love with her, though."

It suddenly all made sense, his unpredictable moods, the denial of his feelings, and the things he'd let slip that he shouldn't have.

He'd tried so hard to keep me at arm's length to obey Kay's instructions and save himself a broken heart when I had to leave, but as the grains of sand in our hourglass conspired against us, he couldn't resist the pull towards me.

"Once I was an Informed, my memories flooded back," Alfie said. "Before I died, I'd been in denial about Sophia, William, and your father's deaths, hiding the telegrams from Annie."

He stood and slowly started pacing the room, fingers interlocked in a white-knuckled grip, betraying his inner turmoil as he cast his eyes downward. "Several estates nearby had been commandeered by the army, painting themselves as bombing targets. Which was why late one evening, we were bombed, and a huge fire ensued," he said. "I woke to the high-pitched squeal of the bomb before Red Rock shook to its foundations."

"But if Red Rock was destroyed, how are we still here?" I asked.

"Remarkably, the foundations remained unbroken," he said. "That's what's important. If the foundations and the property's boundary remain intact, then to the dead, it'll appear how they always remembered it, regardless of its actual state. However, when the house fell to Harrison Reynolds-Woodbury, he renovated it anyway."

Alfie's voice grew ragged as his chest rose and fell sharply. "I considered letting the fire take me and joining your family, but I remembered Annie," he said. "The air was black with smoke, and by the time I reached her, she was already dead. I couldn't just leave her to burn, so I smashed her bedroom window so I could breathe and make my escape, ripping sheets into rope and lowering her down before climbing down myself."

As Alfie's pacing neared me, I reached out. Squeezing his hand, I locked eyes with him. "That was incredibly brave."

Alfie was barely able to meet my gaze as he hung his head. "My body gave out shortly after I collapsed on the lawn, but as I clung to Annie's lifeless body, sobbing, I felt like a failure. Your family all died heroes, and I... I couldn't even save Annabelle."

As the dense fog that had enveloped Alfie's character lifted, his intricate personality was unveiled, exposing the complexity and depth of the man within. The self-imposed guilt that consumed him following the tragic deaths of both him and Annabelle was the actual reason for his lack of self-esteem.

I couldn't begin to understand how negatively the continuous loss of everyone he loved had affected him. Those memories, coupled with the knowledge that he was the sole keeper of the truth, had left an indelible mark on him, suffocating him.

Kay butted in, prodding a perfectly manicured finger on his shoulder. "You didn't bomb this house. You couldn't fight because of your lungs, and you *still* ran through a burning house to try and save Annabelle. We'd have preferred to have left you uninformed so you wouldn't have had to remember, but you were the most suitable Guardian to keep Harper here."

I frowned, slurring as the brandy took effect. "What, like a prisoner?"

"Not at all, but we couldn't have you disappearing and joining The Ungrounded. But be honest with yourself; you've dreamt about the war ending but never really *wanted* to leave, have you?" Kay said. "Alfie's no jailer; he's only meant to stop you interfering with the living. Which, by the way, Alfie, that whole Ouija board business? That's *exactly* what we talked about."

Chapter Seven

Alfie hung his head like a scorned child, avoiding her penetrative gaze.

My eyes narrowed as I clung to any opportunity to poke holes in Kay's story. "You say I can't leave my...grounding. But I leave every day, and I've not become an Ungrounded. Maybe I'm an exception to..."

"There are no exceptions," Kay interrupted. "The gamekeeper's cottage is within the property's boundary lines, so you've been able to live in both."

"So, now I know the dangers. Can't I just obey the rules and stay?" I asked, my brows rising hopefully.

Kay shook her head sternly as she refilled her glass, the crystal decanter tinkling against the glass. "Nope. Someone has been targeting The Spirit Borns and wreaking havoc in the afterlife. That hand you felt in the séance?"

I instinctively ran my hand over my arm, revisiting the memory of the frigid fingers touching me in the ballroom.

The sharp shift in Alfie's voice conveyed his unease. "That was Beau?"

Kay nodded. "That hand belonged to one of his psychics. They've been searching the afterlife for you for years. Now they've felt your presence and know where to find you; it won't be long until they come looking." Kay's eyes twitched towards the windows. "If they still feel your presence here when they arrive, they'll destroy Red Rock to unground you before we can bring you back, and your family will be caught in the crossfire."

"Are they the voices I've been hearing?" I asked. "These psychics?"

"No. What you're hearing are reverberations of the living," Kay said. "Spirit Borns are more susceptible to them."

"But the crying in Sophia's room? And the piano?"

"A fundraiser was held here the other night; that was where the music came from. And the crying is what we call a residual haunting—an echo of a moment in time steeped in emotion," Kay said. "Penny, the Lord and his sons *are* here, but you died centuries apart. You wouldn't see each other until you're both Informeds."

I glanced at Alfie, the cogs in my mind whirring at full speed. "So, does that mean..."

"Yes," he nodded. "I see other Informeds. We tend to keep our distance and stick to the areas of the house we don't use, but I've been known to play the odd game of catch with the children from the garden."

"And the Lady?" I asked, unconsciously flinching.

Kay arched one brow. "Decent afterlives aren't reserved for murderers, Harper."

"The footsteps I heard during the storm, were they an echo of Penny searching for her baby?"

Kay marched loudly across the floor, her noisy heels replicating the sound I'd heard precisely. "I check in on you occasionally and chat with Alfie about your well-being. Most of the sounds you've heard are just the living. To them, *you're* the thing that goes bump in the night."

"Then you were there during the séance, too, right? I heard your footsteps."

"Informed Groundeds can spot things from our world that we use for communication, like Ouija boards, but Handlers can communicate with all spirits, Informed or Uninformed," Kay said. "Another Spirit Born informed me of your plans, so admittedly, I tried to scare you into stopping it." Her face softened as a regretful smile pressed her lips together. "And I *am* sorry about the glass."

I frowned. "*You* broke it?"

Kay returned to her perch on the windowsill and pulled the heel of her shoe into her lap, dusting away the shards of glass embedded into the leather. "And ruined a perfect pair of Jimmy Choos in the process. I figured Alfie would get the damn hint and remember the risk that Beau poses to you all."

Her glare shifted to Alfie, her fierce eyes blazing behind her knitted brows.

Alfie shook his head. "I never should've let it happen. I know how dangerous Beau is."

"Why? What's his problem?" I asked.

"He disagrees with The Spirit Borns' policies about passing on The Ungrounded," Alfie said.

"I'm not even sure if I agree with it," I shrugged. "When spirits are passed on, you said they go to the...?"

"The Infinite," Kay said. "Spirits are sent straight there after being touched by a Spirit Born. But nobody comes back from it, so we've no idea what it's like. It could be heaven or hell, or it could just be nothingness."

"Isn't that, I don't know, unethical?" I asked.

Kay approached me and squeezed my shoulder with a sickeningly artificial smile. "A lot of Spirit Borns feel uncertain about it at first, but Ungroundeds are barely human anymore. They'll attack anyone they

Chapter Seven

encounter, emotionally incapacitating them, causing physical injuries, and in extreme cases, death."

I shuddered, rubbing the chill from my arms. "So, the scariest ghosts imaginable. That's all you had to say, Kay, scariest ghosts imaginable."

"I'll tell you more about it when we're safe," Kay said. "But we need to get moving. If you're here when..."

My body tensed as I shrank away from Kay. "I can't just leave with you."

Alfie took my hands, his eyes pleading. "You've no choice; Beau will destroy Red Rock and unground us all if he senses you here."

I bit my bottom lip to stop it from trembling. "When?"

"Tonight," Kay said.

"*Tonight?*" I snapped, my eyes widening. "Why does this Beau care about one Spirit Born staying in her afterlife? I've never done anything to him."

"He knows how important you are to us," Kay said. "Each Spirit Born is granted a talent, something to help them fight The Ungrounded and exact justice over the rulebreakers. Yours could be crucial to ending our war with Beau. It's why his psychics have been searching for you—to unground you before The Handlers can bring you back and build our defence."

I stared into my lap, wet spots marking my dress as tears fell unashamedly, leaving my cheeks damp and my vision blurred.

Alfie pulled up a chair beside mine, pulling my chin upwards with his thumb until my gaze met his. "Harper, as much as I want to, I can't give you the life you deserve. You'll have a real future this way. You'll travel the world like you've always dreamt of."

As I choked back a torrent of emotion, I turned to Kay. "What happens if I stay?"

"Beau will destroy the house," Kay said gravely. "You'll all become Ungrounded and wind up in The Infinite. And without your help, Beau would destroy countless more afterlives. We need you, Harper."

I turned back to Alfie, my voice trembling. "Then come with me."

Alfie shook his head, a pained smile winkling his eyes. "I can't, sweetheart; only Spirit Borns can cross over planes. I'm where I'm meant to be."

I sniffed, leaving mascara smudges on the back of my hand as I wiped my eyes. "Then I have to say goodbye. I..."

Alfie spoke softly as he cupped my face. "You can't. What would you even say?"

"I... could say I... wanted to travel, or..." I stuttered.

"Sophia would never let you go alone. And if she leaves, we'll never get her back," Alfie said. "Kay and I have already created a cover story that won't rouse suspicion. You leave before everyone wakes, and I'll explain that your relatives tracked you down but that you've promised to return soon. If I tell your family I've met them and ensured they're good people, they'll believe me."

I picked up my glass, my hands shaking so hard that brandy spilt over the rim onto my fingers as I took a sip to steady my frayed nerves, suffusing the air with its rich scent. "Sophia will be devastated."

"She'll understand," Alfie nodded. "They all will."

"Can I ever come back?"

Kay sighed loudly, puffing out her cheeks. "You died here in your first life, so it's possible. But you've got a whole life to live in the meantime. You may end up with a family of your own that you'd prefer being grounded with."

Alfie's face contorted with emotion as he turned away, his eyes fixed on the floor. Bringing a clenched fist to his mouth, he tried to steady his breathing, squeezing his eyes shut as if trying to block out the world around him and find a moment of peace.

Kay bowed her head and headed towards the door. "I'll let you say your goodbyes."

Alfie's eyes burst open, widening with panic. His movements were swift and decisive as he positioned himself between Kay and the door, facing his palms towards her. "Wait, Beau can't get here right away. He doesn't have anyone like Lola in his pocket. Just give us until dawn. *Please*. I could never see her again," he said, his voice breaking. "I... I love her."

As Kay crossed her arms, avoiding eye contact with Alfie, I was grateful for the momentary silence. It gave me the space I needed to fully register Alfie's confession, to breathe in every word, and to make each syllable a part of me. Something to provide comfort in the arduous times ahead.

Kay finally broke the silence, groaning as she rolled her eyes and clicked her tongue against the roof of her mouth. "Just sober her up before we leave. And be back here before Annabelle wakes up."

Alfie's smile was immediate. "Thank you."

"I'll watch out for Beau from our side in the meantime," she said, her tone laced with irritation. "But if I notice anything, I'm coming straight back, no arguments. Is that clear?"

Chapter Seven

Alfie nodded animatedly. "Crystal."

Kay savoured the remaining drops of her brandy and got up to leave, her heels clicking loudly as her coat billowed behind her. But as she neared the door, her form grew semi-translucent, looking almost ghostly. The air around her seemed to shimmer as if it were alive with energy.

With a gentle burst of light, she vanished, leaving Alfie and me in an uneasy silence. The only sound was the rhythmic ticking of the grandfather clock.

I stood and started pacing, running my hands through my hair. "This is just unbelievable," I said. "And Kay's so...mean."

Alfie chuckled. "She's alright. She'll look after you and update you on how the world has changed. A lot of time has passed."

"How much time?"

Alfie's Adam's apple bulged as he swallowed. "Nearly eighty years."

The floor felt unsteady, contorting, and disintegrating beneath me. As bright spots developed behind my eyes, I steadied myself on the mantlepiece, feeling listless.

Alfie pulled a chair towards me, its legs groaning against the hardwood floor. "Sit down. I can make some coffee, and we can talk."

I shook my head, my hair flicking my eyes. "No, I can't handle any more talking. I just want my last moments to be with you."

Alfie's thumb traced a tender path across my cheek, his face betraying a bittersweet mixture of melancholy and affection. "I know, sweetheart, I'm here."

I ran my hands over his chest, feeling his muscles tensing beneath my touch as I peered up at him through my eyelashes. His touch felt comforting, yet it carried a hint of sorrow that lingered in the air like a haunting melody.

"No, I want to be *with* you."

I knew what I was asking of him, and feeling undaunted, I was adamant that it was what I wanted, my conviction growing stronger with each passing moment.

It was an overwhelming prospect; one I wasn't entirely sure I was ready for. However, as I looked into Alfie's eyes, I knew I couldn't leave without consummating the tumultuous relationship that had tested my character for eighty years. The intensity of our bond had reached its crescendo, and I was determined to see it through to its inevitable conclusion.

"Please, Alfie," I whispered. "Just take me upstairs."

Chapter Eight

As we apprehensively awaited Kay's return to the library, we snipped off a lock of my blonde curls for Alfie to keep with him always. The smell of my perfume still lingered on it as it shimmered in the morning light.

Our bodies remained entwined in a tight embrace, cherishing the last of each other's affection. Alfie's stormy eyes fixed on mine as he toyed with my hair. While I felt slightly improper, barefoot, my dress crumpled, with wild hair and smeared makeup, I finally felt like a fully-fledged woman. Alfie's declaration of love had brought me serenity and infused me with a confidence I'd never felt before.

At six a.m., we heard Kay's clicking heels growing louder. Alfie's grip on my waist tightened as Kay materialised in front of us, her form semi-transparent before becoming solid.

An empathic smile creased Kay's face. "Sorry, Harper, time's up. It's too risky to stay any longer."

Alfie handed me the books he'd gifted me for my birthday and tucked my hair behind my ear. "Take these, my own little Alice in Wonderland." He pointed at my neck. "And look after that necklace."

I pressed my lips together to stop them trembling as I fingered the jewels around my neck. "I will," I nodded.

His smile grew as he let his tears flow freely, his eyes sparkling with admiration. "I'm so proud of you; I told you you'd do amazing things one day."

Alfie stepped forward and kissed me, his lips parting mine urgently, hungrily, as Kay awkwardly averted her eyes.

I reluctantly broke away from Alfie's embrace and moved towards Kay. Alfie clung to my arms, then my hands, then my fingers as if begging me to stay.

"What do I need to do?" I asked, my eyes apprehensive.

Kay smiled, holding out her hand. "Just take my arm."

My hand quivered uncontrollably as I reached forward.

Chapter Eight

Immediately, my ears buzzed with the sound of rushing blood as nausea crashed over me.

The room began to spin as though I was caught in a perpetual pirouette or the endless swirl of a wave, yet our feet remained motionless.

Alfie fell to his knees, his face in his hands. However, my head couldn't keep track of his form, and within seconds, he and the room became a blur of colours as a shrill ringing reverberated through my ears, filling my head and then my entire body.

Kay's voice cut through the noise. "You're a good man, Alfie."

Little by little, the world around me disintegrated. As the ringing increased, disorienting me further, the room seemed to drain of all colours, turning every shade in the library grey. My every muscle felt painfully tense as shimmering white light enveloped us.

As static charged the air, I could feel every hair on my body stand to attention. I grasped Kay's hand tighter, my nails digging into her palms as a scream broke through the racket.

Pain shredded my forearms like I had been branded with a glowing poker, but as I glanced downwards, I couldn't see my own body or even Kay's beside me. All I could see was the white light, its intensity permeating every corner of my consciousness.

The pain gradually subsided to a dull ache, like an echo of what once was, and the colour returned. But as soon as I realised that Alfie was gone, my vision blurred with tears as the impact of his absence hit me all at once.

The ringing noise faded, but as streaks of beige and brown returned, I couldn't follow them. The swirls of colour and shape twisting in a vortex around me made my stomach churn. I closed my eyes, hoping the darkness would ease my sickness, but it didn't.

When the ringing stopped, and the world felt stable again, I opened my eyes. My gaze darted around the room like a cornered animal, cautiously taking in the shadowy, impersonal space.

The room was plain, with two single beds lit only by the bedside lamps, giving it a cosy, albeit dull, ambience. The furniture, although functional, was made of cheap pine and lacked any real character.

The most imposing feature in the room was the large black screen mounted on the wall, which seemed to dominate the vanilla artwork beside it.

As I noticed Kay's hand clamped over my mouth, I realised that the scream I'd heard had been my own.

Kay stroked my hair as she gently removed her hand. "You're okay. Don't scream," she said.

I blinked repeatedly, spots mottling my vision. "What...where are we?"

"A hotel in London. We'll be staying here until you're updated."

As the room became motionless, a fresh wave of nausea overtook me. My hand flew to cover my mouth, my eyes watering as the sharp tang of bile hit my tongue.

Kay tore the priceless book from my arms and spun me 180 degrees. "In there!"

With a forceful shove, she sent me crashing into a small bathroom. The fluorescent lights hummed overhead, glaring over every surface as she set the book on a nightstand. As I collapsed onto the white tiles and heaved into the porcelain, Kay appeared, holding back my hair.

I gasped for breath. "I'm...sorry."

"Don't be," Kay smiled. "It happens to most Spirit Borns when they return."

She soaked a cloth in the sink and pressed it to my brow, gently peeling away strands of hair plastered to my clammy skin.

"It's the sulphur. Of course, drinking your body weight yesterday can't have helped."

As I slumped onto the floor, I inspected my forearms, turning them over. "My arms, they..."

"Burned?" Kay interrupted. "I thought they might. It's normal; we call them markers. When you're near a spirit, the veins in your arms will turn dark blue or black, but only Spirit Borns can see them. As you were given life, you sensed Alfie's presence. It won't always hurt like that. Usually, it's an itching or tingling sensation."

Rubbing my temples, I stumbled from the bathroom and collapsed onto the nearest of the two single beds. "My head's pounding. Is that normal, too?"

The tiniest smile curled around Kay's lips. "That's your first hangover talking. You've never felt pain before, so it'll be a shock to the system. I'll grab you some painkillers while I'm out."

"Out?" I frowned. "You're leaving me here? Now?"

She tossed a card, a small plastic device, and what looked like miniature headphones into a handbag. Throwing it over her shoulder and heading for the door, she spared a glance around the room, patting her pockets.

Chapter Eight

She rolled her eyes. "Don't be such a baby, I won't be gone long. We weren't expecting you yet, so nothing's ready. You'll need modern clothes, and you're in no fit state to join me," she said. "Besides, you can't go anywhere until you're updated."

I frowned, my eyes narrowing. "You and Alfie keep saying that. What is it?"

"It's exactly what it sounds like, genius," Kay said sharply. "It's a term we use. A lot has happened in the last eighty years. You'll need a basic understanding of it before going out in public, or you'll stick out like a sore thumb. And with Beau hunting you, it's imperative you blend in."

I shot a cautious glance towards the window, its panes reflecting the dim light of the room, making them appear almost opaque.

The cityscape beyond was a monotonous expanse of concrete and steel, a dreary canvas of lifeless grey that seemed to stretch forever. The persistent drone of traffic outside, a relentless hum that seemed to permeate every corner of the room, was already starting to wear on my nerves, shattering the peace that I had grown accustomed to at Red Rock.

Rubbing warmth into my limbs, I turned to Kay. "How's it so late already?"

"Our clocks run oppositely to keep the living separate from the dead and limit the number of paranormal encounters. So, Alfie's starting his day while we're finishing ours," Kay said. "It's why you all thought the house came alive at night. But even though you've technically just woken up, coming back is strenuous, so you'll feel lethargic."

Working out the kinks in my neck, I scoffed. "Lethargic? I feel like I've been hit by a bus."

Kay rummaged through a brown leather weekend bag and pulled out some nightwear.

"I've got you some pyjamas and toiletries, though I didn't have time to buy anything else."

"Thanks."

She fetched a small plastic box from the nightstand. "This should keep you entertained while I'm gone. Televisions started becoming popular in your day, but I know you didn't have one at Red Rock. You'll be using it often, so familiarise yourself with it. It's the quickest way of completing your updating and learning modern language and culture. We'll start from the end of the war and watch everything we can. News, documentaries, and movies until we reach the present. Sound good?"

Struggling to keep up with Kay's pace, I shrugged. "Uh, sure."

She handed me the plastic box. "This controls the Television."

Feeling the buttons beneath my fingertips, I felt intimidated by my sudden introduction to the digital world. "Don't people read anymore?"

"Yes, but that takes time we don't have," Kay said.

As I awkwardly pressed a button on the remote lying flat on my palm, Kay let out a muffled giggle.

My facial expression turned sour as my brows furrowed. "What?"

"Nothing," Kay said, waving her hand. "It's just like watching Bambi learn how to walk."

My frown deepened. "Who?"

"I just mean it's bizarre. I'd forgotten what it's like with a new Spirit Born. It's kind of beautiful, really. Here..."

Kay reached for the remote, her fingers skipping nimbly across the buttons.

The TV stirred, filling the room with a kaleidoscope of vibrant colours and sounds as I gripped the bedcovers beside me, my entire body tense. She pressed another button, and lines of text filled the screen, each character crisp and clear against the dark background.

"The Wizard of Oz sounds like the perfect first-night movie," Kay said. "It'll keep you busy while I'm gone."

Her tone shifted, emphasising each word. She raised a finger as her eyes locked onto mine. "I've got a key, so *don't* let anyone in, no matter who they say they might be. And if you think of anything you need, call me. My number's on the notepad by the phone."

"But how will..."

She pulled a small screen from her bag. "Virtually everyone on the planet has a mobile phone now, so you'll always be able to contact me, no matter where I am," she said. "I'll buy you your own tomorrow."

Kay pushed another button on the remote and headed out, her heels silenced by the worn carpet. She paused at the door; her fingers curled around the handle as her eyes lingered on me. Her lips curved into a smile that radiated a palpable sense of pity.

As the door slammed shut behind her, the thud reverberated through me like a shockwave. Kay's empathetic expression left an indelible impression on me, one I couldn't shake off easily. It was as if that one pitying look had the power to unmake me, unlocking the floodgate of emotions I'd been trying to suppress.

Chapter Eight

My cheeks grew damp as I tasted saltiness on my tongue. My body shook with sobs that seemed to take over my whole being as I was enveloped by sorrow's raw vulnerability.

For the first time since the dark secrets surrounding my upbringing had been exposed, I was alone. Without the pressure of expectations, I could process my feelings in a way that was genuine and unrestrained.

Stumbling into the bathroom, I wrinkled my nose as the acrid smell of vomit lingered, mixed with the overpowering scent of lemon air freshener.

The only colour in the almost sterile white bathroom came from the bottles of shampoo and makeup artfully arranged beside the sink, illuminated by the bulbs surrounding the mirror. The unforgiving lights seemed to flicker with each beat of my heart, making the bathroom feel more like an interrogation room.

I grabbed some tissues and washed my face, wincing at the superficial scratches on my cheek that, now I was alive, I felt. Glancing at the bleary-eyed mess staring back at me from the mirror, I barely recognised my own reflection. I felt like a stranger in my own skin, lost and alone in a world that had suddenly become unfamiliar.

My dress hung lifelessly from my curves, creased and unkempt. Mascara ran in muddy veins down my ashen face. My entire body shimmered with a thin sheen of perspiration that clung to the dress in dark patches, highlighting the areas where the fabric was sticking to my skin.

I placed a hand on either side of the sink, my fingertips blanching white as I gripped the cool porcelain. Steadying myself, I stared straight into my blue and green eyes. "You can do this," I nodded. "You're a Reynolds-Woodbury, for Christ's sake. Act like it."

I closed my eyes and took a deep breath, allowing the words to sink in. Yet my mind remained consumed by thoughts of my family.

Throes of guilt surged through me as I imagined how my family was handling the news. I could almost see the creases on Alfie's furrowed brow as he struggled to explain. I imagined Sophia's tears as she inevitably stormed to my cottage, seeking confirmation and her devastation at finding it empty.

Craving a distraction, I was grateful when the television filled the room with jovial music. Enamoured by the melody, I drifted into the bedroom, my eyes fixed on the screen.

With a sense of reverence, I carefully removed my necklace and placed it on the nightstand, lovingly tracing the jewels as they sparkled in the soft lighting. I closed my eyes, trying to block out the memories associated with the necklace that tried to invade my mind.

The memories continued to pulse beneath the surface as if waiting for a moment of weakness to resurface. I turned my back to the necklace; its power was too great to confront.

As the pictures on the screen moved seamlessly, I was drawn into a world of vibrant colours and captivating sounds, momentarily forgetting about the world outside. I barely tore my eyes from the screen as I slipped into the pyjamas Kay had left me. A heavy downpour rattled the unfamiliar windows, each raindrop racing to reach the bottom.

Feeling the chill of the room seeping into my bones as goosebumps prickled my skin, I climbed into the nearest bed, pulling the soft bedding to my chin. But despite the film's uplifting plot, I felt numb, as if I was watching the story unfold from a distance.

When the credits rolled, my body sank deeper into the mattress as my mind danced in that sweet spot between being awake and dreaming. Longing for rest, I buried my head into the bulging pillows, letting their softness embrace me as I let myself drift away.

Hours later, I was jolted awake as the door slammed shut behind Kay.

She dumped a handful of bags onto the carpet and shook out her umbrella, flicking rainwater across half the room. She shrugged out of her jacket and laid it over a chair, her damp blouse clinging to her skin.

Delving into one of the bags, she pulled out two boxes and tossed them towards me. "Painkillers. And something to help you sleep. Make sure to take both. You need plenty of rest."

I examined the boxes; one was blue and labelled paracetamol, and the other was plain white with no markings whatsoever.

I rubbed my eyes. "What's in the white box?"

"I just told you. Something to help you sleep."

"I mean, what..."

Kay interrupted sharply. "So, did you like Dorothy?"

"Uh, yeah," I said, yawning. "Will I be watching films like that during updating?"

"A few, but we'll mainly be watching documentaries. But considering your passion for history, I'm sure they'll pique your interest."

I tore open the painkillers and took two. "How long will it take?"

"That depends on you. Maybe a few weeks," Kay shrugged. "Then you can go out alone and meet the others."

Chapter Eight

I frowned, my jaw agape. "I'm stuck here for *weeks*? I can't even take a walk, or...?"

Kay raised both hands, her brows knitted. "Absolutely not. You cannot leave this room. Beau knows our procedures and what to look for when a new Spirit Born returns. Even though Red Rock's safe, he'll still be searching for you."

"Why?" I huffed, tossing the boxes angrily onto the nightstand. "If I'm back, hasn't he missed his shot?"

"If I know Beau," Kay glared, pausing for emphasis, "he'll think you could be useful to him."

"Am I?"

"You could be immensely powerful, yes," she said, her tone intense. "Beau's very influential; he'll want to use that power against us rather than for us."

I gazed into my lap as my shoulders hunched. "I don't have any kind of power."

Kay's lips twisted into a slow smirk. "Not yet, you don't. But there's a fire inside of you waiting to be born."

Chapter Nine

As the first light of dawn crept over the horizon, I felt the weight of exhaustion clinging to my body like a heavy blanket. I stretched my limbs, feeling my muscles slowly come to life. The sound of traffic grew louder and more insistent, a constant hum that seemed to resonate through the city's streets, signalling the approach of rush hour.

As I stared at the flaking white paint on the ceiling, something felt off. Besides the apparent change in my surroundings, something else was different. I propped myself onto my elbows, my eyes narrowing, trying to pinpoint the source of my unease.

The sudden realisation struck me like a bolt of lightning. The voices that had incessantly plagued my mornings had disappeared

With my newfound peace, I felt able to focus on what was important, and every detail of the unfolding morning felt crisp and clear.

My focus shifted around the room, settling on Kay's empty bed, already neatly made.

The sensation of anxiety crept up on me, coiling into a knot under my ribs, as I heard a whisper emanating from behind the bathroom door. I crept closer, tucking my hair behind my ear and turning towards the closed door.

Kay's tone was barely audible but conveyed a sense of urgency and concern. "Possibly what we thought," she whispered. "Yes, last night."

Kay's feet drummed an anxious beat, her heels clicking loudly on the tiles as she paced back and forth in the small bathroom. However, only hearing one side of the conversation made deciphering it impossible.

"While she was sleeping, so we'll need to take precautions." Her voice sharpened with a harsh bite. "I *did!* That's what I don't understand." There was a pause, then another impatient response. "That's unlikely; Lola cleared the place before Harper arrived... No, it's safer for her here...Okay, I'll keep you posted."

Chapter Nine

The metallic lock on the door rattled. As my breath caught in my throat, I darted back to bed. By the time Kay had re-entered the room, I had thrown the bedding over myself.

I rubbed my eyes and yawned, channelling my inner actor in a way that would have made Sophia proud.

Kay's smile appeared forced, as if she were trying too hard to appear pleasant. Her eyes, however, remained guarded and unyielding.

A creeping sense of fear began to take root within me as doubts swelled in my mind. If I couldn't trust my Handler, the one person who was supposed to guide and protect me, then who could I trust?

She handed me a steaming cup of cheap, instant coffee. "You're awake. I just ordered breakfast. How did you sleep?"

"I had some weird dreams about Alfie," I shrugged. "I tossed and turned all night, but that's probably more to do with this hotel. It's not exactly homely."

Kay waved her hand dismissively. "It's only temporary. We'll find you your own place once we find you a job."

"I thought being a Spirit Born was my job?"

"Being a Spirit Born is a *calling*," Kay said. "You won't earn any monetary repayment for it, so you'll need to find a way to pay your bills between assignments."

I let out a derisive scoff, rubbing my temples. "Who in their right mind would employ *me*? My family educated me, but I have no qualifications, no references."

Kay winked as she brought her coffee cup to her lips. "That's nothing The Handlers can't falsify."

"But if I turn up to a job without having a clue what I'm doing..."

"I'm not saying go and work in an operating room or courthouse," Kay interrupted. "Just choose something simple you could learn on the job and go from there."

"So, never strive for anything meaningful?"

Kay cocked her head towards me, a slow and deliberate move that conveyed her impatience. "Don't put words in my mouth, Harper," she said, her tone flat and emotionless. "If you want to get a degree, it's possible, but you'll still need to keep a roof over your head, meaning night school is your only choice. Our eldest Spirit Born, Amy, is a doctor, but it's taken her twelve and half years, and she still hasn't finished her residency."

My brows shot up. "Really, a doctor?"

Kay wagged a finger dismissively. "I wouldn't suggest it. She literally never stops working. God knows how she's managed to juggle everything, but The Handlers respect how hard she's worked to get where she is, so we try not to use her in the field unless absolutely necessary."

"And the others? What do they do?"

"Most haven't shown such a dedicated work ethic as Amy. Finding real careers that'll give employees every weekend off can be tricky. Most have chosen simple roles and have worked their way up from the bottom."

My brows rose as the corners of my lips twitched downwards. "I'm only a Spirit Born on weekends? That doesn't sound too bad."

Kay shook her head as she typed furiously into her phone, her eyes never leaving its screen. "You're a Spirit Born twenty-four-seven, but yes, we only usually need you at weekends," she said. "During the week, The Handlers will interview witnesses and compile cases, then on Friday evenings, we meet to discuss them and send you out to them."

I half-chuckled, half-scoffed. "You get all that done in one weekend?"

Despite my attempts to catch her eye, she remained focused on her phone, her lips curling into a smirk of amusement. "Several of our Spirit Borns' talents help investigations run effectively."

I pulled my legs up and sat cross-legged on the bed. With a thoughtful expression, I rested my chin on my hand. "What *are* everyone's talents? And mine?"

"We don't know yours yet. And as for the others..." Another sly smirk inched across her face. "You wouldn't believe me if I told you." Kay paused, glancing up from her phone and meeting my gaze. "Uh, is there a reason you're not dressed yet?"

I inhaled sharply, my nostrils flaring as I closed my eyes and let out a frustrated sigh, shifting my focus to the bulging plastic bags of clothing Kay had purchased for me.

As I rummaged through the bags, my fingers brushed a soft cotton T-shirt and a pair of black jeans.

I held the jeans against my frame, my eyes narrowing as I examined the tag. "This can't be right."

Kay looked at the jeans, then at me. "What's the problem?"

"The tag says they're my size, but they're tiny," I said, tugging at the hems. "They'll never fit."

Kay shrugged nonchalantly. "That's skinny-fit jeans for you."

Chapter Nine

My glower was instant as I dug through the bags, searching for better-fitting trousers. "The word "skinny" in anything I'm supposed to wear, pardon the pun, doesn't fit."

"I'll save you the job of looking; they're all like that," Kay said, impatiently waving me towards the shower. "It's what all youngsters wear nowadays, so get used to it."

As warm water cascaded down my body, I could smell the faded remnants of Alfie's aftershave swirling down the drain as I showered the last of Red Rock away. The saltiness of bitter tears blossomed across my lips as I dried myself off, the scents of home replaced by the citrus shampoo Kay had bought me.

I eyed the jeans hanging from the towel rail with scepticism as I squeezed the moisture from my hair. They fit more like leggings than traditional jeans, but nonetheless, after some hopping up and down on the spot as I pulled the waistband over my hips, they fit like a glove—a tight, uncomfortable glove.

The oversized T-shirt was thankfully the opposite. Its cut exposed one shoulder, the cotton hanging comfortably from my bust in a way that balanced out the skin-tight fit of the jeans.

I emerged from the bathroom, the bitter aroma of cheap coffee filling the room as Kay gestured towards a steaming cup beside the remote control. "Ready to start updating, darling?"

My jaw tightened until my teeth ached, and my shoulders bunched around my neck as bleak tears pricked my eyes. Sophia had always called me darling and hearing her moniker for me on anyone else's lips felt wrong.

It was just a cruel reminder of the sister I'd abandoned, and that name served only as a reminder of the guilt that gnawed at me relentlessly.

As the tiny hairs on the back of my neck rose, I felt a subtle shift in pressure, like the air was charged with static. Behind me, the bathroom lights flickered erratically as though they had suffered a short in their wiring. As twitching shadows were thrown onto the gloomy walls, I felt trapped within the confines of my emotions.

Speaking between my teeth, my nostrils flared. "Don't call me that."

Kay's reaction was both swift and unexpected. She held up her hands, facing her palms towards me as if she were being held at gunpoint. "I'm... I'm sorry."

"It's what Sophia called me, *just* Sophia."

Kay swallowed, trying to hide the tremor in her voice with layers of professionalism. "I know," she nodded. "It just slipped out. I'm sorry."

Over a room service breakfast, Kay remained edgy, barely touching her food. Her eyes continually drifted to the bathroom, her brow marred with deep creases as she chewed her lip.

Even as she explained my syllabus, referring to the extensive list she'd written on the notepad on her nightstand, her focus seemed to waver. Her eyes darted back and forth between the list and her phone as it emitted an incessant stream of alerts.

As I clumsily navigated the remote to find the first documentary on Kay's list, she pulled on her coat and started packing her handbag.

"You're leaving again?"

Kay remained fixated on her phone, her demeanour distant. "I've arranged for room service to bring your meals at one and six."

"Where are you going?" I frowned.

"I'm meeting the other Handlers and have some errands to run, not that it's any of your business. Just start working through the list, and I'll be back soon."

"But..."

The shrill ringtone of Kay's phone interrupted me. She answered, holding it to her ear with her shoulder. "Yes, I'm leaving now." She covered the speaker with her hand as she glanced at me, her tone betraying her impatience. "Do you need anything before I go?"

I shrugged, puffing out my cheeks as I sighed heavily. The truth was, I needed so much from Kay—support, guidance, advice—but her dismissive mannerisms made me feel like my needs didn't matter.

I shook my head, trying to conceal the overwhelming sense of loneliness creeping through my veins like a sickness as the door slammed shut behind her.

Alone again, I summoned the courage to part the heavy curtains and take my first proper look at the new millennia I'd been thrust into.

The rain had stopped, but every surface was soddened as if no amount of warmth would ever dry it out; the grey concrete turned almost black as dampness seeped into its pores.

The sheer number of buildings, shops, and businesses surrounding the hotel was stifling. In the tight confines of the city, barely an inch of space was left unfilled.

Chapter Nine

In the distance, the sharp points and clean lines of imposing skyscrapers rose majestically into the heavens, dominating the skyline and looming over the city like concrete sentinels.

Despite the chaos of vehicles and pedestrians hurrying to their respective destinations, the city was alive with an unmistakable energy, an electric buzz that filled the air.

The environment was the polar opposite of the world I'd grown up in, with nothing familiar, nothing green or alive in sight. I was used to nature and the scents of each changing season. But instead of the sweet fragrance of blooming flowers and fresh pine, the air was thick with exhaust fumes.

I turned to Kay's list, starting my updating from the end of World War Two. However, knowing my entire family had been its victims only made the grainy images of the front lines that much more emotional.

As I watched, I couldn't help but imagine the faces of William and my father on every fallen soldier that lay strewn across the blood-soaked beaches of Normandy. Each life lost stood as a testament to a story left untold, a family wrought with grief, and the unfulfilled promise of a future that would never come to pass.

After lunch, I became engrossed in the details of Hitler's suicide, feeling relieved that the tyrant had met his demise. But I learned early on in my updating that good news ebbed and flowed with the bad, like a sinister tide that never ceased flowing.

After the credits rolled on a documentary about the Holocaust, the room fell eerily silent. I unclenched my fists and rubbed the deep, crescent-shaped marks in my palms.

I slowed my breathing and ran my hands through my hair, my heart pounding shakily. As rage simmered within me, the bedside lamps flickered for the fourth time that day, casting their intermittent glow on the walls.

I reached for the switch to the lamp, my brow furrowed as Kay swept back into the room. My body instinctively turned rigid, and amidst the roar of my heart, skipping a beat in my ears, there was a brief sizzling sound, like something in the lamp was burning.

Kay's expression was bright as she tossed her bag onto her bed and shrugged out of her jacket. "Sorry, didn't mean to make you jump," she smiled. "Good day? Where did you get up to?"

"The Holocaust."

Kay's smile turned sympathetic as she squeezed my shoulder. "Tough to watch, huh? Are you okay?"

I sighed, my eyes watering as I peered up at her. "Just tell me it gets better."

Kay pressed her lips into a thin line. "Every decade is marred by some sort of tragedy, but the Holocaust? Yeah, that's the worst, kid. And I'm sorry you were alone for it. Are you at least starting to feel at home?"

"As much as one can in a hotel, I suppose," I shrugged. "This place is miserable."

Kay raised her brows as she caught my gaze. "You're only here for a few weeks. Try *living* in them. The Handlers travel so much that we never really settle anywhere."

"Really? I could never live like this permanently. And don't even get me started on the lamps," I said, batting the lampshade. "They've been flickering all day. It's been driving me crazy."

Kay peered around me and looked the lamp up and down. "They look fine to me."

I rolled my eyes. "Of course, they stop now."

As I slowly stirred, my eyes struggled to adjust to the flickering lamp beside me, casting an almost hypnotic light into its shade.

Kay was bustling around the room, gathering her things and preparing to leave again in what was quickly becoming routine—a continually revolving door of her disappearing and reappearing. But the lack of explanation for her prolonged absences left me with an uneasy feeling that I couldn't shift from the pit of my stomach.

I couldn't help but notice the exhaustion etched on her face and the bags under her eyes that she tried to conceal with layers of caked-on makeup.

Bleary-eyed, I growled, hitting the lampshade before burying my head under my pillow.

"What did that lamp ever do to you?" Kay chuckled.

I lifted the pillow from my face, my expression a picture of irritation. "Disturb my sleep, for starters," I groaned. "Doesn't the hotel have a handyman who can take a look at them?"

Kay pressed her lips together, nodding slowly as she rubbed her chin. "Yes, actually," she said. "I'll bring him later. Just don't touch them in the meantime. They might be faulty. Now, I need to interview a witness, so I'll be out for a while."

My brows knitted as my shoulders deflated. "Again?"

"My world doesn't stop just because you've arrived, not to mention I wasn't…"

Chapter Nine

"Expecting me for a while," I interrupted, rolling my eyes sullenly. "Yeah, I got that."

The lamps flickered once more, casting erratic shadows across the ceiling.

My jaw clenched as annoyance teetered into anger. As I reached for the light, Kay's hand shot out, her reflexes unnervingly fast. Her fingers encircled my wrist with an almost bruising grip.

Her gaze met mine with an unyielding intensity. "You're letting inanimate objects get under your skin. Now, *don't* touch them. I don't want to have to explain to the other Handlers how my Spirit Born got electrocuted."

In one fluid motion, she gave my wrist a final squeeze and tossed it forcefully towards me. I caught it in my other hand, rubbing the marks left behind by her nails.

Just as she had the day before, Kay hesitated in the doorway, pulling her bottom lip between her teeth. Her eyes shifted back and forth between her phone and the lamps, then back to me as she typed furiously.

I frowned, my gaze fixed on her. "What?"

Kay's head shot up from her phone, flashing me a contrived smile as her tone grew high-pitched. "Nothing, just keep working through the list."

As I watched her strutting into the hall, her thin coat billowing behind her, my lips pursed, and my eyes narrowed. I was meant to trust Kay implicitly, yet within days, she'd changed from the composed woman I'd met at Red Rock into someone secretive and evasive. But in my enforced seclusion, I was powerless to do anything about it.

As the lamps continued to twitch, the circuits humming loudly, I rubbed my temples. Reaching for the painkillers Kay had bought me, I noticed the other box, the prescription sleeping pills, with no label or markings on the box. I'd not touched them since I'd returned.

As I changed for the day, I noticed something else. Despite knowing I'd left Red Rock barefoot, having abandoned my shoes in the ballroom after the seance, Kay hadn't provided me with any footwear whatsoever.

It was as if she was deliberately restricting my movements, ensuring my obedience. Each passing day felt more stifling than the last, as if the very air in the room was becoming heavier to bear, and I couldn't help but wonder how much longer I could endure it.

I'd left one spiritual prison only to find myself trapped in an all-too real one. Only now, my captivity was far lonelier. My only solace was knowing

Alfie trusted her. As I repeated those words like a mantra, the lights buzzed and flickered, highlighting the room's bland walls and soulless artwork.

Growling through my frustration, I defied Kay's orders, turning the lamp off at the sockets.

I flipped the switch back and forth, yet nothing happened. The unsteady lighting remained, throwing uneven shadows against the walls.

I pinched the bridge of my nose as I sighed and blew my fringe out of my eyes. I couldn't think with the continual faulty lighting, neither could I wait an entire day for the electrician to arrive to fix it.

I reached into the lampshade to remove the bulbs, my fingers twisting and turning slowly, warily.

But the culprit was already gone, leaving an empty space where it should have been. The metal components gleamed in the dim lighting as if waiting for a replacement to take its place.

I tried to shut out the perplexity of it all and come up with a rational explanation. However, Kay's peculiar and secretive behaviour had sown seeds of doubt that had taken root deep within me.

Knowing she could return at any time, I started searching the room.

I flicked through the list Kay had written until I reached the back page and spotted Kay's cursive handwriting.

The word "Sparky?" had been jotted in Kay's looped, cursive handwriting. A reminder, I imagined, to arrange an electrician.

I paused, my brows knitted as I tilted my head. "She didn't write this this morning," I muttered. "She must've written it before I'd said anything. She knew about the faulty lamps before I did."

Feeling my confusion mounting, I flung open every wardrobe door and every drawer. Every nook and cranny were empty, save for a mini fridge at the bottom of the wardrobe.

I meticulously searched Kay's luggage and turned out her pockets. Each item of clothing was folded and organised with military precision, but it was as if she had deliberately removed all traces of her existence from her belongings, leaving me no trail of breadcrumbs to follow.

I slumped onto the bed defeatedly and shot a scowl at the television screen, beginning to abhor its very creation. Then, a glint of light danced across the room, drawing my attention to the top of the wardrobe.

Squinting, I reached upwards into the shadows and wrapped my hand around the two objects catching the light, the circular glass clinking gently against one another as I pulled them toward me.

Chapter Nine

Hidden where I clearly wasn't meant to find them were two light bulbs, about the right size to fit into the empty lamps.

I huffed a heavy breath through my flared nostrils. "It had to have been Kay. No one else has entered the room since I returned. "And" I added slowly. "Talking to yourself is one of the first signs of madness."

I tried to concoct a logical explanation; perhaps the hotel staff had left spares before I arrived. But as I ran my hands over the smooth glass, the lack of dust on them and the simultaneous disappearance of the lamps' bulbs was all too coincidental.

When the lights twitched again, I felt my eyes twitch with them. I glared at the television's continual reel of tragedy and balled my fists. Letting out a primal scream, I hurled the remote control towards the screen, missing my target and knocking open the small fridge in the wardrobe I'd left ajar.

The small plastic door flung open, and a cool gust of air escaped, carrying with it the enticing aroma of the snacks and alcohol inside.

My mind instantly conjured fantasies of indulgence as the temptation to forget about my worries ran through me. I needed a reprieve from the thick knot of anxiety twisting my stomach.

I pooled the fridge's offerings on my bed, the glass bottles tinkling on the over starched bedding. I twisted the cap off a small glass bottle of whiskey and downed it straight, relishing the fiery burn of the liquor as it scorched my throat and settled warmly in my stomach.

I turned my attention to the snacks on offer, ripping open packets of chips and nuts, the plastic wrappers crinkling loudly in the silent room. I devoured their contents greedily, washing them down with sip after sip of various spirits.

As I drank my second and then third bottle, I felt the alcohol coursing within me like a rebellious fire. As my vision blurred, defiance stirred in my veins. It was a feeling I'd never succumbed to before, yet it felt like it had always been inside me, waiting for the right moment to emerge. It felt like it belonged with me, as if it had found its true home.

Tossing Kay's hallowed list onto the floor, I switched the television to some random comedy series. The sound of audience laughter filled the room, and I felt a faint smile tug at the corners of my mouth.

It was only a temporary respite, but it was better than nothing. Despite the distraction, I yearned for something more than the sound of canned laughter. I craved human connection, the kind of interaction that could only be found in real conversation.

As I poured the last of the fridge's alcohol, a bitter-tasting red wine that stained my coffee cup, the phone Kay had bought me beeped.

18:08—Kay: Sorry I'm late. I'll be back soon; I'm just fetching the electrician. Kay.

Had I not been intoxicated, I probably wouldn't have dared even consider disobeying Kay's rules. But something inside me snapped, and a sudden urge to flee the confines of the claustrophobic room overtook me.

Using the excuse that I was out of alcohol and driven by a sense of recklessness, I tidied up my appearance, pulled the tags off my new leather jacket and slipped it on.

I stumbled into the hall to find the hotel's bar to continue losing myself in the numbness that alcohol provided, unconcerned by my lack of footwear or money.

Chapter Ten

The shimmering lights in the lift flickered incessantly on the trip down. I shot them a glare, rolling my eyes. "Does anything in this hotel work?"

Even as the lift shook with metallic groans and vibrations, I was too focused on my escape to pay much attention to the defects.

The mirrored walls reflected my unmoved expression as I remained rooted to the spot, lost in my thoughts and driven by my goal. It wasn't until a sudden, loud ping echoed through the lift that I snapped back to reality.

As the lift doors parted, the sounds of the bustling front counter spilt into the small space. But before I could take a single step, I found myself face-to-face with Kay.

The moment her eyes met mine, her conversation with the young man beside her trailed into silence, and a wave of palpable hostility washed over her. Her piercing gaze held me in place, her nostrils flaring as she took in my appearance, her anger emanating like a visible aura around her.

Slowly, she folded her arms. "Where do you think you're going?"

"The bar," I slurred, shrugging one shoulder.

Kay looked me up and down, mouth agape. "Are you *drunk?*"

"No," I lied, narrowing my eyes. "That's why I'm going to the bar. You coming?"

The man beside her stifled a laugh, glancing downwards to hide his growing smile. Kay shot him a warning glance, conveying her disapproval without uttering a word as she spun me around and shoved me back into the lift. She and the electrician followed closely behind, standing in uncomfortable silence as the lift slowly returned to our floor.

The heady scent of the electrician's cologne was almost overpowering in the confined space, the blend of vanilla and sandalwood commanding my attention and enveloping my senses as he towered a foot over me.

He leaned casually against the mirrored wall, tucking one foot behind the other as his broad shoulders tested the seams of his snug T-shirt and flecks of mud drifted from his work boots onto the rich carpet like snow.

Noticing me staring, his striking emerald eyes slowly looked me up and down as the tiny shards of amber peppered within them shimmered. "What?"

"You're the electrician?" I asked.

His handsome features twisted as he turned his head, wafting a hand in front of his face. "Yeah. Jesus, what have you been drinking?"

"Everything in our mini bar."

His sandy hair shimmered under the lights as he shook his head, his voice laced with sarcasm. "Clever."

His neatly stubbled jaw tightened as he rubbed the back of his neck, drawing attention to the tattoos adorning his biceps, a swallow in mid-flight, its wings extended, while thorns and lilies added complexity and depth to the artwork.

I'd imagined that electricians wore overalls or at least carried tools, but he had neither. He was dressed casually in weathered dark jeans and a pristine black T-shirt. The only part of him that matched a workman's typical attire was his chunky boots and gloves, both splattered with paint and wood shavings.

His hands, however, caught my attention. Partially hidden by the gloves, black staining that resembled soot spread towards his wrists as he extended one towards me. "Harper, right?" he said nonchalantly. "I'm Hunter."

I nodded, feeling all too aware of my intoxication as I reached out. As his fingers enclosed mine, I felt sudden a jolt of electricity that seemed to run through my entire body. It felt like a bucket of ice-cold water had been doused over me, making me feel immediately alert, like my every nerve was on high alert as a magnetic pull, which made me feel more alive than I had in a long time sang from my every cell. Instantly, the lights went out.

At that moment, everything seemed to fade away—the hum of the air conditioning and the machinery's whirring. It was just the two of us, suspended in time, lost in the current that flowed between us, and in the darkness, the impossible felt obtainable.

Just as suddenly as it had begun, the moment was over. The lights abruptly flickered back on. Hunter pulled his hand away as if he had been burned and I was left standing there, feeling a strange sense of loss, as if something important had slipped through my fingers.

Chapter Ten

Kay's frown was beyond intimidating as she exchanged steely glances with Hunter, her frown contorting her face. His gaze drifted up and down my body again as his chest heaved breathlessly.

As we entered the room, Kay's eyes darted to the chaotic pile of scattered wrappers and empty bottles. Her hands instinctively found their way to her hips as her lips formed a thin, disparaging line. "We'll discuss this later."

Despite her obvious embarrassment, Kay retained her composure, exhibiting a level of professionalism that was truly impressive as she guided Hunter towards the lamps.

As he started fiddling with the wires, I took a seat on my bed, cocking my head and raising my brows. "You might need the bulbs," I said, smirking.

For the first time since I'd known her, Kay stuttered. "Uh...the... flickering kept waking me up, so I removed them."

"But how were they still working?" I asked.

Hunter stopped moving, his body stiff as his gaze shifted between me and Kay. His brows raised as his eyes fixed on Kay's. She stared straight back, subtly nodding as if silently urging him to respond, her every movement slight and nuanced.

Finally, Hunter broke the awkward silence, his eyes avoidant. "Uh, if the fixtures get hot enough, they might glow slightly."

Despite my lack of knowledge regarding contemporary electrical appliances, I immediately became sceptical of Hunter's response. Perhaps it was the way he spoke or the ambiguity in his tone, but something about his explanation didn't sit right with me.

"And the lift?" I pressed.

"That'll have to wait until the hotel's quieter to service it," Hunter said.

I narrowed my eyes. "Don't people use stairs anymore?"

Hunter took a deep breath, a slight growl vibrating deep within his chest as his jaw tightened.

"Yes. I just think the wheelchair users may struggle with them. Don't you?" He thrust out his hand impatiently. "Do you have the bulbs?"

I scowled, carefully pulling out the bulbs and handing them over, but as I sat back down, I stumbled, the floor rushing towards me at a dizzying speed.

Reactively, Hunter reached out and caught me before I hit the ground, steadying me. My fingers instinctively gripped his forearm, feeling the tension in his muscles as his gaze met mine, seeming to fix me in place.

Their vivid green colouring seemed to contrast a darkness that lay within them, one that spoke of a hidden pain that I understood well.

However, his wry smile vanished, replaced by an intimidating seriousness, yet a strange desire pulsated from the depths of my stomach that seemed to charge the air with static.

Behind us, the sudden noise of the television startled us both. Its white noise and the mess of colourless dots on the screen made it difficult to concentrate on anything else. He set me on the bed and rubbed his skin where my hands had gripped the sinewy muscle, raising every hair on his arm.

Gesturing to the remote at the very end of the bed, Kay mumbled. "Sorry, I... leant on the remote."

Hunter blinked and shook his head, almost as if clearing his vision as he refocused on his task. "The hotel suffers from dampness, which affects the electrics. There's nothing wrong with the circuits or cables, so there's nothing I can do."

"You can't fix a broken lamp?" I scoffed, cocking my head. "What kind of an electrician are you?"

Hunter's glare was immediate, his eyes narrowing as he spoke through gritted teeth. "An exceptionally good one, actually. Not that you know a *thing* about the subject."

"Then let's just leave the bulbs out," Kay shrugged.

Hunter shook his head, running his hand through his hair. "I wouldn't. They can be good indicators for...problems," he said carefully. "Besides, you'd only get into trouble with the hotel."

I frowned. "Don't *you* work for the hotel?"

Hunter's eyes, the exact shade of my one green eye, drifted to mine. "I'm freelancing," he said, smirking. "Nice meeting you, sort of."

Kay sighed, leading Hunter to the door. "Thanks for coming anyway. I'll show you out."

Hunter glanced at the rubbish littering my bed, then at me as he walked towards the door. "Hope it was worth the hangover."

"Trust me when I say it most definitely was," I said.

A faint but noticeable smile played at one corner of his lips as he strode into the hallway, his gait purposeful but unhurried.

Chapter Ten

Kay leaned back into the room from the open doorway. "I'll be right back."

With a soft click, Kay closed the door behind them. Their muted conversation faded but didn't disappear completely, lingering in the air like a delicate perfume.

Left with an insatiable sense of curiosity, I felt drawn to the door like a moth to a flame. I peered through the peephole, unable to resist the urge to catch another fleeting glimpse of the enigmatic electrician.

A few doors down, Kay's restless feet carried her back and forth as her hands gripped her hips, fingers digging into her delicate blouse. Her eyes were fixed on the carpet, as if searching for an answer that lay hidden in its tired fibres.

Hunter, on the other hand, stood with his back against the wall, his arms crossed casually over his chest as he rested a foot against the wall, knee bent.

He had a relaxed, almost nonchalant air about him as his gaze followed Kay's pacing back and forth. "You keep her locked up like that much longer, and she's going to lose it. We've seen that look before," he said, brows raised pointedly.

Kay glanced upwards, shaking her head. "God, don't remind me," she muttered, rolling her eyes. "And you're sure it's not..."

"Positive. There are a couple of jumpers higher up, but everything else is residual. Is it really happening every night?" he said, wincing sympathetically.

"All night, every night."

"What about the medication?" Hunter said.

Kay let out a frustrated sigh. "She won't take them, and I can't exactly force them down her throat, not with what she could do to me. I thought taking the same precautions as we did with..."

"She's nothing like the others," Hunter interrupted. "She's far more powerful. And keeping her caged like this is dangerous. All that energy will manifest itself eventually. I can feel it coming off her in waves. You need to get her somewhere quiet, like yesterday."

Kay's brow furrowed as she chewed her lip. "We've done things this way for centuries."

As Kay neared Hunter, he gripped her shoulder, forcing his gaze on hers. The intensity in his eyes and the tone of his voice conveying a sense of urgency. "But you've never had anyone like her before. If you're committed to taking her on, you need to throw out the rule book. But right now, she's not in control. She's endangering everyone around her."

"Maybe you could take her for a while, just temporarily," Kay said, her eyes widening pleadingly.

"And burn down another one of my houses in the process? No thanks," Hunter scoffed. "Besides, she needs stability, not to be passed around like a child."

Kay pressed her lips together, nodding once sharply. "Then I want you to help Dominic train her."

Hunter rolled his eyes, crossing his arms. "You know I hate it down there. Dom can handle her alone."

"But you'll be able to help her in ways nobody else can and make life safer. Please?" Kay said, clasping her hands together.

A heavy silence filled the air, the awkward stillness between them palpable as Hunter squeezed his eyes closed. He let out a long sigh that seemed to reverberate through the silence as he pinched the bridge of his nose.

"Fine," Hunter huffed. "Only if you promise to let her out. Just be careful about it. If Hannah's right, she'll be a paranormal magnet. I'm surprised you've not had stragglers knocking your door down already."

Kay frowned, shaking her head. "She's not ready. She's only just got back."

"The hotel's packed, Kay. If she snaps, it won't be pretty. Just give her some time to herself *out* of the hotel. Have you found a place for her to live on the outskirts of the city yet?"

"She needs a job first."

He raised his eyebrows, checking his watch. "That can wait. This can't. Look, I'm late meeting a client. See you both Friday?"

"It'll just be me."

Hunter's brow furrowed as he shrugged. "Why? We could really use her help; it's getting bad out there. She needs to learn at some point."

Kay's head shook with a finality that left no room for doubt, her expression conveying her decision. "Not yet," she said, her voice resolute. "Thanks for coming. I... I just had to make sure it wasn't anything else."

Hunter flashed a teasing grin as he strolled casually towards the lift, his hands tucked in his pockets. "No problem. I'll send you my bill in the post."

As Kay made her way towards the door, I scrambled to tidy up the mess I'd created and restore some semblance of order in the room. With a knot

Chapter Ten

tightening in my stomach, I prayed that my half-hearted show of regret would lessen the severity of the scolding that was undoubtedly coming.

As the door opened, Kay's genuine smile caught me off guard. "Sorry, I had to show him to the foyer," she lied. "About this..." Her voice trailed off as she nodded to the empty bottles.

I stared at the carpet, bracing myself. "I know, I crossed a line."

Kay's expression softened, and an empathetic smile brought a radiance to her face that was nothing short of beautiful. "Yes, you did, and you put yourself at risk, but...I understand. You've been under immense pressure. Please just clean up your mess, and *don't* do it again."

The last thing I needed was for Kay to become even more secretive, so I thought it in my best interests to keep everything I'd overheard to myself.

But despite Hunter's unapproachable and detached demeanour, an inexplicable discernment inside told me I could trust him more than I could Kay, whether it's because what I'd overheard hinted that he, too, was a Spirit Born.

Within his eyes, I saw a relatable sadness, one that suggested that the anguish I was suffering was an old friend of his. It was as if we shared an unspoken bond, a connection that only other Spirit Borns could understand.

As Kay changed for bed and washed the makeup from her face, a pang of guilt tugged at my emotions. Her eyes bore the evidence of her weariness, ringed with dark shadows that sullied her features. As soon as she lay down, she drifted off to sleep, her body desperate for rest, and after what I'd heard, it was clear I was to blame for her exhaustion.

I settled into the soft embrace of my bed beside her, trying to dispel the doubts festering within me surrounding Kay's continual lies. As I grabbed the remote control and turned off the television, the flickering glare of the lamp reflected the light off something that, in my hazy state, I hadn't noticed Kay bring into the room earlier.

Discreetly tucked behind the wastepaper bin, overflowing with the remnants of my drinking binge, was a small, red fire extinguisher. Its colour contrasted sharply against its drab surroundings as its polished nozzle pointed directly toward me like a stainless-steel finger.

Chapter Eleven

After my minor altercation with the minibar, which had left me with a headache that would've crumbled Everest, Kay and I settled into a comfortable routine.

Following Hunter's advice, she negotiated a mutually beneficial agreement with me in which I would receive free time as a reward for achieving certain milestones in my updating.

With the promise of freedom on the horizon, the palpable tension simmering between Kay and me began to fade, and our petty disputes became less frequent.

However, as I made strides, Kay struggled. She'd wake increasingly lethargic, relying on endless jars of coffee to function, her hands trembling with the caffeine as she caked layers of makeup onto her face to conceal the evidence.

As the days ticked by, the malfunctions in our room increased. The lights would flicker sporadically, and the air conditioning would blast freezing air in the middle of the night. And every morning, I'd find that the fire extinguisher had crept closer to my bedside.

When my first day of independence arrived, I was almost giddy as I felt the spring breeze kiss my cheeks. I straightened my leather jacket, the collar nestling comfortably against my neck as I ignored the uncomfortable rub of the combat boots Kay had finally bought me.

As I made my way down the sweeping front steps of the hotel, my eyes were hypnotically drawn to the display of leaflets on a wooden stand just inside the entrance. I felt a shiver of anticipation run down my spine as I recognised one of the attractions.

Nestled between coupons for theme parks and zoos was a pamphlet advertising Red Rock. The scars of a bombing were etched deep into its facade, a thick zigzag running across its once pristine surface. But despite the damage, the house had been lovingly restored and pieced back together.

Chapter Eleven

I cast a wary glance over my shoulder, scrutinising every face in the foyer to check Kay wasn't watching me. Once I was sure the coast was clear, I snatched one of the leaflets, stuffed it into my pocket, and headed towards the nearest train station.

When my phone's GPS indicated that Red Rock was only a short journey away, a plan started taking shape in my mind as a spark of nostalgia ignited within me.

Returning home so soon may have been impulsive, but the magnetic lure of its familiar embrace was too compelling to resist. I longed for the comfort of the familiar sights and sounds that could transport me back to a simpler time and briefly help me forget about my chaotic new life.

My stomach roiled with apprehension as my image stared back at me from the window. As I questioned the recklessness of my plan, the train seemed to answer, gently rocking me and lulling me into an almost trance-like state as it rumbled along the tracks.

With my faith in Kay wavering, her assurances about my family's safety were starting to feel hollow, like a thin veneer hiding a deeper truth. The only thing that could curb my paranoia was visiting Red Rock myself.

As I watched the overwhelming concrete jungle morph into the serene countryside that I knew so well, the shifting colours created a mesmerising display of natural beauty that soothed my anxiety and replaced it with a sense of anticipation.

The verdant greens of the landscape and the bright blue skies overhead all came together in a perfect symphony of colours.

In the distance, I could see the old house nestled in the valley, waiting for my return, its solemn exterior conveying a sense of grace and dignity. After a short taxi ride from the station, I felt my cheeks burning as I heard that familiar crunch of gravel underfoot.

With the passage of another eighty years, the house had undergone a transformation, appearing more refined than ever before. The masonry had weathered, and the young ivy from my afterlife had flourished, its lush tendrils climbing the walls and reaching across most of the building like outstretched fingers.

The bombing had left a thick fault line running through the old and new rock, resembling a deep battle scar that spoke volumes about the building's past. Despite the damage, the house still stood tall and proud, like an old friend who had withstood the storms of life and come out the other side.

I lifted my gaze towards the sky, the sun's warm rays shining down on me as my eyes were drawn to the intricately carved granite aces. I couldn't help but smile as the four card suits were effortlessly cast onto the ground, their shadows dancing playfully at my feet.

Then, as if pulled by an invisible force, my gaze drifted toward Alfie's window. In his world, it was two a.m., but still, I waited below, watching. I felt a sense of detachment, as if I was the only person awake in a sleeping world.

I nodded, willing myself forward. "They'll be asleep," I muttered below my breath. "They wouldn't dare walk the halls at night after the seance."

I joined the end of a line of tourists waiting to go in, trying to ignore the clenching ache in my gut at being so close to Alfie, yet worlds apart.

As I rifled through my purse for the bank card Kay had given me, in my peripheral vision, Alfie's curtain twitched as a form passed through the light within.

My focus jerked upwards, my brows furrowed as I stared at the window, but there was nothing but an expanse of glass reflecting the world outside. The chatter of the tourists around me faded into a distant hum, as if I was listening to them from underwater. My feet felt rooted to the ground, unable to break free of the moment.

Finally, a man coughed loudly behind me, dragging me from my reverie and urging me forward.

A simple front desk had been erected in the foyer next to the stairs. The chequered floors, polished to a high shine, gleamed under the warm light of the chandelier.

The gilded mirror by the door reflected an almost ethereal amount of light around the room. I recognised one of Sophia's landscapes on the far wall. Her impressive skill was evident in every stroke of vibrant colour, evoking a sense of nostalgia that warmed my heart.

An upbeat guide, her name reading "Sasha", stood behind the desk, smiling warmly. "Are you taking the tour?" she asked. "There's one in ten minutes."

I handed over my new bank card, nodding.

As Sasha processed my payment, my eyes drifted towards the grand staircase, feeling an irresistible pull. He was up there. *Alfie was up there.*

I ran my hand along the polished mahogany handrail, tracing every dent and groove with my fingertips as I ignored the red velvet rope crossing the bottom step.

Chapter Eleven

"Can I look around while I wait?" I asked, my tone hopeful as my eyes remained fixed on the stairs.

Sasha smiled, her chocolate eyes sparkling as she reached across the stairs and rested her hand on the banister. "Yes, but upstairs is closed. It's just offices and storage up there anyway."

Begrudgingly, I made my way to the library. Every door was marked with green fire exit signs, and each available socket was occupied by electric heaters, circulating stale air and the scent of ancient books as the fireplace sat a dormant relic.

Velvet ropes cordoned off the spiral staircases and bookshelves, rendering the vast collection of literature purely ornamental. My father's desk, which had once anchored the room, had disappeared altogether, leaving a solemn void where it once stood.

Red Rock's preparations for the viewing public had come at the cost of its charm and character, stripping it of its homeliness and replacing it with an almost sterile feel. But it was still home.

I turned to the painting above the fireplace, its edges marred by scorch marks, a painful reminder of the bombing. I'd always admired Sophia's work, and the portrait of my family and Alfie in the library was my favourite.

I admired the realism of her work. Whilst many artists painted their subjects to look like professional models or china dolls, Sophia left no crease or freckle forgotten. She meticulously ensured that each expression appeared natural, pouring so much of herself into her work that it felt like a part of her had been embedded into the canvas.

The olive-skinned guide, Sasha, appeared at my side, her raven hair glistening in the light as she admired the piece. "Isn't it stunning?" she said, crossing her arms. "The artist's work is all over the house, but we've never been able to identify them."

A proud smile tore through my cheeks. "It's Sophia Reynolds-Woodbury."

"I thought she was an actress," Sasha frowned.

"She was, but she studied art too. Check the back of the canvas." I nodded towards the portrait. "She was always so self-conscious about her work that she never signed the front but always put her initials on the back corner."

"Really? I just wish we had more."

"She often hid her work. Put her on stage, and she'd glow, but with a paintbrush in her hand, she was insecure. I imagine any pieces in the attic would've been damaged by the fire but check the cellar. You might get lucky and find some that aren't stained red."

"We've kept the stains in the cellar a secret. It's off-putting to tourists," she said quietly, leaning closer. "How do you…"

"My…relatives worked here in the forties. I've heard a lot of stories," I interrupted. "But I haven't visited for a while."

Sasha checked her watch. "Then welcome back," she smiled. "And thanks for the tip. I'll make sure to check the painting."

With a gentle clearing of her throat, Sasha began the tour. A small crowd gathered around her as she chatted informatively about the library's individualism and how it had narrowly escaped destruction. She guided us towards the ballroom in a memorised recital that weaved a rich tapestry of Red Rock's history and the Reynolds-Woodbury lineage. A lineage that no one would ever know I was a part of.

Even in the light of day, surrounded by people, my mouth turned dry as I revisited the room where I'd first heard Beau's name, the faceless man who posed such a grave threat to me, my family, and The Spirit Borns.

Unconsciously, I traced my fingers over the spot where one of his psychics had grabbed me. Feeling the prickle of goosebumps rising on my skin, it was as if the room held onto the memory of that encounter.

The ballroom had been prepared for a wedding, the classical surroundings colliding with an air of modern romance. Delicate pastel flower arrangements were scattered around the room and on each of the neatly laid tables, permeating the room with fresh nectar.

The space had been spared any severe damage after the bombing. The only lasting evidence was the faded smoke stain that clung to the ceiling.

We continued through the house and passed the staircase. I hung back from the crowd, letting them flow around me like a stream of water around an immovable boulder.

When I looked up, I felt that pull, that familiar feeling I couldn't quite define. It was part excitement, part trepidation—a sense that something I needed awaited me there.

With Sasha's voice trailing into the distance, I noticed the unattended front desk as the rope cordoning off the staircase taunted me. I took a deep breath and ducked beneath it, feeling the plush velvet brush my neck as I crept upstairs.

Chapter Eleven

As I climbed the staircase, the change in ambience was palpable. The second floor felt like entering a desolate wasteland devoid of any semblance of character.

Each room had been gutted, stripped of any adornment or furniture. In their place were rows of filing cabinets, stacks of boxes, and collections of broken and battered furniture.

The air was thick with the smell of old wood and dust, and as I walked through those lifeless corridors, it felt like I was walking through a graveyard, a place where the memories of my family's past lay buried and forgotten.

Only two rooms appeared to be in use. The smell of a freshly brewed pot of coffee wafted from a guest bedroom at the end of the hall, which had been converted into a staff kitchen. And the other was Alfie's, the only room upstairs that I could safely venture into.

I stood in his open doorway and smiled. In the middle of the room proudly sat my father's desk, littered with invoices and curling receipts, as a computer screen provided the only light in the room. Metal shelving filled with office supplies lined the walls, making the room feel claustrophobic.

Despite finding the room empty, seeing the room's purpose satisfied my curiosity that the movement I'd seen had likely been a staff member and nothing more.

I closed my eyes and sighed, trying to block out the shelving and papers and remember the room as it once was. I wasn't sure what I expected or hoped to see, but finding the empty room still stung.

But as I turned to leave, my breath collected in delicate plumes around me, their ashen colouring distinct as they lingered in the shadowy hall. The hairs on the nape of my neck rose, tickling my collar as I rubbed at the sudden itch prickling across my forearms.

I drew up my sleeve as my markers developed. An inky, tree-like stain spread across my skin, its dark branches blossoming from my inner elbow, splaying outward as they neared my wrist, discolouring my veins.

I tried to hide the nervous flutter in my voice as I whispered into the shadows. "Alfie?"

As my markers darkened, I cursed my selfishness for coming back. If I came across anyone but Alfie, their afterlives would be over.

"Stupid, stupid, stupid," I muttered, shaking my head.

I reached for the door handle, and a familiar scent enveloped me—the infatuating scent of vanilla and sandalwood I'd washed away weeks ago.

I slowly closed my eyes, feeling it fill my lungs as I took one hungry breath, rendering me bewitched by its spell, unable to move or speak.

An ethereal whisper drifted across the room. "Harper?"

I nodded breathlessly as my eyes swept across the room. "Yes, I'm here."

Alfie eerily passed through a filing cabinet from where, in his afterlife, his bed was. His form was clear and crisp, identical to any living being.

I could see the outline of his pyjamas, the gentle curves of his toes poking beneath them, the highlights of his tousled hair, and the vivid blues of his watery eyes.

"Am I dreaming?" he said, blinking.

"No, I'm really here."

His eyebrows rose. "Why? Is something wrong?"

"No," I shook my head. "I just had to check you were okay."

Alfie swiftly crossed the room, his arms outstretched. "I... I thought I'd never see you again."

I recoiled, facing my palms outwards. "Stop. We can't touch, remember?"

"Of course, I didn't think." He dropped his hands awkwardly at his sides. "I've got so much I want to ask you. "If you're here, does that mean you've finished updating?"

"Not yet, I'm just having a break."

"So, your talent...is that...?"

"I don't know what it is yet," I said. "But I think it has something to do with electricity."

Alfie rubbed his eyes, pointing upwards. "That's what woke me. The lights started flashing."

"God only knows how it'll help us," I chuckled. "But Kay's not exactly been forthcoming with information."

Alfie looked towards the hall expectantly. "Is she here? Can I talk to her?"

"She doesn't know I'm here. Today's the first day I've had to myself."

A heavy silence permeated the room as every beat of my heart rang in my ears. Alfie's eyes never left me and seeing him and being unable to touch him was torturous. The distance between us seemed insurmountable, an abyss I couldn't cross. Yet, every fibre of my being itched to run to him and feel his arms around me, consequences be damned.

Alfie glanced around the room, wincing and rubbing the back of his neck. "How's Red Rock looking?"

Chapter Eleven

"Good," I nodded. "A few battle scars, but it adds character."

"And how have you been? You look well."

I hated the forced chitchat. It felt like all the progress we'd made in our relationship had been undone, like the walls we'd broken down had been rebuilt and were back to polite conversation and longing glances.

It was as if the intimacy we had shared had never existed. My only evidence that it was ever even there sparkled from my nightstand. The necklace was a continual reminder of the love I had lost.

"Updating has been...lonely. I've not done much else," I shrugged, almost ashamed that my new life was so insignificant. "How's everyone else?"

"They were upset you left without saying goodbye, but that's understandable. We've been keeping Sophia busy." Alfie's eyes fell to the floor. "But she's only just stopped crying."

As my eyes welled with tears, my guilt enveloped me like a blanket of regret. Alfie's face tensed with empathy, looking equally as pained. Unable to comfort me physically, he changed the subject, adopting a lighter tone to ease the tension hanging in the air.

He smiled, trying to catch my gaze. "You look different."

I glanced at my outfit—skinny jeans, leather jacket, and chunky combat boots—and shrugged, my mind still preoccupied with thoughts of Sophia.

"What're the other Spirit Borns like?" he asked.

"I haven't met them yet. Apparently, I'm not ready," I said. "We only have assignments on weekends, meaning I'll have to get a real job, too."

"Kay told me. But you'll have a proper life like you always wanted." Alfie smiled, but it didn't reach his eyes.

"I liked my old life."

"You would've always had to leave eventually. Perhaps it's better this way, not getting too...involved."

My clenched jaw and balled fists betrayed my emotions as they threatened to spiral out of control. As if responding to my pain, the computer on the desk beside me sprang to life, churning through streams of paper that scattered haphazardly onto the floor.

I closed my eyes and steadied my breathing, trying to calm myself, but the computer seemed intent on defying me, spitting out meaningless pages of text and graphics that only seemed to reflect my inner frustration.

Alfie approached me cautiously, his wide blue eyes pleading. "Look at me, Harper," he said. "This is hard for me, too. You get to experience the world, and I'm stuck here waiting for you to return—if you return."

"I swear I'll be grounded to Red Rock again. Then, when I become Informed grounded, we'll be together again," I said. It's my paradise."

"It was mine too, but without you..." he whispered, "... it's purgatory."

I turned away, closing my eyes as my voice turned gravelly. "Don't."

"You know full well that if we'd have been together longer, you never would've left, and Beau would've found you eventually," Alfie continued. "Besides, The Spirit Borns need you. Kay needs you."

My eyes filled with a venom I never wanted Alfie to see in me. "I don't want to do anything for her," I snapped. "I don't trust her."

"Since you were born, she's only been excited to work with you. You know, to find out if it's all true."

I frowned, my eyes narrowing. "If *what's* true?"

"I... I thought she would've told you by now."

I pointed towards my cheeks, flushing with frustration. "Does this look like the face of someone in the loop?"

He stared at his feet silently and knotted his hands, his eyes avoidant.

"Alfie," I growled. "If *what's* true?"

Alfie raised his hands submissively. "Alright, alright There's this Spirit Born; her talent is seeing things before they happen. Kay said that she's had two premonitions about you. One is that you'd bring peace to the afterlife and a better understanding of The Ungrounded."

"And the other?"

He paused, huffing a short breath through his nose. "The other was that you would rebel against your Handler's rule alongside Beau."

"Then which one's true?"

"Nobody knows. Whatever happens will be up to you. I promise that's all I know," Alfie said, shaking his head. "But you won't find answers about your future by looking backwards. I know you'd never side with that monster.

The brief silence was broken by the sound of footsteps approaching. Peering through the gap in the door, I spotted Sasha ducking her head into each room, searching for her lost visitor.

"I've got to go," I said.

"Wait, don't leave like this."

"I have to," I whispered. "Someone's coming."

Alfie's eyes widened as his shoulders slumped, his tone laced with disappointment and fear. "Will you come back?"

Chapter Eleven

I glanced at Alfie, my bottom lip trembling. It felt like we were saying our final goodbyes all over again, and looking at his deflated posture and stormy eyes, I knew he felt the same. "They've closed the upstairs," I said, "I don't know if I can get up here again."

"Then I'll sleep downstairs," he said, his voice shifting from disappointment to desperation. "Just promise you'll come back."

"You can't live like that."

He sliced his hand through the air. "If it means seeing you, I don't care."

"I do," I whispered. "Look, the guide's here, I can't stay."

As Sasha spotted me, I could do little more than nod a subtle goodbye to Alfie. Her shoulders relaxed as she met my gaze, her eyes tracing my body from top to toe.

Sasha glanced into Alfie's room, frowning. "Who were you talking to?"

"I... had a phone call," I lied.

"I told you; you shouldn't be up here." Sasha curled her finger, beckoning me to follow her down her hall. "I've been looking everywhere for you. After the tour, I checked that portrait, and you were right."

"Good," I smiled. "Maybe you can add it to your tour or something. The family suffered such tragic ends, it only seems right."

"You know, during our research, the locals mentioned a curse," Sasha half-chuckled as she rolled her eyes. But it seemed a little farfetched."

"The curse was born when materials to build the house were quarried from this valley, disturbing an ancient battlefield that had stained the stones with blood. Whenever it rained heavily, the stones would bleed, flooding the cellar with claret-coloured water."

"Sasha's eyes widened said. "Eww, is *that* what that is?"

I smirked. "Supposedly."

"We assumed it was run off from some clay or something."

"It might well be," I shrugged. "But it's where the legend originated from. For desecrating countless war graves, the family was cursed never to have any of its children survive into old age under Red Rock's roof until their debt was paid. But with the staggering number of children that have perished here, you can't help wondering if there's any truth to it. The only Reynolds-Woodbury children to survive were the ones who'd been sent away."

"Creepy," Sasha shuddered. "We've no idea what even happened to Sophia; she just vanished. Locals just said she was another victim of Red Rock. We didn't know what they meant at the time, but now it makes sense."

"The truth is, she volunteered as a nurse in the navy during the war, but her ship was torpedoed, and she didn't survive."

"Really?" Sasha smiled. "Aren't you informative? We only found partial records on the family from The War Office and nothing on Alfred. We know he died during the bombing, but we just assumed he was a deserter."

I grit my teeth, trying to keep my tone even. "He wanted to serve but had chronic asthma."

When we reached the foyer, Sasha stopped behind the front desk, her eyes narrowing thoughtfully as she leaned forward, her elbows resting on the polished counter.

"This may be a long shot, but we're desperate for another guide. I don't know if that would appeal to you, but the visitors would love your touch of personal knowledge. I need another history buff on the staff."

I had to get a job somewhere eventually, but in the back of my mind lurked the risk my presence posed to my family. As I listened to Sasha's chatter about the job's hours and wages, I couldn't shake the nagging doubts in the back of my mind.

I knew my family's routines, and with my markers, I was sure I could evade them. And if it meant seeing me regularly, Alfie would do anything in his power to steer my family upstairs before my shift began at ten.

Of course, Kay would be furious, but if it meant my family had a permanent protector, I didn't care. I couldn't trust her to do it for me anymore.

"It's a small team," Sasha said. Our accountant, Lucie, oversees events, and we have a night cleaner and gardener."

"I'm actually looking for work, but I've got another...job at weekends," I answered carefully.

Sasha smiled at me expectantly, biting her lip. "We can work around that."

As I climbed into my taxi to return me to the station, planning how to enthusiastically impress on Kay the benefits of the role, my thoughts were interrupted by the pounding of angry feet.

A petite woman in a sharp suit, sporting a perfectly trimmed bob, stomped towards the front desk. "Sasha! Who's been messing with my computer?"

Chapter Twelve

Kay glanced up from the laptop balanced on her knees as I dumped the pile of books I'd bought on my way home onto my nightstand. "You're back late."

"Just doing some exploring, some shopping."

"Well, don't go crazy with that bank card. It's for essentials only," Kay said. "You need to make money to spend it, kid."

"Well, in that case, I've got good news." I smiled tentatively as I sat on the bottom of her bed. She arched an eyebrow, silently urging me to continue, but her expression remained unreadable.

"I've found a job."

Kay immediately shook her head, her lips pressed into a severe line. "It's too soon. We'll discuss it once you've finished updating."

"But I've already accepted the position."

"Okay," she answered slowly as she set her laptop aside. "Where?"

I sheepishly pulled the crumpled leaflet from my pocket and handed it to her, my eyes cast downwards.

"You went *back*?" she spluttered, her eyes widening. "Spirit Borns are banned from revisiting their groundings."

I threw up my hands, slapping them against my thighs. "How am I supposed to know?" I snapped. "You never tell me anything."

"No." She shook her head and tossed the crumpled leaflet onto her nightstand as if it had personally offended her. "Absolutely not."

"Please, just listen. My family will be asleep during my shifts. I've got my markers, and Alfie can help."

Kay sighed heavily, pinching the bridge of her nose. "Harper, he can't help you anymore. And seeing someone you love that you can't touch or talk to will just be heartbreaking for you."

"What're you talking about? We spoke just fine."

"Spirit Borns can't converse with spirits. You must have been imagining things."

"I didn't imagine an entire conversation, Kay," I said sharply. "I thought it was what we did."

Kay started pacing back and forth, her bare feet padding against the worn carpet as her fingers clenched her hips. "Only psychics can communicate, and even then, the messages are unclear," she said. "Spirit Borns are enforcers, staying impartial. You can be an enforcer or a communicator, never both."

"Maybe this is how I heal the afterlife? By talking to them."

Kay's eye shot sharply to mine. "Who told you that?"

I cocked my head and raised my eyebrows. "Who do you think?"

"Damn it, Alfie," she muttered. "You honestly heard that much detail?"

I nodded. "Does that mean communication is my talent?"

"No." Kay paused, chewing her lip. "But perhaps they're connected."

She dug around in her bag and retrieved two plastic gadgets. One was circular, a few inches in depth, with several lights encircling an antenna. The other was rectangular, equipped with a small screen and a few buttons.

"So that we know spirits understand our warnings and judgement, Spirit Borns use these. REM pods." She held up the circular device. "And the Ovilus." She held up the rectangular device. "REM pods will sound whenever a Spirit is near and can be used with yes or no questions, the Ovilus has a word database from which spirits can choose phrases. Don't ask me to explain how they work because I wouldn't know where to start. But your ability to communicate could be related to your talent."

"Can Hunter do what I can do? I overheard you two talking."

I watched her carefully, praying she'd be honest as I looked for any hint of dishonesty.

"Everyone calls him Sparky. He really is an electrician by trade, hence the nickname, but his talent also relates to electricity. He can alter electrical currents and redistribute power. I thought he might know if..."

"The lamp was broken, or it was me," I interrupted.

"Yes. Some features of your talent may share similarities with Hunter's, but each Spirit Born's talent is unique and rarely repeated. This means you won't be like anything we've seen before. We suspect your talent is *creating* energy."

"Which is the one thing spirits hunger for, right?" I said. "I've been doing my homework."

Chapter Twelve

"Good," Kay smiled, offering a short nod of approval. "You're like a giant battery to them, which might be how Alfie had enough strength to communicate with you, but it also makes working at Red Rock risky."

I pressed my palms together, my eyes wide. "I'll be careful, I promise. And if Beau..."

"Beau won't be a problem at Red Rock anymore," Kay interrupted. "One of his lackeys already checked it out. Now that they no longer feel your presence there, they'll leave it alone, meaning it could be your ideal hiding place, working somewhere they've already checked. But I have some conditions."

Kay's pacing slowed as she listed demands on her fingers. "First, you're to finish updating," she said. "Second, we make it safe for your family. I want REM pods hidden in every other room, and if you hear one, you're to leave the building. Do you understand? I don't care what you're doing or how bizarre it may look. If you hear one, you bolt."

I nodded. "Understood."

Whilst I was grateful my proposal hadn't descended into another argument, I had expected greater resistance. Kay's fingers closed around my shoulder with a grip that made me wince, her nails leaving tiny crescent-shaped marks.

She leant closer, her treacle-coloured eyes fixed on mine, and spoke with a low but forceful voice that brooked no argument. "Finally, you *will* keep me updated about your discussions with Alfie," she said, emphasising each word with a squeeze.

"Of course," I nodded, a smile inching across my face. "Thank you."

Kay released me and poured herself a drink. "How's he doing? I assume you weren't stupid enough to seek out any of the others?"

"Of course not. Alfie's okay—heartbroken, but okay. I can't get over how real he looked," I said, squinting.

"Ghosts see Spirit Borns clearly, too, you know."

"Even Uninformeds?" I frowned.

"Yep. And if an Informed Grounded is old enough and has enough energy, they'll see the odd living person, too."

"And The Ungrounded?" I said.

"Yes, they see us...you, too," Kay said. "But it's unclear how much they understand."

I titled my head thoughtfully, my brows knitted. "You say Ungroundeds are dangerous, but how do we deal with them?"

"They can't be reasoned with, so Ungroundeds are sent straight to The Infinite as a preventative measure; no offence is needed. Groundeds get two warnings, but serious offences can constitute immediate passing on."

I sat cross-legged on my bed and rested my chin between my interlaced fingers, feeling the creases of my palms pressing against my skin. "What constitutes a serious offence?"

Kay's reply was nonchalant as she shrugged one shoulder. "Possessions, overpowering, physical harm that has permanent repercussions, stuff like that."

"Is sending Ungroundeds to The Infinite without a trial ethical? I mean, who judges them?"

"The Handlers," Kay answered, avoiding my eyes as she swirled her whiskey glass. "If they had committed similar crimes in life, they would've been imprisoned, but there's no jail on earth that can hold spirits. They need to be put somewhere."

I let out a nervous chuckle, hoping Kay wouldn't withdraw from me. "You know this is the most we've talked about this stuff? It's kind of nice."

The silence seemed to stretch on forever as her eyes met mine, narrowing slightly as her face remained a stoic mask. When she finally spoke, her voice was careful, measured. "It's been challenging knowing how to handle you."

I woke abruptly, sitting upright, my spine painfully rigid. Thrashing my hands wildly in front of me, my eyes snapped open as my chest heaved, fighting for every lungful of oxygen.

My limbs trembled with residual adrenaline as I struggled to banish the lurking memories of my nightmare to the deepest recesses of my subconscious.

Kay loomed over me, equally as tense as she lingered beside the fire extinguisher, its nozzle within easy-reaching distance. "Another nightmare?" she said. "What was it this time?"

I rubbed the chill from my arms. "A lightning storm. The ground at my feet was charred, soot climbing my legs." I frowned, shaking my head, praying the movement would shake free the most unnerving details. "And blood everywhere. On my hands, the floor..."

Kay's voice wavered with an uncharacteristic tremble as she spoke, her eyes avoiding mine by retreating into the bathroom. "It was just a dream."

Chapter Twelve

After a solid month of intensive education, the Friday finally arrived when I'd be attending The Fort. But as I imagined what awaited me, all I could see was Hunter's face, sparking waves of nauseating apprehension.

His emerald eyes had pierced through me like a blade, and at that moment, it felt like he already knew all there was to know about me, all my hopes and fears, my dreams and doubts, as if he could see right through me.

The memory of the literal spark I'd felt when we touched replayed in my mind on a loop. As I looked into Hunter's eyes, I saw a reflection of my own desire staring back at me, like we were one soul divided.

Kay crumpled the final page of the list into a ball and tossed it into the bin. "You are officially updated," she said, each word slow and deliberate.

"So, I can come to The Fort today?" I asked, trying not to bite my lip.

"It's what I promised, isn't it?"

My grin was immediate.

Kay raised one brow, a smile lifting one cheek. "Trust me, you wouldn't be looking so pleased with yourself if you knew what was in store for you. Now, get a bag packed. Lola's picking us up shortly."

I tilted my head, smirking. "Knowing how big a fan you are of efficiency, I packed last night."

"Then why's Alfie's necklace still on your nightstand?"

I narrowed my eyes. "I figured it might be a tad overkill, don't you? Or are you wearing a diamond tiara to the briefing?"

Kay snapped the velvet box containing the necklace shut and proceeded to smack me in the head with it. "Use your head, dummy," she said. "Neither of us will be here for a few days. Do you really want to leave it lying out to tempt the housekeeping staff?"

Rubbing my temple, I glared at Kay. She took great pleasure in dismantling any clever one-liners or comebacks I had up my sleeve, almost as if it were a sport to her. Her smug grin only served to amplify the animosity I felt towards her.

I couldn't help but feel that whenever I opened my mouth around her, I was putting myself at risk of being knocked down a peg or two. Every time, it felt like a personal attack on my intelligence, and I longed for the day when I could finally be rid of her.

"Will it take long getting to The Fort?"

Kay chuckled, her lips curling into a knowing smile. "Nope."

"Because that's not vague," I said, frowning.

"You asked me a question; I gave you an answer. Next question?" Kay said sharply, cocking her head as she raised her brows.

"What makes you think I have a question?"

"You always have a question," Kay retorted. "So, out with it."

"What'll happen when we arrive?"

"You'll meet our Precognitive, Hannah. She's the one who had the visions about you. And Gia, our Psychometric, will assess you. She'll be able to confirm your talent. You'll meet everyone else, too, but after the briefing, they'll head off on assignments."

The lamps flickered. "I'll be *assessed*?"

"Don't panic," Kay said, fixing her lipstick in the mirror. "Hannah can tell by looking at you if you're who she saw, and Gia identifies talents through touch."

"Then what? I go out on assignment?"

Kay laughed as she shook her head. "Lord, no. You'll be training with our Dream telepath, Dominic, for at least the next few weeks. He'll put you into a dream state to learn."

Sitting on my bed, I tried to imagine the scenarios and possibilities. "So, if it's a dream, anything could happen?"

"Anything and nothing," Kay shrugged. "You'll be challenged mentally, but physically, you can't be harmed because none of it is real."

There was a knock at the door. A flutter of adrenaline surged through me as my eyes locked on the door. I clenched the bedlinen into vice-like fists beside me, my knuckles blanching white. As my shoulders tensed, the lighting in my vicinity shimmered vibrantly as if keeping pace with the heartbeat of the room.

Kay faced her palm towards me as she answered the door. "Calm down, it's just Lola."

As the door creaked open and closed, a petite young woman glided into the room, exuding an aura of self-assurance that seemed to radiate from within. Her dark, artfully messy hair was streaked with a bold flash of red, framing her doe-like chestnut eyes, which sparkled with the kind of mischief that hinted at playful rebellion.

Her faded band T-shirt and ripped jeans clung to her slender frame, and her waiflike arms jingled with mismatched bracelets, adding a touch of bohemian flair to her outfit.

Lola acknowledged Kay with a polite nod before approaching me. Each step was measured and calculated as if she were treading on thin ice, and

Chapter Twelve

any misstep could lead to disaster. The tension in her body seemed at odds with the warmth radiating from her face.

She swept her heavy side bangs out of her eyes and smiled. "Harper, right? I'm Lola." She tilted her head sympathetically. "Let me guess, freaked?"

"That's one word for it," I said.

Kay heaved her leather weekend bag onto her shoulder and turned out the lights. "Are we the last?"

"Almost," Lola nodded.

"You collect everyone?" I asked. "Doesn't that take a while?"

Lola glanced at Kay, frowning. "You've not told her?" She rolled her eyes and turned to face me. "My talent is teleportation. It only takes a few seconds."

My blinking eyes widened. "I'd assume you were joking had it not been for everything I've witnessed over the past few weeks," I chuckled. "Will we all...travel together then?"

"No, sweetie," Lola said. "Transporting twelve Spirit Borns and Handlers in such quick succession is *exhausting*. On pick-up and drop-off days, I transport everyone individually. I'll take Kay first, then you."

Kay adjusted the straps of her bags and rested a hand on Lola's shoulder. "Just relax. I'll be waiting for you on the other side."

Lola pursed her lips and squeezed her eyes closed as if trying to block out the world around her. A deafening ringing pulsated through the room, growing progressively louder and sharper, like a thousand tiny knives piercing my ears, rendering my thoughts scattered and incoherent.

Despite my best efforts to block out the noise, it grew louder and more persistent by the second, like an unwelcome guest who refused to leave.

The air in the room seemed to vibrate, causing ripples in the glass of water on my nightstand as the air prickled with static.

It was over in one or two seconds. At the sound's crescendo, Kay and Lola's silhouettes pulsated as one, their outlines turning semi-transparent like ghosts melting into the air.

When they disappeared completely, thin wisps of smoke trailed behind them. The ashen plumes curled and twisted together in a mesmerising pattern that gradually dissipated into the room like a fading mist. Long after Kay and Lola had vanished, a crackling of palpable energy lingered, raising the fine hair on my forearms.

My limbs felt painfully rigid as I edged forward, waving my hand through the empty space. As the ringing faded, a bolt of lightning tore through the sky, illuminating the room with a blinding white light. The lamps flickered on and off like the erratic flashes of a camera, each burst of light illuminating the room in a different way.

I closed my eyes, focusing on the rhythmic pitter-pattering of the rain on the windowpanes. "Chill, Reynolds-Woodbury," I told myself.

As I filled my lungs with soothing breaths, the ringing resumed, building and building until Lola reappeared in front of me, standing exactly where she'd just disappeared from, minus Kay.

She glanced around the room, her eyes falling on each dazzling light. "You...okay?"

I nodded, but as Lola's lips curled into a sympathetic smile, I shook my head instead.

She took a seat on the bed next to me. "I know. We've all been there."

After a moment's silence, the erratic lighting settled. "Your talent is... incredible," I said.

"It wasn't always. I'd end up in the strangest places at first. With practice, I've essentially been promoted to our Uber," Lola chuckled. "But it comes in handy with spirits that try to evade us."

"They try and escape?"

Lola nodded. "Yep, just like how criminals avoid the police, I imagine."

"You think of them as criminals?"

"Only if they've hurt people."

"What about The Ungrounded?" I asked.

"They're a... grey area," Lola said slowly. "And it's not something we have the time to debate right now. Kay's waiting, and she's one Handler I *don't* want to get on the wrong side of."

Lola stood, holding out her hand and cocking her head towards herself with a subtle nod.

"What do I need to do?" I asked.

"Just put your hand on my shoulder and try to relax. It's initially a little disorienting, but don't panic—I've got you."

As I reached forward, the lights overhead flickered erratically. Lola's gaze shifted from the lights to me, concern etched on her face. "Clear your mind," she said. "And keep breathing. Feel the air in your lungs. Focus on the feeling of your hand on my shoulder and count aloud backwards from ten."

Chapter Twelve

"10...9...8..." I began, fighting to keep my voice even.

"Good."

"7...6...5..."

"That's it," she nodded. "Stay calm."

"4...3..."

I could see Lola's lips moving, but the persistent ringing that had returned gradually drowned out her voice, pressing itself into every corner of my mind until it pulsated through my entire being.

"2...1..." I yelled.

I closed my eyes as a flash of light enveloped me. For a split second, it felt as if my body had become weightless, like the earth had lost its gravitational pull. My fingers tightened around Lola's shoulder, desperate to hold on to something tangible amidst the disorienting chaos and fearing that if I let go, I'd end up lost in the ether.

After a moment, I could feel the weight of my body and the pressure of my feet planted on the ground again. As the noise subsided, I opened my eyes and found Kay's directly in front.

She held a wastepaper bin towards me. "Do you need to throw up?"

"What?" I frowned, my face twisting confusedly. "No."

As the room swirled into focus, the blood drained from my face. My hand clutched Lola's shoulder, keeping myself upright, my fingers embedded into her clothing.

Kay wrestled my grip from Lola and led me to a bed in the corner of the room. "Here, sit down."

"Just rest a minute and get your bearings," Lola smiled as she disappeared into the hall. "You did great, Harper."

Kay handed me a bottle of water. "It's only uncomfortable the first time. It's the same as your markers...I imagine."

"Doesn't anyone here drive?" I chuckled in between gulps of water.

"Well, it's quicker and helps keep our location secret. Beau discovered our earlier base, so we had to move."

I glanced around the simple room. The bed was covered in maroon, fur-trimmed blankets. The walls and floor were made of bare stone, lending the space a rustic feel, softened with wall hangings and rugs that brought colour and texture to the room.

A few pieces of mahogany furniture filled the space: a dresser on which Kay had dumped my belongings, including the fire extinguisher I hadn't noticed her pack, a dressing table facing the lead-striped window, and a nightstand. Two armchairs faced a simple fireplace on the other side of the room, filling the space with the scent of charred wood.

It took me a moment to notice the exposed wires protruding from holes that had formerly housed the overhead lighting fixtures. Instead, candles and oil lamps had been placed on every surface, but with the sun still streaming through the partially stained-glass windows, reflecting dashes of colour onto the floor, they weren't yet necessary.

I frowned as I turned to face Kay. "There's no electricity in my room?"

"It's just a precaution. I can't be here to watch you twenty-four-seven."

I closed my eyes, a wry smile twisting my lips. "Mm, sounds heavenly."

"Funny." Kay gripped both of my shoulders. "Now, are you ready to meet the others?"

Chapter Thirteen

The inescapable clicking of Kay's heels ricocheting against the stone was the only sound as she marched ahead down the winding corridors, head held high as I struggled to keep up.

My anxiety was palpable, like a living beast that darted from my body in jittery bursts and affected every chandelier and light sconce we walked by. Each fixture glowed intensely before fading to its usual lustre once we'd passed.

Kay glanced over her shoulder, her tone scolding. "Calm down."

"I'm *trying*," I said, gritting my teeth.

We descended a large staircase into a reception area. The scattered Persian rugs provided the only relief from the monotony of the grey stone.

To the left of the reception area, a long hallway stretched out before us like a never-ending maze as long-dead nobles stared down at us with lifeless eyes from the splintered frames lining the walls.

To our right, an imposing set of oak doors, ornately carved with interwoven roses and acorns, towered over us. The hum of polite conversation could be heard on the other side of the thick wood.

Kay turned to me with a sharp nod and threw her weight against the doors, the ageing hinges letting out a drawn-out, almost guttural groan as if resisting her force.

As the doors opened, all conversation momentarily stopped as I felt the weight of twenty-two pairs of eyes bearing down on me. Yet, somehow, I managed to rein in the effects I was continually having on the lights. The simple chandeliers overhead in the ancient banquet hall only flickered briefly on my arrival.

As I threw a silent prayer of thanks into the heavens, I forced my shoulders back, my head held high, as I remembered my heritage and the kind of woman I'd been brought up to be.

I craned my neck, taking in the room's vaulted ceiling. Despite the hall's size, with no windows to let in fresh air or natural light, the air was musty with the smell of age-old cobwebs.

Spirit Born

The room felt stagnant, creating a sense of claustrophobia that seemed at odds with the hall's dimensions.

In place of windows, the walls were adorned with portraits of military legends in full uniform, their medals gleaming, exuding authority as their judgemental eyes seemed to pierce straight through me.

The flames of the large fireplace, its tiles blackened by the passing centuries, danced across the surface of the varnished tables that had been arranged in a circular formation.

Around the tables, twenty-four bulky wooden chairs towered a foot above their occupants, some of whom were smiling welcomingly, others seeming indifferent to my arrival, the conversations around the room resumed.

The Handlers had claimed one side of the circle, each bearing a striking resemblance to Kay, in elegant attire befitting their roles.

On the other half, the Spirit Borns had taken up their position. The boys had gathered in one-quarter of the space while the girls took up the remaining quarter.

As I made my way towards the only unoccupied seat in the room next to Lola, I noticed Hunter's gaze fixed on me, following my every move across the room with unwavering focus as if he were trying to decipher the very essence of my being. His expression was a mask of stoicism, but within his piercing eyes, I saw glimmers of amber, like flickers of sunlight dancing atop a verdant sea.

A leather motorcycle jacket hung from the back of his chair, and matching biker gloves lay on the table, each mark and scuff hinting at countless adventures and close calls. I could almost smell the faint aroma of oil and petrol lingering on the fabric as I passed.

A thick leather cuff encircled Hunter's wrist, and his silver thumb rings caught the firelight. But it was the tips of his fingers that caught my attention. They were coated in a fine black powder resembling soot. The strange powder gradually faded as it neared his wrists, contrasting his warm skin tone.

As a rush of heat flooded my body, flushing my cheeks, Hunter's unabashed staring left me feeling completely exposed.

Responding to the anxiety threatening to overtake me, the lights flickered, though thankfully, it was so subtle that only Hunter seemed to have noticed.

Chapter Thirteen

Without turning his head, he glanced upwards and then at me. His eyes narrowed as he silently mouthed the word "breathe."

Following his instruction, I took a deep breath and exhaled slowly, blowing my fringe out of my eyes as I noticed Lola elbowing her neighbour. Her face lit up with a knowing smile, as if she understood something I didn't.

I continued to my seat, past a pair of stunning girls bearing a sibling-like resemblance, a mousy-looking girl lost in a tattered Jane Austen novel, and the doctor, still wearing her white overcoat, bent over a stack of paperwork, her brow furrowed as she chewed the tip of her pen.

But while the girls were somewhat welcoming, some of the boys seemed downright hostile.

Two immediately caught my attention as their dark eyes scanned my body from top to bottom. They exchanged sly smirks as they whispered to each other, their slouched postures reeking of immaturity and disrespect.

One boy, his shaggy hair falling haphazardly into his eyes, exuded an air of nonchalance as his muddy boots rested carelessly over the arm of his chair.

From a distance, I noticed an orange glow dancing across his hand, like he was rolling a flame over his fingers like it was a coin. He leaned backwards, holding my gaze as he rubbed his fingers together to manipulate the flame's intensity.

The flickering light was reflected in his eyes as he clicked his fingers, directing the flame with ease into a silver lighter that rested on the table.

He nudged the blonde boy beside him, his hair pulled into a tight top knot. He had been focused on the table, twirling his index finger a few inches above its surface and creating a miniature vortex of what appeared to be dust. However, once distracted, the dust collapsed onto the table, and he blew it in my direction in one intimidating breath.

As I took my seat beside Lola, the girl on my other side introduced herself. Her bleach-blond waves tickled my forearm as she enthusiastically shook my hand.

She sat cross-legged on her chair, dressed like she was headed to the beach, not a briefing, in an oversized T-shirt and frayed denim shorts. "I'm Hannah, our precognitive," she smiled.

"So, you're the one with the visions?" I said, glancing towards the unwelcoming boys. "Can you predict what their problem is?"

Hannah's voice was a gentle lullaby that soothed my anxious mind. She placed a comforting hand on my arm as her eyes met mine. "Oh, honey," she whispered. "They're scared of you."

Kay abruptly rose from her seat, the screeching sound of her chair scraping against the stone floor and echoing through the room. She cast a warning glance around the circle, and the girls put away their books and paperwork and as the boys fell silent in a routine that seemed to have been rehearsed a thousand times before.

"Everyone, this is Harper." Kay's gaze swept across the room and lingered on the unwelcoming boys, her brows drawing together in a fierce glare. "Sawyer, sit up straight."

I couldn't help but smirk. Despite all my handler shortcomings, I could at least trust Kay's ability to call someone out for behaving like an offensive dick.

In response, Sawyer rolled his eyes and shifted his leg, crossing his arms across his chest like a petulant child.

Kay returned her attention to the rest of the circle. "Let's start with introductions. But keep it simple. We don't want to confuse her," she said. "Boys?"

The first of six boys, the blond sitting with Sawyer, cleared his throat. "I'm Beck." He waved half-heartedly. "I'm telekinetic. I move stuff with my mind."

Beck automatically turned to his unfriendly friend. Sawyer's body language conveyed a sense of boredom as he reclined in his chair, his dark hair partially obscuring his eyes.

"I'm Sawyer, a pyrokinetic. I control fire," he said.

Sawyer slowly cocked his head towards the next in line. He was slightly older, smartly dressed in a suit which was starting to look a little tired as his tie hung from his breast pocket.

He smiled, nodding politely. "I'm Theon. I'm telepathic."

"These are not the droids you're looking for," Beck sniggered.

Theon's jaw tightened as he glanced at the ceiling with a look that said, "Give me patience."

An unshakable fear crept into my thoughts: the possibility of Theon revealing my innermost secrets to Kay, and I couldn't deny the vulnerability that came with it.

Chapter Thirteen

As I tried to repress thoughts about Hunter and force my attraction towards him into the darkest shadows of my mind, a prickle of heat danced across my chest as if my body seemed resolute on betraying me.

But the more I tried to push them away, the more the thoughts seemed to linger, like a nagging voice that refused to be silenced.

Another boy flashed a warm smile, his hazel eyes and thick Irish accent proving an endearing combination. "I'm Dominic," he said. He was dressed smartly, wearing a tailored shirt rolled up to his elbows and a lanyard around his neck, suggesting that, like the doctor, he had come straight from work.

"I'm a dream telepath. I'll be training you, so you'll soon be sick of me."

As Dominic pivoted his head towards Hunter, his face remained impassive, leaving no trace of his inner thoughts. As I focused on his eyes, I couldn't help but recall that first meeting when a single glance was enough to ignite an electric spark between us.

Hunter's voice was as monotonous and unreadable as his face. "We've met."

"I know," I said sharply. "I was there."

One corner of his lip twitched upwards. "I just didn't know if your little drinking binge affected your memory."

"You seemed to think it was pretty funny at the time," I said.

He furrowed his brow and tilted his head, as if considering every angle of his next response. "I'm ergogenic."

"Electricity, right?" I commented dryly. "I'd never have guessed."

Half of his mouth grinned, and his eyes narrowed further as he leaned forward, his fingers interlaced atop the table. "How *was* that hangover, by the way?"

A tense silence hung in the air, punctuated only by muted giggling between Lola and Hannah. Hunter finally averted his eyes, impatiently turning to the next person in line to continue.

The last boy seemed more intensely focused than the others. He sat up straight, displaying the same level of concentration one would expect from a seasoned job interview candidate.

The timbre of his voice carried an unmistakable hint of a distant American heritage, his accent a curious blend of Southern dialects. "I'm Captain Daniel Graft, 66th Calvary, Ma'am," he said, offering a polite nod. "But everyone calls me Cap or Captain. My talent is Xenoglossy. I can understand any language."

Without giving me a moment to process the boys' introductions or even remember their names, Kay turned to the other half of the room, raising her brows expectantly at Lola.

"Girls?" she said.

Lola wore a teasing smile as she rolled her eyes and shook her head. Her tone was playfully nonchalant, intended to rouse a giggle amongst her peers. "Christ, this feels like a morbid AA meeting or something," she teased. "I'm Lola, and I'm a Spirit Born. I've tried to stop, but I just can't help myself," she said with an exaggerated shrug.

Kay's glare was immediate.

Lola raised her hands. "Okay, okay. I'm a Teleporter. You've seen me in action."

Hannah was next, her bare toes wriggling as she turned her body towards me. "I'm Hannah, our Precognitive. I can identify potential risks on assignments, working closely with our Retrocognitive here, Aida." Hannah gestured to the girl beside her.

The dull colours of Aida's clothes made her almost fade into her surroundings. However, judging by her mannerisms, she seemed to prefer it that way. She nervously gnawed her lips while her eyes twitched restlessly. As she pushed her thick-rimmed glasses onto her nose, Hannah nudged her, smiling and nodding encouragingly.

When she finally spoke, her timid voice was barely audible over the sounds in the room. "I'm Aida, our Retrocognitive."

"So, you see *past* events?" I asked.

Aida nodded and looked down, focusing on her hands twisted together on the table. As the next girl started speaking, her posture visibly relaxed, and she released the breath she'd been holding.

The doctor tucked her pen behind her ear and smiled as she brushed the rebellious strands which had escaped her neat bun from her eyes. "I'm Amy, our psychic medic," she said. "But I'm also a professional doctor."

The eldest of The Spirit Borns' crumpled baby-blue scrubs and white overcoat, along with the dark shadows beneath her eyes, hinted at the gruelling demands of her profession.

"I'll patch you up after training and after any scraped knees or twisted ankles on assignment," Amy continued. "And I'm the most experienced Spirit Born here, so if you ever have any questions, just ask."

The last in line leaned into the table until she could meet my gaze, her honey-blonde hair cascading over her shoulders. She was dressed similarly

Chapter Thirteen

to me, with the addition of unique accessories that gently sparkled in the firelight.

"I'm Gia," she said, a subtle French purr to her accent. "I'm our psychometric. I can identify paranormal talents."

Kay cleared her throat and interlaced her hands on the table as she turned to face me. "Harper, are you ready?"

"Now?" I frowned. "With everyone here?"

My question went unanswered as Gia approached me, holding out her hand and smiling. I could feel the weight of the others' collective gaze as they leaned closer, their expressions a mixture of caution and curiosity.

As I wiped my slick palms onto my jeans and extended my hand, the overhead lights shuddered ominously, casting an unsettling glow over the room.

The hum of fluctuating power provided constant background noise, like a warning of impending danger. I could feel the nervous energy radiating from those around me as cautious looks were exchanged around the room.

One of the Handlers, a fashionable-looking blonde, turned towards Hunter. "Would you mind?"

With a nod, he closed his eyes. His brow furrowed as he outstretched his fingers, the tendons in his arms straining with the effort. As he spread them wide, pulsing energy radiated from his fingertips, causing them to glow and smoulder with a pale amber light.

As the light grew stronger, the power in the room around us seemed to dim in comparison until I could only see the intense glow surrounding his fingertips.

When the light from his fingers faded, the overhead lights returned to normal. As I watched him, I couldn't help but wonder if he had been doing that since the moment that I'd walked in.

As Gia neared me, I met her gaze. "Will it hurt?"

"Not at all," she smiled.

My shoulders tensed as I braced myself and took Gia's hand. She closed her eyes, her fingernails digging into my skin as her grip tightened. Suddenly, her eyes flew open, revealing a wild and vacant stare.

As her lips twitched, the bloodshot whites of her eyes were revealed. I turned to Kay for reassurance, my mouth agape, but she and everyone else in the room maintained an unwavering gaze on Gia. All except Hunter, who mouthed the word "breathe" to me repeatedly.

I felt myself turn cold as Gia's eyes eerily rolled back into place. Her eyelids fluttered as she regained consciousness. My stomach raged with nausea as she repeatedly blinked, her face emotionless as she stumbled back to her seat.

She pulled a bottle of water from her bag and downed its contents as if she'd just run a marathon. Glancing at Kay, she nodded.

Despite Sawyer's frosty greeting, I was still startled by his unexpected outburst, which reverberated through the room with its volume. His words hit me like a shock wave. "Hannah was right?" he spat. "Then get rid of her."

"She could destroy us all," Beck added. "She's clearly not in control."

Hunter's jaw tightened. "None of us were at first. I distinctly remember you looking at me like that once."

"Of course, *you'd* defend her," Sawyer smirked.

"That's got nothing to do with it," Hunter said. "Where do you think she'll end up without us?"

"What makes you think we've got any hope of controlling her?" Sawyer said. "She's wild! She could destroy everything we've rebuilt here!"

"With Beau breathing down our necks, perhaps we need a bit of wildness?" Lola said. "She could be our only hope of beating him and regaining control of the afterlife."

"She'll be just as useless against Beau as we all are," Beck said. "And to make her out to be some sort of paranormal messiah isn't just stupid; it's suicidal."

Lola's cheeks started to turn pink as her voice grew louder, belying her petite frame. "Since when do we turn away our own?"

"Since she could end us all with a snap of her fingers!" Sawyer said, clicking his fingers.

My nostrils flared as my eyes narrowed, anger boiling inside me. "If you're that scared of me, Sawyer, perhaps it's in your best interests to not piss me off?"

Sawyer blinked, his jaw wide as Hunter smirked, the strange amber shards within his eyes shimmering.

Kay raised both hands as she rose to her feet. "Enough squabbling," she said. "Before you ostracise her, Sawyer, there's something else you should all know—something nobody foresaw. She can *talk* to the dead."

Beck threw his weight into his chair and crossed his arms. "Bullshit."

Chapter Thirteen

"Are you disbelieving a Handler?" Kay said, her eyes vicious. "Aida, would you care to take a look?"

Aida's talent wasn't as disturbing as Gia's. She merely turned her face, her eyes closed as her lips disappeared into a firm line.

She opened her eyes, fiddling with her sleeves as she nodded. "It's true," she nodded. "She spoke with her dead ex."

"Who cares?" Sawyer said. "Give me an Ovilus or a spirit box, and so can I."

"That's not the same, and you know it," Lola snapped. "Besides, you're hardly poster boys for control. Beck can only move what, *dust* since his little breakdown, and Sawyer gave someone third-degree burns for turning him down in a bar."

"And you're so perfect? You're essentially our Uber," Sawyer scoffed, sarcastically pointing his thumbs up. "By the way, remind me to give you five stars."

Lola glared at Sawyer, her jaw tightening. The sound of her hands slamming on the table ricocheted through the air like a gunshot as she shoved her chair from the table. Immediately, my ears started ringing as she disappeared and reappeared by his side.

"And our bouncer!" Lola said, grabbing the neck of his shirt and disappearing, leaving Sawyer's seat empty.

A few seconds later, Lola reappeared in her seat, straightening out her hair and clothing, but Sawyer was missing. Kay pursed her lips and shook her head, eyes fixed on Lola.

"What?" Lola shrugged. "He causes problems every weekend."

"So," Hunter said slowly. "Are we going ahead with Harper's training?"

"Yes," Kay nodded. "Her introduction in The Empty Room starts tomorrow. Amy, you're to stay behind in case you're needed, and Lola, you're staying too to help Harper settle in. Once you've completed drop-offs, come straight back. No sightseeing. And because we're keeping so many behind, there are only two assignments this weekend."

Kay pulled a stack of files from her bag and passed them around the circle. Each Spirit Born opened their file with expressions ranging from intrigue to boredom, as though the process was a tedious chore.

Even though I wasn't attending either of the assignments, as a beige file landed in front of me, I followed suit and scanned the text and images within.

"And after some concerning insights from Hannah," Kay continued. "We'd prefer safety in numbers."

"What did you see, Han?" Hunter asked.

"Beau's been ungrounding spirits in vast numbers, so The Ungrounded population is increasing swiftly. Buildings of historical significance have been torched in four major cities."

Beck frowned as he carefully watched Hannah. "I thought you couldn't see him anymore?"

"I can't. He's too well protected," Hannah said. "But I can see the people working for him. I also watch the news, dumbass."

"Did see you where he'll hit next?" Hunter said.

"Not yet, but he's up to something big."

Kay's tone shifted, growing deeper, and commanding the circle's attention. Her eyes scanned everyone with a sense of purpose, as though trying to convey the weight of her words through her gaze. "Remember, he knows everything about us. So, watch each other's backs, and if you suspect he's at either location, *leave*. I don't want to hear about any half-baked revenge plots gone awry," she said. "Group A is Theon, Sawyer, Beck and Gia, and Group B is Captain, Aida and Hannah. Group A is a semi-high-profile case, an incubus gaining strength at Nevada State Prison. A televised group investigated there recently, but there was an encounter they couldn't show on TV."

I leaned towards Lola, whispering. "What's an incubus?"

Lola's face tensed as she winced. "It's a spirit who assaults women in their sleep."

"Since then, other groups conducting overnight explorations have suffered serious assaults," Kay said. "But the more notoriety a location gets, the more enticing it is to investigators."

"Have we identified the spirit?" Theon said.

"Aida didn't get a name but saw he was incarcerated for murder and rape. If he's interacting with the living, he must be an older Informed Grounded, but the prison's massive, with plenty of hiding places, so it won't be an easy grab," Kay said. "The inmates are mostly Informeds and are fiercely protective over one another. But if you can find him, a past warden could be of help. He's often seen in his office; blueprints are in your files. Your cover is the usual drill. You are paranormal enthusiasts on an investigation, so keep a camera nearby for show. Any questions?"

Chapter Thirteen

The members of Group A shook their heads, pawing over their files as a sense of anticipation hung in the air. The files were meticulously prepared, each page detailing the prison's history and providing descriptions of the infamous prisoners still active within its walls who could threaten the assignment's success.

Faded black-and-white photos of prisoners in grubby black-and-white smocks sat atop their criminal careers, providing a haunting visual record.

The final pages were dedicated to the graphic accounts from victims that described the sensation of hands inside their sleeping bags and icy breathing on their necks. Their words were so graphic that I could almost picture the scene in my head, sending a shiver down my spine.

Kay's stern pacing around the circle jolted me back to reality, the sharp click of her heels echoing through the room. "Group B will be going to Ettington Park in Warwickshire. Staff and visitors to the hotel have documented hauntings there for decades, but higher levels of activity than normal have been reported recently," she said. "The Informed Grounded we're after is an Italian officer who died whilst incarcerated at the POW camp that was on the property during the war. He's given a child a nasty head injury, and it's his final warning, so he's going to the Infinite. Captain, please translate any EVP responses you receive. Questions?"

The members of Group B remained silent, casually flipping through their files like it was a holiday brochure. And in a way, it was. Ettington Park was an exceptional five-star hotel, boasting gothic architecture and fairytale-like towers that could make even Red Rock feel inferior.

Kay nodded once. "Good. Grab your stuff. Drop-offs start in ten."

As I entered my room with Kay, I could feel my body relax as I took in the peaceful silence that enveloped the space. The golden light of the setting sun filtered through the curtains and cast a warm glow over the room, inviting me to unwind.

I let myself collapse onto my bed, sinking into the soft blankets as I let out a long sigh, feeling the weight of the day lift off my shoulders.

"That went well." I laughed nervously. "Is every briefing like that?"

"Pretty much. Some of the others have struggled to readjust, so they don't play well with others."

A smirk twisted one side of my mouth. "You don't say. So, what happens now?"

"The teams head to their locations and spend tomorrow learning the layout, ready for the assignment on Saturday night. Occasionally, an extra night is needed, but that's rare. Then, on Sunday, Lola collects everyone for debriefing. As for you, you'll start training tomorrow morning."

I sighed, rubbing my temples. "But I've no clue where to even begin."

"Well, electricity's a form of energy, so we're hoping Hunter can teach you how to control it to make life safer for everyone, but no one can teach you your true talent. Nobody has, or ever will, have this talent but you. It'll be up to you to reach your core and the potential within it."

"My *core*?"

"The heart of your talent. Finding it will require a discovery or sacrifice which proves you understand your talent and what it means to be a Spirit Born."

"What if I hurt someone during training?"

Kay took a seat on the bed beside me. "You can't. Remember, none of it is real, hence why we call it The *Empty* Room," she said. "Everyone's experience within it is unique. You'll be tested, but it's not real, so it doesn't matter if you fail. Tomorrow will just be an introduction."

As I dressed for bed, I admired the view as fog rolled around the mountainous, snow-capped peaks outside. We were completely isolated, with no other houses or even roads visible. The verdant moss and wildflowers bordering it had even taken over the pebble-ridden dirt track leading up to the ancient fort as if nature had reclaimed it as its own.

I craned my neck at my window at the heart of the fort, trying to take in every detail of the building. I could just make out the battlements on each corner, with two simple towers reaching into the heavens that gave the fort an air of strength and protection.

Only one other light was visible in the row of bedrooms, like a beacon in the stillness of the night. From its open window, I heard the gentle strumming of a guitar accompanied by the purr of a skilful, poetic voice.

Although I couldn't make out the lyrics clearly, the tone of the song was steeped in a kind of sorrow that tugged at my heartstrings, as if the singer were pouring their soul into the night.

As the sun dipped below the horizon, the shadows stole the light and stars shimmered like diamonds behind the wispy, semi-transparent clouds. Lulled to sleep by the amorous music, I dreamt of Alfie and of fire.

Chapter Thirteen

In my dream, I stood barefoot on a scorched earth, watching as flames spread uncontrollably from my feet, devouring everything in their path.

Chapter Fourteen

As the first rays of sunlight filtered into my room, I was startled by a knock at the door. As I checked my appearance in the mirror, I could hear the low hum of Hunter and Dominic's voices on the other side of the door, their words barely audible through the wooden barrier that stood between us.

Meeting my eyes in the mirror, I took a deep breath. "You're a Reynolds-Woodbury," I whispered. "You can handle this."

When I opened my door, Dominic met me with a reassuring smile, his eyes conveying a sense of calmness that at once put me at ease. Hunter, however, was the complete opposite.

Despite offering me support during the briefing, his demeanour was cold as he shoved his hands into his pockets. As his eyes locked onto mine, I could see the tension in his jawline and the stiffness in his body growing.

"Sleep well?" Dominic asked.

"Not really," I sighed. "Bad dreams."

Dominic shrugged one shoulder. "Don't worry; that seems to be the norm here. When Hunter first arrived, he had these crazy nightmares about lightning."

Hunter frowned, slapping Dominic with the back of his hand. "Dude!"

"Whoops," Dominic said innocently.

Dominic's accent made anything he had to say adorable. However, Hunter was clearly fuming with him for divulging a part of himself that he clearly preferred to have remained a secret. His jaw tightened so hard I swear I heard his teeth grinding.

"So, Harper, are you ready for your first training session?" Dominic said.

I puffed out my cheeks, sighing heavily.

Hunter impatiently started walking down the hall, his muscular arms swinging so quickly that his tattoos became a blur of colours. "We'll take that as a yes," he said.

Chapter Fourteen

As we strolled towards the staircase, the lighting gently ebbed and flowed in sync with my every step. The warm, yellow glow would dim as I slowed my pace and immediately brightened as I quickened it.

I was finally beginning to grasp the necessity for my room's lack of power, especially with the nightmares that had left my sheets damp with sweat.

"We usually work one-on-one," Dominic said. "So, having two trainers inside one mind will be interesting."

"You sure there's enough room in there?" I chuckled.

"Why? Are you narrow-minded?" Hunter commented dryly, arching one brow.

We passed the foyer and continued down another flight of stairs into a large, modernised cellar that mismatched the rest of the property.

As my eyes darted from side to side, I couldn't shake the feeling of unease creeping up inside me as we approached the open door of a white padded room at the far end of the cellar.

However, it wasn't the prospect of entering The Empty Room that made me feel so unnerved; it was the sight of the dozen treatment rooms that lined the hall leading to it. The fluorescent lights that buzzed overhead seemed to amplify the silence.

The rooms looked untouched, with the smell of fresh paint lingering in the air. Each small room was equipped with a bed, stainless steel cabinets and glass-fronted cupboards stocked with various medicines and clinical instruments, disinfected and organised with a surgeon's precision.

Simply put, The Handlers had recently built a miniature hospital in their basement as if they were preparing for war or the onset of some deadly outbreak.

I chewed my lip, trying to hide my apprehension. "Do you...use these treatment rooms a lot?"

"Cuts and scrapes mainly, or the occasional twisted ankle running around in the dark on assignments," Dominic said. "When Sawyer and Hunter first arrived, we got the occasional burn or shock, but nothing too serious. We used to have just one treatment room, but recently, we expanded."

"Why?"

"Because..." Hunter began, but he paused when he noticed Dominic's subtle headshake and fell silent.

I let out a frustrated sigh, realising that Kay wasn't the only one withholding information from me. It felt unfair that Theon's talent could penetrate every part of my mind, yet I was kept in the dark about so much still.

I couldn't help but feel like an outsider looking in. It was like the other Spirit Borns were on one side of an impenetrable glass wall, and I was on the other, banging on its surface to be let in and become a part of their world.

"So, how does this work?" I said, changing the subject. "Kay hasn't explained much."

"No surprises there," Dominic said.

"You'll lie down on the bed with me," Hunter said.

Immediately, Hunter's cheeks flushed, and his eyes widened as Dominic tried to suppress the smirk creeping across his face.

Hunter waved his hands and corrected himself. "Next to, you'll have a bed *next* to mine."

"I'll put you into a dream-like state and enter your consciousness through touch. It'll be like a continual dream you can't wake up from," Dominic said. "Kay and Aida have given me a comprehensive overview of your afterlife, which will help me guide you towards experiences that could be productive. However, having two trainers will exhaust me faster, so we'll need to take regular breaks. And because our sessions will be shorter, you'll need more of them."

Hunter rolled his eyes, his voice laced with sarcasm. "Great."

As we reached the open door to the padded room, the anxiety coursing through my veins made my entire body hum with nervous energy. I couldn't shake the sense that something terrible was about to happen. It was like standing on the edge of a cliff, looking down into the abyss.

Hunter's face seemed to soften with concern as he waited for me to cross the threshold into The Empty Room.

He pointed upwards to the flickering overhead lights. "You good?"

"I'm sorry, I can't control it," I said.

He chuckled. "Thanks, Captain Obvious. I'm guessing that's why I'm *really* here."

The room's only light source emanated from a large strip hanging from the ceiling by two chains, filling the space with a clinical whiteness. Two white leather examination beds occupied most of the space, each with a pillow at its head, looking pristine and sterile in contrast to the faded brown armchair between them.

Chapter Fourteen

The brown leather armchair supplied the only colour in the room. Its faded arms and sagging seat would've looked more at home in someone's lounge than in a padded room.

As I approached one of the beds, Hunter began jumping up and down on the spot, shaking his hands and stretching his neck as if preparing to enter a boxing ring.

Despite his clear reluctance, he finally lay on the bed, staring up at the ceiling and repeatedly clenching and releasing his fists. As he did so, tiny flecks of the black dust on his hands fluttered onto the mattress like black snow, distinctive against the white leather.

I lay on the bed opposite him, trying to distract myself. I counted the ceiling tiles and scrutinised every crack and crevice within them.

As Dominic was busy downing water, the lights flickered aggressively, their circuits buzzing progressively louder until the sound felt inescapable.

My eyes flicked towards Hunter, steadying his breathing with measured breaths while my own became erratic as I struggled to push back the rising tide of panic.

I glanced at the blackness of Hunter's fingertips as they moved, almost in slow motion, bridging the gap between us.

As his fingers connected with my skin, squeezing my forearm with his massive hands, I felt that spark between us again. The hallway was suddenly illuminated by a shower of sparks as the bulbs closest to The Empty Room exploded.

The air was filled with the sound of tinkling glass fragments as they rained down onto the floor, casting a glittering carpet of light on the linoleum while the acrid smell of burnt filaments lingered.

Unfazed, Hunter squeezed my arm tighter, leaving a trail of ash on my skin. He leaned towards me as Dominic closed the door to The Empty Room, his eyes cautiously scanning the broken fixtures and debris littering the floor.

Hunter's eyes locked with mine, his voice a reassuring purr. "You've got this," he said. "Just breathe."

As I nodded, a feeling of doubt and fear clung to me, but the fact that Hunter was with me gave me a strange sense of security.

He'd barely spoken to me since we'd met, and when he had, his voice had always held undertones of sarcasm and bitterness. However, he never left me to face my burdens alone whenever he saw me struggling.

Dominic sat in his armchair between us and cleared his throat, diverting my attention from Hunter. "Harper, I want you to focus on a time and place you're familiar with, somewhere you feel safe," he said. "When you have that place in mind, close your eyes and say, "Come with me". You'll be able to interact with your surroundings, but any people you meet other than me and Hunter can't see or hear you."

Dominic placed his hand on Hunter's and my shoulders, closed his eyes, and drew his brows together in concentration. I took a deep breath and thought of the only place familiar to me. Despite its ominous past, Red Rock was the only place I had ever felt secure, and I latched onto those memories with all my might.

"Come with me," I whispered.

There was a brief silence, with only our heavy breathing breaking the stillness. I felt no physical sensation, pain, ringing in my ears, or even a feeling of lightness.

My body went into a state of numbness as if it were protecting me from the impact of what was to come. I could hear distant sounds and muffled voices, but they didn't make sense. All I could focus on was my breathing, which seemed to be the only thing keeping me grounded.

Dominic's voice finally broke the silence. "Open your eyes."

I opened one eye, flinching. I only opened the other when I saw that the colourless walls of The Empty Room had transformed into Alfie's bedroom. His bed covers were soft beneath me as Hunter and Dominic waited patiently by the door.

But the moment Hunter's eyes met mine, the girlish flushes that spread through me like wildfire only filled me with guilt. I'd spent eighty long years loving Alfie relentlessly, yet here I was, in his bedroom, feeling a strange crush developing for another man.

The birdsong and the rich smell of bacon wafting upstairs suggested it was morning. I rose, tracing my fingers along the bed towards the nightstand.

Noticing the brandy glass balanced atop a stack of books, I chuckled. "It's so real," I said. "Yet... it's not. Alfie would never balance drinks on first editions."

"I can never recreate absolute truth," Dominic said. "Today is about showing you what's possible and saying goodbye to your afterlife."

"I won't be searching for my core here?"

Chapter Fourteen

"You won't find your core during training. It'll be somewhere in the real world, but your training will prepare you for finding it."

"But how can I help on assignments if I don't understand my talent?"

"You can still pass on spirits and be of help without it. Just look at Beck." Hunter said.

"Every session is different, but this place," Dominic said, motioning to our surroundings, "is somewhere we'll never return to."

"How do I know what to do?" I asked.

"The location and scenario will guide you," Dominic said.

A gentle hum of violins began playing downstairs, pulling me hypnotically towards the source of the sound. As we made our way downstairs, flower arrangements filled every alcove and rose petals littered the floor, creating a dense path that rustled underfoot.

As Dominic and Hunter trailed behind, I followed the petals. As I caught sight of myself in the baroque mirror in the foyer, the flowers suddenly made sense.

My outfit had been replaced by a wedding dress, the gems on its bodice projecting spots of light across every surface like I was surrounded by a thousand sparkling stars.

I paused by the mirror, marvelling at the dress that fit me like a glove. The laced corset pulled me in at the waist, flowing into a billowing skirt with a train that Dominic and Hunter paid careful attention not to stand on.

Dominic leaned closer, whispering. "Harper, we should keep moving."

I nodded, trying to dispel the disappointment that was consuming me. It felt cruel, revealing to me what I had always yearned for but could never have.

As if Mother Nature sensed my discomposure, Red Rock fell into shadow as unnaturally dark clouds blotted out the sun and jagged streaks of lightning split the sky.

Hunter visibly recoiled with each strike, his eyes flickering ceaselessly. There was little Dominic could do to reassure him; something about lightning terrified him to his core.

However, as the sweet notes of the Wedding March filled the air, my focus was drawn away from Hunter. I followed the petals towards the ballroom, almost in a trance, as the chandeliers overhead flickered with each step.

Despite seeing no musicians present, the Wedding March continued, urging me down the aisle.

Chairs had been arranged in neat rows. Most of them were empty, except for five in the front row. The occupants sat with their gazes fixed ahead, oblivious to the bride's arrival.

Knowing who was in those seats, my pace quickened to a jog. Hunter and Dominic struggled to keep up as the chandeliers trembled erratically before showering us with sparks.

Hunter glanced overhead. "Stop her," he growled. "This is too much for her."

Dominic held Hunter's shoulders back as he struggled to break free. "No, she needs this. Just let it play out."

I reached the front, my heels skidding on the polished floor as I focused on my family. They were each elegantly dressed, their hands resting lifelessly in their laps. Alfie sat closest to the aisle in a crisp black suit, a corsage pinned to his lapel.

Their gazes were fixed ahead, eyes devoid of any emotion. There was no hint of joy nor a trace of sorrow, and their bodies remained completely motionless as if frozen in time.

I crouched by Sophia and reached for her hands, stiff as tree branches, as I sobbed into her lifeless lap. "I'm sorry I left. I had no choice."

Seeing them so unemotional, especially the vivacious Sophia, broke me. I collapsed backwards; my body wracked with sobs.

Wrapping my arms around my knees, my dress rustled as I rocked back and forth, my chest heaving. Dominic and Hunter shielded their eyes from the lightning piercing through the veil of murky clouds.

"This isn't working," Hunter snapped. "Look what this is doing to her!"

He disentangled himself from Dominic's grasp and jogged forward. He knelt beside me and lifted my chin with his thumb until his emerald eyes found mine. "Harper, just *breathe*," he said. "Our first sessions are always like this. They're a chance to say goodbye to your afterlife. It's why we'll never return here."

I glared back at him, tears streaking my face. "It's cruel!"

"It's *closure*. Goodbyes aren't meant to be happy, but sometimes they're necessary." Hunter's rough fingers cupped my face. "Just say what's in your heart. Or if you'd prefer, we can just leave, but I know you can't see or talk to the rest of your family, and you'll never get this chance again. But whatever you choose, we can't stay much longer."

My sobbing eased, and I could feel the oxygen in my bloodstream once more.

Chapter Fourteen

Hunter nodded. "That's it. Just breathe."

He sat with me in silence until I regained my composure, then took a seat with Dominic a few rows back. Sniffing, I wiped my eyes and approached my family, kissing each of their foreheads and running my hands over Sophia's hair.

Out of the corner of my eye, I spotted Dominic nodding at Hunter, who was defiantly shaking his head. Though no words were exchanged, it was evident that the two had differing opinions in some sort of silent disagreement.

As I approached Alfie, he didn't behave like the others had. He twitched and stood, wringing his hands before awkwardly outstretching them as he forced his lips into an awkward smile.

Although not identical, his self-conscious mannerisms were close enough to the Alfie I knew.

Remembering what Dominic said about recreating absolute truth, it was still better than the soulless copies of my family members sitting beside him.

More importantly, I could touch him one last time. Of course, I wouldn't really be in his arms, but I could at least close my eyes and remember a time when I was.

Dominic's unblinking eyes fixated on me intently while Hunter stared into his lap. I threw myself into Alfie's embrace, knocking him slightly off balance. Electrical fixtures shattered, and circuits popped as I ran my hands through his hair.

As his lips met mine, the energy between us seemed to charge the entire house. The flickering of the chandeliers increased in intensity as the lightning outside grew closer, flooding the space with white light.

His grip on my waist tightened. At that moment, all the lonely years we'd spent pining for each other fell away like the wilting petals of a flower, and inescapable chemistry took over, vibrating through us.

I longed to stay there, never leaving The Empty Room, but as if the replica of Alfie sensed our dwindling time, he pulled away, sighing.

In an unusual display of affection, something he'd never done before, he pressed his forehead to mine as his fingers roamed my hair.

Dominic's voice drifted towards me. "We're out of time, Harper."

I grabbed Alfie's clothing, pulling him closer, hoping to delay the inevitable. But he stiffened, pulling away and returning to his trance-like state in his seat.

As my arms hung painfully empty, Hunter finally looked at me again, his eyes wide and anguished. When he and Dominic stood, the world around me disintegrated.

The luxurious golden hues of the ballroom gradually faded until no colour remained as my wedding dress fragmented into confetti-like pieces.

Like a reversed snowfall, the pieces pulled away from my body and floated upwards, revealing the band T-shirt, ripped jeans and combat boots I'd entered The Empty Room in.

It was as if the dress had fulfilled its purpose, and now it was time for me to move on to the next phase of my life.

"Harper, wake up," Dominic whispered.

When I opened my eyes, the Empty Room swayed into focus, but it was in shadow, with the lifeless lights gently swinging from the ceiling. Hunter quickly sat up, scowling at Dominic, slowly shaking his head, his eyes fierce and untameable.

I grabbed Dominic's shirt, my voice tinged with desperation. "You have to send me back."

"I can't." Dominic smiled sympathetically. "The more you return, the harder it is to leave. That's why we only do this once."

Hunter huffed loudly. "Can I go now?"

"Yeah, just grab the light on your way out," Dominic said, refocusing on me. "I know it may not feel like it now, but there *were* positives to this. The power at Red Rock went crazy when you kissed Alfie, so he may be linked to your core."

Hunter stepped off his bed, and the sound of crunching glass echoed around the room.

He glanced overhead and then at Dominic as he crossed the small room and reached for the light switch, flicking it back and forth. But there was nothing. Using the torch on his phone, he peered down the darkened hall of the cellar.

Hunter's phone illuminated his knitted brows. "The basement's bulbs have blown—all of them. How's that possible? She only busted one before we came in."

"Harper, you can leave. Go get some rest," Dominic said. "We'll try to fix the lights and hopefully fit in another session later."

Dominic ushered me towards the door. I crept through the darkened treatment rooms towards the stairs, my arms wrapped tightly around myself.

Chapter Fourteen

Despite their hushed tones, I could still hear echoes of Dominic and Hunter's voices resonating throughout the cellar.

Hunter's voice was a low growl. "Not cool, man."

"What? You got to play the hero, didn't you?" Dominic said.

"I don't *want* to be a hero," Hunter replied, his pacing clear from the crushing of broken glass. "I was doing fine until she arrived."

"We all knew she was coming, so what's the big deal?"

"Because I like to think my life is under my own control and not preordained," Hunter snapped.

"Is that why you're pushing her away? Because you need to be in control of your life?"

"My life is my business, but what happened in there wasn't okay. If you ever do that again, I'm *done*. You got that?" Hunter said. "What are you going to do about this mess anyway?"

The sound of broken glass being scuffed gave the impression that Hunter had kicked it across the room.

"Maybe it's just a coincidence," Dominic said.

"If it was anyone else, I might agree, but not her. You can't seriously be considering putting her back in here?"

"We can handle a few burst bulbs," Dominic replied, his tone nonchalant.

"You don't understand. I was working so hard to keep her contained, and she still trashed the place. And while she was out cold," Hunter said. "You honestly don't feel the energy coming off of her."

"Energy is your department, not mine. You'll just have to join me for each session to be safe."

"And skip months of assignments?" Hunter scoffed. "Besides, you don't understand. Training her like this won't work. The damage might look minor, but that's just her first session. And look at the state of you. You're exhausted. How do you think she'll be weeks down the line? How do you plan on controlling her whilst keeping everyone else safe?"

"So, what are you suggesting?" Dominic said.

Stillness lingered for a moment, making the silence almost tangible and adding to the already palpable tension.

Hunter's voice was laced with an air of gravity as he finally spoke. "I'm suggesting we build a bigger hospital."

Chapter Fifteen

Dominic and Hunter didn't return after training, meaning the damage I'd caused was far more extensive than simply replacing a few bulbs.

As a result, I had lain awake most of the night, tossing and turning over my experiences in The Empty Room and the drama afterwards.

Upon returning from the bathroom the following morning, I was relieved to be greeted by a friendly face.

Lola sat with her feet on my bed, ankles crossed, leisurely reading a novel from my nightstand.

She snapped the book shut and flashed me a bright smile. "There you are."

"Is... everything okay?" I asked.

"Kay sent me. Dom's exhausted, and Hunter's still fixing the lights, so training's off for today. What the hell happened down there anyway?"

I shrugged. "Honestly, I've no idea."

"Well, whatever you did, I'll make sure to have you handy next time I fancy escaping training," Lola smirked. "Kay suggested we get out of here for a bit before debriefing, so have you got anything we could cross off your new-life bucket list?"

I frowned confusedly. "My new-life bucket list?"

"You know, things you've been dying to try or places you want to visit?" Lola bit her lip, clenching her fists at her sides, virtually bouncing with enthusiasm.

My mind wandered to the places I'd dreamt of exploring with Alfie. However, the memories of The Empty Room lingered in my mind, turning any thoughts relating to him bittersweet.

Instead, I remembered Sophia's photo album, which documented her enviable adventures: Central Park in the snow, the white cliffs of Dover, riding horseback on the beach.

Then, for a reason I didn't understand, my mind was flooded with an image of Sophia and Nick at Coney Island.

Chapter Fifteen

Her radiant blonde hair swayed in the wind as the pair laughed in front of a rollercoaster that dominated the skyline.

The image was so vivid I could almost taste the salty tang of the sea air and hear the distant seagulls crying overhead.

"Are there any rollercoaster's nearby?" I asked, chewing my bottom lip.

Lola's brows rose, and the edges of her lips twitched as she nodded in approval. "I like your style," she said. "You ready to go now?"

Grabbing my phone and leather jacket, I nodded.

"Oh, one more thing." Lola dipped her hand into her jacket pocket and pulled out a small plastic medication bottle. The pills softly rattled as she held them towards me. "Amy and Kay told me to give you these."

My eyes narrowed as my brows drew together. "What are they?"

"They're for anxiety."

"I'm not an anxious person," I said.

Lola smiled. "I know. They're just an extra failsafe if things go wrong while we're in public."

"But..."

Lola rattled the bottle at me until I accepted them. "Just take them," she said. "Kay will only give me hell if I don't. Besides, they might get you out of a sticky situation."

"Did you ever take them?" I asked.

Lola's eyes widened as she nodded animatedly. "Oh yeah. When I was new, I ended up in all sorts of crazy places until I calmed down and cleared my head."

I watched Lola carefully but saw no traces of insincerity on her face. After a moment's contemplation, I tucked the pills into the pocket of my leather jacket, not that I ever planned on taking them.

"Now I've transported you once; there's no need for countdowns," Lola said, holding out her hand. "Are you ready?"

I braced myself and reached out. After a flash of brilliant light and a brief moment of weightlessness, we reappeared in an empty bathroom cubicle peppered with graffiti. I wiggled a finger in my ear and shook my head to clear the disorientation as the ringing faded.

As we entered the bustling theme park, my senses were immediately bombarded with a chorus of squeals from excited youngsters. The air was thick with the sugary scent of candy floss and popcorn, and the rides' neon colours and flashing lights soaring over our heads dazzled my eyes.

Lola looped her arm through mine, the sounds of chatter and laughter enveloping us as we headed into the crowds. "So, you must have a million questions," she said.

"Where were you grounded?" I asked.

"A tuberculosis hospital. My mother was pregnant with me when she got sick, and we both died during childbirth."

My face softened as I smiled sympathetically. "I'm sorry."

"Don't be. Remember, it didn't look like some derelict building. To us, it was a modern hospital. And everyone who had been sick wasn't anymore," Lola said, shrugging one shoulder.

"It was like we'd found the miracle cure."

"And nobody ever wondered why their families never visited?"

Lola arched one brow. "It was a TB hospital, Harper. People rarely had visitors when they were alive."

"Couldn't you and your mother ground yourselves anywhere else?"

"Remember the *rules*," Lola said "you can only be grounded where you've lived, died, or were born. For me, I had no other option, and my mother never would've left me alone. But she's...not around anymore."

"She was ungrounded?"

Lola's demeanour shifted, and she nodded in silence as her eyes fell to the floor. Her body language betrayed the weight of her grief, her bubbly persona giving way to sorrow that hung heavily in the air.

"Were you an Uninformed Grounded like me?" I asked, trying to shift topics. "I felt like such an idiot for not realising sooner."

"Most of us were Uninformed. I only learned from another patient, so I blabbed to my mother and received a warning."

"*You* got a warning?"

She nodded, raising her chin proudly. "Yep. I'm the only Spirit Born to have ever received one. That was decades ago, though." Lola paused, pursing her lips and pulling them thoughtfully to the side. "Now...can I ask *you* something?"

"Sure."

Lola's eyes narrowed. "What's it like talking to your ex? Can you actually hear him, or is it like an EVP?"

"It's like any normal conversation. Why?"

Lola's tone lowered as she met my gaze. "Because The Handlers have never allowed rule-breaking before. So be careful."

"I know. I can't touch Alfie without..."

Chapter Fifteen

"That's obvious," Lola interrupted. "I mean there'll be a reason Kay's letting you work at Red Rock. You might inadvertently drag Alfie into something he never should've been a part of."

My brow furrowed. "You know about my job?"

"Everyone knows. It's impossible to keep secrets with Theon, Hannah, and Aida around," Lola said, pulling me towards her with a reassuring squeeze. "But we always have each other's backs. You'd be surprised how many secrets we've managed to keep hidden from The Handlers over the years."

Lola's words carried a weight that I couldn't ignore. She had a point, I'd been surprised Kay had let me take the job, so I had to consider the possibility that there was more she wasn't telling me.

However, Lola's insightful nature was a beacon of comfort in an otherwise murky situation. And with Hunter's unpredictable and confusing behaviour, ranging from supportive and endearing to emotionally detached, Lola was becoming a much-needed source of support and guidance.

Seeing the apprehension on my face, Lola's features softened. "I'm sorry. I shouldn't have said anything."

"No, I'm glad you did. I've just been so preoccupied with my grief that I can't think straight." I sighed, resting a hand on my aching chest. "Does it ever stop hurting? Missing your family, I mean?"

Lola shrugged, smiling compassionately. "Not really. But if you surround yourself with people and experiences that bring you joy, the pain will lessen over time. And that starts today."

I feigned a smile as Lola tugged me into her petite frame and coaxed me towards the end of a long queue. "Didn't you mention a rollercoaster?" She grinned.

The masterpiece of modern engineering ahead of us was far more advanced than the rickety ride depicted in Sophia's faded photograph.

The neon orange track was elevated high above our heads, crisscrossing over the paths of visitors, creating a web of vibrant steel.

As we joined the queue, a train of cars packed with screaming thrill-seekers barrelled down the sharp drops and banks, their legs flailing above our heads, sweeping in one direction and then the next, creating a rush of wind that flurried our hair as they flew past.

Lola stood on her tiptoes, craning her neck to peer over the heads of those queuing as she pointed to a side gate for the fast-track entrance. "There!"

As visitors were distracted with their phones and engaged in conversations, Lola transported us to a gap near the front of the queue.

I glanced around, chewing my lip. "What if someone saw?"

"Nobody's paying attention," she shrugged. "And if anyone had seen, they'd only invent some logical explanation. So, are you nervous?"

"No."

Lola cocked her head, pointing upwards to the ride's twitching lights. "Then what's up?"

"I don't know, I guess I feel...guilty doing this without my family."

"Look, H," Lola said. "Can I call you H?"

Although I was unsure how I felt about my name being reduced to a single letter, I nodded. Something about it felt familiar, almost comfortable.

"Your family has already lived their lives," Lola smiled, her warm brown eyes sparkling as she leaned towards me. "It's time you did the same."

An attendant showed us to a car at the front of the ride as the smell of oil and burnt rubber hung in the air above the track. The restraints were clamped over us, constricting my chest until I could barely breathe or reach Lola's outstretched hand.

The gears clicked loudly as the ride began its ascent. Suddenly, we were launched forward with such speed that my breath was snatched away, leaving me gasping for air.

My hair became a tangled mess around my face as we abruptly stopped, our dangling limbs jostled by every sharp movement of the cars.

Passengers shot confused glances at one another as we surged forward again in short bursts. As the bulbs lining the track dazzled and burst one after another, Lola's grip tightened around my fingers, and I realised the ride's behaviour wasn't normal.

On the paths below, concerned visitors shielded their faces from falling glass as they pointed upward, and beside me, Lola's eyes widened. Her face froze as her expression quickly turned from excitement to alarm.

The occupants of the cars behind us started screaming, their voices steeped in desperation as they pleaded with people below for help.

As we approached the first loop, rising fifty feet in the air, a deep groan bellowed above our heads, vibrating through the ride's metal framework as the hydraulics holding the restraints in place started to creak open.

The screaming around us intensified, growing louder and more frantic, and cries of "I love you" could be heard being exchanged behind us.

Chapter Fifteen

I knew my nerves had caused the harrowing scene unfolding around me, but now it had begun, I had no idea how to stop it. The restraints that held us in place seemed to loosen further with every beat of my heart.

Within moments, they had grown slack enough for Lola to wriggle around and face me. Her face was ashen as she clung onto the ride's framework with one hand and squeezed my fingers with the other.

"Harper!" she yelled, her eyes unblinking. "Sweetie, calm down!"

I fumbled towards my pocket. "The medication! You can reach..."

"There's no time for that," she interrupted. "Just get your shit together."

I squeezed my eyes closed, trying to shut it all out. "I don't know how!"

"Yes, you do. You did this, and you can undo it. Just breathe."

Breathe. A vivid image of Hunter's face filled my mind, mouthing those exact words to me, and his deep voice echoed comfortingly through my mind. *You've got this.*

"In through your nose and out through your mouth," Lola ordered.

As we shuddered towards the first loop, onlookers stared up in horror, some making frenzied, pre-emptive calls to the emergency services. Others tried to convince their loved ones to jump before we got any higher, promising faithfully that they'd catch them.

"Just get us out of here!" I pleaded, my voice barely audible over the groaning of metal.

"The hydraulics are shot. If we leave now, everyone will fall. You can do this, Harper, just focus."

"Then you go. Save yourself."

"I'm not leaving you," Lola yelled. "Now, take all that hurt and pain you've suffered the last few weeks and direct it towards the rails. Draw power from the lights...from the entire park if you have to, then let go and push us back to the start. Make Alfie proud."

I closed my eyes, trying to silence the screams that seemed to slice right through me as I imagined telling Alfie that I'd succeeded in fixing my mistake, that I had rescued everyone I'd put in danger. But nothing happened. When I pictured Alfie's face, I felt nothing, just a strange, hollow numbness.

Then I squeezed my eyes closed harder and envisioned Hunter.

Breathe.

I pictured his face, the shadow of stubble grazing his jaw, his sandy hair, the curve of his lips, the flex of his muscles, and his blackened fingers.

The lights across the park spluttered out in waves, surging towards the stricken ride. I imagined the intensity of his eyes, the same emerald green as one of my own, and the golden flecks within them that seemed to shimmer with his mood.

Breathe.

An intense wave of heat coursed through my body, extending into my fingers and toes. Instinctively, I stretched my hands and feet towards the track, and with one final metallic groan, the movement of the restraints ground to a halt.

You've got this.

"That's it!" Lola shouted, nursing a look of cautious optimism. "Now let go!"

I recalled that first touch, that spark, as I released a guttural scream.

I could feel the heat building inside me, growing more intense with each passing moment, until a searing blaze threatened to consume me.

Ignoring the pain, I focused on the energy coursing through me, building and building, until it became a searing heat.

I stretched out my fingers and clutched them into claws. Jagged streaks of vivid light burst from my hands like miniature lightning bolts, crackling and sparking as they flew towards the track.

The park became a blur of colours as the cars flew backwards and curled down the loop, whipping my hair around my shoulders. The screams were momentarily stunned into silence, and seconds later, we were back on the platform.

As Lola and I panted loudly, hysterical crying erupted behind us. The shrill whine of sirens was getting closer as park workers sprang into action, talking into radios and helping traumatised patrons from the cars.

Overcome with emotion, relatives clambered over barriers and flooded the platform, embracing their loved ones in tearful embraces.

Lola's trembling hand grabbed my shoulder. "*Now* we can go."

We reappeared in the empty Spirit Born lounge. My vision blurred as I swayed, feeling light-headed, while Lola collapsed onto a sofa in front of a lifeless television, her head in her hands.

"I'm... so sorry," I stammered.

Lola's voice quivered with regret as she shook her head, her eyes fixed on her feet. "It's not your fault. I didn't think about your talent." Lola bashed her palm against her forehead. "I never think."

Chapter Fifteen

When she finally looked at me, her eyes widened as they tracked up and down my body, the blood draining from her face. "Oh God...Harper."

The acrid smell of burnt hair and flesh polluted the air around me, making my stomach churn with nausea. As the adrenaline in my bloodstream dwindled, pain seared through me.

My hands shook uncontrollably as tendrils of smoke spiralled around my face. Thick, black and red zigzagging burns charred my arms, each streak carving through raw skin towards my fingers like gruesome veins shrouded in soot. Whilst I couldn't see them, my feet felt equally as damaged.

Lola's tone turned high-pitched as she stumbled over furniture towards the door. "I'll... I'll get Amy."

"No," I said, my chest heaving. "Hunter. Where's Hunter?"

My injuries reminded me of his blackened fingertips, and I knew I owed him a debt I could never repay. Without my inexplicable connection to him, without his previous support, I doubted I would've had the strength to fix the damage I'd inflicted and avert disaster.

Lola frowned confusedly. "Probably in his room."

"He'll... he'll know what to do."

"No, you need a doctor," Lola said, facing her palms towards me. "Just don't move, okay?"

She sprinted into the hall, screeching Amy's name. But I had to know how to endure my talent. I needed to know if I'd be subjected to agonising pain whenever I used it or if it would fade with time, like our markers. More importantly, I needed to know if I was dangerous.

I could feel every step of the climb as I made my way up the stairs, my legs crying out in agony with each movement, sending spasms of pain shooting up my legs.

I reached out for anything that could help me stay upright; the railing, the sconces, the furniture. After making it upstairs, I grew listless as red spots danced around the edges of my vision.

Halfway down the hall leading to the bedrooms, I heard the gentle plucking of guitar strings and a voice so effortlessly entrancing that it was otherworldly.

As I continued down the hall, the music grew louder until I could make out the words being sung. They spoke of love and longing in a way that tugged at my heartstrings, and the vibration of the guitar's strings added depth to the melody.

I finally reached Hunter's room. He sat with his feet up on his bed, playing an acoustic guitar, as black as a raven's wings.

Clinging to his doorframe, I caught my breath. He stopped singing but remained focused on the guitar strings as they released small clouds of black dust.

"What do you want?" he asked impatiently. "Broken something else?"

My lungs burned as I tried to form words. My vision grew hazy, and I felt my consciousness slipping away like sand through my fingers.

"I *said*, what do..." Hunter's eyes finally shot towards me and widened. "Jesus Christ."

He sprang from his bed, tossing his guitar aside, causing a dull twang as it hit the floor. He crossed the room with three purposeful strides as his voice softened.

He carefully swept one hand behind my legs and the other behind my neck as he lifted me off the ground. "It's okay, I've got you."

The oaky scent of his cologne enveloped me as he carried me to his bed and laid me down, his muscles taut beneath his shirt.

"We need to get those boots off," he said.

"No, my feet are burnt too," I said, tears cutting through the ash mottling my face.

"I know. And I *know* it hurts, but we have to," Hunter said, his tone soft as his brow furrowed. "If we wait, they'll mould to your feet."

He pulled a large toiletries bag from his dresser and fished out some surgical scissors and a few glass bottles. After setting them on his nightstand, he rattled several pills into his hand and held them to my mouth with a bottle of water.

"For the pain," he said, smoothing my frazzled hair. "They're a special concoction of Amy's, so they'll work quickly. They'll make you a little woozy, but trust me, you won't want to remember this anyway."

Hunter worked quickly, cutting sections of leather and rubber and gently peeling them away from my raw skin. As I grimaced in pain, the overhead lights flickered intermittently, casting shadows around the room, but in my exhausted state, I suspected it wasn't my doing.

"You're flashing me," I said.

Hunter glanced at the lights, then at me, raising one brow. "What's to say it's not you?"

"Because it's not, is it?"

The corner of his lips twitched upwards. "No comment."

Chapter Fifteen

"Will using my talent always hurt like this?"

"At first."

"Then?"

"If it's anything like mine, it gets easier," he shrugged. "What happened anyway?"

"We went out, but I... Lola's going to hate me," I said.

"She'd never hate you."

I cocked my head, watching Hunter carefully. "But you do, don't you, Hunter?"

"Everyone calls me Sparky around here."

"Well, I'm not everyone."

"No, you're certainly not," he chuckled. "Why'd you think I hate you?"

"After training, you were so angry."

"I just feel a little...out of control around you," he muttered, avoiding my gaze. "I wasn't angry at you, just the situation. Dom asked too much of me."

Heavy footsteps could be heard pounding towards us. Lola swept in breathlessly, followed by Amy, carrying a large doctor's bag. Hunter stepped back, rubbing the back of his neck and streaking his skin with ash as he allowed her through.

"I've removed most of her shoes," Hunter said, "and I've administered pain relief."

Amy's eyes widened as she pressed a stethoscope to my chest, the metal cool against my skin. "That stuff I made you? Damn it, Hunter, she's half your size."

"I just thought," Hunter mumbled, the concern on his face growing.

At the door, Lola wrung her hands. "How can I help?"

"Go and tell Kay," Amy said.

"Sure," Lola nodded. "Harper, I'll stop by your room when Amy's finished treating you, okay?"

"We shouldn't move her now," Amy said. "It'll only worsen her pain. She's staying here for tonight."

"But her room's...safer," Lola said, subtly gesturing to the shimmering lighting.

"It's not her. Harper's energy levels are depleted, and Hunter's overmedicated her." Amy tossed her stethoscope over her swan-like neck and turned to Hunter. "Dude, *chill*. She'll be fine. Take a breather or something."

"I'm not leaving her," Hunter said, crossing his arms.

Amy smirked as she applied a blood pressure cuff to my arm. "That was quick."

"Shut it," Hunter said, his jaw rigid. "It means nothing."

Amy faced a palm towards him. "Then calm yourself. And keep her awake until I'm done."

She removed the blood pressure cuff, crouched by my side, and held my hand for several minutes. I winced, instinctively trying to pull away, but I didn't have the strength to fight her off.

As Amy closed her eyes, her mouth set in a firm line, a strange warmth radiated from her hands into mine, making my fingertips tingle.

She carefully set my hand on the bed and retrieved a tangled mess of plastic tubing and needles from her bag to start a drip.

Her hands moved with steady coordination as she untangled the plastic tubes and connected them to the IV bag. Throughout it all, the strange warmth from her hands seemed to linger like a soothing balm.

She passed a bulging bag of fluids to Hunter to hold up as he rolled his shoulders and steadied his breathing. When the flickering lights had settled, he pulled up a chair beside me and whispered into my ear.

"So where did you guys go, a power station?" he chuckled.

My eyelids fluttered as I mumbled. "A... ride."

"You can't sleep yet," Hunter said, tapping my face firmly.

"Hunter, you're practically slapping the poor girl," Amy said. "Just take her hand. This one's mostly done. Just be gentle."

"But her feet? She needs to be mobile."

"I'll get to them," Amy said. "I just had to get a line in."

My hand looked miniature in Hunter's as he cupped it, carefully avoiding the drip. "Your hand, H," he said.

"Really?" Amy smirked. "H?"

"It just slipped out. It means *nothing*," Hunter growled.

Amy raised both hands. "Just making an observation."

"*Harper...*" Hunter said "your hand feels a little better, right?"

I squinted at my scorched limb. Although it still seemed raw and painful, the crisp burns had faded to a pinkish hue, with darker discolouration at my fingertips.

"I need five," Amy said, rubbing her temples. "...just keep her awake."

"Why?" I mumbled, glancing to the doorway as Amy disappeared into the hall. "Is she angry, too?"

Chapter Fifteen

Hunter smiled, smoothing the hair clinging to my brow. "Nobody's angry. These things happen when you're new. She just needs to regain her strength."

Even heavily medicated, I gritted my teeth and writhed in pain, leaving Hunter's sheets spotted with blood as bottles of medication and snaking curls of bandaging littered the bed.

"You said a ride?" Hunter said, clearly trying to distract me from the pain as he wiped my tears away with his thumb. "What was it, a car...train?"

"A rollercoaster."

"You don't do things by halves, do you?" he chuckled. "What happened?"

"I thought of..."

"Alfie?" he interrupted, his eyes cast downward.

"My sister," I answered. It felt like my throat was coated in sandpaper, causing each word to emerge with a sharp, rasping quality. "I panicked, and the restraints opened, but Lola made me fix it."

"And what made you seek out me rather than our resident doctor?" Hunter asked.

"I figured you knew what to do. And I wouldn't have been able to fix it without you."

His brows knitted together confusedly. "I'm sorry?"

"I imagined your voice saying, 'breathe,' and it felt like you were there with me."

Hunter slowly cocked his head, leaning back in his chair as a smile eased across half of his face, his eyes fixed on mine. "Glad I could be of assistance."

I sighed, covering my face with my hands. "What'll everyone think? Sawyer and Beck already want me out as it is."

"Well, thankfully those morons aren't in charge. Just remember you *fixed* it, and fixing our mistakes receives high praise here. We've all made a few, and not many of us managed to solve them as you did."

A feeble smile wrinkled my eyes. "Are you always so positive about everything?"

I heard Kay's stilettos clicking loudly in the hallway. The sound echoed through the corridor, growing louder and more distinct with every step. When the footsteps stopped, the humming of Kay and Amy's voices could be heard.

Spirit Born

"Sounds like your Handler's here," Hunter smirked as he released my intertwined fingers. I watched him gently place my hand on the bed, feeling a surge of disappointment as Kay entered. Her focus was immediately drawn to the closeness of Hunter and me.

She swept to my bedside, feeling my brow. "Christ, I thought you were going shopping or something."

"I've told her the parachute jump tomorrow is off," Hunter grinned.

Kay's expression was stern and unmoving as she glared back at him. "Not funny. Well, I'm here now; you can leave. I've set up a bed for you in The Spirit Borns' lounge."

Hunter frowned, his thick bicep bulging as he held up my fluids. "I'm staying."

"She's *my* responsibility," Kay said, thrusting out her hand impatiently. "Now give me the bag."

"She can stay your responsibility, but I'm not leaving. I'm not breaking any rules by being here."

Unused to being challenged, she stumbled over her words. "But it's... inappropriate for you to be here."

"How is it?" Hunter said. "I'm supporting a teammate, nothing more."

Kay's unrelenting glare bore into Hunter without mercy. "Do I need to fetch your Handler?"

"Do it," Hunter shrugged dismissively. "I'll tell Annie the same thing. I'm staying."

Amy re-entered, wheeling a squeaky IV stand. Her eyes shifted back and forth between Hunter and Kay, her expression resembling that of a weary teacher observing two bickering schoolchildren.

"Enough!" Amy snapped, facing a palm to them both. "If you're going to argue, do it elsewhere. Hunter knows what he's doing, Kay. He's fine watching her." Amy turned her attention to me, her voice softening. "Now, Harper, how are the hands feeling?"

I squeezed my hands into loose fists, my fingers trembling. "A little better."

Amy took the bag of fluids from Hunter and attached it to the stand. "Good. I'll start your feet next, wrapping them in bandages soaked in a special salve we developed for Hunter. You'll heal in hours, not weeks."

"You'll have to excuse us for debriefing, Kay," Hunter said.

Chapter Fifteen

"Lola's in shock, so she's in no fit state to travel. The teams will return tomorrow. Since you're in... good hands, Harper, I'll update the other Handlers," Kay said.

Her gaze lingered on Hunter as she made her way out of the room, her eyes drifting from his head to his toes. Meanwhile, Hunter pulled up a chair beside me and took my hand.

As Amy began the delicate process of wrapping my feet in sticky, citrus-smelling bandages, the room fell into an uneasy silence.

"Hunter, how do I control this?" I asked, trying to hide the desperation in my voice.

"How can I ensure I won't hurt anyone?"

Hunter puffed out his cheeks as he sighed. "Well, it's becoming clear that your family triggers you, so you've got to try and push them from your mind, just temporarily."

"That'll be pretty hard now I'm working at Red Rock."

Deep lines shredded Hunter's forehead as he frowned, blinking repeatedly. He jarred his head backwards and shook his head as if trying to shake off a persistent thought. "Are you crazy?" he said, releasing my hand as the overhead lights brightened dramatically.

Amy nodded upwards, her tone low. "Hunter," she warned.

"I'm serious. Are you certifiably insane?" Hunter said, his voice growing louder. "Why take such an unnecessary risk?"

I shrugged one shoulder. "It's my home. I've never felt out of control there."

Amy finished wrapping my legs, trying to act like she wasn't there. "I'm all done," she said, packing her bag and edging towards the doorway. "You can sleep now but keep off your feet until tomorrow. And Hunter, if there are any problems, fetch me."

Alone with Hunter, looking in an absolute state with my limbs coated in sticky bandaging, I felt exposed and vulnerable. His eyes bored into me, and I could feel his gaze assessing me from head to toe.

"You took the job to see your boyfriend again, didn't you?" he said. "Even though he can't hold or care for you anymore?"

"Why do you even care?"

"I don't. I mean... I do, but..." He sighed, closing his eyes. "I just don't want you clinging to your grief."

"Why? My grief is my own business."

"You're a good person, but that ache—it's something I wouldn't wish on my worst enemy. I want better for you."

My eyelids fluttered feebly, feeling weighted with lead. "I can't... I just..."

"Shh," Hunter soothed, his fingers brushing my cheek. "Just sleep now, H."

The flickering lights overhead cast an eerie glow over Hunter's bedroom. I lay my head on his pillow, enveloped by the scent of his cologne.

As I succumbed to the pull of unconsciousness, I closed my eyes and allowed myself to sink into the softness of the bed.

At that moment, I could've sworn I felt the warmth of his breath on my face as he leaned in close, pressing his forehead gently against mine.

Chapter Sixteen

Hours later, I became aware of two familiar voices in the background. I could hear the gentle cadence of Amy and Hunter's conversation. My eyes felt too heavy to open, so I remained still and listened quietly.

"Have you been here all night?" Amy asked.

"I couldn't leave her alone," Hunter said.

"Here, you want some coffee?"

"God, yes." Hunter yawned loudly. "She's been out of it all night, so hopefully, she won't be a total mess for debriefing."

"She's actually going?"

Hunter chuckled. "You think anyone's going to stop her? Besides, she's paranoid everyone hates her."

"Why? She's incredible. She just needs to be more careful; this was serious. Far worse than the states you got yourself into."

"She didn't know what she was doing. But Lola still got her to save everyone like *that*," Hunter said, clicking his fingers.

"Look, it'll stay between us, but I overheard you discussing what really helped her yesterday. So why are you keeping your distance? You know what Hannah saw. Why fight it?"

"It's not like we could ever do anything about it. And I don't know if we could ever be safe around each other. You saw the lights last night. It's been years since I've been on edge like that."

"It was a pretty stressful situation," Amy said. "Anyway, I wouldn't have put you down as a stickler for the rules, and Harper clearly isn't either."

"After what happened with Hannah, can you blame The Handlers for being careful?" Hunter's voice turned deep. "Besides, Harper's in love with someone else."

"Yeah, a *spirit*. And once The Handlers get whatever they're after, they'll be separated. But none of it makes sense. Surely, he'll only hold her back?" Amy said. "What has Hannah said?"

"She's been sworn to secrecy about anything Harper-related. She only told me about her other vision because it involved me."

"Poor kid. There are so many rumours about her circling," Amy said. "But nobody knows the truth."

"I heard Kay on the phone earlier, though, ensuring the other Handlers that Harper will be well enough to attend next weekend's assignment."

"What?" Amy said, the higher tone in her voice betraying her surprise. "Where?"

"I'm guessing that big job Hannah's seen brewing."

Amy sighed. "Christ, another mass un-grounding? But why put Harper out there so soon?"

"They're clearly fixing her up to be one of our big guns. And if her family is entwined with her core, it'd explain her job at Red Rock," Hunter said.

"But they can't just wind her up and point her at Beau already. Besides, she'll be as useless as we are against him. He's too well protected."

"Maybe, but they're putting a lot of faith in her that she can fix everything," Hunter said.

"Then stop pushing her away. *Help* her so something like this doesn't happen again. And get her away from Red Rock," Amy warned, her voice grave. "Something about that place is dangerous for her. Aida's terrified of it. And whenever anyone asks Hannah about it, she turns pale and runs for the nearest exit."

As I slowly opened my eyes, I noticed Hunter sitting comfortably in the armchair beside Amy, savouring his coffee by the crackling fire. The warm glow of the firelight flickered gently across his strong jawline, and as he locked eyes with me, a profound longing stirred within my chest, yearning to be satisfied.

Hunter set down his mug, coffee sloshing over its rim, and crossed the room as Amy followed.

"How are you feeling?" Hunter asked.

Amy waved a penlight across my eyes. "Are you in any pain?"

Flexing my limbs, I winced. The effort required to move my arms and legs felt like a struggle, as if my body resisted any attempt to loosen up. "A little," I said.

As Hunter offered me his arm, I sat up with a groan. I glanced at the thready, vein-like scars lightly marring my arms that reached into my fingertips.

Chapter Sixteen

"How's Lola?" I asked.

"She stopped by earlier," Hunter said. "But everyone's getting ready for debriefing now."

I tugged at his arm, carefully lowering my legs to the floor as I gritted my teeth. The pain was noticeable, but it was bearable enough for me to walk with some support.

I tugged myself free of my drip, leaving a trickle of blood from the pinprick mark on my hand. "I'm going," I said.

"Stop that." Hunter's jaw tightened as he struggled unsuccessfully to reconnect the drip. "You're staying put. Amy, can you set up another drip, please?"

Despite being half a foot shorter than him, I squared up to Hunter defiantly. "I'm not going to debrief clinging to a drip stand."

"Uh, she actually doesn't need it anymore anyway," Amy interjected, raising her finger like a schoolchild.

"Not helping Doc," Hunter growled.

I stood shakily, cocking my head. "Perfect, let's go."

"Didn't you say nobody could stop her going?" Amy smirked, brows raised.

"*Not helping Doc,*" Hunter repeated, his tone growing increasingly frustrated.

"You can't keep me here. I'm the reason everyone's back late," I said, wincing as I planted my hands on my hips, the tenacity in my eyes unwavering.

Hunter's eyes narrowed, and a hint of a smile played on his lips. "Are you always this stubborn?"

"Persistently so."

"You're infuriating," Hunter growled, throwing up his hands as the lighting twitched with his mood. "Fine! Just do yourself a favour and change first. You look bloody awful."

I cringed as I tugged at the hem of my shirt. The fabric gave way beneath my fingers, disintegrating into a cloud of dark ash that drifted to the floor like snowflakes.

Hunter helped me to my room and paced impatiently in the hall, his heavy steps echoing like a rhythmic heartbeat as I changed. Looking in the mirror, my appearance startled me.

My face was ashen, and my hair was a mess, with strands sticking out in all directions. My eyes were bloodshot, and the bruise-like shadows beneath them spoke of the trauma I'd suffered.

My white cotton T-shirt had been scorched black and grey, and the remaining material was tattered, revealing glimpses of skin beneath. Flakes of ash created a dull film that covered my entire body, with darker streaks on my cheeks and hands that I imagined had rubbed off from Hunter.

As I cleaned my face, my eyes wandered to my limbs and the intricate branch-like scars etched onto my skin. The pinkish scars darkened towards my toes and fingertips, contrasting with my pallid complexion.

I unceremoniously tossed the used face wipes on the dresser, wrestled my dishevelled hair into a bun, and covered the burns with a hoodie and jeans.

Hunter pounded on the door. "We've no time for your beauty regime, princess," he barked. "We've got to go."

"One minute!" I yelled, my voice strained with irritation.

My body felt uncooperative as I staggered towards the door and opened it, my head still spinning.

Hunter smirked as his eyes ran up and down my frame. "For someone who just blew herself up, you look... okay," he said, offering his arm like a formal escort.

We headed downstairs in silence, the air heavy with unspoken tension. As I reached for the door handle to the briefing room, Hunter placed his hand over mine.

Hunter shifted his weight from foot to foot, avoiding my gaze and revealing a rare nervousness that contrasted with his usual brooding demeanour.

His emerald eyes finally met mine. "While you were out of it, I put my number in your phone," he said.

"Why?" I frowned.

He shrugged, tensing his shoulders as his face contorted into an offended scowl. "Everyone's telling me to be nicer to you. And it's...lonely being new."

I nodded as his piercing gaze locked with mine, sending a shiver down my spine. At that moment, it felt like he could unravel my innermost thoughts with a single glance.

Chapter Sixteen

As we entered the briefing room, I felt the weight of twenty-four pairs of eyes fixated on me. The silence was so dense that the following gasps felt like explosive bursts, shattering the stillness.

Around the table, jaws dropped in disbelief. The other Spirit Borns' expressions revealed a mixture of shock and confusion as they blinked rapidly.

I held my head high as Hunter helped me to my seat, pulling the heavy chair beside Lola out for me, the wood groaning against the stone floor.

Hunter squeezed my shoulder, a smile tugging the corners of his lips. He flashed a comforting wink and silently mouthed the word "breathe" as he headed to his seat.

Sawyer was the first to break the silence, his eyes narrowing as he tilted his head at me. "Our motel was infested with cockroaches the size of rats, so why the extra overnight?" he said, his voice laced with sharpness. "You look utterly fried, Harper, so I'm guessing you're involved."

"Don't start," Hunter warned, his jaw clenching.

"So, you're her mouthpiece already?" Sawyer scoffed. "That didn't take long, did it?"

Hunter's body grew rigid, his muscles visibly tensing as he slammed one fist onto the table and pointed with the other. "I'm warning you," he growled.

"Temper, temper," Sawyer chuckled sarcastically. "Well, we don't need a confession from either of you." He held out his phone, displaying a shaky video of the rollercoaster incident uploaded onto YouTube. "It's everywhere on social media."

"Did she hurt you, Lola?" Beck asked, his voice softening. "Is that why you couldn't pick us up?"

"Do I *look* hurt?" Lola replied sharply. "I was just...freaked. We could've died, but Harper saved everyone."

Sawyer gripped the table, leaning into the circle. "Yeah, after creating the situation in the first place."

"*I* created it!" Lola turned towards me and reached for my hand, her eyes glistening with tears. "I wasn't thinking, and I'm *so* sorry, H."

I smiled and silently nodded, mustering all the strength I had left to squeeze her hand.

Sawyer continued, his voice echoing around the room. "Regardless! She's already wreaking havoc."

"Quit shouting. My head's pounding," Beck moaned, rubbing his temples. His dishevelled appearance was marked by bloodshot eyes and a pallid complexion.

Kay intervened, raising her hand. "Enough! Yes, there was an incident. But neither Harper nor Lola could be identified. Authorities have blamed a power surge from a faulty transformer. The only injuries sustained were Harper's, and she'll heal. It could've been far worse, had it not been for Lola's direction."

Theon cast a quick glance at Hunter before his eyes shifted to me, a questioning look in his eyes. I gazed back, feeling a surge of warmth in my chest as I silently begged him to keep Hunter's unintentional support to himself.

Theon's lips curved into a half-smile as he nodded so subtly that only someone paying close attention would have noticed. I felt a wave of relief as my body relaxed.

"Lol's, you *told* her to do that?" Sawyer said.

"Whatever she said helped Harper avoid disaster, so let's leave it at that and get on with debriefs", Amy said, checking her watch. "I've got rounds in an hour."

Beck's eyes widened as he glanced around the circle. "But she can't stay here. You must all realise that? She didn't hurt anyone this time, but..."

"Look, I shouldn't have taken her there," Lola interrupted. "You all trust me, right? Well, I trust *her*. We've all done things we thought were unforgivable, yet we're still here. And despite all the chaos, Harper fixed it."

"Which is more than most of us have managed," Hunter added.

Lola's Handler, Cameron, sat on Kay's right side, his piercing grey eyes carefully assessing the situation with a mixture of concern and authority. "Harper's staying," he said. "End of discussion. Now we've all got places to be, so can we continue? How was Nevada?"

"Hot," Beck huffed.

Cameron rolled his eyes. "Other than the weather."

"We followed your advice and visited the Warden's quarters with EVP recorders," Theon said. "Eventually, we got a cell number."

"Did you get a name?" Kay asked, holding her pen poised over her notepad.

"Patrick McKenna," Theon said. "A serial rapist and murderer who died on death row."

"And how did you catch him?"

Chapter Sixteen

A devilish glint flashed through Beck's eyes as he nodded towards Gia. "Live...bait," he said.

"*Not* my idea," Gia said. "But I settled on his bunk, and after a few hours, he couldn't help himself."

"Any response?" Kay asked.

Gia shook her head. "No, he just grabbed me, and that was it. Good riddance," she shuddered.

"And the extra overnight?" Kay asked.

"We were only an hour out of Vegas, so we headed for the strip and crashed in some dingy motel," Beck said. "But we were that wasted we'd have slept anywhere."

A Handler with long blonde waves cascading down her back which looked like she'd just walked out of a salon blew a short breath through her nose. "You're working. Try and show a little professionalism, boy."

Beck raised his hands. "Hey, we did our job, Jules. We passed on Rapey-old-whatshisface, so who cares if we blow off a little steam."

"And three hundred dollars," Gia sniggered.

Jules' unblinking glare was instantaneous.

"What?" Beck shrugged. "I got a bonus at work."

Kay pinched the bridge of her nose. "Moving on. Group B, how did you fare?"

Captain sighed. "Not good." He looked almost as dishevelled as Beck. His shirt was crumpled, and dark shadows lurked beneath his tired eyes. "There was *way* more activity than we've ever documented there."

"Ungroundeds?" Kay frowned.

"Yeah, but not just the odd straggler," Captain answered. "It was chaos. We only got two responses on the Ovilus all night and no decipherable EVPs."

"Maybe they were just drawn towards the energy levels at the hotel?" Hunter shrugged.

Hannah shook her head, her expression grave. "Not that many."

"How many are we talking?" Kay asked.

Captain's brows rose. *"Dozens."*

The oppressive stillness of the room magnified the groaning of wood as several individuals shifted in their seats. Even The Handlers' eyes were unsettled as they stole glances at one another.

"The EVPs were incomprehensible," Hannah continued. "But when we asked where all the Ungroundeds came from, the Ovilus said 'strange' and 'visitors.'"

"This seemed planned," Captain said. "The hotel is reputedly haunted, so it's already on our radar. Beau knows we won't leave it unattended."

Kay raised a hand, flashing that sickeningly fake smile I despised. "Let's not jump to conclusions. The Handlers will investigate further. What happened with the POW?"

"We couldn't locate him, but honestly, we had bigger fish to fry," Captain answered. "But we took out some of The Ungrounded."

"Then we'll ensure a show of force this weekend," Kay said, nodding sharply. "How many Ungroundeds were left?"

"Another twenty-five at least," Captain said.

Sawyer turned towards Hannah, his brow tense. "You didn't see this coming, Han?"

"Only partially," she replied, shaking her head.

"Regardless of how this mess was caused, *everyone* will attend this weekend. We'll need all hands-on deck for this one," Kay said, nodding once.

Hunter's gaze shifted towards me, a war of apprehension and concern brewing in his eyes. "But Harper's..."

"*Everyone will attend*," Kay interrupted, her jaw tightening.

Beck's eyes widened as his voice echoed through the room. "That's insane! She blew herself up *yesterday*, and you want to take her on assignment?"

"I understand your concerns," Kay said. "But with that many Ungroundeds, we can't afford to leave anyone behind, and with Beau still looking for Harper, we can't leave her alone. Besides, her communicative abilities might prove helpful."

"We'll book your rooms," Cameron said. "And since we already know the assignment, we'll head straight there and conduct the briefing at Ettington this weekend."

"If there's a plan, can we wrap this up?" Amy said, rechecking her watch.

Sawyer's hand shot into the air. "Shotgun."

Lola materialised behind his chair, and with a mischievous smirk, she slapped the back of his head. She vanished again in a blur of movement

Chapter Sixteen

and reappeared beside Amy. "What part of 'She's got rounds', don't you understand?"

Amy gathered her things and looked at me. "Harper, take it easy for a few days."

"I will," I nodded. "And thank you."

"No problem. I've given Kay some ointments that'll aid recovery. If you have any issues, call me." Amy smiled as she took Lola's arm and vanished.

"Everyone else, you're dismissed," Amy's Handler, Emma, said.

As The Handlers shuffled papers and chatted quietly, the Spirit Borns rushed to the door. Several made hasty calls to their employers, lying about heavy traffic or family emergencies.

As I stood up, Kay gestured for me to sit back down. "Don't move, Harper. When Lola gets back, you'll be next," she said. "I'll collect your things."

As Kay chatted to the Handlers, she kept one eye trained keenly in my direction, watching me closely as Hunter crouched beside my chair and rested a hand on my knee.

His emerald eyes sparkled in the firelight as his aftershave enveloped me. "Get some rest," Hunter said softly. "Try not to blow anything up this week, and if you need anything, I'm around."

I nodded toward the other Spirit Borns, babbling excuses down their phones. "Aren't you worried about calling your boss?"

He smirked, shrugging, and winking in one slick move as he walked away. "No. Where I work, I *am* the boss."

The emotions swirling within me were a tangled web of conflict. I still loved Alfie, or at least part of me did.

But my attraction to Hunter grew with each magnetic interaction. The desire for him felt inherent and primal, as if it had been intricately woven into my every seam.

However, the only way to unravel the mystery of what The Handlers wanted with Alfie was to remain close to him despite the lingering echo of Dominic's post-training warning that reverberated through my mind.

"The more you return, the harder it is to leave."

Chapter Seventeen

With Amy's treatment, my injuries faded within days. As the wounds closed, delicate pink scars formed, winding their way across my limbs like branching tree limbs, the intricate patterns of markings each as unique and oddly beautiful as a spider's web.

Despite the harrowing ordeal, Kay's frequent disappearances became increasingly conspicuous. She would vanish before dawn and reappear late at night, hidden by the veil of darkness.

In spite of my curiosity, she remained steadfast in her refusal to disclose the secrets of her whereabouts and activities, creating a palpable sense of separation, like an outsider peering in through frosted glass. However, over time, I had become resigned to the futility of attempting to extract any meaningful information from her.

As I embarked on my first day working at Red Rock, a feeling of gratitude enveloped me. It wasn't simply the familiarity of being home or even the joy of seeing Alfie; it was the yearning for human connection that had built during the solitary hours confined to the four walls of my hotel room, and I was eager to break free of the feeling of restlessness that had begun to take hold of me.

I made my way down Red Rock's familiar driveway as the property seemed to unfold before me. My cheeks grew warm, and my pulse raced with anticipation as I found the reassurance of Sasha's comforting smile awaiting me at the front desk.

"Welcome back," she said, cocking her head towards the stairs. "Follow me. You can complete your initial training in the office."

Sasha led the way, pointing out paintings and sculptures with all the finesse of a seasoned tour guide. Meanwhile, my self-consciousness overtook me as I was preoccupied with adjusting my clothes and hair.

Despite applying multiple layers of foundation and blush, my efforts were hopeless in concealing my complexion's ashen hue after the weekend's

Chapter Seventeen

events. It was as if my skin was drained of all vitality, reminiscent of someone who had just weathered the flu.

As Sasha whirled around Alfie's room, heaving a collection of folders from the shelves, and stacking them on my father's desk, I lingered in the corner, trying to ignore the persistent itching on my arms.

I didn't need to pull up my sleeves to know that my inky markers would be blossoming across my skin, twisting in and out of my scars like vines as I scanned the room, scrutinising every shadow for any hint of Alfie.

Sasha winced sympathetically as she rested her elbow on the tower of folders she'd made, drawing my attention towards her. "Your first week will be pretty dull," she said. "You'll need to read everything in these. It's mostly historical information about the house that you'll need to know by heart. The rest are just health and safety nonsense. And if you need a break, there's a staff kitchen down the hall."

"Harper?"

Alfie slowly emerged from behind the cabinets, his form as solid and distinct as the living beings around him, so real that I struggled to fight the impulse to reach out and touch him.

His face lit up with a beaming smile as his chest heaved breathlessly. "You're back?"

I felt the warmth of my breath on my lips as I pressed them into a rigid line, and as I closed my eyes, I felt Sasha's gaze fixated on me.

"What's wrong?" Alfie said, his smile fading as his shoulders fell.

"I know, boring, right?" Sasha continued. "But once you're finished, you can start shadowing tours."

"It's not that. I'm just so pleased you've given me the opportunity to *work here*," I nodded, praying Alfie got the hint. "And thanks for showing me around."

Sasha frowned confusedly. "Uh, no problem."

"Oh, you're not alone?" Alfie said, stepping back. "But are you staying?"

"So, I just...read?" I asked, hoping that laying it all out for Alfie would appease him. "Here. Alone?"

Sasha answered slowly. "Yeah, like I said."

"I'm sorry," I chuckled, chewing my lip. "I'm just nervous."

"It's fine," Sasha smiled, the warmth in her tone setting me at ease. "I have a tour starting, so I'll just be downstairs if you need anything. Any questions?"

"No, I'm fine."

Alfie's hair fluttered over his forehead as he released his held breath. "Thank God, I've been so worried."

"I'm okay, *Sasha*," I said, my eyes widening at her.

Sasha's confused frown returned as she awkwardly waved and closed the door with a lingering sense of unease. Her concern was evident, no doubt regretting the decision to hire such an eccentric new employee on a whim.

Sweeping the beads of sweat glistening from my forehead, I sighed as I collapsed into the office chair behind the desk. "She's gone," I said. "How are you?"

"Just tired. I've barely slept in case you returned," Alfie replied, his bare toes clenching as dark rings marred his face, betraying his fatigue.

"You need sleep, Alfie. What'll the others think?"

"That I'm broken-hearted?" Alfie shrugged, his eyes falling to the floor.

"I'm so sorry."

"Harper, don't you dare apologise. You didn't ask for this," he said, his brows drawing together as his eyes met mine. "Did I hear you mention a job?"

Valuing the change of topic, a timid smile pinched my cheeks. "I've been hired as a tour guide."

"Then you'll be here all the time? That's fantastic," Alfie grinned. "And who better to show people around Red Rock than someone who's actually lived here?"

"Not that I can tell them that."

"What did you tell them?" Alfie asked.

"That my family worked here and shared stories about the place."

"I can't imagine Kay approved."

"Not initially, but she's been surprisingly supportive. She's just concerned about the risks."

Alfie took a measured step back. "Well, we know not to get too...close."

"Yes, but I'm worried about my family, too. If we cross paths, it'll be game over. Do you think you can get them to bed earlier?"

"If it means you'll stay, of course," he nodded. "But honestly, nobody wants to stay up past nine since you left anyway, especially after the whole seance fiasco."

"Good. I start at ten, but I'll be working downstairs. Kay's dropping off some REM pods today; they'll alert me if anyone's close," I explained, raising my brows and forcing my gaze on him. "We *must* keep everyone safe. I've put enough people in danger already."

Chapter Seventeen

A crooked smile brought a devilish charm to Alfie's lips. "Harper, you couldn't endanger anyone if you tried."

"I *didn't* try." Tears pricked my eyes as the computer on the desk sprang to life, repetitively opening random search pages.

"It just...happens," I said. "It's happening right now, for Christ's sake."

"I'm confused. The only thing you seem to affect in the afterlife is the lighting. That's what woke me."

I ran my hands through my hair, sighing. "Well, my talent affects everything here."

"So, you know what it is?"

"It's dangerous. I create energy."

Alfie reached for my shoulder and immediately stopped himself, squeezing his fingers together awkwardly at his waist. "But you'll learn to control it."

"I could've killed people, Alfie." My voice trembled. "My friend Lola took me on a rollercoaster, and I broke the restraints. People were screaming, but Lola made me fix it."

"And did you fix it?"

My eyes fell to the floor, avoiding Alfie's gaze. "Yes," I sniffed. "My hands and feet were charred in the process, but we have this Spirit Born doctor who healed me. And another, Hunter, watched over me."

I swallowed, suppressing the rising nausea as the familiar hum of Hunter's name on my lips stirred a swarm of butterflies in my stomach, their delicate wings creating a tempest of emotions.

"He sounds like a good chap," Alfie smiled, though the expression didn't reach his distant eyes. "He must be fond of you to look after you like that?"

"Maybe," I shrugged. "He tended to me all night in his room."

Alfie shifted, his brows drawing together disapprovingly. "You slept in his *room*?"

"It wasn't like that. I was injured, and Hunter just...stayed."

"So, you're getting close?" Alfie probed.

"I don't know," I shrugged. "But..."

Raising his hand, Alfie's eyes seemed to gain new clarity as if he'd just awakened. "I'm sorry, Harper..." he said, his voice struggling to find its strength. "...you shouldn't need to explain yourself to me. It'll just take time for me to adjust."

Alfie always avoided difficult discussions, headed for the door, his eyes fixed downwards. "I just...need a moment."

"Alfie, don't leave like this."

The squeak of ungreased wheels echoed softly as I rolled my office chair in front of him, blocking his exit.

"Let me through," Alfie said, his jaw tightening. "Please don't make me a prisoner in my own bedroom."

"Are you coming back?"

He nodded, a sad smile returning to his face. "I'll always come back for you, Harper. I'll just grab a drink in the library and let you work for a while."

I attempted to distract myself with the binders, but having lived and breathed Red Rock for eighty years, reading them was merely a tedious exercise, and as a result, the drama of my life crept into the fringes of my mind.

I couldn't begin to imagine Alfie's pain. I was exploring a new world while he watched from the sidelines, anchored in place and time. And seeing the anguished look on his face as I divulged the events and encounters of my new life only stoked a fire of guilt that I couldn't extinguish.

Long shadows began to crawl across the desk, casting a dusky hue over the pages before me. But as I opened my third binder, paying little attention to the mind-numbing text, the floorboards in the hall groaned, jolting my attention from the dead to the living.

"Harper, you've got a visitor." Sasha's cheery voice filled the room as she peered around the door. "Your boyfriend's brought you lunch."

I frowned confusedly, eyes narrowing. "My *boyfriend?*"

"Hey, sweetheart." A familiar voice purred, making my stomach instantly coil into knots.

Hunter's shadow dwarfed Sasha as he stood behind her, out of her line of sight. A wry grin played on his lips as he conspicuously winked and pulled a REM pod from his backpack, his blackened hands covered by thick gloves and a pencil balanced behind his ear.

Tiny flakes of sawdust drifted from his tight black T-shirt as he adjusted the strap of his bag. Leaning casually against the doorframe, crossing one foot behind the other, the soft clinking of metal echoed as the tools on his low-slung belt knocked against one another. He slid his hands into the pockets of his paint-splattered combat trousers as his playful, emerald eyes found mine.

I felt my cheeks flush, bringing a rush of colour to my pallid complexion as I quietly appreciated the simplicity of Hunter's rugged masculinity.

Chapter Seventeen

"How's your first day going?" Hunter asked.

"Uh...all the better for seeing you," I said slowly.

Momentarily resting her hand on Hunter's bicep, a smile broke across Sasha's face. "You guys are adorable," she said. "I'll leave you to it. Harper, you can take your lunch now if you like."

"Lovely meeting you," Hunter called.

He folded his arms, cocking his head as his keen eyes watched Sasha's retreating figure. Then, with one brow arched inquisitively, he turned to me.

"All the better for seeing you?" Hunter chuckled. "What are you, the big bad wolf of imaginary girlfriends?"

"Shut up," I said, my lips twitching with a suppressed smile. "You caught me off guard."

"I'd have texted, but I figured the look on your face would've been priceless. Kay sent me with some kit for the house."

He pulled a padded lunchbox from his work-battered bag and tossed it onto the desk. "And she told me to feed you. Lucky for you, I make a mean BLT."

"I'm a vegetarian."

Hunter rubbed the back of his neck. "Oh, uh..."

"I'm kidding," I grinned. "You're not the only one who can make jokes. Thanks."

His eyes remained pinned on mine as he ambled towards me and perched on the edge of the desk, his knees grazing mine. "So, any issues with your talent?"

"Why, are you Kay's spy?" I said, my eyes narrowing teasingly.

"Christ, no," he chuckled.

"Then no." I shot a frustrated glance at the screen on the desk. "I sent the computer a little crazy earlier, but nothing more."

"You're probably drained from the weekend. It takes me a while to get over incidents, too. You look better, though. And the scars look kind of badass." His knee nudged mine playfully. "What caused the computer issues? You sure you weren't just being a moronic forties girl in a twenty's world?"

"It's rude calling your imaginary girlfriend a moron. It was nothing. Alfie just wound me up."

Hunter's countenance shifted as a subtle frown manifested on his face. "You talked today?" he asked, his tone betraying his curiosity.

"I can't exactly ignore him."

"In a house this big, surely you can avoid him?" Hunter said, fiddling with his tool belt.

"Yeah, but this is his *bedroom*."

Movement at the edges of my vision diverted my attention to the doorway. I squeezed my eyes closed, cursing under my breath and wishing the ground to split open and engulf me as I noticed Alfie.

As Hunter followed my gaze towards him, Alfie swayed visibly, holding a glass of scotch in one hand and a half-empty bottle in the other.

His bloodshot eyes, glassy with emotion, narrowed accusingly at Hunter. "Who's this?" Alfie slurred.

With a smile that radiated sincerity, Hunter nodded once. In contrast, Alfie glared back, lips pursed.

"Alfie," I said. "This is Hunter, the Spirit Born I was telling you about. Hunter, this is Alfie."

"Nice to meet you, mate. I've heard a lot of good things about you," Hunter said, regardless of the fact he couldn't hear Alfie's reply without me.

"He's who helped you? This...this *roughneck*?" Alfie sneered, casting a critical eye over Hunter's appearance. "Well, tell him thanks. I'd shake his hand, but..."

Alfie held out his hand, only to snap it back, chuckling as he stumbled into the room.

"He said to thank you for looking after me," I repeated, my eyes cast downwards as I fiddled with my sleeves.

"You hear that much detail?" Hunter said.

"I hear everything."

"Don't talk about me like I'm not here," Alfie half shouted. "Make sure you tell him *everything* I have to say."

"Jesus, Alfie, and what do you want to say, exactly?" I snapped, crossing my arms. "I'm all ears."

"You tell him there's nothing we don't talk about. Tell him I know *everything* about you."

"No, Alfie. You're drunk."

Hunter smiled sympathetically as he caught my eye, "Is he always like...this?"

"No, never."

Alfie waved his hand towards the door, sloshing his drink wildly. "If I'm that bad, then leave me to sleep in peace."

"I *can't*," I said, gritting my teeth. "I'm meant to read here."

Chapter Seventeen

Alfie scowled at Hunter, then at me. As his movements grew increasingly erratic, we instinctively recoiled, trying to avoid grazing Alfie and accidentally sending him to The Infinite, which only pressed Hunter's body so close to mine that I could feel the heat radiating from him.

Jealousy was an alien contrast to the embodiment of gentleness I'd loved in Alfie, and it looked ugly on him. It pained me to bear witness to it so early on in my new life, and it cast a shadow of unease that, more and worse, would surely follow.

But despite this, all I could concentrate on was Hunter's warmth, which cast a comforting glow over my mind and consumed my thoughts with what could be.

"You're kicking me out?" Alfie snapped, his eyes widening.

"Yes, you can sleep it off in my old room."

Alfie pointed aggressively at Hunter; his face twisted as he stumbled past. "Tell him he's not welcome here."

Hunter's reactions were swift, smoothly sidestepping Alfie and sliding virtually into my lap, thus preventing Alfie from barrelling into him.

"Easy, mate," Hunter said, his voice a gentle purr.

"Tell that Spirit Born bastard I'm not his mate!" Alfie yelled, the sudden volume like a splash of icy water as he raised his chin aggressively.

"No!" I snapped, my fists clenching. "I'm not repeating your drunken ramblings. You've embarrassed yourself enough."

Alfie sipped his whiskey. "I swear to god if he's here tomorrow..."

I stood, nostrils flaring as my knuckles blanched white. "You'll what? Scold him to death? You lay a finger on him, and you're gone, so drop it."

Alfie finally conceded, lurching into the hall and ranting incomprehensibly under his breath. Even though our door remained open, the reverberations of Alfie's door slamming in his world echoed through the house as I slumped into my chair, running my hands through my hair.

"I'm so sorry."

As Hunter squeezed my knee, the room seemed to fill with static. "Don't apologise," he said. "He's just not coping without you. It's understandable. Maybe it's too hard for him to see you moving on. That's if... that's what you want?"

My gaze slowly lifted, and my stormy blue and woodland green eyes found Hunter's. When his eyes were on mine, they seemed to envelop me, making me the epicentre of his universe, and it was a place I never wished to leave. Something about their attention made me feel formidable, dangerous, even, as if I held an unyielding power in his presence.

In his eyes, I was beginning to find a particular security as I began to understand the suggestion that the true sense of home I so desperately sought was, in fact, not tied to a specific place but a person.

"Around him, I feel one way. But around...others..." I said carefully. "...I feel different. I feel alive."

"Oh, the irony in such a notion."

Hunter tugged off his gloves with his teeth, releasing a cloud of dust that shimmered in the light. He crouched beside me, lowering himself until our eyes were level.

The printer churned through its paper as he interweaved his bare fingers with mine, and the overhead lights shimmered vibrantly. However, our focus remained on each other, preferring the oblivion we found in the other's eyes to the bustling activity around us.

Despite barely knowing Hunter, his hand in mine felt like it belonged there, as if his coarse fingers, leaving a faint trace of ash on my skin, had found their way home.

"Would it change anything if I said I won't fight it anymore?" Hunter said, the golden shards in his eyes sparkling like the soul of a dying fire.

"Is that meant to mean something?"

His voice was barely audible as his hand squeezed mine. "Maybe not to you, but perhaps you should ask around," he said. "And whenever you're ready, H, so am I."

As he started pulling away, I tugged him back towards me in a moment of mindless spontaneity.

My chest prickled with heat as I felt overcome by the need to satiate the hunger that I'd harboured for him since we'd first met. His movements stilled, and a smile slowly eased across the contours of his face.

His hand slipped behind my neck, moving in tandem with my own as though we were one body. As I toyed with the minute and delicate hairs on his neck, his lips met mine, playing with them softly at first, then desperately, as his thumb grazed my jaw.

As nearby bulbs fizzed and threatened to burst, my fingers tangled in Hunter's sandy hair. I imagined that his level of control, combined with my exhaustion, were the only reasons we weren't showered with sparks.

The kiss escalated as my body craved a distraction, and Hunter obliged willingly. He lifted me from my chair, and my legs wrapped instinctively

Chapter Seventeen

around his waist. Holding my weight with one hand, Hunter swept the binders from the desk, leaving them splayed open on the floor as he laid me down.

Everything about the situation was wrong, from desecrating my father's desk to Alfie passing out down the hall and my employer's running tours downstairs. Still, the risk only made it all the more gratifying.

The promise of releasing the sexual tension that'd been building for weeks gave me little resolve to stop it, and Hunter's appreciative moans suggested he'd been waiting for me for far longer than I knew.

"We can't do this here," Hunter panted, his breath warming my ear.

"Shh, stop talking."

I tugged up his shirt, revealing perfect ridges of definition, but as my hands ran up his back, his muscles flexing as my nails raked his skin, the marching of footsteps echoed in the hall.

Hunter jerked upright, focusing on the door before his gaze returned to me. Silently, we frantically picked up the binders strewn across the floor and piled them back onto the desk in a haphazard heap. As the footsteps neared, Hunter curled his finger towards him.

Pulling up the hem of his shirt, he licked the cotton before gently wiping the ash from my face and neck. A gesture that, in its ease and tenderness, was utterly adorable.

Sasha appeared at the doorway, focused on her phone. "Are you guys alright?" she asked. "We had a power cut downstairs."

"We're good," I nodded, my cheeks burning as Hunter adjusted his clothing.

"Everything's fine," Hunter added. "I can check the breakers if there's a problem?"

"That's sweet of you to offer, but we've got it covered. Just one of those days, I guess," Sasha sighed. "We had books flying off shelves in the library earlier, too. Super creepy."

As Sasha returned down the hall, leaving us alone, Hunter's gaze returned to me.

"You think it's Alfie?" I asked.

"I wouldn't have thought he was strong enough yet. But if he has enough energy or is worked up enough..."

"And he's getting both from me," I interrupted.

"That may be why nothing's happened here talent-wise. Alfie's consuming all the energy you're projecting," Hunter said. "It could be a violent mix for the living caught in the crossfire."

"Should I just quit?"

"That's your decision, H. Look, whatever this is..." he purred, gesturing to himself and then to me. "I'll never tell you what to do or how to think, not that you appear to need any guidance anyway. Just be careful. Do you know how to set up the REM pods?"

I nodded. "Kay showed me."

"Then I'll leave you to your work," Hunter said, his eyes lingering on me as he disappeared out of sight.

After work, I found Lola leaning against the doorway's marble pillars, casually filing her nails.

"Thought you might need a ride." She tilted her head, smiling sympathetically as she looped her arm through mine and pulled me out of sight of my new employers. "Rough day?"

"A little. One minute, Hunter and I are all over each other on my desk, and the next..."

Lola gasped, excitedly gripping my arm. "You're kidding. I take it you don't share an office without anyone?" she chuckled.

"Hunter didn't tell you?"

"He's not one to kiss and tell—or kiss at all, really. To my knowledge, he's never had a girlfriend. He mentioned he met Alfie, though."

I rubbed my forehead. "God, it was so embarrassing."

"Hunter's a decent guy; he understands. Maybe it's the shared drama of the weekend or whatever, but since then, his attitude has totally changed. He's got your back something fierce. And this...*heat* between you, trust it. That kind of thing doesn't come around often."

"He said he'd stop fighting," I said, catching Lola's eyes as I frowned curiously. "Do you know what he's talking about?"

"He actually said that?" Lola beamed.

"What does he mean?"

Lola glanced around, checking that we were alone before we reappeared outside my hotel room.

"Well, Hannah had a vision."

"Christ," I interrupted, rolling my eyes as I wiggled a finger in my ear to ease the ringing. "I feel like every other Spirit Born-related sentence starts with "Hannah had a vision."

Chapter Seventeen

Lola raised her brows. "Just listen," Lola pleaded. "Years ago, she had one about you and Hunter that even The Handlers don't know about, that whatever happens, regardless of rules or consequences, Hunter would end up with a girl of great power. One whose name would be a single letter. But you know Hunter. When Hannah told him, he said it was nonsense."

"Because he wants to feel in control?"

Lola nodded. "Exactly."

"So now what?"

"That's up to you. You could try fighting it yourself, but it sounds like it might be a little late for that. Besides, Hannah's never been wrong."

Despite the distraction of Kay's rare presence over dinner, my mind remained preoccupied with the day's events. And once thoughts of Hunter had flooded my mind, they were impossible to escape.

I felt almost in a daze, caught in the fringes of sleeping and waking as I twirled my hair, savouring the oaky notes of Hunter's cologne that clung to my fingertips.

My mind wandered to the places those hands had been as my unfocused eyes gazed into space, trying to recreate the enchanting greens of his unflinching eyes within the small confines of my hotel room.

"Hey," Kay said, clicking her fingers in front of my face. "Are you okay?"

"Yeah...why?" I answered, shifting.

Kay pointed to the scramble of hazy dots on the TV.

I closed my eyes and conjured the timbre of Hunter's voice—a deep rumble that disturbed my chaotic thoughts and brought me clarity.

You've got this...breathe.

"Perhaps this will distract you," Kay said, settling back onto her bed.

Grinning, she slid a printed pamphlet towards me, showcasing a flat on the outskirts of London.

The property was a first-floor, one-bedroom flat in a large Victorian house. Red posies bloomed between the neatly trimmed hedges in the front garden.

The kitchen had been recently refurbished, and scratch-proof stickers were still peeling from the appliances. Black and white chequered tiles covered the floor, and a breakfast bar, complete with two chunky wooden stools, separated the kitchen from the open-plan lounge.

The living room's bay window let a stream of golden light pour into the room, casting an inviting glow over every surface and illuminating dust particles delicately floating around the pillow-lined bench beneath the window.

The free-standing Victorian roll-top bath in the bathroom was the room's focal point, with its brushed silver feet sitting atop a small platform. After months of showers at the hotel, I couldn't help but visualise myself up to my neck in white foam as my toes and fingers wrinkled.

The bedroom resembled the lounge, with a smaller fireplace. On the opposite wall, a series of floor-to-ceiling mirrored wardrobes, each embellished with ornate silver handles, gave the space a sense of opulence and space.

I could feel Kay's keen eyes boring into me as she sipped her whiskey, her every movement measured as I examined the final pages.

I gnawed my lip, sensing the gravity of the decision that seemed to linger tangibly in the air. Seizing the opportunity before me meant liberation from Kay's relentless scrutiny and the independence to chart a path that was entirely my own. However, I was acutely aware that embracing freedom meant facing the risks that cast a dark shadow on the way ahead, and I wasn't entirely sure I was ready to confront them alone.

"Do you think it's safe?" I asked. "Living with other people?"

Kay nonchalantly shrugged her shoulders. "Well, you like Lola, right?"

"Yeah, why?"

She leaned over, her tone uncharacteristically playful as she pointed to the pamphlet. "Guess who lives downstairs?"

"No way!" I gasped, my eyes widening as a wide grin spread across my face.

"I hope you don't mind, but I've already paid the deposit," Kay said, her face tense as she braced herself for resistance. "I just thought you'd like having a friend nearby, you know if..."

"If I blow anything up," I smirked. "So, she's my escape plan?"

"When we saw it listed for rent, The Handlers thought it would be perfect. If anything...happens, Lola can get you somewhere safe out of the city. But if you don't like it..."

"Are you kidding?" I interrupted, crumpling the leaflet to my chest. "With Lola downstairs, it's perfect."

I closed the gap between us and wrestled Kay into a hug, despite her arms, as always, remaining un-affectionately pinned at her sides, her body rigid as she resisted.

Chapter Seventeen

"Then I'll pick up the keys tomorrow," Kay said, shrugging out of my embrace. "There's an allowance on the bank card I gave you for resettling, so you'll need to start picking out furniture."

After eagerly texting Lola to arrange a shopping trip, I idly scrolled through my contacts until I saw the familiar name that made my heart race uncontrollably.

In an instant, my thoughts were shrouded by a rich tapestry woven from memories and desires that burst to life with vibrancy.

> *22:32 - I've got a flat! H xx*
> *22:35- Hunter: Sorry, gorgeous. I'm an electrician, not a mechanic. Lol. Congrats, where is it? X*
> *22:43 - Above Lola. H xx*
> *22:46 - Uh-oh! Your neighbours will love you two. Well, I'm always available for desk shopping if you need one. I'm sure we could rearrange a few more. How's after work on Thursday? X*
> *22:47 - I could be tempted. H xx*
> *22:49 - Hunter: Tease.*

"What are you two girls gossiping about over there?" Kay smirked, undoubtedly noticing the telltale blush creeping across my cheeks.

"Nothing...." I shrugged casually, suppressing a grin. "Just...furniture shopping."

Chapter Eighteen

When I arrived at work the following day, I noticed Alfie's haunting silhouette standing rigidly at his window. He wrung his hands as he watched me approach, his pallid form almost luminous against the shadows. Every step up the stairs reverberated through me like a drumbeat in my chest, and a cold sweat gathered on my palm as I anxiously pushed open the door to his bedroom.

"Are you alone?" Alfie asked.

Avoiding his gaze, I nodded as I removed my leather jacket and settled behind the desk. His dishevelled appearance gave me pause—his ashen, unshaven complexion stood in stark contrast to the pronounced rings beneath his eyes, which had grown so pronounced that I could see them clearly across the room.

"I'm so sorry," Alfie said, fiddling with his heavily creased pyjama bottoms. "I was struggling, and I..."

"It's okay," I interrupted. "I didn't consider how working here could affect you. I never should've taken the job; it's unfair to you."

"I don't care. After spending the morning in a dimly lit room, downing black coffee..." He softly chuckled as he rubbed his temples. "...I watched your family. They talk about you constantly, imagining where you are and what you're doing. But I'm the only one who knows the truth. And that's a *gift*, Harper. I see that now."

"But it's not right. Hunter said..."

"Oh God, that chap yesterday?" Alfie said, cringing. "Please send him my apologies. You know I'm not like..."

"I know. And he understands. But he's worried you're falling apart."

"No," Alfie said slowly, batting his hand breezily. "I survived losing my parents, losing my second family, and being bombed. Well, sort of. I'm from tough stock."

"You don't have to pretend with me, Alfie. It's okay not to be okay," I said, opening a binder.

Chapter Eighteen

"You know, it's still so strange seeing you like this," Alfie said, his eyes tracing my body. "Sometimes I'll see parts of your surroundings, but right now, it looks like you're hovering mid-air, pretending to read."

"I know the feeling," I said. "I still have to pinch myself whenever I see you drifting through the furniture."

I paused, shaking my head in an attempt to clear my cluttered thoughts. It was a familiar scenario with Alfie. He would smoothly transition to a different topic whenever a difficult conversation arose.

"Stop changing the subject."

"Okay, look, I'll admit it's hard," Alfie said. "My entire existence, you're the only person who has ever understood me. And now we're back together; I can't imagine losing you again."

"But I'm not, am I? With you, I mean." I turned my face, hiding the tears on the brink of spilling down my face. "You shouldn't think of us as being a couple anymore."

"Why?" His brows knitted together as he paced into my line of sight. "Has something happened that I should know about?"

I'd always been Alfie's without contention. But now that he'd met his rival, it seemed evident that the internal struggles and insecurities that had plagued Alfie's life had followed him into his afterlife.

The burden of truth weighed heavily on me, compelling me to confess what had happened with Hunter. However, considering the fragility of Alfie's current state, I couldn't help but worry about the impact my confession would have on him.

"We can't even touch each other," I said, each word a struggle. "We can't..."

Alfie's voice filled the room as he crossed his arms, his jaw clenching with tension. *"Has something happened that I should know about?"* he yelled.

I loved Alfie profoundly, and a part of me always would, but I couldn't waste the next chapter of my life pursuing a man I could no longer have

As my new life began to take form, filled with the warmth of friendship, the fulfilment of a job, and the comfort of a home, I came to the profound realisation that lingering in nostalgia would only unravel everything I'd been so anxious to build.

Chasing ghosts was my calling, but I could no longer chase this one, not in the way he wanted me to.

"Look at me, Harper," Alfie growled.

Spirit Born

My eyes fell into my lap as I squeezed them shut, wet spots mottling my shirt, while Alfie's voice softened, taking on a pleading tone.

"*Please*. Look at me," Alfie said.

I finally met his gaze. "Hunter," I whispered.

"The Spirit Born from yesterday?" Alfie frowned. "What about him?"

I remained silent, my heart aching with heaviness. As a look of realisation swept across Alfie's features, his bottom lip quivered. Slowly, he shook his head, running both hands through his hair as he turned his face.

"And he had the audacity to come here and... what, rub it in my face?" Alfie said, nostrils flaring. "I *knew* there was something off about him."

"You were so drunk you barely knew your name," I said defensively. "Besides, it hadn't...happened then."

"Then when did it happen?"

"After you stormed out," I mumbled, my fingers nervously tracing the cracks etched into the worn surface of the desk.

"So, it's my fault?"

"No. Yes," I stuttered. "I... I don't know."

"I think you need to figure out what you want, Harper."

"Says the king of blowing hot and cold?" I scoffed.

"That's not fair, I *always* wanted you."

"Then what were you so afraid of?"

"*This!*" Alfie yelled, flinging his arms outwards. "I knew you'd always leave and that I'd have to stay. And even though it torments me, I still wait at my window all night, every night, waiting for you to return."

He inched closer, his voice hoarse with emotion as his eyes glistened with unshed tears.

"I don't sleep...I barely eat," he whispered. "And when I woke up in the woods yesterday, all I could think of was getting back here to apologise when *you're* the one that really needs forgiveness."

"I know, and I'm..." I paused, frowning. "Wait, why were you in the woods?"

"I figured I stormed off and passed out there," Alfie shrugged.

"But the woods are past the boundary," I said, my eyes widening. "How did you get back?"

"It was all a blur. I just remember my feet dragging against the leaves and waking up on the doorstep at dawn."

"And you didn't become an Ungrounded?" I asked. "How long were you gone?"

Chapter Eighteen

"A few hours maybe, I'm not sure."

"And you're still...yourself?"

"I guess so."

I'd been avoiding looking directly at Alfie, but as I finally mustered the courage to do so, I couldn't help noticing the striking changes in his appearance. His cheekbones jutted out in angular points from his unshaven face as his crumpled pyjamas hung loosely from his hips, and his tousled hair seemed heavy with grease. For the first time, he actually looked like the ghost he was.

Even considering Alfie's admission to a lack of sleep and nourishment, the extent of his sudden transformation prompted me to question whether being temporarily ungrounded, if that were even possible, was the cause.

Whatever was to blame for his markedly changed appearance, I felt obligated to protect him and ensure he didn't stray again. But in his unhinged state, feeling betrayed by my confession, I had no idea how he'd behave anymore.

"I never expected you to remain alone forever. But I only just got you back," Alfie sighed, making for the door.

"Wait," I pleaded, my eyes wide with concern. "We need to talk about how you got back to your grounding. It's important."

"More important than breaking my heart?" Alfie answered, his voice breaking. "I can't even look at you right now."

"Knock, knock," Sasha announced.

Alfie noticed my attention shift towards the door. He shook his head, his movements swift as he disappeared through Sasha and out of sight.

"Are you okay?" Sasha asked, smiling as she planted a cup of coffee on the desk, its inviting aroma enveloping the room. "I thought I heard voices."

"Sorry, family emergency," I lied, waving my phone loosely in the air.

"Well, if you ever need to talk, I'm always around." She winked. "Anyway, I better go clean up the mess downstairs."

"Mess?"

"Lucie didn't tell you?" Sasha leaned in closer, her eyes narrowing and tone lowering as if sharing a piece of water cooler gossip. "We keep finding books dumped everywhere in the library. And our night cleaner, Holly, is pretty spooked. She thinks something is messing with her, so we checked the CCTV, and they were. Books flying off the shelves by themselves. So, it seems we have a resident ghost."

As Sasha disappeared into the hall, wiggling her fingers spookily, I closed my eyes and pinched the bridge of my nose. Alfie had seemed weary and dejected since I'd left, but this was different. His demeanour had never been aggressive or destructive before, especially in a place he treasured so much.

The haunting image of Alfie's eyes remained with me, burned into my memory like an old photograph. Once a sparkling oceanic blue, they had transformed into a lifeless, dull grey that seemed to retreat into the shadows of his face.

I could only hope that now that he had somehow returned home, he would find healing, if it were possible for a ghost to do so. But despite my prayers for his recovery, I couldn't shake the growing nervousness gnawing at me, stirring thoughts of whether my family shared the same concerns over his sudden deterioration.

After work, Lola had transported us somewhere pitch black. With my knees squeezed into my stomach, my chest tightened as the metal of the claustrophobic wire cage surrounding us cooled my skin.

As my eyes adjusted to the darkness, I made out piles of fresh-smelling blankets and pillows heaped on top of us, creating a cosy cocoon that obscured our view of the surroundings.

"Lols, I'm seriously beginning to doubt your relocation choices," I muttered, half grinning. "As soon as we climb out of here, people will see us."

"Trust me, it won't matter," Lola said.

"Where the hell are we?"

"Well, you wanted to go furniture shopping, right?"

Lola's hand shot up dramatically, like some sort of zombie of soft furnishings, scattering pillows into the aisle. She clambered out of the display, extending her hand and inviting me to follow her as if she were leading me into another world.

Nearby, a woman gasped and clung to her trolley before haughtily strutting off, while an amused employee chuckled and shook his head as he continued to stack shelves.

"You know you can get kicked out for that?" he smirked. "I've been here a while, though; you've been in there for ages."

Chapter Eighteen

As Lola dragged me towards the trolleys at the front of the brightly lit store, she flashed a wide grin back at the employee. "We're a very dedicated team,"

"Dare I even ask what that was about?" I asked, arching one brow.

"A while back, there was this craze where people played hide and seek here, but they started hiding in such crazy places that management put signs up banning it," Lola explained. "But you still get occasional weirdoes like us doing it."

I rolled my eyes. "You know, I really worry about the modern world sometimes."

"I know, right? Our generation created penicillin, and millennials invented this."

"Give us time," I said, elbowing her gently. "You sure we'll find everything I need here?"

She nodded cheerfully, tugging a trolley towards her tiny frame. "Yep. Everything but electronics, but I'm sure Hunter can help with that tomorrow."

"Sounds like a surefire way to break a shit load of TVs," I muttered.

I couldn't help but notice the strikingly modern feel of the furniture on display. The clean lines and bold, clashing colours starkly contrasted the earthy atmosphere I was used to at Red Rock. It only reinforced the feeling of shedding my skin and starting anew.

Despite my lack of knowledge about current trends, I found myself inexplicably drawn to certain pieces, paying little attention to whether they harmonised with each other.

At the checkout counter, as I eagerly signed the delivery form for the larger pieces of furniture, Lola precariously manoeuvred one of the two trolleys we'd filled towards the door. As its wheels wailed a high-pitch screech under the weight of our purchases, Lola was barely visible behind the piles of furnishings and appliances as she scanned the shadowy car park for a secluded spot to transport everything to my new flat.

Are you sure you'll manage all that?" I asked.

"Have you seen the size of Hunter?" Lola smirked. "I'll be right back."

In my new lounge, the vague stacks and rows of cardboard boxes created the illusion of a miniature cityscape nestled within the confines of the room. As we sat on the floor and assembled the smaller pieces of furniture, our conversation naturally drifted to our expectations of the upcoming weekend, intermingled with our shared frustration with Sawyer and Becks' unwarranted hostility towards me.

"They've always been like that," Lola said. "Sawyer had a tough time updating, and Beck's just his sheep, but we kind of understand why. Beck spent most of his afterlife alone. His brother left him when Beck was six to find the rest of their family, but of course, once he became an Ungrounded, he didn't return, so when Sawyer took him under his wing, Beck was grateful."

"That still doesn't excuse their behaviour."

"Of course not, but you know they won't let up about you and Hunter now they've gotten a rise out of him. He's one of The Handlers' golden boys, so those two morons have just been waiting for him to screw up."

I sighed, blowing my fringe out of my eyes. "Maybe we should just get it over with and confess?"

"Are you kidding? The Handlers would freak. Spirit Borns can't date; it's against the rules," Lola said, shaking her head vehemently. "So, are you officially together then?"

"Honestly, I've no idea."

The ambient lighting overhead dimmed and flickered erratically, creating shifting shadows that enveloped the room. As our conversation about Hunter unfolded, the interplay of light and shadow intensified, adding a layer of depth to our exchange.

"Chill," Lola soothed, rubbing my arm. "Stop worrying about Alfie."

"I'm not," I huffed, driving a screw into place on the side table we were building. "It's...Hunter."

"Oh," she said slowly. "But I thought your core related to Alfie?"

"That's what Hunter and Dominic said." I chewed my lip. "Is it possible to have more than one core?"

Lola gazed thoughtfully into the shifting shadows, her brow furrowed. "I've never heard of it before," she said. "But cores are often linked to our strongest emotions. Maybe it's not specifically Alfie, but how you feel for him. The emotions behind the person and relationship."

"But with Hunter, it's all so much stronger, the lights...the electricity..."

"Then maybe your talent is telling you how you feel about both of them?" Lola said, her tone carrying a hint of curiosity.

"But what if losing me makes Alfie's condition worsen?"

"Look, unless you get hit by a bus tomorrow and can return to Red Rock, there's nothing you can physically do to help him anymore." Lola's warm smile conveyed her compassion as she tucked a loose strand of hair

Chapter Eighteen

behind my ear. "He has to help himself now. Just give him space until he's adjusted. I've no idea how he made it back to Red Rock, but in his current state, I doubt he'd manage it a second time."

"I know. I just don't understand why he'd be so reckless; he knows the rules."

"Have you considered it could've been...intentional?" Lola said cautiously, her face tense as one eye narrowed.

"What, like some sort of paranormal suicide?"

Lola handed me another screw and nodded. "It happens. Some want to forget, and others have been around so long they just want it over."

I shook my head adamantly as my brows drew together. "He'd never want to be one of The Ungrounded. I know him; he wouldn't want that for himself."

"You *knew* him. And now you're apart, it's like he's a different person. But I've got to ask, aren't you curious why Kay still wants him in your life?"

"Of course I do, but whatever she's after, our fight shouldn't become his. He deserves peace."

Fuelled by fast food, we finished assembling the smaller pieces of furniture. Conversation with Lola was effortless, and her quick wit continually brought laughter and positivity that I desperately craved. She told me about her adventures as I hung on to every word, spellbound by the extraordinary sights she had witnessed, all thanks to her remarkable talent.

She had been inside the Vatican, Buckingham Palace, Area 51, and the White House's Oval Office (before Secret Service officers drew their weapons and prompted her to make a swift exit). And, of course, she'd snooped around her favourite celebrities' houses, carefully selecting small souvenirs of no monetary or sentimental value to build the collection of oddities showcased in her flat downstairs.

From the depths of Lola's being radiated a relentless thirst for adventure, and her captivating, larger-than-life presence seemed to burst at her seams, evoking nostalgic memories of Sophia.

While I could never fill the void my sister had left, nor would I ever wish to do so, having a dependable friend provided me with the companionship I'd longed for since my return.

I'd had no idea how to soothe the ache I'd been burdened with since losing my family, but Lola's unwavering optimism and contagious enthusiasm led me to believe it all started with letting the right people into my life.

Even when our conversation turned to more disconcerting matters concerning The Handlers' expectations on assignment, Lola maintained a certain balance and cautious optimism that prevented my anxiety from spiralling out of control.

"The way my handler, Cameron, describes our work is that we're enforcers. Just like the police, we don't decide the law, but it's our responsibility to uphold it," Lola explained. "But there's no court system for what we do because no jail can hold a spirit, save for The Infinite. It's why there are such firm laws about groundings, so we can keep an eye on the rule breakers whilst preserving the afterlives of the deserving. But as for the assignment at Ettington, it's who put all those Ungroundeds there in the first place that we need to watch out for."

"Beau?" I shifted as a chill tickled my spine. "You think he's behind it?"

Lola nodded sharply. "Absolutely. Especially with how this assignment's just been exploding. I've been nipping The Handler's back and forth from there all week. They're still trying to figure out what the hell is going on and how he did it."

"Do you think he'll show?"

"Possibly," Lola shrugged. "He's been quiet for a while now, which makes me nervous. And what better way to discover our new strength than by getting us all on one assignment? He already knows everyone else's abilities, so he'll be itching to discover yours."

I leaned in closer, my eyes unconsciously narrowing. "But how does Beau know so much about us? Could someone be feeding him information from within The Spirit Borns?"

Lola's face froze, her brows knitted together. She repeatedly blinked as if trying to process what she had just heard. Her movements were slow and deliberate as she set down her glass and pivoted to face me.

The gravity of her expression mirrored the sternness I'd only witnessed once before during the roller coaster incident, sending an involuntary shiver down my spine.

"Jesus," Lola said slowly. "You don't know, do you?"

"Know what?"

Lola's frown deepened, casting a shadow over her warm features as her chocolate-coloured eyes darkened. "Harper," she said. "Who did you think you were replacing? You're The *Thirteenth* Spirit Born. You were never meant to exist."

Chapter Nineteen

After Lola revealed Beau's true identity, I felt overwhelmed with a profound sense of isolation. By the time I got back to the hotel, Kay was gone, out doing who knew what, but rather than returning fatigued and tense, she now rarely returned at all.

Instead, she sent occasional texts checking in, and with each one, I struggled to fight my insubordinate nature and respond with a barrage of expletives for failing to explain everything about Beau's background. However, it wasn't a conversation I wanted to have via text or over the phone. I wanted to look into her eyes and see her reaction when I told her I knew she'd been keeping things from me.

At work, even Alfie remained absent, though I would still feel an apprehensive shiver tickle my spine every time the gravel on the driveway crunched underfoot. It was as though his presence lingered, and I felt his eyes tracing my path, continually watching me. But wherever he was hiding, he was at a far enough distance that he was out of range of the REM pods and my markers.

I didn't know what was more unsettling, seeing him in the state he'd been in or not seeing him at all. As a result, I found myself perpetually consumed by the concerns of whether he was recovering or slipping further into oblivion.

When Thursday arrived, the vine of loneliness I'd felt ensnared by loosened its suffocating grip as the anticipation of meeting Hunter at the steps of Red Rock filled my mind with a mix of nervous energy and anticipation.

With every passing minute, knots tightened in my stomach. I envisioned our conversations, meticulously crafting charming anecdotes to impress him. Yet, deep down, I knew that the moment Hunter's emerald eyes met mine, my carefully rehearsed words would scatter like leaves in the wind, lost in the rapid thumping of my heart against my ribs.

I found Hunter leaning casually against a restored vintage motorbike, its polished chrome attachments catching the light as his dark jeans and black leather jacket contrasted the gleaming metal and fading autumn sun on the horizon.

As I felt my nerves bubbling inside me, the bike's headlights burst into full beam. Reactively, I raised my hand and shielded my eyes.

"Hello to you, too," Hunter chuckled.

"Don't you have a car?" I asked, furrowing my brow as I fought to suppress a smile.

Hunter held a sleek black helmet towards me. "Yep. And a van. But this is more fun."

"You sure you're not just looking for an excuse to have my arms around you?"

"That too," he smirked.

Apprehensively, I accepted the helmet, lifting my gaze to meet his through my lashes.

"Don't look at me like that, H," he grinned, cocking his head towards the bike. "You'll be fine."

"I don't even know how to get on that thing."

"Ooh, the big bad Thirteenth isn't afraid of a little motorbike, is she?" he teased, towering over me as the golden shards in his eyes sparkled. "Come here."

As his hand slipped around my waist, he pulled me close and gently lifted me as I swung my leg over the bike. He carefully shifted my body towards the back of the seat and paused.

A wicked grin lit up his face as he slowly ran both hands down my thigh, gently squeezing as they reached my ankle, raising it a few inches until the heel of my combat boots sat on the footrest. He slowly walked around the bike, his eyes fixed on mine with every step, and repeated the process with the other leg, his touch sending ripples of electric desire through me.

"Feel good?" he asked.

"As comfortable as one can be on a death trap, I suppose."

Pulling an extra pair of gloves from his back pocket, he took my hands in his and tenderly secured them over mine. As I pulled my helmet on, I felt my chest rise and fall with every breath.

Hunter swung his leg over the bike and, with a swift kick downward, sent leaves scattering in the exhaust's wake as the growl of the engine reverberated through the air. He revved the throttle, and I instinctively

Chapter Nineteen

wrapped my hands around his waist, feeling the strength fluttering through his muscles.

He pulled on his helmet and glanced over his shoulder. "Hold on tight. I don't fancy suffering Kay's wrath by damaging you."

"I think I'm already pretty damaged."

I couldn't see the gentle curve of his lips, but the intensity of his eyes, blazing from behind the dark plastic of his visor, suggested he was smiling. "Aren't we all a little damaged?" he said.

Hunter turned the throttle with a smooth twist of his wrist, causing the tyres to kick up gravel onto the lawn. The sudden acceleration shifted my weight backwards, prompting me to squeeze his waist tighter. Over the hum of the engine, I could hear him chuckling. He briefly interlocked his fingers with mine, offering a reassuring connection, before resuming control of the handlebar.

The wind danced through my hair as I savoured the exhilaration of being on a motorbike for the first time. Headlights streaked by in flashes of white lights, and as we manoeuvred through the bustling traffic, the slightest shift in Hunter's muscles sent shivers of excitement through me.

His careful placement of me on the bike and the gentle fastening of my gloves exuded a surprising sensuality, infusing the mundane task of picking me up from work with an air of suggestiveness.

The intensity of our attraction was so potent, so profoundly rooted in chemistry, that it almost frightened me.

When we were together, it felt like my logical side was overpowered as the left side of my brain took over, seeking out primal pleasures without considering the consequences.

Hunter's hand would find its place on mine at every set of traffic lights, silently soothing me until the lights, flickering in response to my nerves, turned green.

But with Hunter by my side, I felt reassured. If I were to lose control, he possessed the power and self-control to contain my surges of energy, preventing me from causing a scene. We were like two puzzle pieces fitting seamlessly together. However, I had yet to consider what would happen when my abilities surpassed his.

We arrived at an industrial estate bustling with various showrooms and superstores, their bright facades illuminating the space. After parking in a secluded corner, Hunter turned off the ignition and gracefully dismounted the bike. He then carefully removed my helmet, taking a moment to tuck a stray lock of golden hair behind my ear.

The sun dipped below the horizon, casting a rich hue across the sky as a river of desire surged through me. I chewed my lip and lifted my gaze to meet Hunter's, feeling the hunger for him creeping through my veins like a growing flame that awakened every cell in my body.

As the atmosphere crackled with mounting tension, the streetlamps responded and flickered to life, flooding the area with vivid, artificial light. I squeezed my eyes shut, attempting to soothe my racing thoughts. However, the longer we lingered under the streetlamps, the more intense their glow became, piercing my eyelids as the faint hum of faltering circuits permeated the air.

Hunter edged closer, brushing his thumb down my cheek and guiding my face towards him. "Hey, it's okay," he hushed. "I've got you."

Hunter's gaze shifted towards the streetlamps overhead, his focus unwavering as they slowly dimmed. As his hands came to rest on my shoulders, I could see a faint amber glow breaking through the worn seams of his gloves. Amidst the urban backdrop, all that could be heard were the sounds of passing traffic.

As his eyes lowered to mine, my lips bridged the small gap between us and unexpectedly met his, taking him by surprise.

His hands traced the contours of my face and slipped around my neck as he pulled me closer, his lips parting and brushing softly against mine. The soft moans that vibrated from him suggested he appreciated each delicate touch as I tasted the faint flavour of peppermint chewing gum on his breath.

He pulled away, breathless, and held my gaze as the golden sparks within the forests of his irises shimmered like scattered stardust. Then it struck me; they only came alive when he was excited or angry, as if his emotions kindled miniature fireworks within his eyes.

"This is insane," Hunter said, a smile playing on his lips as he shook his head. "You know we shouldn't be doing this."

I nodded. "I know. Lola told me."

"I've never disobeyed the rules before. And I know this shouldn't be wrong, but lying to Annie doesn't feel right. How do you manage it with Kay? Don't you feel guilty?"

I chuckled, "I never obeyed Kay to begin with. She's kept so much from me to earn my respect. But where does that leave us?"

Chapter Nineteen

"I guess it leaves us with a secret," Hunter half smiled.

"But won't Theon..."

"We don't leak each other's secrets," Hunter interrupted, his fingers lost in the waves of my hair. "The question is, are you okay living like that, being my secret?"

I shrugged one shoulder, the corners of my lips twitching upwards with them. "If you're okay being mine?"

He nodded without hesitation. His lips curled into a playful grin as he casually threw me my helmet. "I'm not carrying your crap for you though," he said, winking.

"You've got two hands," I replied, with a smile too broad to refrain.

"My spare hand has places to be."

As we crossed the parking lot, I felt the warmth of Hunter's fingers as they slipped around mine, our gloves interweaving effortlessly. To avoid inadvertently channelling my abilities in unwanted ways, I consciously focused on the minute details of our surroundings. The aroma of the freshly trimmed bushes nearby and the distant buzz of traffic served as welcome distractions as we ventured into the electronics store on the hunt for a suitable TV for my new flat.

"I feel like you know everything about me," I said. "But I know nothing about you."

He paused, towering over me, his eyes narrowing teasingly. "And yet you still want to do this? So *reckless*, Miss Reynolds-Woodbury."

"Tell me about your afterlife," I continued, undeterred.

"I was lucky; I had a pretty good one. My family owned a little cinema."

"So, you lived off of popcorn and soft drinks?" I teased.

A small chuckle erupted within him that made my heart buzz with frenetic energy. "Something like that," he said. "We had a little flat above it in the 30s. I spent my childhood playing hide-and-seek in the seats with my sister and watching movies from the projector room."

"Then what happened?"

"I had a wonderful father, but he made some rather unwise investment choices and fell into debt. To keep the cinema open, he got a loan from some rather nefarious people," Hunter explained. "But we cut corners wherever possible to keep up with the repayments. That was, until his final payment."

I squeezed his hand, my lips curling into a compassionate smile. "You know we don't..."

"No, I want you to know," Hunter interrupted.

As we strolled toward the television displays, I couldn't ignore the fact that his body visibly tensed up, the seams on his leather jacket creaking with unease.

"After closing one night, two men arrived for the money we owed. A stocky man in a suit with gold rings on every finger and a tall, thin man with greasy hair and bony fingers. They tied my dad to a chair on the front row to rough him up, but they went too far. My mother was putting me and my sister to bed, and by the time we heard the commotion, it was too late."

My mouth hung open as I struggled to find the right words. "I'm... I'm so sorry," I stammered.

"The thugs couldn't leave any witnesses, so they then turned their violence towards us," Hunter continued. "The thin man grabbed my mother, and the other grabbed me and my sister. The last thing I remember was my mother's screams as we were dragged away. Then everything went black."

I chose my words carefully, my eyes narrowing. "So, it was your father's fault?" I asked, pausing by a TV to read its features absentmindedly.

"Yes and no," Hunter explained. "My father only missed his final payment to help someone else, so he earned a decent afterlife with us through that sacrifice. You see, there was a girl who worked for us who'd continually turn up for her shifts beaten black and blue. But whenever she tried saving money to escape her abusive boyfriend, he'd find it and threaten to kill her if she tried to leave. So, my father handed her enough money from our safe to start over."

"But the police..."

"Were useless," Hunter interrupted. "The girl's boyfriend's father was a chief inspector who continually downplayed his son's crimes. But the girl escaped, and my family ended up together for ninety years, so it all turned out okay. My parents and sister are still at the cinema, and my Handler, Annie, tells me they're happy." Hunter bobbed his head. "And after a while, I could appreciate the positives of my new life. I have a business I've built from scratch, a home almost paid for, and a calling I adore."

Hunter's eyes remained fixated on the threadbare carpet. His furrowed brow revealed a mind wavering on the brink of being consumed by the sorrows of the past. To pull him back to the present, I steered the conversation to a more optimistic subject.

"You own your own home already?" I asked.

Chapter Nineteen

A lopsided smile eased across his face. "I couldn't afford much, so it was just a shell when I bought it, but it's nearly finished now. I did most of the work myself." Leaning closer, his grin turning mischievous. He lowered his voice to a near whisper and winked knowingly. "And it's helped never needing to pay an electric bill. Though the streetlamps by my house are always out for some curious reason."

"I've never even considered things like that," I answered, arching my brows.

"You're new; you're only focusing on the basics right now, which I imagine Kay's been drilling into you."

"Ugh, Kay," I groaned as we passed a salesperson purposefully eyeing his watch.

"Trouble in paradise?"

"She doesn't tell me anything," I said. "Like the fact that I'm Beau's *replacement*. The thirteenth? I only found that out from Lola."

"Kay didn't tell you?"

"No," I said, "and Lola's so scared of Kay that she won't tell me anything else."

"What do you want to know? I kind of had a front-row seat to most of the shit he did."

I chewed my lip, pondering the burning questions lingering in the dark recesses of my mind. "What happened for Beau to hate us so much?" I asked, eyes narrowing.

"He wasn't always the monster he is now. He actually started out okay," Hunter shrugged. "I returned shortly after he did, so we grew close. He even moved in with me."

"How the hell did that happen?" I spluttered.

"We kind of fit, just like you and Lols have. But Beau and I were vastly different people with vastly different talents. Mine is aggressive, whereas Beau's is defensive. He could create psychic barriers to protect us from paranormal influences and the harm that The Ungroundeds can cause." Hunter sighed, his demeanour turning sombre as he cast his eyes downwards and shook his head. "But we didn't realise how harmful that talent could be if it were ever used against us until he left."

"Then how did our protector end up our enemy?"

"Beau was always kept on the sidelines, safeguarding us from a distance," Hunter answered. "Consequently, he became isolated and resentful that he was never used in the field."

"But he could still pass on spirits, right?" I asked.

"Of course, but The Handlers insisted on keeping him separate; it wasn't until his power grew that we understood why." Hunter locked eyes with me, his grip on my hand tightening. "Beau didn't just suppress the abilities of spirits, but *any* paranormal influence, including ours. Eventually, nobody could use their talents around him at all."

"So that's why Hannah can't see him?"

"Exactly, but I think a part of her doesn't want to see what he's become anyway," Hunter said. "He stripped us of everything that made us special, so everyone avoided him. The Handlers kept him at the old fort, having him protect the teams from afar. Alone, he started delving into past assignments and researching the Ungrounded, arguing that we were making the wrong calls."

"He sounds obsessed," I scoffed.

"He was. He even turned on me and moved out, saying I'd become a "yes man"." Hunter rolled his eyes, a look of resented frustration on his face. "His Handler persevered, insisting they could still use him. They were just trying to help, providing him a place where he'd be understood, but they only fuelled his anger. Soon, incidents started occurring on assignments where Beau refused to protect us anymore. Some of us suffered possessions, and even Lols succumbed to an insidious depression after an attachment. She refused to leave her flat for weeks."

My hand drifted to my mouth as concern knitted my brows. "Was she okay?"

"Eventually," Hunter nodded. "After that, things went quiet with Beau. He had grown too powerful for Lola to transport, so he fell off the radar for weeks at a time. Nobody heard from him until things took a sinister turn." He swallowed and took a deep breath as his voice grew hoarse. "Beau's Handler, Laura, turned up dead in her hotel room."

My eyes widened. "Beau killed her?" I whispered.

The hair on my arms stood to attention as I felt the colour drain from my face. I knew Beau was dangerous, but the revelation that he was implicated in his own Handler's murder added a chilling dimension to his character. The faceless villain I'd conjured in my mind suddenly took on a more sinister persona, and the depth of his interest in me and my abilities unsettled me to the core.

"We know he visited her. However, Laura died of head trauma, so we'd no idea whether it was murder or some kind of accident," Hunter

Chapter Nineteen

continued. "He was assigned another handler, Kay, hoping to resolve his issues and have him return to service, but it didn't work. And no matter where they were, Hannah and Aida couldn't see him anymore. They had no idea where he'd been or where he was headed. Lola even took Hannah and Aida to Australia to try and gain enough distance to use their talents to track him down, but after Laura's death, it seemed like his abilities just exploded."

"But Hannah and Aida used their talents fine when..."

"I know. They can see everything and everyone else, but Beau became invisible to them," Hunter said. "And once the Australia trip fell through, they gave up searching."

"So, how did he become a threat again?"

"Around six months later, we arrived for briefing, and he was there waiting for us. He warned us to cease all action against The Ungrounded because using The Infinite as punishment was unethical," Hunter said. "He claimed that during his absence, he'd procured a group of followers from the spiritual community, talented psychics and fanatics who were prepared to challenge us if we resisted."

I chuckled sarcastically. "I can't imagine The Handlers bowing to his demands."

"They didn't," Hunter shook his head, brows raised. "And while Beau had always been a very charismatic person, nobody believed he could gain such a following so quickly."

"Did he freak out when you refused?"

"Quite the opposite," Hunter said. "He always hid the rage coursing within him well below the surface. He just said if we ignored him, we'd suffer. Then he left."

"He just *left*?" I frowned.

"He was always the master of his fury, only unleashing it when absolutely necessary. But we realised how serious he'd been a few days later." Hunter's tone lowered, his eyes darkening as he fiddled with his gloves. "I was at work rewiring some dusty old house when Lola turned up, completely inconsolable. Her grounding had been destroyed, and her mother and all the other patients at the TB hospital had been ungrounded."

"Lola told me her mother was gone," I said pensively. "But she never said how it happened."

"She doesn't like to talk about it, even to me," Hunter said, half shrugging. "At first, we thought it was just a tragic accident, but gradually, the number of tearful, bloodshot eyes and trembling hands clutching crumbling tissues around the briefing table only grew as everyone else's families met the same fate."

"So, yours are..."

"No, mine's okay," Hunter said, nodding thoughtfully. "Three families were spared: Dom's, Hannah's, and mine."

"Why, you three?"

"I was his best friend, one of the only people who tried to support him," Hunter said. "As for the others, Dominic helped him master his craft, so Beau always felt he owed him for that. And Hannah...well, she and Beau are the reason relationships within The Spirit Borns were forbidden. And deep down, I think he assumed Han and I would leave with him. Hannah nearly did."

"But she seems so loyal?"

"She was...is," Hunter said, quickly correcting himself. "But she loved him. He gave her the peace she couldn't find anywhere else. Hannah's visions come anytime, anywhere, and are often immensely painful. But Beau's talent kept hers dormant, so she could finally feel normal."

"That's so sad."

"It is. But Beau and Hannah's determination to be together nearly destroyed The Spirit Borns. Hannah's always been an enormous asset to The Handlers, and her relationship with Beau took her out of action completely."

I couldn't help but draw parallels between the peculiar bond Hunter and I shared and Beau and Hannah's. If ever I felt my body haemorrhaging energy uncontrollably or teetering on the brink of igniting a blaze, Hunter was a source of safety and stability, able to suppress my talent and bring me back to myself—for now, at least.

"If she loved him, why did she stay?" I asked.

"I think she doubted her decision at first, but once Beau started his backlash against us, she knew the man she loved had transformed into someone she didn't recognise," Hunter said, an air of resignation in his voice. "And there was a period just before Laura's murder when Beau was incapacitated by some bizarre illness. So, we've always wondered whether Hannah saw something when he was weakened about what he would become that helped her renounce her love. But she's never confirmed nor denied it."

Chapter Nineteen

"But he's just a man, or... Spirit Born, rather. Can he really be *that* dangerous?" I frowned, my scepticism evident in the furrow of my brow.

Hunter abruptly stopped in the aisle, his towering figure casting a shadow over me. The leather of his gloves squeaked softly as he squeezed my hand tighter as if trying to convey the importance of his words through his touch. His face turned still, and the luminous sparks within his eyes flickered out.

"He knows everything about us and despises what we stand for. Most of us were so terrified he'd turn up on our doorsteps that we moved houses, even work addresses. Doc had to move hospitals twice after strangers turned up looking for her. And we're certain he's behind Laura's death, so his boundaries between right and wrong have been forever broken," Hunter warned, his eyes fierce and impassioned. "He'll stop at nothing to get what he wants, which, right now, could be you. Hannah's been having visions of you for years, long before Beau gained full strength, and they shared everything, so he likely already knows how important you are to us."

"But what does he want?" I asked, eyes narrowing. "What's his end goal?"

"He wants us gone and complete freedom in the afterlife, regardless of the risk to the living."

"Is that such a bad thing?" I shrugged.

"Think about the assignment in the States, the Incubus. Would you like a spirit like that roaming free, ruthlessly assaulting women?" Hunter pressed, his piercing eyes fixed on mine. "But the living are defenceless against what they can't see. We're the only ones who can help."

"But isn't Beau contradicting his own principles?" I said. "Why create more Ungroundeds when he knows we'll send them straight to The Infinite?"

"He views them as expendable soldiers, a necessary sacrifice to defeat us. He's trying to overpower us, and he's succeeding," Hunter nodded, a bittersweet smile on his face as his eyes reflected a mixture of determination and sadness. "You saw the arguing during briefings and debriefings. It never used to be like that. The more overworked we are, the more likely the chain of command will collapse. And even though The Handlers won't acknowledge it, it's obvious he's orchestrating this scenario at Ettington to get us all out in the open and test The Thirteenth's strength. He won't stop until he finds you."

"Why?" I asked, raising my eyebrows. "Why would he still be looking for me?"

"You're the biggest threat to him, which makes you either an asset or a target," Hunter said. "You're his opposite; you create while he destroys and consumes. Beau's an exceptional strategist. He might want to take you out before you grow too powerful. Or he might even try to get you to switch sides, leaving The Spirit Borns defenceless."

"I'd never..."

"I know, but he's very charismatic, very influential," Hunter interrupted." You'd be a coveted prize to him. You're the only thirteenth Spirit Born created, there'll never be another. Your talent is so extreme for a reason, H, to eradicate the mistake made before you."

As my gaze dropped to the floor, I noticed Hunter tilting his head, a smirk forming on one side of his mouth. With a gentle touch of his thumb, he lifted my chin, guiding my eyes to his. He briefly closed his eyes and let out a deep sigh, as if the air around us was laced with an intoxicating aroma.

"Those eyes, H. One ocean blue, one emerald green," Hunter said, his voice deep and resonant, like the purr of a contented jungle cat. "You could convince a man to do terrible things with those eyes. It's like when you came into being, you couldn't decide what you wanted to be, so you chose to be everything at once."

His eyes moved slowly up and down my body, his gloved hand caressing my cheek as he leaned in, pressing his forehead against mine.

"You really don't see it, do you?" Hunter said, drawing back, his eyes holding mine unwaveringly. "You have more power than the entire team combined. You're here to *save* us, not to mention, turn my world upside down. I'd like to say I'm going to let you, but honestly, I don't think I have any control over the matter."

Thanks to eighty years of Alfie's rejection, my confidence had been completely shattered, rendering me hesitant to accept compliments, always doubting their sincerity. When Hunter looked at me with his penetrative green eyes, eyes that seemed to already know me, it felt as if he was seeing through my exterior and exposing the broken soul within. Despite this, I remained steadfast in my denial of the notion that my unrefined abilities made me anything other than dangerous.

"You have this electricity, this...grace," Hunter continued, his eyes narrowing ever so slightly. "I feel it whenever you're near."

Chapter Nineteen

A nearby salesperson coughed loudly, looking again, more impatiently, at his watch. When I tore my focus from Hunter and looked around the store, I noticed we were the only customers left. A team of weary-looking employees, with their coats on and bags thrown over their shoulders, stood huddled by the semi-shuttered door, waiting for us to complete our purchases and leave.

We quickly selected a basic television, laptop, and accessories and arranged their delivery. As we profusely apologised to the staff for delaying them, the metallic rattling of the shutters echoed through the quiet car park as they were slammed behind us.

"So," Hunter said, checking his watch as we ambled toward his motorbike. "It's still early. Do you want to go anywhere else? Or have you got somewhere you need to be?"

"Well, Kay's probably still missing," I replied.

"She'll be tied up at Ettington; all the Handlers are."

"In that case, I have a ton of furniture that needs building," I said. "Are you good with a screwdriver?"

I'd never anticipated feeling so at ease being exposed to the traffic and the raw bite of the elements so quickly, so easily. As I dropped my keys onto the breakfast bar of my new flat, the adrenaline of the ride lingered in my veins like a potent elixir. Every nerve in my body hummed with electric energy, as if I could feel the pulse of the city resonating within me.

Hunter placed his sleek helmet beside my keys as if it had always belonged there. He tilted his head, the corners of his lips subtly curving upwards, and casually leaned against one of the two stools at the breakfast bar. "So, did you enjoy the bike?"

I ran my hands through my hair, embracing the wildness in its lengths. "God, yes."

A mischievous smile played on Hunter's lips. "Then there's a present for you in your closet."

I frowned confusedly as Hunter immediately continued. "I might have had Lola nip inside earlier."

I nodded slowly, my brow relaxing. "Like a housewarming present?"

"Not quite." He bit his lip as he nodded towards my bedroom, a playful glint in his eye. "Take a look."

I narrowed my eyes, a half-smile on my lips as I navigated through the maze of cardboard boxes and limbs of half-assembled furniture to reach the bedroom.

Standing before the mirrored closet, I hardly recognised my own reflection. Clad in my biking gloves, gripping my helmet, my cheeks glowed with the thrill of newfound passion, and an unshakeable smile seemed ingrained into my face.

Even my posture exuded confidence, my back as straight as a rod, bearing a head held high. The woman before me was a far cry from the demure orphan I was at Red Rock. I had shed the constraints of my afterlife and had emerged as someone new.

"Are you lost in there?" Hunter called. "I know the place is new, but..."

I couldn't help but chuckle as I cheekily replied, "Shut up," my tone playful.

As I opened the mirrored doors, the rich scent of supple leather drifted from the wardrobe. Inside hung a fitted biking jacket and matching trousers, the elbows and knees heavily padded. The jacket was adorned with various badges of unfamiliar motoring brands, but what captured my attention were the distinguishing stripes running the length of each arm: a thin cobalt blue one on one arm and a forest green on the other.

I set my helmet down, pulled off my gloves with my teeth, and ran my hands over the jacket, eagerly breathing in the earthy aroma of the leather.

Hunter appeared, leaning against the doorframe. A subtle smile eased across his lips as he watched me. He folded his arms and casually tucked one foot behind the other. "What do you think?"

I sighed, unable to find the right words.

"I had the jacket specially made."

"I guessed that." I finally answered, my fingers tracing the striping that matched my eyes. "It's...beautiful."

I crossed the room, my steps muffled by the plush, cream carpet. Wrapping my arms around Hunter's waist, I pulled him into me, feeling the warmth radiating from him as he gently rested his chin on my head. I felt miniature in his embrace as he towered almost a foot over me.

"Thank you," I said, my voice muffled against his chest.

Hunter made short work of finishing the furniture that Lola and I had started building. He effortlessly secured screws in place as I handed them to him, trying not to admire the way his muscles expanded and tensed with every turn of the screwdriver.

As we worked and talked, we seemed to naturally grow closer, like a flower reaching for the sun. However, as it got late, my phone buzzed incessantly with messages from Kay, asking where I was and who I was

Chapter Nineteen

with. When I replied that I was safe in my flat with Hunter, it only seemed to ignite panic within her.

She started calling repeatedly until, in frustration, I turned my phone to silent. But not wanting to spark doubts within Hunter's mind, I chose to keep my concerns about Kay pushing me towards Alfie and away from Hunter to myself until I had discovered why.

Hunter checked his watch, a disappointed smile pinching one cheek. "If I keep you out much later," he said, "Kay will only show up banging the front door down."

"That's if she even comes home tonight," I said, blowing my fringe out of my eyes. "Is your Handler controlling like this?"

"Annie? God no. But Kay changed after she failed with Beau." Hunter padded into the kitchen and perched on one of the bar stools as he reached for his chunky biking boots. "I'd better get you back. Kay's *not* a woman I want to get on the wrong side of."

"Am I not worth risking the wrath of the mean lady?" I said, my eyes narrowing teasingly as I approached him.

His eyes were glued to my every move as I ran my hands over his chest and peered up at him. He half-closed his eyes, inhaling deeply as he dropped his boots, landing on the floor with a thud. As he gripped my waist and pulled me closer, the circuits and fixtures around us droned loudly, and I could feel their vibrations in the air while the lights overhead shimmered like the stars through clouds.

I felt Hunter's deep tones hum against my skin as his lips grazed my neck. "H, *breathe*," he soothed. "Let's not trash your new flat before you've even moved in."

He moaned softly, his lips vibrating against mine as his kiss grew deep, searching. He lifted me onto the breakfast bar, clattering an empty wine bottle into the sink as my legs closed around him like a pincer, pulling his hips into mine.

As the scent of his cologne hung like a cloud over us, I laid back on the counter, propping myself up on one elbow. Hunter's kisses traced the contours of my body, stirring a wave of giggles as his stubble grazed my stomach and hip bones. The lights shuddered with me like they were laughing too. Hunter stopped briefly, glancing up at them and grinning with the knowledge that their intensity guided him in the right direction.

But as Hunter's lips met mine and my fingers tangled in the spun gold of his hair, I felt a subtle shift in the atmosphere. My ears began to ring as a small shadow loomed over us.

Lola shielded her eyes with her hands and spun to face the front door, though I could see blossoms of scarlet skin peeking between her fingers. "Crap, sorry!" she exclaimed.

"Jesus Lols, you couldn't have knocked?" Hunter snapped, the frustration evident on his face as he straightened his clothing and ran his hands through his tousled hair.

"I'm sorry, but it's Kay. She's freaking out, calling nonstop," Lola said, her gentle voice unusually tense. "I promised I'd come and check if you'd left yet. It was the only way I could convince her not to come down here herself."

"She's back?" I frowned. "I thought she was at Ettington?"

"She was," Lola nodded, sheepishly chewing a nail. "She called me over there out of the blue to bring her home an hour ago."

I felt my teeth grinding as my jaw clenched. With my nostrils flaring, I stormed into the bedroom. There wasn't time to change into the biking trousers, but I threw on my new jacket and zipped it up, the force of my movements catching my curls in the teeth of the zipper. It fit perfectly, moulding to every curve of my body, but I didn't have the opportunity to admire it. My nails pressed crescents into my clenched palms as I stomped back into the living room.

"Don't be mad at me," Lola pleaded, her doe-like eyes brimming with innocence as she stood pigeon-toed in her cartoon-patterned PJs. "She sounded distraught," she continued.

Feeling the weight of her distress, I squeezed her shoulder, offering as much reassurance as I could muster. "I'm not mad at you, Lola, I promise," I replied earnestly. "I just need a word with my Handler."

As we pulled up outside the hotel, the rumble of Hunter's engine faded, replaced by the shrill alarms of several nearby cars piercing the night air. The flashing indicator lights cast an amber sheen on our skin, and the repetitive beeping of horns reverberated off the buildings in a cacophony of sound. Ignoring the scene I was causing, I pulled off my helmet and

Chapter Nineteen

marched into the foyer, the chandeliers overhead shimmering with my mood.

Hunter grabbed my hand and pulled me towards him, removing his helmet one-handed in a fluid motion. "H, stop," he urged. "Look what you're doing. *Breathe.*"

I huffed in and out loudly once, with a look that said, "Happy?" But it did little to calm my flaring talent.

His chin lowered, eyebrows raised. "Not good enough."

"Well, you can..."

"No, I want *you* to fix it," he said.

A smile spread across half of my mouth, lifted by Hunter's unwavering patience. As Hunter gazed into my eyes, I breathed steadily. In my mind, I conjured the only person I knew could dampen the fire in my heart: Alfie.

Once the lights had dimmed to a gentle flicker, Hunter simply closed his eyes and nodded. He held my hand tightly, almost fearfully, as we walked to my room in silence. Upon reaching my door, he tenderly pressed his lips to my palm and slowly, reluctantly, let go.

As we entered, Kay was pacing the room with her hands on her hips, her eyes wider than I'd ever seen them. She threw the phone in her hand to the floor. "Where the *hell* have you been?" she demanded.

"I told you," I replied, gritting my teeth. "We went shopping."

Kay's eyes darted between me and Hunter. "Just the two of you?"

"Yeah, Hunter helped me buy a TV."

Kay's nose wrinkled in disdain as she appraised Hunter from head to toe, a look of almost disgust crossing her features. Her sharp eyes narrowed as they locked onto his with intense scrutiny. Hunter stood his ground, meeting her gaze with an unwavering stare, his posture stiff and resolute.

"You think that's safe?" Kay snapped.

"Hey, she did just fine," Hunter said.

Kay ignored Hunter, fixing her gaze on me. "You should've told me before. I'd have taken you."

"She needs companionship, Kay. Friends," Hunter interjected, his tone pleading for understanding.

"She *has* companionship."

"An ex-boyfriend in the afterlife?" Hunter scoffed. "You seriously think he's helping her in his state?"

"What *state*?" Kay interrupted, glaring at us each in turn with a look that demanded answers. "What have you two done?"

"Nothing," I said, my voice rising. "Alfie's gone way off the deep end. He's destroying himself all on his own."

The atmosphere crackled with static as the radio and TV suddenly burst to life, filling the small space with a cacophony of sound and colour. The bulbs encircling the bathroom mirror brightened to the point of disintegrating.

Reaching for the fire extinguisher, Kay raised one palm towards me. "Harper, calm down," she said. "We're just talking."

"You keep that away from her," Hunter snapped, speaking through his teeth as he stepped forward. "It's not her."

Kay's gaze shifted from me to Hunter. As I watched her, I saw the realisation dawning that the situation was slipping out of her control. Her tone softened to the sickly sweet one I abhorred—forced and often laden with lies, grating against my every nerve.

"I just want to know what happened," she said.

Hunter rolled his shoulders and regained his composure. The TV and radio fell eerily silent as I threw up my hands. "Alfie's lost it," I said. "He saw Hunter when you sent him to Red Rock and flew into a rage."

"So, what? He's heartbroken?"

"I wouldn't know; he's avoiding me," I shrugged. "He's been trashing the house, frightening the staff. And he... he managed to leave the grounds without being ungrounded."

"Agai..." she began, then trailed off with a fake cough.

Hunter and I exchanged a glance before redirecting our attention to Kay.

"But he's back now, right?" Kay asked, her tone betraying a hint of panic.

"Yeah," I answered slowly, my frown deepening. "But it's like Alfie's fading, and you don't seem surprised."

"Kay, do you know something?" Hunter said, his leathers squeaking softly as he crossed his arms. "Because I saw him today when I picked up Harper, and she's right, he's starting to look like an Ungrounded."

Kay remained silent, her face tight with frustration as she threw on her coat and quickly stashed her phone and keys into her bag.

"Where are you going?" I asked.

"Where do you think?" she snapped, looking at her watch with furrowed brows. "I'm going to talk to Alfie. *Alone.*"

Chapter Nineteen

As she strutted towards the door, I swiftly reached out, seizing Kay's arm and drawing her close, causing her to stumble. "Why all the sudden interest in him?" I demanded. "Why are you letting me break all the rules to work alongside him?"

"Take your hand off of me," Kay growled.

"Why is he so important?" I continued, my voice reaching its crescendo, desperate for an answer, any answer.

The fabric of Kay's black trench coat slipped through my fingers as she wrenched her arm free and straightened her clothing. Breathing heavily, she reached the door and yanked it open. Bathed in a halo of warm light from the hall, Kay paused and glanced over her shoulder. "Because we need him," she whispered before the door slammed closed behind her.

Chapter Twenty

Alfie's sombre silhouette remained absent from his window, but I knew he was there, somewhere. It felt like his very essence had woven itself into the fabric of the air, lingering like a subtle wisp of smoke. The updates from Sasha and Lucie only intensified my unease and shrouded Red Rock with an inescapable shadow of dread.

Our night cleaner, Holly, was seriously injured on shift, and despite my curiosity, my new colleagues were hesitant to divulge any details that could unsettle their latest hire.

I wandered the halls aimlessly during my breaks, hoping to find Alfie. I waited for those ebony splinters of my markers to emerge, but my skin remained frustratingly pale against the rich backdrop. In his absence, I managed to complete my training ahead of schedule, and by the Friday before I was due to head to Ettington, I began shadowing Sasha's tours and running errands.

As I collected flyers from the front desk, I was preoccupied with lingering anxieties about the assignment that night. Suddenly, an icy breeze surged through the hall. I rubbed the gooseflesh from my arms, feeling an unsettling chill creeping down my neck as my breath collected in milky clouds around me. The air turned frigid, and as my forearms started tingling, a faint, trembling voice pierced the silence in the deserted hall.

"Harper?"

I squeezed my eyes closed, a wave of self-directed reproach washing over me for my negligence. Despite my unwavering focus on my markers for what felt like an eternity, I had become lulled into a false sense of security by their absence.

Unbeknownst to me, I'd allowed Alfie to creep up within a few paces behind me. Slowly, I turned towards him. My eyes widened, and I had to clench my lip between my teeth to stifle a gasp.

Chapter Twenty

Looking impossibly frail, his unwashed pyjamas dwarfed his meagre figure. His sharp collarbones and ribs seemed capable of piercing his delicate skin, and his weathered wrinkles marred his face.

The vibrant colouring of his eyes had all but disappeared, veiled with a chalky hue resembling cataracts. The vacant look within them gave the impression that his presence was merely physical, a shell devoid of the spark that had once defined him.

I glanced up and down the hall, ensuring we were alone. When I turned back to face him, his twisted, skeletal fingers were reaching toward me as he feebly shuffled closer.

"You're here," Alfie said.

I swallowed, forcing a timid smile. "Yeah. Are you okay?"

Alfie opened his arms and edged closer. "I've been waiting for you."

I stepped back, purposefully creating some distance between us while keeping my eyes on his outstretched hands. "What are you doing?" I whispered.

"It's alright; I can hold you again," he nodded, his words at odds with the icy detachment in his gaze. Even his voice was cold.

"We can't, okay?" I said, emphasising each word as if speaking to a child.

"They said just once."

My brows furrowed. "Who did? Did Kay see you?"

"No touching," Alfie scolded himself as he wagged his finger, his eyes darting back and forth, unable to settle on any particular spot for more than a second. "Yes, a lady came," he added, his words tinged with uncertainty.

I drew a shaky breath, fixing my eyes on the ceiling to hold back the tears threatening to fall. "What did Kay...the lady say?" I asked, my voice wavering.

"That I can touch you. Just once," Alfie answered.

I shook my head, my hair a flurry of curls around me. "But then you'd disappear. You don't want that. My family needs you."

"Family?" Alfie's eyes narrowed. He paused, jerking his head back and blinking repeatedly as if struggling to refocus his gaze.

When he spoke again, he seemed aware, and although weary, his tone still carried the familiar essence of Alfie. "Harper? What are you doing here?"

I shrugged. "Working."

"Then why are you crying?" he asked, tilting his head.

"I'm not." I sniffed.

"Then you were just about to cry, I know that look. What happened?" Alfie pressed.

"It's nothing," I said. "You just... weren't yourself for a moment."

Alfie sighed, running a hand through his thinning hair. *"Again?"*

"It's happened before?"

"I think so," he mumbled, his eyes falling to the floor. "Sometimes I wake up in strange places. Like I'm sleepwalking."

"Did you leave Red Rock again?"

Alfie shrugged one emaciated shoulder. "I'm still here, so I'm guessing no."

I heard Sasha's voice echoing down the hallway, calling out my name. As my attention shifted towards her, Alfie's face fell.

"You have to go?"

"I'm sorry," I whispered. "My lift's here."

Alfie's gaze swept past me, and he looked down the hall. "Can I speak to Kay? I need to see her."

"She's not here," I said, staring at my feet.

A pained expression overtook Alfie's features. "Oh," he said. "Hunter?"

"Lola, too. We've got an assignment," I said, trying to soften the blow. "But why do you need to see Kay? You only saw her last night."

"I did?" Alfie frowned. "I... I don't remember."

"Try. Did she really tell you to touch me?"

"Why would she say that?" He rubbed his temples, the deep grooves between his brows betraying his confusion. "No, I'd remember."

Sasha called again, her voice growing insistent.

"I've got to go," I sighed. "But if Kay returns, don't listen to her; she can't be trusted. And you're not yourself right now."

As I drifted down the hall, Alfie shuffled in the opposite direction, nodding silently. The only sound from him was the repetitive whisper, "Just once, just once," he muttered incoherently under his breath until he faded into the shadows.

When I saw the familiar depths of Hunter's eyes, the dam inside me that held back my tears crumbled. Sobs wracked my body, and with each convulsive release, I gasped for air as I struggled to regain control.

As Lola waited in the passenger seat of his van, Hunter leaned against the bonnet, his smile fading as he simply opened his arms, his features brimming with concern and heartfelt sympathy.

Chapter Twenty

I barrelled into him and buried my face in his chest, seeking refuge in his warmth. Hunter said nothing as he rocked me back and forth, tenderly running his fingers through my hair, leaving the blonde strands streaked with black ash.

He didn't need to speak, didn't need to ask, "What happened?" Having seen Alfie himself, he understood my pain without needing an explanation. When my tears subsided, he slipped an arm around my shoulder, gently guiding me into the van where Lola was ready with tissues.

Neither Hunter nor Lola could fathom any explanation as to how Alfie was slipping in and out of an Ungrounded-like state. Our only hope of helping him lay with The Handlers, but my strained relationship with them did not help matters.

However, now that my flat had been transformed into a liveable space, we could at least finally move the last of my belongings from the hotel, freeing me from Kay's web of apron strings.

When Lola left to transport Hunter to Ettington, I couldn't sit still. I restlessly paced my flat, methodically unpacking and repacking my bag as anticipation and trepidation fought a battle within me for supremacy.

After a few minutes, the newly unwrapped glasses in the kitchen cabinets began to tremble against each other, creating a soft clinking sound. Simultaneously, my ears started to ring, gradually growing louder and more pronounced.

Lola materialised beside me, extending her hand. "Ready?" she smiled. "The lobby's packed, so I'm dropping you in the ladies' room in the foyer. And you'll be sharing a room with me."

With my overstuffed, soft leather bag slung over my shoulder, I took her hand. In an instant, I was transported to Ettington, crammed into a spacious toilet cubicle, the scent of expensive citrus cleaners teasing my senses.

Pushing open the cubicle door, I stepped into the luxurious Victorian bathroom. The grandeur of a bygone era embraced me at every turn, each surface shining and every fixture gleaming as crystal chandeliers cast light onto the gold-gilded mirrors. A low whistle escaped me.

"Wait until you see the rest of the place," Lola winked before disappearing to collect the next Spirit Born.

I checked my appearance in the mirror, even though Hunter had just seen me ten minutes ago, not to mention at my absolute worst back at Red

Rock, bawling with mascara streaking my cheeks. Nevertheless, I couldn't help but fluff my hair like a lovesick teenager.

I couldn't care less what the others thought of my appearance, but Hunter was different. When we were together, there was an inherent magnetism that told me I was everything he wanted, like he was Icarus, and I was the sun. But when we were apart, the question "Am I enough?" rolled around my mind like a marble in an empty jar, thanks to the lingering insecurities Alfie's denial had sired.

As I sifted through my makeup bag, my fingers brushed against an unopened blood-red lipstick. The vivid hue captivated me, yet it remained untouched, serving as a poignant reminder of Sophia. Confronting my reflection in the mirror, I hesitated momentarily, feeling the weight of emotion well up within me.

I uncapped the lipstick and carefully applied its pigment to my lips, each stroke a deliberate act of reclaiming a piece of myself. The striking contrast of the deep red against my fair complexion told a tale of resilience, a silent narrative to those who understood the complexities of my past.

"Don't fear the past," I said, "embrace it."

Little did I know that when I stepped into the foyer, I'd rarely be seen again without that vivid flash of red.

Nestled amidst the serene hills of the Warwickshire countryside, Ettington epitomised the majestic allure of a large country estate in rural England, and every aspect of the property, from the sprawling grounds to the exquisite architecture, had been meticulously arranged to embody its elevated status and privilege.

The lobby walls were panelled with polished oak and decorated with a curated collection of portraits showcasing the previous owners and local landscapes. As the setting sun's golden rays flooded through enormous windows, the crystal chandeliers scattered the room with a mesmerising brilliance.

The Spirit Borns collected so far were scattered amongst the guests lounging on leather Chesterfield sofas, casually browsing home and country magazines. Meanwhile, Kay and Beck's Handler, Tom, checked us in at the front desk, their faces mirroring the tension in their postures.

As Hunter chatted to Dominic, his eyes found mine, a subtle smile teasing one corner of his lips. Before I could even acknowledge him, Kay's sudden change in expression caught my attention as she turned towards me. The sharp clicking of her heels echoed through the air as she stepped

Chapter Twenty

into my path. Silently, she handed me a keycard and gestured toward the sweeping staircase.

Upstairs, the grandeur transitioned from breathtaking to sumptuous comfort. Cream sofas enveloped a polished coffee table in front of a wide flat-screen TV. Beyond a graceful archway, two beds were adorned with towels folded into elegant swans, resting gracefully atop impeccably arranged linen.

As Lola's off-key singing echoed from the bathroom, I settled onto the sofa with a coffee to delve into Ettington's file.

Several disturbed guests had reported attacks in their rooms, with their injuries documented by photos of angry scratches and purple welts eerily resembling finger marks. Additionally, a concerned family informed staff that their four-year-old son had made an invisible friend who, according to the child, followed him everywhere during their stay, telling him to "do bad things".

Interviews with various staff recounted persistent feelings of being followed, with one employee claiming she felt like the prey of an invisible apex predator. As I read on and learned of the more severe injuries suffered, I couldn't blame her.

The accounts narrated a concerning string of near misses and lucky escapes. A porter was pushed down a flight of stairs, resulting in a fractured skull. The pool was temporarily closed when a woman nearly drowned after being held underwater. And after a wedding, the bride was adamant she'd been shoved almost clean over a balcony.

I was struck by a surprising surge of compassion for Kay. Throughout every one of her infuriating absences, she'd been diligently interviewing dozens of witnesses and struggling to unveil the truth lurking behind Ettingon's glamourous exterior—the darkness within the light.

As I swallowed hard, I couldn't shake the disquieting parallels I noticed between Ettington and Red Rock. Suddenly, I felt like a child again, running from the shadows, afraid to turn out the lights.

By the time Lola and I entered the function room that The Handlers had hired for the weekend, we were the last to arrive.

A horseshoe of tables and chairs circled the room, facing a whiteboard on which The Handlers had sketched a rough diagram of the building in thick black marker.

As Lola and I settled into our seats, I stole a glance at Hunter, searching for reassurance in his eyes. He sat there, breathing deeply, his intense gaze fixed towards the front of the room. A subtle furrow formed between his brows as a faint ethereal glow shone from his clenched hands beneath the table.

I sighed, pressing my lips together. I hated that he had to work so hard just to shield me from my lack of control over my talent.

"Now everyone's present, we have some news," Tom began, his tone low. "There's been a death."

Around the table, eyes shifted, and cautious glances were exchanged. Some chewed their nails or bit their lips, while others leaned towards their neighbours, sharing hushed whispers.

Tom raised his hand, and immediately, the room fell silent. "When we arrived yesterday to finish interviews," he said, "we were informed about the sudden death of a staff member."

"By an Ungrounded?" Amy asked, her eyes narrowing with scepticism. It was the first time I had seen her without her white overcoat. As she pulled her cardigan closer to her chest, she clearly missed the shield of her uniform. "I thought that was impossible," she continued.

Tom nodded. "It's rare, but it happens. The victim, Andrea, unexpectedly committed suicide."

"But if she harmed herself, then it wouldn't be an Ungrounded, right?" Lola asked, her eyes darting to each Handler for confirmation.

"Yes and no," Kay said. "Andrea had no reason to kill herself. She'd just been accepted into Oxford and had a loving family."

"Is there any family history of mental illness?" Amy asked, pen poised over her notepad. "Or was there any evidence of self-harm?"

"No history of mental illness, but yes, there were marks on the body, all of which were under three weeks old," Tom explained. He passed around a series of graphic black-and-white photos of a thin, lifeless arm crisscrossed with healing scratches. Immediately, the harsh reality of my calling as a Spirit Born hit home.

"When did things start getting worse here?" Gia asked.

"A month ago," Kay said. "Andrea's family claims that paranormal activity started occurring in their home around the same time."

Chapter Twenty

"After a week, the activity in the house died down," Tom explained. "But Andrea's demeanour underwent a dramatic shift. She became depressed, haunted by vivid nightmares. She distanced herself from her friends, and before long, she stopped sleeping, eating, and going to work."

"Her doctor prescribed sedatives and anti-depressants," Kay added, "but..."

"Anti-depressants take weeks to start working," Amy interjected, her tone sombre.

Tom nodded. "After Andrea took the sedatives and finally slept, her parents checked her laptop, searching for clues about what had caused her decline. They found that her search history was filled with questions about stalking and suicide. Additionally, hotel staff confirmed that before Andrea stopped going to work, she claimed she felt watched even when she was alone."

"So, what are we thinking? Did a spirit follow her home from the hotel and form an attachment?" Hunter asked.

Kay nodded, but she refused to look at him despite answering his question. "Exactly. We think she was in stage three of possession, possibly fourth," she said.

A collective gasp filled the room as the Spirit Borns either shook their heads or flinched in reaction.

Dominic bowed his head. "Stage three? Poor kid barely stood a chance."

"With numerous reports of extreme violence here, it was evident even before Andrea's death that these are not your average Ungroundeds. Therefore, we have been investigating the local area, attempting to establish their origin," Kay said. She pulled a thick file from her briefcase and dumped it onto the desk, its weight sending vibrations through the table. Holding up a photo of a large property, she continued, "And we came across this place."

"Shit," Theon muttered under his breath, slowly pushing back from the desk and folding his arms. Around the room, audible groans and creaking chairs beneath shifting bodies added to the tension.

I leaned towards Lola. "What is it?"

"We've been there before," She replied glumly. "Like, a lot."

Kay paced back and forth in front of the whiteboard, her hands behind her back, exuding the authority of a general commanding her troops. "Hatton County Lunatic Asylum, now known as Central Hospital. The violence here mirrors the behaviour of many of the dangerous patients once committed there."

"So, with Hannah's assistance, we paid a visit and headed to the secure wing," Tom said. "But it was empty."

"*Just* the secure wing?" Captain asked, frowning.

Kay nodded. "We asked some of the Informed Groundeds in another area of the hospital where the secure wing patients were, and the only responses on the Ovilus were 'strange' and 'man'."

"They're crazy people," Sawyer scoffed, "everything's strange to them."

Lola rolled her eyes. "Maybe you should visit; you'd fit right in," she growled. "Moron. They had similar responses *here* last weekend."

Ignoring the bickering, Kay continued. "The EVP we captured supports the Ovilus' response."

Reaching into her coat pocket, she retrieved a small recorder and pressed play. The room fell silent as everyone leaned in.

From the tiny speaker, Kay's voice emerged in an almost mechanical cadence, easily recognisable despite the slight distortion in the grainy sound quality. "Where are the patients from the secure ward?" she asked, pausing between questions. "Why did they leave?"

Kay glanced around the room expectantly. "Hear it?" she asked. The Spirit Borns nodded in response, their eyes widening slightly.

"Hear what?" I frowned, eyes narrowing.

After increasing the volume, Kay rewound the recording and pressed play again. Following her questions, a faint noise permeated the silence, but it was impossible to discern, merely a shadow of a sound.

"That mumble?" I asked.

Kay approached me, holding the recorder to my ear. "Listen closely," she said.

With the volume turned up to the maximum, Kay's voice boomed so loudly that the recorder's speaker quivered, but I could finally hear the response.

"Where are the patients from the secure ward?" Kay asked.

A trembling, ethereal voice whispered back. "Gone."

"Why did they leave?" Kay asked.

"Not leave, taken," came the haunting response. The words seemed to linger in the air as I ran my hand up and down my arms, rubbing the goosebumps from my skin. I locked eyes with Kay and nodded.

Chapter Twenty

"Then this *was* Beau?" Lola said, the soft edges of her voice sharpened with anger. "And he's gotten someone else killed?"

"Who else could it have been?" Captain said, brows raised. "I told you as much last week."

"But if he touches them, they're gone," Gia said. "And if the rest of the patients were still there, the building's foundations were clearly intact. How could he have done this?"

Every pair of Spirit Born eyes were glued to Kay and Tom as they awaited an explanation.

"He chose a vulnerable group, who could be easily riled up and coerced into leaving," Kay said. "Our best guess is that he's informed them and lured them outside, where his psychics guided them to the hotel. They've just stuck around here due to the high energy levels. The hotel is fully booked all year, so there's plenty to feed off."

"If Beau has enough followers and psychics to control that many of The Ungrounded, then aren't we underestimating his numbers here?" Beck frowned. "How can he control that many spirits, especially crazy ones at that?"

Tom shrugged. "We don't know for sure. But it's likely he used a hell of a lot of electromagnetic pumps to keep The Ungroundeds' attention."

I raised my hand like a pupil in an overcrowded classroom. "One question," I said. "If there are no staff to watch the patients anymore, why haven't the secure wing patients left already? Or at least explored the rest of the hospital?"

Hunter turned his body towards me, leaning in to meet my eyes. "Spirits abide by the rules they followed in life," he explained. "Uninformed Groundeds' afterlives will mirror their earthly lives."

I rubbed the bridge of my nose. "But in the report of the prison, spirits roamed the grounds too."

"A prison's different," Hunter said. "The inmates do everything together, sharing space throughout the building. A psychiatric hospital is different. Even without staff, they'll stay put. Think about Red Rock. The fear of the war kept you there. For me, it was the responsibility of running the cinema one day. For Lola, it was fear of infecting others with tuberculosis. An Uninformed will *always* find a reason to stay because it's where they're meant to be."

"Still, it must be a pretty long trek between the two locations," Amy said. "Especially towing Ungroundeds."

"By foot, it's only four and a half hours," Kay answered. "But even with EM pumps, it would've taken days."

"Hold on," I said, "what are EM pumps?"

"Jesus, Kay," Sawyer chuckled sarcastically. "Haven't you bothered to tell her anything?"

Kay made no response, but I noticed a slight blush tint on her cheeks. She knew as well as I did that, she had dumped me at our hotel with no information, no clues about who or what I was or what I had been returned from the grave to do.

"Electromagnetic pumps," Tom explained. "They create an electromagnetic field which a spirit, Grounded or Ungrounded, can use as energy. So, if Beau had enough of them, The Ungrounded would follow him, even though they won't understand where they're going or why."

"Even if Beau's bolstered his ranks," Kay added, "they couldn't have managed them all at once. They've probably been bringing over a few at a time for weeks."

"It's obviously a trap," Captain remarked.

Kay raised her and turned her face. "It's not."

Captain leaned into the table, awaiting an answer. "Then why all the effort?"

"Most of The Handlers have been here all week, and there's been no sign of him or his psychics," Kay said dismissively. "Beau probably turned tail and ran when he realised we were in town."

"Respectfully, Kay," Captain responded, arching one brow. "That doesn't answer my question."

My lips twisted into a crooked smile as I savoured the sense of triumph. One by one, the other Spirit Borns were finding their voices and challenging The Handlers, echoing the rebellion stirring within me. Their questions were the first whispers of dissent, destined to become a roar.

"He wants to prove that he's upping his game and getting organised while we chase our tails," Kay said. "But Beau wouldn't bother showing up here. He's seen enough of our investigations to know what happens. He uh... he..."

The colour drained from Kay's face, the cogs in her mind whirring as she glanced at me. But in a room full of people who knew the truth, it was impossible for her to backpedal into another lie.

Chapter Twenty

"He... uh... is a Spirit Born?" I said, my tone harsh. "I heard. Thanks for the heads-up, by the way. Real helpful." I grinned mockingly as I gave two sarcastically exaggerated thumbs up.

Kay shifted uncomfortably, dismissing my sarcastic remark as she redirected her attention to the rest of the group. "Well, he'll be finding all this incredibly amusing somewhere. But not here."

"We can't just let him get away with causing another death," Lola snapped, her eyes shimmering with uncharacteristic darkness as a storm brewed within them.

Tom's lips curled into a sympathetic smile. "You're all defenceless around him," he remarked gently. "Confronting him without knowing his numbers and without a plan would only put you in danger."

"Until we figure out how to handle him, it's business as usual," Kay added. "Which reminds me, business cards are in the back of your files if any guests inquire about the investigation, but we've bought out as many rooms as possible to give you space to work, so there won't be many."

"Once the bar calls last orders and the guests are in their rooms," Tom said, "head out."

"But have there been any incidents in the rooms?" Aida asked timidly. Her voice was barely audible compared to everyone else's.

"A few scratches here and there," Tom replied. "Most reports have come from communal areas. However, that doesn't mean The Ungrounded can't use the rooms to hide in. If Lola's too busy to get you inside, the keys for the additional rooms we've booked will be in the equipment room. Additionally, if an Ungrounded slips into an actual guest's room, leave a REM pod by the door so Harper can spot when it leaves on the monitors."

Sawyer's jaw slackened as his brows knitted together. "Wait, she's not actually working the assignment?"

I noticed Hunter's jaw tighten, but Lola was the one to speak. "What did you think she's doing here?" she quipped, tilting her head. "Having a nice little break in the countryside?"

"She's only managing the equipment room," Kay answered, raising a placating hand.

"That's smart," Beck sneered, "put the girl who can't control a light bulb in a room full of electronics."

I clenched my fists, feeling my blood boil at Sawyer and Beck's comments. The glow from Hunter's hands grew brighter, his fingers trembling as the overhead lights flickered just once. I closed my eyes and took a deep breath, slowly filling and emptying my lungs while conjuring the low, reassuring cadence of Hunter's voice in my mind, repeating the words like a mantra.

Breathe.

You've got this.

"It's our only option," Kay said, her jaw set with a look that said, "Don't test me".

Beck folded his arms. "The other Handlers can't babysit her somewhere?"

"We're busy compiling files for your next assignment, not to mention a *mountain* of paperwork on this one," Kay answered sharply. She turned to the map on the whiteboard. "Use tomorrow to familiarise yourself with the property. And remember, there are several innocent Informeds here too; they are *not* to be touched."

Tom raised one long, rigid finger. "But the POW we were here for originally is still at large," he said. "He's not a priority, but if you spot him, don't let him escape. Captain can translate any EVPs if needed."

"If there are no further questions," Kay paused, awaiting a response. She was met with silence as she began shuffling papers into her briefcase. "In that case, everyone, please have a late night tonight. You're dismissed."

I twisted my body towards Lola, frowning in confusion. "Did she say *late* night?"

"It's to get ourselves into a nocturnal sleeping pattern," Lola nodded.

Hunter and Dominic waited by the door. As Kay's eyes traced my path out of the room, Hunter kept his hyper hands tucked in his pockets as if he needed to restrain himself from reaching out and touching me.

The four of us slowly ambled down the hall, and when we were out of Kay's earshot, Hunter turned to me, an almost childlike giddiness on his face. "Dom and I are ordering a pizza and watching a movie," he said. "If you two don't have any dinner plans, do you want to join us?"

Lola smirked. "As long as I don't have to defend pineapple on a pizza as being the devil again."

"It *is* the devil!" Hunter snapped, with a playful glint in his eyes.

"It's freaking delicious, is what it is," Lola replied.

"Wait, won't Kay freak if she catches me and Hunter in the same room?" I frowned.

Chapter Twenty

Lola looped her arm through mine. "She's handling twelve Spirit Borns," she said. "Tonight, her main focus will be getting an extremely drunk Sawyer and Beck away from the bar."

As our foursome split up at the top of the stairs to return to our individual rooms, Hunter's face seemed to glow, and a crooked grin spread across his lips. He walked backwards, cheerfully calling down the hall, "We're in room 209. We'll get the pizza; you bring the booze."

Chapter Twenty-one

Behind closed doors, Hunter and I sprawled out on the sofa in his room, his arm draped around me, delicately caressing my shoulder and leaving shimmering black streaks on it as we ate, drank, and chatted.

As the credits rolled on our third film at 2 a.m., I caught Dominic and Lola exchanging a mischievous look. Their smiles grew broader, their expressions hinting at a shared secret as they stood.

Lola swiped a half-empty bottle of whiskey nestled amidst the pizza crumbs and discarded glass bottles cluttering the coffee table. They staggered tipsily towards the door, the effects of the alcohol evident in every step.

Dominic's Irish tone slurred as he confidently announced, "We're going for a walk."

"A walk? Now?" I frowned.

Lola nodded animatedly. "Yep. A really long, really far walk."

"So," Dominic said slowly as he grabbed Lola's hand, "see you at breakfast?"

I glanced at Hunter, but he wore the same perplexed expression as I did. When I turned back to challenge Lola and Dominic, my ears were ringing softly, and they had vanished.

A subtle smile danced at the corners of Hunter's lips. He fixed his eyes on mine, the golden shards within them twinkling like the flickering light of a candle.

He tucked a lock of hair behind my ear and trailed a delicate arc along my cheek with his thumb, every touch leaving faint traces of ebony. He drew closer and planted a hungry, lingering kiss on my lips, each sensation etching a vivid memory in my mind.

The bittersweet taste of alcohol lingered on my tongue as I stood unsteadily, feeling my breath catch in my chest. With a sense of urgency, I tugged off my combat boots and straddled Hunter's lap, running my fingers through his tousled hair.

Chapter Twenty-one

Despite the luxury of time, I found it impossible to resist the magnetic pull of the moment, unable to slow down our escalating passion.

The distant rumble of thunder filled the air as Hunter lifted me from the sofa and carried me to the bed, my legs locked around his waist.

But as he gently lowered me onto the plush sheets, my heart raced against my ribs. My every nerve crackled with energy as I teetered on the brink of losing all self-control, inches away from tumbling over the edge.

The bedside lamps flickered intensely, casting erratic shadows across the walls. In the bathroom, the bulbs exploded in bright flashes, leaving glass tinkling against the spotless tiles.

Hunter pressed his forehead to mine, his voice a soothing murmur. "H, I've got you," he said. "Are you sure you want to do this?"

With a mixture of yearning and unwavering resolve, I reached for the waistband of his jeans. "God, yes," I breathed.

"Then stop rushing," he said, nodding toward the lights. "I think that's what's triggering all this. I can help, but you've got to give me a hand, okay? Just keep your eyes on me."

I squeezed my eyes shut and buried my face in my hands. "I'm sorry."

"Stop that," Hunter scolded softly, gently prying my hands away. "Just focus on me," he said. Slowly, he ran his hand up my arm, and my body tingled responsibly. "Focus on your physical feelings and not your emotions. Block everything else out."

I drew in a deep breath, letting Hunter's seductive aroma become a part of me. Concentrating on the physical sensations, I anchored myself in the present moment, forcing the tangle of nervous energy within me into the distant corners of my mind.

I focused on the intensity of his eyes, the colour of the soft moss on the cobblestones of my old cottage, and the sparks that danced within them, each flicker reflecting his ever-changing emotions. I thought about how his every touch aimed not only to please me but also to strengthen our bond.

The vibrations of energy resonating between us and the serenity that his stability brought me told me that he had always been mine and that, despite my history with Alfie, my fate had always been intertwined with Hunter's. It was as if our connection had always existed, transcending time and space, inescapable and absolute.

❖

I opened my eyes just before Hunter. I felt the gentle pressure of his hands around my waist as his soft breath played with my hair. My limbs, sore in the most satisfying way, unfurled as I welcomed the dawn.

Hunter let out a satisfied moan, his lips curling into a smile on my skin. "Hiya, trouble."

"Hey," I sighed. "I don't ever want to leave this bed."

He turned me onto my back, his fingers carefully sweeping my hair from my eyes, each strand glistening with ebony. "You kill me," he whispered.

Hunter's phone began vibrating across the nightstand. With a frustrated groan, he reached across me to answer it, breaking the spell between us.

"Hey, Lols... Fine, just give us a minute," Hunter said, the disappointment in his voice clear as he hung up, pouting slightly. "Lola's on her way. Kay's doing the rounds."

He reclined against the plush headboard, the soft ripples of a sheet cascading over his lap as he casually propped one hand behind his head.

His emerald eyes traced my every step as I enveloped myself in a blanket and hurried about the room, gathering my scattered clothing into a messy heap.

After finding my combat boots, Lola and Dominic appeared. Dominic politely shielded his bloodshot eyes, grinning from ear to ear as he headed straight to the bathroom.

He walked by fist-bumping Hunter as he passed, and didn't acknowledge the crunch of the shattered bulbs under his shoes in the bathroom.

"We've got to go," Lola said, her voice slightly hoarse. "Kay will be at our door any minute."

Lola took my hand, and Hunter's eyes sparkled. He winked, his lips curving into an endearingly crooked smile as we disappeared.

While the warm water cascaded over me in the shower, I watched the streaks of black dust that had been clinging to my body swirl down the drain, evoking a strange sense of longing within me.

Meanwhile, Lola played a peculiar and provocative playlist from her phone, beginning with "Let's Talk About Sex" and ending with "Two Become One".

The buoyant atmosphere was abruptly shattered by Kay's persistent knocking, which reverberated through the room. As I rummaged for a towel, I overheard her storming in and demanding to know my whereabouts.

Chapter Twenty-one

Despite Lola's protests that I was only in the bathroom, she pounded on the door before barging in.

"Jesus Kay!" I screamed, clutching a towel to my chest. "What the hell are you doing?"

Kay raised her hands, her cheeks blushing as she averted her eyes. "Sorry, sorry," she said. "I just had to know where you were."

"I did tell you," Lola said, cocking her head with her hands on her hips.

"Okay, I'll just..." Kay stammered. "I'm going."

Slamming the door behind her, I huffed loudly. "She doesn't want me anywhere near Hunter, does she?" I said. "She'd prefer me tethered to an unstable, semi-ungrounded spirit."

"Have you figured out why they need him yet?" Lola asked, rattling two paracetamols into her hand and downing them with water.

I gathered my damp curls into a messy bun and shrugged. "Not yet, but I'll figure it out. It's not like Alfie's going anywhere."

"Not if he carries on the way he's going," Lola muttered, brows raised.

"You mean if he leaves Red Rock again?"

"What... no. Because..." Lola paused, frowning. "Kay hasn't told you? Again?"

"I think it's clear by now that Kay doesn't tell me shit," I said. "What's going on?"

Lola bit her lip. "He... he's on his second warning."

"What? How?"

"H, Alfie's been hurting people," Lola said softly, her gaze shifting downwards as she nervously toyed with her nails.

Her words seemed to linger in the air, heavy with the weight of the information I struggled to process. "So, he did hurt Holly," I muttered. "I knew something happened, but I'd been praying it wasn't him."

"Well, you said it yourself. Alfie's losing it."

"Who gave the warnings? Was it Hunter?" I demanded, my voice tense. "Does he know?"

"It was Gia and Theon, and they were both sworn to secrecy. If Hunter knew, he would've told you," Lola reasoned. "There were two emergency assignments this week, both to Red Rock. I only know because I had to transport them there. I didn't mention it because Kay promised she'd tell you. I just assumed you didn't want to talk about it."

I pinched the bridge of my nose and sighed. "It's okay. It's not your fault."

"I didn't see the file, so I don't know the details, but check Red Rock's accident book; it's bound to be documented," Lola suggested. "The victim was hospitalised."

I had never met the night cleaner, Holly, but I felt a strange sense of responsibility for her injuries. "Is she okay?" I asked.

"I've no idea," Lola answered.

Seeing Hunter's smiling face as he waved us over to a corner table in the hotel's restaurant did little to soothe my agitation. The tension etched on my face, my raised shoulders, and the gently shimmering lighting overhead immediately told him something was wrong.

As Lola and I settled into our seats, Hunter's smile faded, and a concerned frown settled on his brow. He leaned towards me, his hand resting on the back of my chair. "What's wrong?" he whispered.

I longed to touch his face and reassure him, but in a restaurant filled with Spirit Borns stealing glances at us, all I could manage was a forced, weak smile.

"Just...Kay stuff," I answered. "I don't want to talk about it."

"Okay," Hunter nodded. "We'll talk later."

"I wonder how long it will be before they storm over," Dominic said quietly, leaning towards Lola.

"What did you do now?" Hunter asked, subtly caressing my arm with his thumb.

Lola grinned. "Well, late last night, both Sawyer and Beck received calls to attend the front desk."

"So off they went," Dominic said, walking his fingers across the table, "stumbling to the foyer in their boxers and bathrobes."

"And the strangest thing happened," Lola smirked, flashing her eyes wide. "When they returned to their room, all their clothes had vanished."

"You didn't," I whispered, my lips curving into a smile.

"Let's just say a local charity shop had a rather generous donation waiting on their doorstep this morning," Lola said, arching one brow.

"And there are a couple of well-dressed statues around here somewhere," Dominic added.

Lola innocently brought her coffee cup to her lips. "Payback's a bitch, right?"

We spent the afternoon touring the expansive grounds. Despite our numbers, even the more seasoned Spirit Borns seemed apprehensive,

Chapter Twenty-one

jumping at every sudden noise and eyeing each car that progressed down the winding drive with careful reproach.

Each member of the team we passed seemed to be in a similar state to ourselves. With peaky faces, they shielded their bloodshot eyes with dark sunglasses as they downed coffee. Yet, the atmosphere was charged with tension. It seeped into me, coiling into a heavy knot in the pit of my stomach.

To distract ourselves, we chatted about Lola's futile quest for a boyfriend, recounting the disastrous dates she'd cleverly escaped from by transporting herself out of restaurant bathrooms.

However, I noticed that Dominic seemed uneasy when the topic came up, and Lola seemed equally disturbed when we discussed his series of one-night stands.

As the sun descended below the horizon, its fading light painted the manicured lawns with an amber glow, stretching long shadows toward the distinguished old house. At that moment, I couldn't help but notice the subtle shift in the energy permeating the entire property.

By the time Lola and I arrived at the equipment room, it was a hive of activity. Excited chatter filled the air, punctuated by the clatter of radios and equipment being collected.

Kay and Tom busied themselves setting up the last of the monitors while half-listening to Sawyer and Beck rambling about Lola's prank, with clothing tags protruding from the backs of their shirts.

Sawyer spotted Lola, his features twisting into a menacing grimace as he pointed aggressively and started storming towards her.

Tom's rigid arm flew outwards, holding Sawyer back. "Leave it," he ordered, pointing him towards the door. "Get to work."

Kay's gaze settled on me as she sauntered over, wearing a sickly-sweet smile—the one she reserved for public appearances or when she sought to manipulate or calm me down.

"Harper," she said, "I've already prepared a pot of coffee for you. Now let me explain how everything works."

I pushed past her towards the monitors, purposely brushing her shoulder. "Lola can handle that."

Hunter and Dominic entered and gathered their equipment with the quiet confidence of experienced professionals. Although I tried to maintain my composure, the bitterness in my tone was unmistakable. Sensing the tension, Hunter kept a watchful eye on me.

"It's been her job so far, hasn't it? Telling me everything?" I continued, fixing a penetrating gaze at Kay. "About Beau. About Alfie."

Kay frowned, looking genuinely confused. "I'm sorry, I don't understand. I'm just helping you..."

"Then help me with this, Kay," I interrupted. "How's Alfie doing since his warnings? Or Holly?"

In my peripheral vision, I noticed Hunter's fingertips beginning to glow with an intensity I had never witnessed before. The monitors flickered as he grasped onto the table to steady himself, his knuckles blanching white.

Kay's face turned to stone as the weight of realisation settled over her features.

Hunter straightened to his full height, his eyes catching mine as he towered over me. "H, whatever this is, you're scaring people," he said quietly.

I looked at the remaining individuals in the room, avoiding eye contact and trying to look busy as they stuffed their pockets with equipment and hurried into the hall as fast as they could.

I felt a sense of shame wash over me, acknowledging that my emotions were wielding too much influence over my talent.

"Kay, just go," Hunter said. "We'll show Harper the ropes."

I turned my back to her and sank into the padded leather office chair opposite the array of sleek monitors. The only sound in the room was the reverberating slam of the door as Kay and the last Spirit Borns exited, leaving a heavy silence in their wake.

Dominic frowned, his focus shifting between me and Hunter. "What's going on?"

"Dude, I'm as clueless as you," Hunter shrugged.

"We'll explain later," Lola said. "You guys go, I've got this."

Hunter crouched by my chair, the concern in his smile reflected in his eyes as he cupped my neck and pressed his forehead to mine. "Breathe," he whispered, softly kissing my hair.

Despite his departure, when the door closed behind him, the lingering warmth of his touch brought me comfort.

Lola sat beside me, giving my shoulder a reassuring squeeze. "I know she's stressing you out," she said. "But we've still got a job to do."

"Hey, what if you drop her in the pool for me, and I give her a little zap," I teased.

Chapter Twenty-one

Lola clicked her tongue. "Electrocuting the bitch is a tad harsh. Maybe rethink your revenge, psycho."

Two dozen cameras had been positioned around the hotel, and a table, slightly sagging in the middle, held the monitors displaying their feeds.

On the grainy images, multiple REM pods flickered to life in the deserted corridors as the Spirit Borns loitered in their pairs, checking their watches and waiting for the last guests to return to their rooms.

"It's simple," Lola said. "If you see something happen, call out the location on the radio and ask if anyone's nearby."

"What if I get an Ungrounded confused with a guest?"

Lola shook her head. "You won't. Spirits won't appear on camera like they do in person. You'll hear noises or see wisps of light and orbs. Initially, it's a little weird, as you won't see what we see," she explained. "But you'll get used to it."

"What about the hotspots where people have been injured? Are they active?"

"Sometimes, but Ungroundeds roam, and once they see us, they scatter. The first few will be easy, but after that, it's a cat-and-mouse game." Lola said, scanning each screen.

I frowned. "Don't you have to go?"

"Once we see something, I will, but I'll be popping in and out all night."

Lola pointed to one of the screens where the continuous light of a REM pod painted the walls an unsettling shade of blood red. As Lola increased the volume for that camera, the distant sound of footsteps gradually intensified.

Suddenly, the camera's tripod began jerking erratically, its focus zooming in and out as if an unseen force was manipulating the buttons. Seconds later, the whole setup toppled over, leaving the camera lens pointed up at the ceiling.

"Quick, call it in," Lola said, nodding towards the radio lying on the desk. "Tell whoever replies that I can take them there."

My fingers fumbled with the radio's buttons, pressing all but the one I needed before finding the orange communication button. "Uh... hi, it's Harper," I said awkwardly.

"Well, duh," Sawyer replied, his sarcasm slicing through the airwaves like a knife.

My jaw tightened, and I took a breath. "There's activity in the south hall on the second floor. Lola can pick up whoever's closest," I answered.

"We're not far," Hunter said. "Lols, we're out front."

"Coming darling," Beck patronised, making kissing noises like a petulant child.

Other teams joined in, the sounds spreading across the radio waves with a contagious energy. However, instead of being malicious, their exaggerated kissing and giggling noises subtly altered the dynamics of Sawyer and Beck's bullying, transforming the moment into something comical.

I couldn't help but love them for it—anything to soften the blow of the duo's exasperating behaviour. I rolled my eyes, an amused smile tugging at my lips as I shook my head.

Hunter's voice crackled over the radio, his tone playful. "You've got to stop calling me at work, though, sweetheart," he teased, prompting another round of ridiculous kissing noises.

As I poured myself a mug of strong black coffee, Lola vanished from my side and reappeared on screen. Her cheerful expression shone through as she enthusiastically waved at the nearest camera alongside Dominic and Hunter.

They materialised again in the second-floor south corridor, bathed in the constant crimson glow emanating from the REM pod. After adjusting the fallen camera, Lola and the boys crept down the hall, each step cautious and calculated.

As they fearlessly advanced towards the adversary only they could see, Hunter extended his hands to each side, splaying his fingertips wide as his entire body tensed.

The atmosphere crackled with power as every light in the hall shuddered and succumbed to darkness in an isolated blackout. Simultaneously, orbs of radiant, white light surged from the light fixtures towards Hunter, briefly illuminating his glowing fingertips before fading.

The trio stood cloaked in darkness, their forms blending seamlessly with the shadows, obscuring their movements from wandering guests. However, the grainy night vision camera still captured them clearly, the image resembling an old black-and-white movie.

As Dominic carefully monitored the Ovilus in his hand, they split up. Lola transported herself to the other end of the corridor, effectively blocking the Ungrounded's escape route while Dominic and Hunter took the other end.

Together, they slowly edged towards the middle of the hall, strategically cornering the spirit as the air resonated with frantic, otherworldly whispers.

Chapter Twenty-one

Resting my chin in my palm, I imagined it was a significantly different experience in person; however, from the isolated equipment room, the act of passing on an Ungrounded was far less exhilarating than I'd imagined.

As they converged in the centre of the hall. Hunter's fingertips began to glow again, shimmering like beacons in the darkness. Through the camera's microphone, I caught the evocative timbre of his voice.

"Look at the light," Hunter commanded, almost a growl. "Keep looking at the light."

Hunter reached forward, his fingers hovering as though they were resting on someone's shoulder. He stood motionless, his gaze locked on the ethereal wisps gathering and dispersing around him. The delicate tendrils swirled and coiled like a tapestry of otherworldly beauty.

Hunter skilfully manipulated the light, gradually diminishing its glow until it rested solely on the tip of one index finger. With a theatrical flourish, he turned towards the camera and imitated a gun with his hand. With each simulated shot, he skilfully returned the light to its origin, gradually re-illuminating the entire space.

Dominic playfully elbowed Hunter. "Showing off for your girl?" he teased.

"Wouldn't you?" Hunter replied.

Hunter smirked as he casually blew the tip of his finger and tucked his hand into his pocket. Absorbed with watching his every move, I was caught off guard by an unfamiliar voice.

Somewhere, the faint, trembling voice of a woman whispered, "What are you doing?"

My body tensed, and the overhead lights flickered in sync with my unease. I scanned each screen, turning up the volume and listening intently to each one as I grabbed my radio.

"Was someone calling?" I asked.

A chorus of "noes" replied.

I rubbed my eyes and refocused on the screens. My brows furrowed as Lola reappeared beside me.

"Did The Ungrounded say anything?" I inquired. "Dom looked pretty focused on his Ovilus."

"Nothing important," Lola shrugged. "Just "doctor". But we record all responses for The Handlers."

Spirit Born

She gestured to a small notebook and pen in front of the monitors. As she topped up our mugs of coffee, I jotted down the response and tucked the pen behind my ear.

"Nothing else?"

Lola frowned. "No. Why?"

"I thought I heard someone say, 'What are you doing?'" I said, absent-mindedly twisting a strand of my hair. "Could I have missed something?"

"The Ungrounded don't talk like that," Lola explained. "You'll occasionally hear the odd word on camera, but only the stronger Informed Groundeds can communicate clearly, and even then, only a recorder can make out their voices."

I arched one brow. "Or me, remember?"

"Did any REM pods light up?"

"I'm not sure," I shrugged. "I was focused on you guys."

"Ogling Hunter, you mean," Lola teased. "Relax. It was probably just interference or a staff member or something."

Lola pointed to a screen showing two individuals jogging down a hallway on the ground floor, their footsteps echoing as they chased a trail of REM pods lighting up in rapid succession. "Look, Theon and Captain have something," she said.

Despite Captain's distinguished military background, he and Theon seemed to lack the precision that Lola, Hunter, and Dominic had demonstrated.

However, as they cornered their spirit in the foyer, sending a haze of mist rolling towards them, I distinctly heard the words "Per favore" whispered in the darkness of the cellars as a nearby REM pod lit up.

"You hear that?" I asked.

"I did," Lola nodded, her tone reflecting her surprise. "That POW must be pretty strong, or hell of a pissed off, for us to hear him like that. He's probably hiding out down there. Tell Captain to go down; he's nearby anyway. The spirit's grounded, so he might give a decent EVP response for The Handlers."

"Sounds like they're seeking vindication," I said. "I mean, can you really express anything decently when you learn you're being condemned to The Infinite?"

"That's why we get so many unintelligible responses. And it's why your ability to communicate is so important," Lola said, squeezing my arm.

Chapter Twenty-one

I smirked. "Something tells me The Handlers won't be too appreciative. If the dead finally have a voice, they'll have to listen to their defence."

"True."

"Cap, are you there?" I asked over the radio.

He answered with crisp professionalism. "Go ahead."

"Head to the cellar, the POW's turned up."

"Yes, ma'am," he answered. "How'd you know it's him?"

"I don't know much Italian, but I know what "per favore" means," I said. "It's all storage down there, so watch your footing."

"Grazie," he said.

Lola turned up the volume on the cellar's screen as Theon and Captain jogged down the stairs. "This one will be slightly different," she said. "While they can't hear his response, the POW can understand us, so with Captain translating, he'll know what's happening. If the Ovilus doesn't pick up a response now, we can review Captain's EVPs later."

Theon hung back as Captain approached a corner of the cellar cluttered with boxes of decaying paperwork. Facing his palms outward in a placating gesture, he spoke fluent Italian into the darkness. The light of the REM pod cast the sharp shadows of broken furniture against the dusty brick walls.

Captain took a deep breath, puffed out his chest and saluted. "Soldato, è ora di unirti ai tuoi compagni nell'infinito," he said.

Drawing my attention from Captain, the unfamiliar voice returned, sharper and closer than before. "Who are you?" it queried.

As a chill raced down my spine, the eerie tone evoked unwelcome memories of the voices that had once plagued my mornings.

"Are you the devil?" the voice asked.

I spun my chair around. A petite young woman stood by the door, barefoot with toes clenched inwards like twisted claws.

Her grey, fraying hospital gown hung limply from her frail frame, smeared with dirt. Her lank hair hung in matted clumps as her hollow, black eyes stared vacantly towards us. As her eyes danced around the room, she clawed at her arms, marred with self-inflicted wounds.

"How... how did you escape?" she stuttered, her tone almost childlike.

Lola cautiously approached her. "It's okay; I'll get her," she said. "With your talent, one was bound to wander in here sooner or later."

"Stay away," the girl ordered, waving a clenched fist, her sinewy arms tense.

I faced my palm towards her. "It's okay. Everything's fine."

"No, it's not," she whimpered, tears carving thick streaks through the dirt on her face. "Everyone's gone."

I grabbed Lola's shoulder, pulling her back. "Wait, she might be able to tell us something."

"Everyone's gone," the spirit repeated.

"From the hospital?" I said. "We know."

"I... I need a doctor."

"You don't need a doctor," I said gently. "You just need rest."

She frowned, glancing towards the windows, her willowy arms wrapped around her body. "I don't like the thunderstorms."

I stole a glance at the window and the starry night beyond. "There's no storm, sweetie."

Lola's eyes shifted back and forth between me and the Ungrounded spirit. "What is she saying?" she whispered.

"She's not making much sense," I replied.

"Will my parents come today?" the girl asked, her eyes wide with a desperation no living being could pacify.

"I don't know," I shrugged. "Maybe we can find them together?"

Recognising the confusion in the girl's disjointed thoughts, I realised my original hopes that she had any valuable information to share were far too optimistic. The kindest thing I could do for her now was to make her end swift.

As I extended my hand towards her, my skin tingled as tiny bolts of electricity danced from finger to finger. It was an entirely new experience. My talent had always been more of a sensation than something visible or tangible.

The girl slowly reached out, her eyes locked on my hands as she frowned curiously at the sparkling waves of energy.

Suddenly, she wrenched her hand back. "No!" she snapped. "He warned us about you!"

"Who did?" I frowned.

As my hand fell limply at my side, the manifestation of energy disappeared, leaving my fingers impossibly ordinary.

"I need a doctor," the girl growled, baring her yellowing teeth. "I want him, now!"

"I'll get him," I lied. "Just tell me, did someone come to the hospital?"

"A doctor."

Chapter Twenty-one

I drew a deep breath, pinching the bridge of my nose. "No, not a doctor, sweetheart, a man."

The sudden exclamation of the girl's voice startled me. "He was a new doctor!" she snapped. As quickly as her outburst came, her tone softened, her demeanour shifting like an ebbing tide. "My parents come on Sundays. Is it Sunday?"

"Yes, it's Sunday. Once we've spoken, we'll go find them," I sighed. "Is that what he said? That he was a new doctor? Did he have people with him?"

"No. But he brought the whispers."

"Did the whispers tell you to leave?" I asked. "How did he get you all here?"

She began hitting her head as she wandered towards the door. "No breaking rules," she muttered to herself.

"Wait," I pleaded, clutching my hands together as I cut off her escape. "Please."

"I'm lost. I need..."

"I'll get you where you need to be," I interrupted. "But please try and remember. What did the new doctor say?"

"He made people disappear. He could make everyone disappear unless..." She trailed off, her bottom lip quivering.

"Unless you left the hospital ....with him?"

She nodded, her dark eyes cast downward as she wrapped her willowy arms around herself. "Don't let them catch you. Hide if they see you," she ranted.

"You mean don't let The Spirit Borns catch you?" I asked.

Lola shook her head, her eyes glassy with sadness. "H, look at her," she said softly. "This is cruel. She's suffering."

"Calm down," I told the girl, holding out my hand. "I won't hurt you. I'll take you to your family now."

As a hesitant smile inched across the girl's ashen face, the uncertainty of what awaited her gnawed at my conscience.

I had no idea what The Infinite was like; nobody did. I was clueless as to whether I was giving her peace or condemning her to some desolate netherworld. However, the imminent danger looming over the living at Ettington forced my hand—she couldn't stay there.

Her eyes darted around the room like a cornered animal as she inched forward, her hand outstretched as if I were her sole anchor in a turbulent sea.

The second her hand closed around mine, the bolts of electricity returned to my fingers, and the overhead lights flickered responsively.

Her eyes found mine, and the vacancy within them diminished slightly, sparking a glimmer of recognition. The rich chestnut brown of her irises reemerged as a faint smile danced on her lips.

It was as though her consciousness had been unshackled, if only for a moment, enabling her to fully experience her last moments. And for the briefest second, her frigid hand in mine felt solid, as though it had physical form.

Sighing softly, she closed her eyes. A sudden gust of air swept through the room, whipping my hair around my face. As a dense, white fog enveloped me, an orb of soft light shot upwards, disappearing through the ceiling.

When the final wisps of fog dissolved into the air, all traces of the girl had vanished, leaving only Lola's wide, unblinking eyes and open mouth fixed in my direction.

I retrieved the pen from behind my ear and thrust my hand towards her. "Pass me that notepad," I said.

Chapter Twenty-two

At five a.m., as the morning sun hazed the room with light, all activity around the hotel had quietened, and only a few teams could boast any success.

Glancing at the monitors, a low growl escaped me as I recognised Kay striding towards the equipment room, her head held high.

"She probably just wants to congratulate you for bagging your first Ungrounded," Lola said.

"I'm not interested," I snarled. The radios reacted to my frustration, squealing with interference.

"Hey, *chill*," Lola said. "*I'll* get rid of her. Just keep watching the monitors."

Onscreen, Lola took Kay roughly by the elbow and steered her down the hall, stopping directly in front of one of the cameras. As Kay jerked her elbow back, I turned up the volume as far as it went.

Lola crossed her arms. "She's every right to be pissed," she said. "You never should've kept it from her."

"You don't understand..."

"No, we understand fine," Lola interrupted. "We understand The Handlers are keeping secrets, especially about Harper."

Kay sighed. "It's not like that."

"Then why is Alfie still around when you forced everyone else to pass on their families when they were ungrounded?"

"But...Alfie's not one an Ungrounded," Kay stammered.

"He certainly *looks* like an Ungrounded. He *acts* like an Ungrounded. So why is he so special?" Lola pressed. "Have you even seen him lately? He barely knows who he is anymore."

My eyes brimmed with visceral tears at the reminder that Alfie was suffering, trapped in the no man's land between being grounded and ungrounded.

Kay squeezed her eyes shut. "I'm aware."

"Then why let it continue?" Lola asked. "Are you studying how he returned to Red Rock or something?"

"We already know how Alfie got back."

Lola threw up her hands. "How? Or is that information you don't trust us lowly Spirit Borns with?"

"I can't trust you not to run straight to Harper with anything I tell you."

"What makes you think Hunter gives a damn about her?"

Kay smirked, slowly shaking her head as she towered over Lola. "You've always been a terrible liar, Lola," Kay said. "I'm not blind or stupid. And I'm telling you, it *can't* happen. Harper will be the death of that boy."

"You think you can keep them apart now?" Lola scoffed. "Anyway, it's irrelevant. We can pass on Alfie ourselves before anyone else gets hurt. Alfie's just getting warmed up, and you know it."

Kay's eyes widened, her body growing rigid. "Don't!" she blurted out. "It would put Harper's life in danger, and we would lose all hope of neutralising Beau."

Kay turned her back to Lola, clutching a clenched fist to her mouth as her chest rose and fell sharply with each breath.

Lola staggered back as if struck, her brows furrowed. "What power could Alfie hold over a Spirit Born, especially one as vindictive as Beau? *Please*, tell us what's going on," she begged. "Why is Harper in danger?"

The pair stood in an uneasy silence; the air heavy with unspoken words.

Lola softened her tone as she tentatively circled Kay, extending an olive branch of forgiveness. "You know, no one blames you for what Beau did."

Kay clenched her fists at her sides and closed her eyes, blocking Lola out and emphasising that she found absolution unbearable. "Lola, stop," she warned, her voice wavering.

"We placed the blame where it belonged," Lola stated. "No one could have foreseen his plans or stopped him."

"That's why stopping him now is so important."

Lola inched closer, her gaze narrowing. "And you know how, don't you?" she asked. "Did Hannah see that Alfie can help us somehow?"

"The more people know, the more dangerous it is for Harper. And don't bother asking Hannah; she won't tell you anything. She wants Beau gone as much as we do." Kay tried trying to barge past Lola, her chin raised. "Enough! Just let me talk to her."

Chapter Twenty-two

Lola's delicate figure tensed as she blocked Kay's path, her eyes blazing. "If you even *try* getting through me, you'll end up somewhere you don't want to be."

Kay's jaw dropped as she looked Lola up and down. "You forget your place, Lola," she snarled. "I'm her Handler."

"You ceased being her Handler when all the lies started. If you go in there now, all hell will break loose," Lola said, pointing down the hall. "So just leave."

Kay slowly shook her head, her voice low. "You've no idea what you kids are doing with her."

"Oh, we don't? "Lola scoffed. "You'd sleep hugging fire extinguishers. But with us, she's stable and happy. And if you understood us at all, you'd know that learning your entire prior life was a lie makes honesty pretty damn crucial in your new one."

"Trust me, I understand that all too well. Just do me a favour," Kay said. "Don't go gossiping. Let me discuss everything with her myself."

"You already have," Lola replied, her lips curving into a sly smirk as she gestured towards the nearest camera. "But you never know; she might have nodded off."

As Kay's gaze narrowed on the tripod, I closed my eyes and centred myself.

Breathing deeply, I summoned the memories from the previous night to the forefront of my mind, letting each vivid detail unfold like a technicolour movie. I had to prove to Kay that I could master more control than she believed me capable of.

The air crackled with energy as bolts of electricity danced across my fingertips, and the vein-like scarring on my arms began to glow with a pale-yellow light. On the monitor, I noticed the lights surrounding Kay and Lola glimmer, hesitantly at first, before a radiant wave of light spread to every bulb in the hall.

As the intensity of my power surged, I could feel the electrical circuits fighting me as I pushed them to their limits, but not beyond. The energy felt like a living extension of my body, something I could manipulate and expand outwards, much like a muscle steadily growing stronger over time. A smile spread across my features as Lola and Kay instinctively shielded their eyes from the glare.

Slightly breathless, I sank back into the embrace of my soft leather chair as the glow of my scars dimmed. When the regular ambient lighting in the hall returned, Kay's silhouette was perfectly illuminated as she spun on her heel, her nostrils flaring as she stormed off.

As we made our way back to our rooms, fatigue weighed heavily on both our minds and bodies, creating a fog that made it difficult to process the issues Kay had raised. It wasn't until we met Hunter and Dominic for dinner that evening that we shared what had been discussed so fervently.

Amidst the soft linking of silverware and expensive porcelain, Hunter lowered his voice, leaning into the table. "Dead?" he frowned. "They're just going to kill Beau?"

"She didn't actually *say* dead," Lola clarified. "But when The Handlers say "gone" that's usually what they mean."

"But how's an Ungrounded going to take on Beau?" Dominic asked.

Lola shrugged. "Kay's adamant he's still grounded."

"Either way, no spirit holds power over a Spirit Born. And nobody seriously believes Alfie's still grounded, do they?" Hunter turned to me, squeezing my knee beneath the table. "H, I'm sorry, but..."

"It's okay," I interrupted, nodding. "I've seen him. I know."

Dominic subtly nodded towards Hannah, who sat on the other side of the restaurant, her eyes occasionally glancing over. "What about Hannah? Do you think she'd tell us anything?" he asked.

"God no, she's been in The Handlers' pockets ever since Beau left," Lola said. "And if Kay's telling the truth about passing on Alfie, she'd never risk Harper's safety by telling us. The more you know about a vision, the more the outcome is affected."

"Do you really think Hannah wants Beau dead, though?" Dominic wondered. "It's one thing wishing it, but another having it actually happen. I mean, they were like the Romeo and Juliet of The Spirit Borns."

"But when he left, her loyalties were seriously questioned, not that Beau gave a damn," Lola tutted as she picked over her dessert.

"No, he loved her," Hunter said firmly, his eyes fixing on mine. "If anything, Hannah broke *his* heart by staying. He wanted to give her normality, and we all know that if she'd gone with him, he never would've gone off the deep end. She kept him grounded."

"If she broke his heart, why was her family left standing?" Lola asked, dabbing her mouth with a napkin. "Beau's not the kind of psychopath that accepts rejection very well."

"He wouldn't hurt her like that," Hunter said. "Ever."

Dominic's eyes widened. "Or she's a spy."

Chapter Twenty-two

"Don't be ridiculous," Lola said, gently slapping the back of his head.

"So, what should we do about Alfie?" Hunter asked. "What Kay said could just be another one of her control tactics."

Lola pulled her lips to one side thoughtfully. "Maybe. But the way she just blurted it out makes me wonder if there's some truth in it."

"What if we pass Alfie on, and it's true?" I asked.

Hunter gently rubbed my hand, his touch leaving a tiny smear of ash on my skin. "Then we'll keep you safe," he nodded. "And find we'll another way to deal with Beau. But personally, I don't see how Alfie can help us. He's a mess."

Only fragments of Alfie's former self remained, but if he could somehow help our cause, the path forward appeared straightforward on the surface. However, beneath this veneer lay a complex web of uncertainties and doubts.

"We wait," I said. "But if Alfie hurts anyone else or says he wants it over, then we pass him on and accept the consequences."

Savouring a sip of my coffee, I couldn't ignore the heaviness in my eyes from hours of relentless screen-watching.

As we embraced the nocturnal rhythm on our second night at Ettington, we made a more determined effort to seek out the dozens of remaining Ungroundeds. However, with so many roaming Ettington's halls, we feared our arrival had merely kicked the hornet's nest.

I sighed wearily, massaging my temples.

Lola's hands appeared on my shoulders. "Are you okay?"

I let out a sharp gasp, my shoulders tense as a sudden squeal of white noise erupted from my radio. "Jesus!" I exclaimed.

"No, just me," Lola winced. "Sorry, I didn't mean to scare you."

Hunter's voice echoed from Lola's radio. "H, is everything alright? We heard a noise?"

"I'm fine," I answered, but no sound came from Lola's radio. I turned it over and shook it gently, hoping to revive it, only to see thin tendrils of smoke unfurling from the scorched battery compartment.

Hunter called again, his voice growing urgent. "Harper?"

"Here, take mine," Lola said, handing me her radio. "Before he has a nervous breakdown."

"Just radio issues," I answered. Wherever Hunter was in the building, I could almost feel his anxiety diminishing.

Lola peered over my shoulders towards the monitors. "So, what's next?" she asked.

"There's a persistent noise in the bar," I said, my finger skimming down the growing list of activity on my notepad. "Then the front lawn."

"I'll grab a team."

I held Lola's radio towards her. "Won't you need your radio?"

"I'll manage. You need it more than me," she said, flashing a smile as she vanished.

I resumed my vigil over the monitors, yawning and stretching life into my stiff neck. Shortly after Lola had left, my eyes narrowed as I noticed a potential problem.

A dark figure leisurely emerged through the back door and settled on the sturdy stone steps, their gaze fixed upon the cascading shadows that danced across the sprawling rear gardens.

Grabbing my coffee with one hand, I picked up my radio with the other. "Is anyone free?" I asked. "There's a guest on the rear steps."

"We were just there," Sawyer dismissed. "It's clear."

I squeezed my eyes closed and tried to rub away the fatigue with my fists. However, when I rechecked the screen, Sawyer was right. The steps were eerily quiet, and the silence was deafening.

I scanned each monitor methodically, but there was no trace of the guest in the surrounding areas either. When Lola reappeared twenty minutes later, I voiced my concerns, bombarding her with a barrage of questions.

"It's late," Lola reassured. "All the guests are sleeping."

"Could it have been a spirit? The way it just vanished was creepy," I said, struggling to suppress a shudder.

"It takes a crazy amount of energy for a spirit to appear as a full apparition on screen."

"Like the amount of energy, I can generate?" I responded, cocking my head.

Lola released a thoughtful sigh. "Okay, what did he look like?"

"I didn't get a good look at him. He was there one second and gone the next." I shifted as a chill tingled through my neck and into my body. "Could it be...?"

"Absolutely not," Lola interrupted. "We've been using our talents all night without issue. If he was here, we'd be the first to know." Her tone

Chapter Twenty-two

softened as she rubbed my arms. "You're tired; your eyes are just playing tricks on you. But I'll swing by the steps en route to my next call and check it's not a spirit, okay?"

I nodded as Lola disappeared from the equipment room and reappeared on the steps. After a brief search, she turned towards the camera, shrugging and shaking her head. But I knew what I'd seen.

While I felt reassured that it couldn't be Beau, the idea of a spirit wandering the grounds with enough power to manifest on screen was deeply unsettling, especially considering the levels of violence attributed to many of them.

I found myself absentmindedly chewing the end of my pen into a mangled barb of plastic as I became preoccupied with searching for the elusive spirit. As Lola grew increasingly busier as the night progressed, the sightings I relayed to the teams became late and chaotic.

Eventually, Hunter and Dominic arrived, their warm, sympathetic smiles conveying genuine concern and understanding.

Hunter sat beside me and smoothly pulled my chair towards him, his knees enclosing mine. "Hey, trouble," he purred. "What's up?"

"Just tired," I sighed.

Hunter arched one brow. "Don't lie, not to me," he said softly. "We've been checking the steps throughout the night, but I promise you, there's nothing." Hunter's thumb grazed my cheek. "Why don't you take a break and clear your head? We can cover you."

"And suffer Sawyer and Beck's berating for throwing in the towel early?" I said. "I'm good, honestly."

Hunter's lips curved into a lopsided smile, revealing a slight dimple on one cheek. "You're so stubborn."

"Just committed," I smirked.

"Which is another word for stubborn," Hunter said. "Okay, fine. I know that look by now. Radio us if you change your mind."

Hunter grasped my neck and planted a kiss on my hair, inhaling my shampoo as he stood and left.

They strolled down the hall, the cameras capturing every word and action. Dominic playfully wrestled Hunter into a headlock and tousled his hair.

"You two, man," Dominic said. "She lights up around you, pardon the pun. You can see who she really is when you're together. She's different around you."

Hunter rubbed the back of his neck. "A good different, hopefully."

"Definitely," Dominic said, slapping Hunter's back. "Stop worrying. You knew this would happen, so just enjoy the ride."

"Hannah mentioned we'd be volatile together, but she doesn't know how or why. All I know is that I feel so out of control around her I can't stand it. And I feel even worse when we're apart."

Dominic shrugged. "That's love for you, mate."

I felt a knot twist in my stomach as my mouth went bone dry. It was the first time love or anything like it had been mentioned, but Hunter didn't rebuff Dominic's comment; he merely continued chitchatting as if it was a known fact between them.

"What about Alfie?" Hunter said.

"She said it herself; he needs to go. He's doing some considerable damage at Red Rock. The Handlers told Gia and Theon they were waiting until Harper's more stable to tell her."

Hunter came to an abrupt halt in the hallway, his face contorted in disgust. "More *stable?* No wonder everyone's terrified of her if that's what her Handler tells people. Makes you wonder what other lies they're telling."

"Yep," Dominic nodded. "I trusted my Handler, James, with everything, but since Harper arrived, he's been so secretive."

"They all have," Hunter said.

"Whatever's going on, Harper's trapped smack bang in the middle of it. And if we pass on Alfie and are wrong, we all need to be prepared to bat for her," Dominic warned. "But she's worth it, right?"

"Definitely," Hunter answered, his gaze snapping sharply towards Dominic's. "She's turned my life inside out, but I just... don't care anymore. About the rules, The Handlers, any of it."

Hunter and Dominic's eyes simultaneously shot to the end of the hall as a nearby REM pod lit up. They took off running, chasing their spirit outside, their boots squelching on the dewy lawn until they disappeared into the shadows.

I slumped into my chair, staring into space. As my thoughts of Hunter consumed me, the atmosphere crackled with static. My body vibrated with energy, my fingers gently sparkling as the room became pressurised with electrical charges.

Controlling my breathing, I expelled Hunter from my mind and refocused on the assignment. REM pods lit up on most floors, and partial

Chapter Twenty-two

apparitions, the misty outlines of feet or arms, could be seen wandering the halls.

But as I reached for Lola's radio, the unknown spirit reappeared, repeating the same behaviour as before, sitting on the steps and gazing into the sparkling night sky.

As I watched him, his outline remained distinct, but his focus shifted. Gradually, he pivoted toward the camera, his gaze unnervingly intense as he locked eyes directly with the lens.

Trying to keep my voice steady, I spoke into my radio. "Guys, I need someone right now. Is anyone free?"

I waited for a reply, but none came.

"Lola. Hunter. Dom?" My voice grew louder. "Anybody?"

Then I noticed the charred battery compartment, the acrid smell of burnt plastic filling the air. My ardent daydreaming had rendered another radio useless, and due to The Handler's orders to leave our phones in our rooms, contacting anyone was impossible.

Impatiently, I tapped my foot against the desk, awaiting Lola's return while the spirit on the steps waited. But as I studied each screen, every team was engaged, a fair distance from both the equipment room and the steps.

I knew I wouldn't need it, but I grabbed a voice recorder to appease The Handlers. After scribbling a note to Lola explaining where I was, I taped it to the screens.

Jogging towards the steps, I ignored the tall, lanky Ungrounded lurking at the end of the hall, shifting his weight from foot to foot. The dead didn't bother me anymore, even the clinically insane ones roaming Ettington.

My sole focus was to reach the spirit that had been powerful enough to appear on screen on multiple occasions and disappear without a trace like smoke.

As I passed through the foyer, the unmistakable outline of the man gradually emerged. Perched on the top step, his silhouette was cloaked in a shroud of thick, swirling smoke that partially obscured him from view, weaving around his shoulders like ghostly tendrils.

I cautiously advanced, holding my recorder in front of me like a weapon. "Turn around," I commanded, injecting confidence into my voice.

His posture straightened as he slowly peered over his shoulder, one half of his mouth twisting into an endearing smile as the smoke cleared.

He casually flicked a cigarette into the bushes, blowing a lungful of smoke towards the lawns as I closed my eyes and cringed.

"Don't shoot," he chuckled. His thick Southern American accent exuded class and sophistication as he slowly stood and turned, his hands raised. "I'm unarmed."

He was a guest, wearing a black sweatshirt, its hood draping over the back of his fitted leather jacket. Caked in thick mud, his boots left distinct footprints on the stone steps as he edged towards me.

His pale blond hair danced in the summer breeze as his ice-blue eyes tracked my every movement.

"I'm sorry," I stammered. "I... I thought you were someone else."

"No problem, miss," he said, his wry half-smile suggesting a delicate playfulness. He nodded to the recorder as he lit another cigarette, the flame from his lighter momentarily illuminating his chiselled features with licks of amber. "What've you got there?"

"A recorder. We're conducting an investigation," I said, patting my empty pockets. "I have a card here somewhere."

His eyes flicked towards the camera, then back to me. "So that's what all these cameras are for?" he asked. "Isn't that an invasion of privacy?"

"We have permission to film," I said. "And it's quiet this weekend."

"That's convenient. You wouldn't want a bunch of leisurely guests like me ruining your shots," he winked, lazily leaning against the wall. "Oh, I'm sorry. Am I in the way? Is that why you're here?"

"No, you're fine."

"So, are y'all on TV?" the guest asked.

"Just the internet, I think," I replied, my cheeks burning.

He arched one brow. "You *think*?"

"I'm new. I'm just manning the cameras."

"Whilst everyone else has all the fun?" he said, teasingly narrowing his eyes.

I shrugged, biting my lip.

"I'm sorry, I'm being rude." He held his crumpled packet of cigarettes towards me, his magnetic eyes brazenly staring. "Would you care for one?"

"I don't smoke," I said, turning to head back inside. "Sorry for bothering you."

"No problem," he replied, raising his hand. "So, if I see anyone else running around in the dark, it'll just be your team?"

I was torn between my duty to return to the monitors and the magnetic pull of the stranger's charm. His engaging banter made it difficult to peel myself away from the conversation and back to my responsibilities.

Chapter Twenty-two

"Or burglars." I chuckled.

"I'll lock up my valuables then, just to be safe," he said.

"Hopefully, it's our last night tonight. If we catch enough...footage," I said carefully. "We won't bother you much longer."

"And what sort of footage are y'all looking for?" he asked, tracing his jawline with his fingers.

I fiddled with my recorder, feeling a flush of embarrassment. "We're ghost hunters," I confessed.

"I see," he said, his brows furrowed. "And y'all believe in that stuff?"

"I was raised in a haunted house," I nodded. "But it's reassuring to know that death isn't the end."

"I suppose it is, the idea there's a place for everyone." The stranger tilted his head, his smile growing. "It's a shame you're leaving so soon, though. We could've had a drink together."

He drew deeply on his cigarette, pulling my gaze towards his lips. There was something about him that was not only attractive but mysterious. Like a rare spark of individuality shone from within him that your average man hadn't a hope mustering.

He smiled, revealing a set of perfect teeth. "Well, if y'all end up staying, maybe you'll meet me tomorrow?"

"That'd be nice..."

"Why do I sense a "but" coming here?" the stranger interrupted.

I half-smiled, glancing at my feet. Realising how close I'd unconsciously inched towards him, I stepped back. "*But* I don't think my boyfriend would like that very much," I said.

"Oh, you're breaking my heart," he said, exaggeratingly placing a hand on his chest. "You've got a boyfriend?"

I nodded, twisting my hair with my free hand.

He clicked his tongue seductively. "Lucky guy," he said.

"Lucky girl," I answered.

The porch light above us flickered, mimicking the butterflies swirling in my stomach at the mention of Hunter and the term "boyfriend" in the same sentence.

The stranger's gaze shot upward, his brow furrowing at the inexplicable flickering of the lights before he fixed his magnetic eyes on me.

I took a breath, replaying the reassuring cadence of Hunter's voice in my mind. As I found my centre, the flickering ceased.

"And he's supportive of your nocturnal pursuits? Running around talking to strange men at three a.m.?" the stranger flirted.

I arched one brow. "You're admitting that you're strange?"

"Aren't we all a little strange?" he answered coolly.

"True," I smiled. "But my boyfriend's here too, so I'm guessing he's pretty supportive."

He smirked, his voice rising in pitch as he crossed his arms. "Is he now. Has your boy got a name?"

"Hunter," I answered.

"Unusual name?"

"Unusual guy," I shrugged. "Look, I'm sorry, but I really should be getting back now."

"Of course. I'd hate to get you in trouble." His tone lowered, purring with the tiniest trace of aggression as his eyes narrowed. "Your boss must be a real bitch."

I frowned, recoiling slightly at the sudden intimidation. "Not really," I lied.

"Is that so?" He paused, focusing on me intently. "I'm sorry, miss. I didn't catch your name."

"That's because I didn't give it," I replied sharply.

Heavy, rhythmic footsteps reverberated through the foyer, accompanied by the sharp staccato of panting breaths drawing nearer. Suddenly, Hunter, Lola, and Dominic tore into view, their hurried footsteps echoing through the open space as they sprinted through the foyer and crowded the steps.

Hunter stepped between me and the stranger and held me to his chest. His body felt rigid, his shirt slightly damp with perspiration as his heart hammered against my cheek. Lola and Dominic looked equally tense; their shoulders raised as their wide eyes flickered restlessly between us.

Initially, his gaze exuded charm and allure, but in a split second, it turned cold and penetrating, emanating a hostility that revealed his true nature.

"Beau, I presume?" I growled.

He briefly closed his eyes and politely bowed his head.

Lola lunged forward, but Dominic held her shoulders back as she writhed futilely against his grip. "How dare you show up here?" she spat. "A girl killed herself over this ridiculous stunt, Beau!"

"That was... unfortunate," he said.

Chapter Twenty-two

I'd never seen Lola's eyes so wild, so untamed. *"Unfortunate?"* she yelled. "Who the hell do you think you are? I've every right to drop you from the Fort's ramparts!"

"Quit raving, Lola. Y'all can't touch me," Beau dismissed. He fixed his icy stare on me, rubbing his chin as he half-licked, half-bit his bottom lip. "But The Thirteenth, she interests me."

"Your fight is with us," Lola warned, still trying to wriggle free of Dominic. "Leave Harper out of this."

Beau clapped his hands once and pointed towards me in one slick motion. *"Harper,"* he said. "That wasn't so hard, was it? A pleasure to meet you, Harper."

"I wish I could say the same, but I'd be lying." I snarled.

As I bared my teeth at Beau, the circuits on Ettington's ground floor sputtered with irregular flashes, each pulse spreading like a creeping vine throughout the entire building, casting the lawns in a mesmerising amber hue.

Beau's gaze drifted over the shimmering lights in the background before turning to Hunter, Lola, and Dominic, cocking his head. "And y'all left her watching the monitors?" He shook his head, tutting disapprovingly. "Shame on you."

"How long have you been watching us?" Hunter demanded. "We've been using our talents without issue until ten minutes ago."

"Do you see Lola transporting or Dominic drifting into his dream state twenty-four-seven? *No,* and I'm no different," Beau answered. "Now that I'm in complete control, I can turn it on and off whenever I please."

"So why are we all here?" Dominic asked. "Why the effort?"

Beau pouted sarcastically. "Well, y'all don't call, y'all don't write," he said. "And y'all ignored my letters, so I had to come see you personally."

"What letters?" Hunter asked, his brow furrowing as his head jarred back.

Beau exhaled sharply, emitting a sound that was part laugh, part huff. "And y'all still think The Handlers can be trusted?" he smirked. "I've been warning y'all to cease action on The Ungrounded for years."

"Shocker," Lola scoffed.

"Maybe the contents of the letters will surprise you," Beau said. "I wrote to The Handlers, warning them that if they ignored me, the first spirits I ungrounded would be your families."

I could feel the tension in Hunter's body as his fists clenched. Lola's eyes widened and glistened with bitter tears, while Dominic's bewildered expression revealed his sense of helplessness. He loosened his grip on Lola's arms, drawing her into a protective embrace.

Beau nodded, brows raised. "They could've saved your mother, Lola. But instead, they did *nothing*."

"They... knew?" Lola stuttered, shaking her head. "He... he wouldn't. Cameron wouldn't..."

"He did," Beau interrupted. "Cameron received a letter just like the other Handlers, detailing who'd be next."

Beau stepped forward, placing a hand on Lola's shoulder, his eyes softening and trying to connect with hers. Her complexion turned ashen, and her entire body quaked as tears cascaded down her face.

As Beau twisted his way into her mind, her warm eyes became hollow pools. Her hand mindlessly reached for Beau's, as if confessing the truth had made him her ally. Despite Dominic's whisperings of support in her ear as he bore her weight, she remained unresponsive.

Time seemed to slow as I watched Beau sinking his claws into her, and fearing I was about to lose my best friend to my worst enemy, I searched my mind for a way to reach her.

"Lola, put the blame where it belongs," I pleaded, recalling the comforting words she had spoken to Kay. "Beau may have given you the truth, but he dealt you the pain, too."

A flicker of life stirred within her eyes as they sharply met mine, and the palpable agony radiating from her made my entire body ache.

She glanced at Beau's hand resting on her shoulder and trailed her gaze along his arm. By the time her eyes locked with his, they were filled with rage, and her nose wrinkled in disgust.

Wrenching her shoulder from Beau's grip, she edged towards me and took my hand, her fingers like ice. Dominic removed his jacket, draped it over Lola and rubbed her shoulders to warm her.

"Well, as entertaining as it's been watching y'all running amuck, I'm actually here for you," Beau said, pointing first to Hunter, then to Dominic. "I had to create an assignment big enough to ensure you'd both be here. And, of course, meeting The Thirteenth was high on my priority list, too."

Hunter frowned. "Why us? We were your friends. We supported you when nobody else would."

Chapter Twenty-two

"That's exactly why I'm here, old friend," Beau said, his lips curving into a nostalgic smile. "I was never certain about my suspicions regarding The Handlers withholding my letters. Hence, I'm here to issue my final demand. Live and in person, so The Handlers can't mislead you. You can make your own decisions for once in your pitiful lives."

My eyes narrowed. "And what's the demand?"

"Same as before. Y'all are to cease action on The Ungrounded," he said. "Or the remaining Spirit Born families will fall."

There was a brief silence as Beau's unnervingly chilling, yet captivating eyes bored into us. Beside me, a wide-eyed look of disbelief shrouded Dominic's face, his jaw quivering as he turned equally pale as Lola. While Hunter appeared not to respond, I felt a shudder ripple through him as beads of sweat shimmered from his temples.

I straightened my posture, lifting my chin defiantly. "And your terms?"

"My *terms?*" Beau said, his eyebrows furrowing slightly as a perplexed smile tugged at one corner of his lips.

"Well, the afterlife needs protection," I said. "There are still Groundeds that knowingly cause trouble. They can't just evade prosecution forever."

Beau nodded, pouting in an overzealous manner that, despite his charm, made my skin crawl. "Absolutely. I mean, just this week, a girl fractured her spine in some big old house after being attacked by a Grounded... or was it an Ungrounded? You know, I just can't remember." He grinned, putting a finger to his lips. "She looks awfully like you, apparently."

Out of the corner of my eye, I noticed Hunter's gaze shift to Dominic in a silent look of panic. But as Beau's eyes bore into me, I didn't want to appear weak by looking away. Our concerns about what he knew about Red Rock or my connections to it had to wait.

"Exactly," I continued, undeterred. "Therefore, the warning system must remain in place."

"Fine, but The Ungrounded are innocent, and things must change to reflect that," Beau said. "The Handlers have to go. They're corrupt."

Hunter stepped forward, pointing directly into Beau's face. "This isn't the way to change things, and you know it," he snapped. "Look at all the harm you've caused. And your lies left Laura's death on *my* conscience."

I furrowed my brow as I looked at Hunter, but his resolute gaze stayed locked on Beau's.

"I've seen your pain, old friend, and I never intended to inflict it on you," Beau said, pressing his hand to his chest in what appeared to be a rare moment of sincerity. "I've heard all about your reclusiveness, your loneliness. But at least you've rejoined the world again. The Thirteenth is proof of that."

"You *are* watching us then?" Dominic said.

"Well, y'all know I've got a few psychics in my pocket. Of course. They're no..." Beau swallowed hard. "...Hannah, but I see enough."

"Look, I don't trust the Handlers either," I said. "But they'll never surrender willingly. It'll take time to get them out. And if we cease action on The Ungrounded, you *must* stop creating them."

"Darlin', if y'all are finally listening, I won't need to unground another soul," Beau said. "And I can be patient regarding The Handlers."

"If we agree to your demands, do you *swear* the remaining Spirit Born families will be spared?" I asked.

I extended my hand, feeling a slight vibration in my fingers as the scars on my arms glowed with a mesmerising, ethereal energy. The radiance drew the undivided attention of Hunter, Lola, and Dominic, who observed the evolution of my talent with a mixture of awe and curiosity.

Before shaking my hand, Beau hesitated, his eyes lingering on the intricate web of scars on my skin. Then, his gaze shifted to the shimmering light beaming from the hotel behind us like a beacon.

I couldn't help but imagine the irritation it must be causing the guests, disturbed from their slumber by the relentless glow that pierced the darkness.

"Out of curiosity, Thirteenth, what's your talent?" Beau inquired, his eyes narrowing. "You can't be another Hunter, so what *are* you?"

"I create energy."

"My opposite. I consume, you create," Beau muttered, rubbing his chin. "Very well, all ungroundings at my hands will cease, your families included, so long as you abide by our agreement."

His hand slipped into mine, shaking it once. His grip suddenly tightened, and he tugged me towards him sharply, my body almost collapsing into his as the rich scent of his aftershave enveloped me.

Hunter, Lola, and Dominic collectively lurched forward behind me, their hands outstretched as Beau leaned close and whispered into my ear, the warmth of his breath caressing my neck. "Remember, Thirteenth, I have eyes and ears everywhere," he warned. "I'll be watching."

As Beau released my hand, a sleek, black SUV pulled up at the bottom of the steps, its tyres softly crunching against the gravel. Leaning into the

Chapter Twenty-two

vehicle, Beau fixed his gaze on me, a solemn expression adorning his face. In the distance, echoes of thunder ruptured a cloudless sky.

Beau nodded directly at Hunter, Lola and Dominic. "Y'all help her now, you hear? Her time will be before you know it," he warned. "And losing someone with such potential would be a tragic waste."

Before I could ask for an explanation, he slipped into the backseat, and the car accelerated down the driveway, spraying us with gravel as we stood motionless.

Hunter and Dominic's faces turned a sickly shade of green, their distress evident as they swallowed hard, appearing on the brink of throwing up. Meanwhile, Lola swayed unsteadily like a slender branch in the wind, her complexion drained of colour.

"Call everyone back," I said breathlessly. "We're leaving."

Chapter Twenty-three

"He's lying," Beck scoffed. "He'd say anything if it meant we'd turn on The Handlers."

Dominic's brow furrowed as he shakily clutched a mug of brandy that Lola had swiped from the bar. "And what if he's not?" he asked.

When we recounted the story of Beau's return, most of the Spirit-Borns stayed eerily quiet, leaving us to wonder whether their hushed reactions resulted from disbelief or sheer horror.

No matter how many times we assured them that we had seen him leave, several individuals continually peered out of curtains and even around the room as if he were somehow hidden amongst us. And the absence of Hannah, coupled with her lack of response to calls on her phone and radio, only served to heighten the palpable tension in the room.

"Then you Beau lovers can endure what we've all suffered," Sawyer said, nodding to Hunter and Dominic.

"You can't be serious?" Aida snapped, her tiny voice catching the room off guard with its uncharacteristic volume. "Enough harm has been caused already."

"So, what can we do to save them?" Captain asked. "Just pack up and leave?"

Beck's eyes widened. *"Now?* You want to leave Ettington crawling with psychotic Ungroundeds? With people committing suicide and being half drowned?"

"I hate to say it, but Sawyer's right," Amy sighed. "We can't leave Ettington like this. But Beau caused this mess. Is he willing to negotiate?"

"We told you; he's gone," I answered. "He said he'd be watching, but even if he's lying, if he swings by and sees it's been cleared, he'll know."

"Then Hunter, Dom, it should be your decision," Gia said.

"This is what he wants, you know that, right?" Theon said, casting his gaze around the room. "For us to make some impossible choice; what's more important, the safety of the living or your families' afterlives?"

Chapter Twenty-three

"Are Kay and Tom still here? We could ask them?" Captain shrugged.

Hunter shook his head adamantly. "We're not involving them. They're the reason we're in this position in the first place. They'll tell us to continue regardless... that they'll *handle* it," Hunter said sarcastically. "Besides, I'm assuming they've left. After the light show that Harper caused, Kay would've been straight down here to find out what happened."

"About that, how did you even manage it?" Beck asked. "Nobody else could use their talents when he turned up."

"I've no idea," I shrugged. "But that's not important right now."

"Can we have the building cleansed?" Amy suggested. "That could protect the living temporarily until we figure out what to do."

"Ettington's enormous," Aida said, chewing her lip. "It'd take weeks."

"Well, whatever we're doing, we need to act fast," Amy advised. "But Gia's right. With Hannah missing, the decision should fall on Hunter and Dominic."

A rare silence fell over the group, each member holding their breath as they trained their attention on Hunter and Dominic. The pair locked eyes with one another as though the solution to their dilemma resided in the other's gaze.

Hunter looked downwards, sighing as he brushed the ash from his fingertips in a self-soothing gesture. "We have to see this through," he said, his voice taut with refrained emotion.

Dominic's eyes widened as he grasped Hunter's collar, his eyes glassy. "I'm begging you," he pleaded. "Don't do this, Hunter. Let's just go home."

Hunter pulled Dominic into his arms, squeezing his thick arms around his neck.

"We have to," Hunter said softly as he pulled Dominic into his embrace, squeezing his thick arms around his neck. "Who would we be if anyone else was killed because we left?"

"But if he comes back..."

"We'll be smart about it," Hunter interrupted, holding Dominic at arm's length. "We'll post lookouts. Beau doesn't know how many we've already passed on, so we focus on the most dangerous ones and leave a few stragglers. Then, if he checks, it'll look like we listened."

I checked my watch. "We've got three hours until sunrise; we've got to be gone by then. We can't risk staying another night."

"Part of the roof is flat; I can post a lookout team there," Captain suggested. "We'll have a bird's eye view if he returns."

"Good. Take one other person with you," I nodded. "If Beau returns or if anyone sees anything suspicious, everyone come straight back to the equipment room. We'll just make out like we were busy arguing and packing."

"And brace yourselves for a rocky debrief," Lola added. "After tonight, regardless of what your Handler says, *don't* accept assignments for The Ungrounded. If anyone caves, it'll all be over for the remaining Spirit Born families. Remember that."

Hunter nodded towards me. "I'll stay and help Harper identify the worst offenders. We can't afford to let any slip past us. Dominic, you can join Gia until Hannah turns up."

As the room slowly emptied, the monitors picked up on the lingering echoes of everyone's private reactions.

Some could be heard muttering various expletives under their breath, while others maintained a stoic composure, flinching visibly at even the faintest sound echoing through the corridors. Nevertheless, a palpable sense of anxiety permeated the atmosphere, affecting them all.

Drawing me back to the room, Hunter squeezed my hand, my body jolting. "Are you okay?" he asked.

"I guess so," I answered, recalling the pale magnetism of Beau's eyes. "I just had no idea he was like that. He was so charming at first. I had no idea."

"Yeah, he's a complete gentleman until he's... not. I meant you're not hurt?" he said, examining my hands and turning them over in his own.

"I'm fine," I frowned. "I'm more worried about you and Dominic. Why?"

"When we turned up, we all tried to overpower him with our talents, but you lit up the entire building like it was nothing."

I shrugged. "Maybe Beau was just having an off day?"

"He doesn't *have* off days." Hunter shook his head, sighing. "I don't think The Handler's ever imagined he'd grow this powerful."

I tilted my head inquisitively. "But you still supported him?"

"He was always alone. I guess I felt sorry for him." Hunter's tone changed, sounding more optimistic as his eyes widened slightly, though I wondered if he was merely seeking a distraction from the stress he was struggling under. "But seeing how you can use your talent around him, maybe that's something we can use against him?"

"What...dazzle him with sparkly lights?" I chuckled.

Chapter Twenty-three

"With practice, what's to suggest you couldn't pull off something like the rollercoaster?"

My brows drew together, my voice sharp as I replied. "Because that nearly killed me."

"You weren't ready, but we can train harder. There's energy in everything. Even the human heart only beats through electrical impulses. You could..."

"I'm not going to kill Beau because you don't know how to handle him," I snapped, drawing back.

"How else do you think we'll stop him? A cancer like Beau won't ever stop trying to destroy us."

I exhaled loudly, shrugging. "I don't know. Beau killed his Handler, right? Let's go to the police. If we kill him, we're no better than he is."

"I *did* go to the police. Repeatedly," Hunter said. "I told them what I'd seen, but Beau squirmed out of it."

"What *did* you see?" I asked. "And why is Laura's death on your conscience?"

Hunter stared at the screens, swallowing hard and ignoring my questions. I hated bringing up his past trauma at such a strenuous time, but I had to know.

I leant forward, trying to catch his gaze, but his emerald eyes looked vacant, unreachable. "Please, Hunter. *Tell* me," I said.

Hunter drew a shaky breath, his tense posture betraying the turmoil within. "I saw him leaving Laura's hotel room, covered in blood."

"But how's that you're fault?" I probed. "What aren't you telling me?"

Hunter's eyes finally snapped toward me. "I took him there, alright?" he said. "Beau and Laura had been arguing, and he was sick, so I drove him to her hotel and waited in the hall. He promised me he just wanted to talk, but when he left the room, he suddenly wasn't sick anymore. And when I saw Laura's body, I felt utterly broken."

"How could the police do nothing with a body in a hotel like that?" I asked.

Hunter's eyes darkened as his jaw tightened. "Because I made the mistake of calling The Handlers first," he growled. "They sent me home saying they'd handle it, but something didn't feel right. So, I called the police myself the next morning, and they said the room was clear. And with The Handlers destroying all the evidence, I had no proof that a crime even occurred."

Hunter hunched over the desk, cradling his face in his hands as his fingers trembled slightly. His broad shoulders rose and fell with each heavy breath, as if they carried the weight of the world.

I caressed his hair, trying to catch his gaze and pierce his veil of sorrow. I wanted to chase away his demons and provide him solace, but he seemed lost.

"I've felt responsible for everything he's done since. None of it would've happened if I'd just called the police first and had him arrested," Hunter said. "I asked The Handlers why they'd covered it up, but they said it would've raised too many questions. And being a new Spirit Born, I believed them. Just please don't think any less of me. I was young and naive."

I sighed, my thumb grazing his jawline. "There's very little you could do that would ever make me think any less of you," I said.

Hunter sniffed and blotted away the tears welling in the corners of his eyes, leaving tiny ebony marks on his face as he regained his composure.

"But if they covered up Laura's murder," I said. "The Handlers will hardly admit to keeping Beau's letters secret."

"Well, we'll hopefully have an ace up our sleeve."

"Theon?" I asked, brows raised.

"No. Whatever the Handlers are, they aren't entirely human. Our talents don't work on them," Hunter explained. "They've only taken advantage of Lola and Hannah's abilities for convenience. But Lola's going to raid The Fort's archives tomorrow."

"You think they'll have kept the letters?" I said.

"After Laura's death, I wanted to know whether it was an accident or murder, so Lols searched the archives then."

I unconsciously leaned forward. "And?"

"Nothing. We figured The Handlers destroyed that information because they were implicated in the cover-up. However, Lola did discover detailed files on everyone, including one two inches thick on Beau," Hunter replied, his eyes continually scanning the monitors. "There's bound to be something down there that can prove whether he was telling the truth."

"Then maybe we can kill two birds with one stone," I said. "Perhaps we can find something on Alfie and figure out why The Handlers need him?"

❖

Chapter Twenty-three

By six a.m., as the sun threatened to inch over the horizon, we'd caught all the dangerous Ungroundeds, except for one. We debated leaving it, but with Captain's reassurance that nobody had been spotted approaching the property or loitering in the grounds, we pressed on.

However, as the morning came alive, each flutter of awakening birds and note of their morning chorus served as a poignant reminder that time was slipping away, like the steady trickle of sand in an hourglass.

I sighed, rubbing my temples. "We're running out of time."

Towering behind me as he stood over my chair, Hunter massaged the tension from my shoulders and planted a kiss on the crown of my head. "We'll make it," he soothed, his eyes never leaving the screens.

The tranquillity of the room was shattered by a sudden, forceful knock on the door. Instantly, our bodies tensed, and our eyes met in silent apprehension before shifting to the door.

I swallowed hard. "What if it's Beau?"

"He couldn't have slipped past Captain," Hunter said, though his tone seemed uncertain.

Hunter swung the door open, and in the hallway stood a tired-looking staff member in a crumpled blue suit, his badge reading 'night manager'.

"Can we...help you?" Hunter asked.

"I thought we could help each other, actually. You're the paranormal enthusiasts, right?" He yawned, running his hands through his dishevelled hair. "We've had to move a guest from their room after some unsettling experiences. They've refused to stay in that room, so I thought you could add it to your investigation." He pulled a key card from his pocket and handed it to Hunter. "And if you've any means of... removing whatever's in there, please do so."

As the night manager disappeared from sight, I grabbed the radio. "We've found the missing Ungrounded. It's ducked into a guest's room, number 102. Lola, come grab the key and a team. Everyone else, start grabbing gear."

Reassembled in the equipment room, the team flew into a well-rehearsed routine of packing as they returned the monitors and devices to their bulky plastic cases, each adorned with peeling stickers from locations and hotels across the globe.

Within half an hour, the room was emptied. The only proof we had ever been there was the stained coffee cups and empty wrappers overflowing the wastepaper bin.

We disappeared to our rooms to pack, each of us glancing over our shoulders, feeling trapped in a perpetual state of fear ever since the bogeyman had paid us a visit.

As Lola silently slipped away to start drop-offs, I frantically stuffed our bags with clothing. The urgency of our departure made me feel like a criminal fleeing for the border after some fantastical heist gone awry.

When Hunter and Dominic arrived, the room was in complete disarray. Empty wine bottles and snack wrappers were strewn across every surface, but we hadn't the time to tidy up.

Lola reappeared, panting. "Ready?"

"Are you okay," Dominic asked, resting a concerned hand on her shoulder. "Do you need a break?"

Lola shook her head. "There's no time. I'll rest when we're away from this damned hotel. Where are we headed?"

"Maybe we can get some sleep and watch a movie or something at Harper's," Hunter suggested. "It would keep our minds occupied until debrief."

Worry had been gnawing at me about leaving Lola on her own, so I nodded. "Works for us."

We took Lola's hand one at a time, transporting us to my flat. It felt as though we had been holding our breath underwater for hours. But once we were in our own space, away from the chaos at Ettington, we finally felt the air fill our lungs again.

Stress visibly faded as tense shoulders lowered, panicked eyes ceased searching, and our panicked hearts settled into a calmer rhythm.

The throbbing in my head was relentless after hours of staring at screens, and the dark smudges on Hunter's temples indicated that he felt the same way.

Despite our overwhelming exhaustion, we were reluctant to part ways with Lola and Dominic to get some much-needed rest. Even though Lola's flat was just downstairs, it still felt too far away in our anxious states.

We brought sofa cushions up from Lola's for Dominic to sleep on while Lola took my sofa beside him. However, every time she disappeared to gather blankets or pillows, she returned with flushed cheeks and raw eyes from tears privately shed.

Once Lola and Dominic were comfortable, Hunter and I settled in my bedroom, kicking off our shoes and climbing into bed. We were too

Chapter Twenty-three

exhausted to change, but the uncomfortable rub of my jeans and the pinch of my bra didn't bother me.

All I allowed myself to feel was Hunter's hands encircling my waist, drawing me closer to him. Despite the threats surrounding us, I found solace as my fingertips traced the contours of his arms, feeling incredibly small and protected within them. However, perhaps that was naive of me, having not yet experienced Beau's true depravity for myself.

Hours later, I sensed the mattress moving and stirred. As I rubbed my eyes and propped onto my elbows, Hunter crept towards the door.

"Hey," I yawned. "Leaving before dawn, hussy?"

He smiled and returned to the bed. "Sorry, H. I didn't want to wake you."

"Are Lols and Dom awake?" I asked.

Hunter brushed my hair from my eyes, one careful strand at a time. "Yeah, I heard the TV come on a little while ago."

I groaned, hiding my face with my hands. "God, I must be a mess."

"You're gorgeous. You might need a new top, though," Hunter chuckled, gesturing to my white T-shirt, its middle streaked with ashy smudges.

I half shrugged. "I never really liked this shirt anyway."

"Wait," he said. He prodded my stomach twice, adding more smudges and transforming them into a crooked smile. "How about now?"

I sighed. "Note to self, buy some black pyjamas."

"Or just no pyjamas at all?" Hunter winked. "I can buy you *plenty* of no pyjamas."

After an invigorating shower, I felt more alert. As I absentmindedly towel-dried my hair, I found Hunter perched on the lone remaining cushion of my sofa. Meanwhile, Lola and Dominic were hidden under the others, leisurely sipping their coffee. Like children at play, they had made a giant pillow fort shrouded in blankets.

A surprised laugh escaped me. "What are you, five? Let me guess, Lola's idea?"

Hunter slipped an arm around my waist. "Actually, it was Dom's, apparently."

"Dare I ask, why?" I asked.

Dominic shrugged as though it was entirely normal for two grown adults to watch TV in a pillow fort. "We just got talking about our families, and mine made them all the time," he said. "But growing up in a TB hospital,

Lola never had. Ergo... pillow fort. Didn't you guys make pillow forts when you were kids?"

"You can't exactly remove the cushions in a cinema," Hunter said. "And our sofa upstairs was just nasty."

"Ours were antiques," I added. "I think if I'd started creating pillow forts at Red Rock, Kay would've had to collect me even earlier."

Dominic enthusiastically patted the cushion beside him. "Then come on in. There's plenty of room."

For a fleeting moment, I hesitated, absently chewing my lip while absorbing the contagious smiles from Dominic and Lola, their faces seeming to illuminate the whole room.

I grinned as I clambered into the comforting embrace of the soft pillows. "What the hell."

Dominic peered out from behind a plush grey blanket. "Hunter?"

"Dude, I'm 6 "3"," Hunter answered. "I'll never fit."

"Add a cushion then. I've been thinking about having an extension built to this place." Dominic joked, glancing around at his creation.

Rolling his eyes playfully, Hunter smiled, adding the last pillow on the couch onto the floor. He squeezed in beside me, the blankets clinging to his head like he was some kind of human tent pole.

The imminent confrontation with The Handlers had weighed heavily on my mind, casting a shadow over the fledgling prospect of forging a new path independently.

This pivotal moment held the promise of a new order but also came with a steep cost. We were all aware that the Handlers would not willingly yield to Beau's demands despite the potential risks their resistance posed to the remaining Spirit Born families.

However, in the face of this impending storm, a brief interlude of immaturity provided a much-needed respite from the intensity of our circumstances.

It was alarming to witness Lola's resilience being extinguished as Beau exploited her grief to control her. I felt a great sense of relief upon seeing her radiant smile again, knowing that Dominic played a significant role in her recovery.

The pair had connected over the weekend, and his efforts to keep her mood light with banter and humour, despite the fear he must have felt for his family's safety, hadn't gone unnoticed.

Chapter Twenty-three

She would occasionally graze her hand along his arm or rest her head against his shoulder, subtly signalling an intimacy that left Hunter and me wondering whether something deeper was blossoming between them.

I wondered if they'd have the courage to challenge The Handlers' rule and develop their connection as we had been doing.

Her responses, occasionally grazing her hand along his arm or resting her head against his shoulder, left Hunter and me wondering whether something deeper was blossoming between them.

Around midday, the shrill ringing of our phones filled the air, a jarring indication that The Handlers had noticed our absence from Ettington. Despite the communication blackout we had implemented among the other Spirit Borns, it appeared to only amplify the sense of panic gripping The Handlers.

As Lola and Dominic slipped away to the archives, the ringing persisted. Meanwhile, Hunter and I kept busy washing and drying dishes side by side in silence.

It felt like they had been gone for hours when, in reality, only twenty minutes had passed before they reappeared.

Dominic dramatically flung a stack of eleven yellowing, dog-eared files onto the breakfast bar. He held Lola close, his arms wrapped around her delicate shoulder as veins of mascara marred her cheeks. I didn't need to speculate about whose file was missing.

Dominic's nostrils flared as he tore a tattered sheet of paper from the file on top, slamming it onto the countertop with such force that the plates and cutlery drying by the sink clattered against one another.

Dominic's lip curled, his eyes dark as he snarled, "They kept the damned letters. Beau's telling the truth."

Chapter Twenty-four

The atmosphere in the room was unusually subdued, considering the usual squabbling nature of the Spirit Borns as we awaited Lola's return with the Handlers.

Most of them sat fiddling with their hands or clothing, glancing apprehensively towards me, Hunter, Lola and Dominic, trying to deduce from our stoic expressions what evidence had been found to verify Beau's claims.

We were determined to expose the extent of corruption among The Handlers. Anticipating that they would likely attempt to deceive others, we devised a plan to initially request the truth from them and keep the incriminating files hidden until they became necessary.

We emphasised to everyone the importance of withholding responses to any questions until we had gathered every Handler.

Despite having a loosely outlined plan, when Lola vanished to retrieve the first Handler, nausea radiated through me like the heat of a fire. As sweat shimmered from my temples, the overhead lights flickered as my apprehension threatened to overcome my control.

Hunter's eyes found mine as he took an exaggerated breath and nodded. As I obediently followed his lead, I couldn't help but notice the subtle signs of strain on his face. Furrowed brows, tightly pressed lips, and intermittent moments of closed eyes revealed the effort he was exerting to either guide my talent or suppress it.

However, when the first handler arrived, the uneasy silence transformed into stifled laughter and averted eyes.

Gia's handler, Liz, appeared in her slippers, with soaking wet hair and a towel draped around her shoulders.

A look of indignation flashed in her eyes as she glared around the room, her cheeks flushing red as she cradled a large glass of red wine in one hand.

She wrenched her damp towel from her body and threw it onto the floor, a petulant gesture that did her no favours in being taken seriously. "What the hell is going on?" she demanded.

Chapter Twenty-four

We remained silent, but Liz could at least find solace in the fact that she wouldn't be counted among the most embarrassed Handlers that day.

A few were as impeccably dressed as always, Kay disappointingly included. However, most were in various stages of undress, arriving with half-finished makeup, their hair twisted into towels balanced atop their heads, or set into curlers.

Another who, judging by the mortified look on Dominic's face, was his Handler, arrived in little more than his underwear. Wearing brightly spotted boxers, he was kept warm by a fluffy pink bathrobe. However, I was left wondering whether that was Lola's idea of a twisted joke or if she had genuinely found him in such an unconventional ensemble.

Gradually, as the room filled, the inevitable ranting grew louder. The Handlers took turns bellowing at us despite Lola's instruction that their questions would only be addressed once all twelve had been gathered.

As Lola took her seat beside me, Liz stooped to pick up her towel, no doubt so she could throw it again later. "Have you lost your mind, Lola?" she snarled. "Is this some sort of prank?"

As some of the Handlers sought to cover their indecency by sitting behind the table, most of the clothed ones, Kay included, remained standing.

Her fists clenched as she circled us like a shark in bloodied seas, but without her insufferable heels, her imposing presence seemed somewhat diminished. Her bare feet merely pitter-pattered across the floor like a child in the kitchen at suppertime.

"I swear to God, that assignment better be finished, and I mean *every* last Ungrounded, or you're all in serious trouble," Kay snapped, pointing to us each viciously. As her accusatory finger settled on me, her features contorted into a nefarious scowl.

Hunter's enigmatic eyes were sullied with anger as he opened his mouth, but surprisingly, it was Beck's voice that broke the momentary silence.

"And what will you do to her, or any of us for that matter?" he said sharply. "We all have lives outside this hellhole, but we do this because it's our calling. But without us, you'd be *nothing*. So quit threatening her."

Despite the lingering sting of the hurtful remarks made by both him and Sawyer when I first arrived, I was grateful for the support. I nodded once towards him in thanks, the smile tugging at my lips conveying my appreciation.

"Why, of all people, are *you* suddenly defending her?" Kay scoffed. "You don't even like her."

"I don't have to like her to appreciate her power," Beck replied. "The way she just lit up Ettington last night was nothing short of incredible."

"So, she blew your cover. Is that why we're here?" Kay asked, her eyes narrowing at me accusingly. "What triggered her?"

Hunter sighed. "Beau. He turned up on the assignment."

Tom frowned, pulling his dressing gown tightly around himself, his lips turning almost blue." But... how? No one can master their talents around him."

"I've no clue," I shrugged. "It just...happened."

"That's impossible," Tom mumbled, glancing at the other Handlers.

Kay's chair scraped loudly against the stone floor as she took a seat and leaned in toward the table. "What happened *exactly*?" she inquired. "Was anyone hurt?"

"No, he was very civil. Very...informative," I answered, my tone detached. "He told me that The Handlers knew The Spirit Borns' families would be targeted first when he started his rampage. He insisted that his actions were solely as the result of your refusal to meet with him."

"We were horrified at the thought," Lola continued, her bottom lip trembling. "And wanted to ask, is it true?"

The Handlers shook their heads in perfect unison, their voices mixing in a nervous, disjointed babble of denial. Despite their attempts to appear composed, their wide-eyed expressions betrayed an undercurrent of panic. Their unblinking eyes stole uneasy glances at one another as their faces paled.

As Cameron reached across the table towards Lola, she recoiled from his touch, squeezing her eyes closed as she turned her face from him.

"We would never do such a thing," Cameron pleaded.

Lola's lips trembled, a silent sob escaping her as a single tear traced a delicate path down her cheek.

"Beau thrives on conflict," Kay asserted, her voice unwavering as she endeavoured to assert authority. "Harper, I know he's charming, but you don't understand what he's really like. You're only inflicting pain on the others by..."

Hunter slammed his fist onto the table as the lights flickered aggressively overhead. "Don't bloody put this on her!" he shouted. "And as she's

Chapter Twenty-four

the only person who might be able to stop him, you might want to show her some respect."

"We have two problems here," Dominic said. "The first is that Beau demanded that we cease all action against The Ungrounded, or the remaining Spirit Born families would fall. And the second, far graver issue, is that we believe you're lying."

"And you *believe* him?" Kay scoffed. "He wouldn't attack the remaining families after all this time."

Lola jerked her head back, her eyes blinking rapidly as her voice cut through the air like a blade. "Excuse me?" she snapped. "He's ungrounded all the others. Do you honestly think he has any issues with eliminating the final three?"

"He spared the final families because he *loved* you. You were his best friend," Kay said, gesturing towards Hunter with a smile that reeked of lies and manipulation. "His teacher," she continued, her gaze falling on Dominic. "And wherever Hannah is, she was his girlfriend."

"Talking of whom, you don't seem too bothered that your prize asset is missing," I remarked dryly. "Not one of you has mentioned her absence."

Her Handler, Sadie, answered, shivering as her soaking hair created a puddle at her feet. "She's safe. She requested a leave of absence."

I frowned, my features twisting into a look of scepticism. "Mid-assignment? Did she see him coming?"

"She can't see him," Sadie said, shaking her head. "And this is the first we've heard of Beau's reappearance."

Kay knitted her hands together atop the table. "So, you're all just quitting because he's turned up spouting lies?"

"You know it's too dangerous to stop passing on The Ungrounded," Tom added.

"He's left your families alone for two years," Kay said, her voice rising as she held up two fingers. "He won't attack them now. He's lying."

I raised my hand, unable to bear any more of her lies. "Fine, dig your own graves," I said. "Just remember, we gave you the opportunity to explain yourselves."

Lola disappeared from beside me and reappeared by the crackling fireplace, her face hidden behind the towering stack of files.

With purposeful strides, she navigated the circle, personally delivering each file before settling back into her seat. She set her own aside, turning her face from it as if repulsed by the sight of it.

The Handlers' eyes widened as they swallowed repeatedly, sweat gathering on their foreheads. In the moments of deathly silence that followed, each Spirit Born opened their files and read their letters as Hunter, Lola, Dominic, and I stared unflinchingly at our Handlers, our hands interlocked atop the table.

The faces of the other Spirit Borns grew ashen, their mouths hanging open as tears welled up in the corners of their eyes. Their hands, clutching Beau's dog-eared letters, shook visibly.

Sawyer's eyes snapped towards his handler, Tom, his narrowed eyes brimming with rage. "What the *hell* is this?"

"Jules, how could you?" Beck snarled, screwing the letter into a ball and throwing it at her.

Sawyer's fury reached a crescendo, and something in him snapped. His face flushed crimson as he lunged across the table at Tom.

As Tom instinctively recoiled into his chair, shielding his face with his hands, Beck immediately reacted. He wrapped his arms around Sawyer's shoulders, restraining him and whispering support into his ear.

Whatever was said soothed Sawyer enough to coax him back into his seat. Beck smoothed his hands over his hair and enveloped him in his embrace as Sawyer buried his face in his hands, sobbing.

You could see the pain in Aida's eyes as her voice quivered, growing louder and more agitated than her usual tone. "You watched me cry myself to sleep for months," she said.

Amy grabbed her file, straightened her overcoat, and purposefully headed for the door. With her head held high, she deliberately averted her eyes from the Handlers. "I'm out," she said, shaking her head. "I can't be a part of this anymore. You're not the people I thought you were."

Hunter stood, blocking Amy's path as he pressed his palms together and caught her gaze. "Doc, don't go. Stay... for us," he pleaded. "If we go after him, things could get bad. *Please*, we need you."

Amy glanced upward, her eyes glassy with tears she wouldn't let fall. She was a woman of little emotion, but even her surgically steady hands shook with the internal anguish that her stoic facade struggled to repress.

After a fleeting pause filled with unspoken emotions, Amy merely nodded and returned to her seat. She pulled a tissue from her pocket and handed it to Gia, who sat beside her, tears glistening in the firelight.

"So, we're going after him?" Sawyer sniffed, wiping his eyes with his fist.

Chapter Twenty-four

"We don't know yet. But respectfully..." I answered, raising my hands. "... you've already mourned the loss of your families. The pain you're feeling now isn't contempt for Beau; it's anger at The Handlers' deceit."

As a surge of raw emotions rippled through the group, some of the Spirit Borns found solace in tearful embraces. Meanwhile, others appeared shell-shocked, staring at their letters in an almost trance-like state.

Kay stood and fixed her eyes on Lola, slowly shaking her head as she paced the room. "You're the last person I thought would break our trust, rob our archives and incite a riot, Lola." Kay huffed, then turned toward me. "And you. Is this what you wanted, a total breakdown of command?"

"We wanted the *truth*," I snapped. "But we knew you'd never give it freely."

"But you... you don't know what he was like," Kay stuttered, steadying herself against the table. "We were..."

"Kaylin, don't," Liz interrupted, reaching for her hand. "There's no taking it back."

Kay released a trembling sigh. "We've no choice."

I'd never heard Kay's full name before; I'd always assumed it was nothing more than the three letters I'd grown to loathe, signifying the gravity of the situation.

As Kay took a deep breath, her gaze landed on the Spirit Borns. It was the first time she appeared genuinely sincere, with a hint of fear evident in her expression.

"We were terrified of Beau," Kay said. "We knew we couldn't give in to his demands, but it was The Handlers he truly hated. He'd already murdered Laura, and we feared what he'd do to us if we ever met with him."

"But you could have *told* us," Amy said. "We're not fools. We can all agree that The Ungrounded population can't be left unchecked, but by keeping it secret, you robbed us of our chance to say goodbye."

"It wasn't your decision to make alone," Lola added, her tone softening. "We should've just beaten him to the punch and sent our families to The Infinite ourselves, so they never would've had to become Ungroundeds in the first place. At least then, we'd still have our old groundings in one piece to remember them by. Beau would never have bothered destroying them if he knew his true target was already gone."

"I know I'd have preferred giving the flag one final salute beside my father, as opposed to what actually happened," Captain said.

"I could've passed on my mother in my arms, with her knowing who I was," Lola said, sobbing softly. "Rather than a vacant shell of a woman who couldn't remember her own name."

"And if we'd have taken back control that way, the other innocent spirits in our groundings wouldn't have been caught in the crossfire," Hunter said. "The patients in Lola's sanatorium...the kids at Sawyer's orphanage...the soldiers at Captain's barracks."

"Withholding such important information caused a ripple effect that could've been halted if you'd have just been honest with us," Lola said. "We'd have been devastated, of course, but we'd have understood."

The lights flickered, casting eerie shadows around the room as Hunter fought to steady his voice. "Instead, you went behind our backs, making decisions about *our* lives," he said.

Cameron reached towards Lola again, his fingers trembling. "I swear to you, Lola," he said. "We thought it was a trap. Laura had only been dead a few months, and it was still so fresh in our minds."

Hunter's Handler, Annie, cleared her throat, her voice hoarse. "After we cleared her hotel room, we were... traumatised," she said. "He even left us a message in blood on the countertop, like he was finger painting. 'Don't look for me'."

Hunter nodded solemnly. "I know. I was there, remember?"

"If you were that scared of him, why didn't you just let the police deal with him?" I asked.

"It's not that simple," Kay said, shaking her head. "Investigating Laura's murder would've led the police straight to us."

A deep frown creased my face as I shrugged. "Would that have been so terrible?"

"A group of young adults with no records...no family, with forged documents?" Kay replied. "You mentioned ripple effects? Well, his arrest would've made one, too. You'd *all* have been arrested and prosecuted. But we were so proud of how well you were all doing. Amy had just started her residency, Hunter's business was finally turning a profit, and Lola, you'd just conquered travelling overseas and were touring the world in your spare time. We didn't want to ruin it."

As much as I loathed the Handlers' deception and the repercussions their lies had spawned, the self-pitying remorse they each grappled with could not be feigned. Each Handler stirred at the mention of Laura's murder, hiding their faces so we couldn't see the extent of their grief.

Chapter Twenty-four

Their fear of Beau was incontestable. They had hidden from him to save themselves, but the price of their safety had been paid by The Spirit Borns and their families.

The Handlers had faced the same inconceivable decision that we had faced at Ettington: what was more important, the living or the dead. And we had made the same choice.

Despite uncovering the reasons behind the Handlers' secretive behaviour, we found ourselves at an impasse. Our opposing stances on how future assignments should be handled stood in the way of progress.

Having lost a friend to Beau's irrationality, the Handlers appeared unyielding in their refusal to negotiate. Meanwhile, the Spirit Borns were desperate that no further afterlives, including the remaining Spirit Born families, be lost.

"Even if we had called the police, Beau's exceptionally intelligent," Kay continued. "He'd have concocted a story or claimed it was an accident, which the evidence suggested could've been possible."

Around the table, a palpable sense of uncertainty hung in the air as everyone seemed unsure how to proceed.

"Ceasing action on The Ungrounded can't be a long-term solution," Kay said, chewing her lip.

"Then we could suggest a treaty allowing us to pass on dangerous Ungroundeds whilst keeping the warning strategy in place?" I suggested. "But whatever we decide, we'll need to meet with Beau to negotiate."

"Agreed," Lola nodded. "Hunter, he was your best friend, maybe…"

"That friend died with Laura," Hunter interrupted. "He'll never listen to me now."

"What about Harper?" Dominic shrugged. "He seemed pretty interested in her?"

"Absolutely not," Hunter refused, slicing his hand through the air. "He's *too* interested in her. If we send her, we might never get her back."

"Or she'll come back in pieces," Beck said.

Hunter frowned. "Dude, that's my girlfriend."

Beck's eyes widened, grinning as he pointed at Hunter. "I knew it."

Across the table, Kay's eyes narrowed into icy slits as she fixed her gaze on me and Hunter. Her jaw clenched with palpable tension, her lips pressed into a thin line, betraying the silent fury simmering within her.

"Look, Harper can use her talents around him, right?" Sawyer said. "Direct the same force you used on that rollercoaster at Beau and…"

"I'm not killing him," I interrupted sharply. "I'm not lowering myself to that."

Sawyer rolled his bloodshot eyes. "Fine, then just rough him up a little, and maybe he'll back off?"

"Or it could make things worse and put Harper in danger," Hunter interjected.

"What about Alfie?" I asked, my eyes fixed on Kay.

"What about him?" she replied stiffly, folding her arms.

"He's important, right?"

"How's a semi-grounded spirit going to help us?" Gia asked.

"I've no idea. Ask Kay," I said. "It's why my file's missing, isn't it? Because there's stuff about Alfie in it."

"It's missing because Alfie's assaults are still being documented," Kay said, her teeth grinding.

"When can I see it?"

"No," Kay answered slowly.

"Why not?" I asked. "Everyone else has read theirs."

"By *stealing* them. Those files aren't meant for you to read," Kay answered, her eyes hardening again, growing colder. "And our interest in Alfie is purely academic."

"He spent his afterlife protecting me, and now he's suffering," I pleaded. "He wouldn't want this for himself. If he's not needed for this fight, then let us pass him on."

"No!" Kay snapped, her eyes widening. "We forbid it."

I stood, slamming my palms onto the table, the sound echoing through the room as my eyes bore into Kay. My nostrils flared as the lighting struggled, and the only reason the table hadn't been littered with shattered glass was because of Hunter, concentrating hard on the other side of the table, his outstretched fingers glowing brightly.

"You *forbid* it?" I yelled.

Kay raised her hands pleadingly. "Think about your family," she said. "If he disappears, Sophia will only run off looking for him, and you know it. Just trust me on this."

"Trust you?" I scoffed. "You're joking, right?"

"Look, we're losing track of why we're here," Dominic intervened. "Gia's right, Alfie can't help, and whatever's going on with him, we've bigger fish to fry right now. We need to agree on who'll meet Beau."

Chapter Twenty-four

I sank back into my seat as Hunter raised his hand to volunteer, followed by Lola, Dominic and myself. However, as everyone else avoided our eyes, picking at knots in the table or rereading their letters, it was clear that nobody else was willing to step forward.

I understood. They each felt powerless against Beau, and the talents that filled them with an unwavering sense of capability and dominance were futile around him.

However, as I opened a discussion about a grading system for The Ungrounded, Dominic held up his phone, ushering silence.

"I've got a message from Hannah," he announced, clearing his throat. "It just says "Go home."."

Hunter checked his phone. "I've got one, too," he said. "Did everyone else get one?"

Everyone, save for The Handlers in their dressing gowns and towels, checked their phones, but nobody else had received the vague message.

"She must know something," Aida said, chewing her nails to the quick.

"Or she's with Beau, and they're trying to lure you away," Beck suggested.

"She didn't go through hell after he left just to run back to him," Gia snapped. "They're not together."

"Look, I agree with Aida," Sawyer nodded. "If Hannah says leave, we should listen."

"But we still have to come to an accord on future assignments," I said. "I think we agree that sending *every* Ungrounded to The Infinite is unethical, especially when we don't know the conditions there. I propose we create an agreement with Beau to only pass on Ungroundeds that have caused harm or who request it."

"But every Ungrounded is a ticking time bomb," Kay said. "They all end up hurting people eventually. They need handling before they reach that point."

I rolled my eyes. "That's like executing someone *before* they've murdered someone. Besides, you don't have a choice," I said, crossing my arms. "We categorically refuse to pass on random Ungroundeds. So don't waste your time creating files for them."

Lola's voice carried a tone of stern determination as she locked eyes with the Handlers. "You owe us this," she said. "You refused to save the other families, but you *will* help us protect the final three."

"And if it doesn't work, we'll admit we were wrong," I added. "Hunter, Dominic and Hannah will say their final goodbyes to their families, and we'll return to doing things your way."

"I'll try to track down Beau on social media to arrange a meeting, and we'll discuss it during Friday's briefing," Hunter said, standing. "But he's expecting us to be home by now. He told Harper he'd be watching, so we'd best take Hannah's advice and leave."

As Lola dropped off the soggy, shivering Handlers and the emotional Spirit Borns, Hunter and Dominic's phones chimed with a second text from Hannah. The message repeated the ominous words "Go home," making the wait for Lola to return feel endless.

She finally reappeared, catching her breath as she clutched the table for support. "Where to?"

"Maybe it's better we just stay together?" I shrugged.

Dominic winced, rubbing the kinks from his shoulders. "Does that mean I'm on the floor again?"

"I've got space for everyone at my house," Hunter suggested, and Dominic's eyes lit up immediately.

Hunter's three-story red brick townhouse exuded a rugged and contemporary charm that perfectly suited his persona.

The interior boasted open spaces where many of the walls had been knocked down, revealing exposed brickwork that complemented the vibrant colour scheme.

Hunter's pride in his home was evident as he eagerly offered me a tour, while Lola and Dominic settled on the sofa, playing video games and exchanging flirtatious banter.

The rooms Hunter frequented most had been fully renovated, a stark contrast to the unfinished halls, where exposed wires splayed from holes in the walls, and the bare floorboards were dusted with wood shavings.

In the lounge, the treated brickwork was complemented by teal walls. A collection of guitars adorned the walls, interspersed with photographs, memorabilia, and weathered road signs gathered from all corners of the globe.

One wall served as a captivating visual diary of his globe-trotting escapades with Lola. It showcased cheerful snapshots of him standing on

Chapter Twenty-four

the Great Wall of China, outside the magnificent Taj Mahal, in front of the iconic Sydney Opera House, and gazing at the breathtaking Golden Gate Bridge.

Finally, a set of comical photos depicted Hunter posing in some of the world's most restricted places.

I observed him perched precariously on the shoulder of the iconic Christ the Redeemer in Rio and resting his work boots on the presidential desk in the White House's Oval Office, grinning as he talked into the phone.

In another scene, he exuded regal confidence as he waved from a grand balcony at Buckingham Palace. Then, there was the surreal image of him inside Fort Knox, his eyes widening in awe as he held a heavy bar of gold. The photos continued on and on, each location more remarkable than the last.

As I ascended the stairs, I was met with his bedroom, spare rooms, office, and bathroom, all harmonising seamlessly with the house's overall style. In his bedroom was a bed so large I worried I'd get lost in it and have to ask for directions.

A room on the second floor caught my attention. It had been refurbished but sat vacant. The walls were painted in deep maroon with gold trim, save for one solid white wall. At first glance, the only furnishings I noticed were a spattering of random beanbags and pillows on the floor.

However, when we entered, I saw the movie projector beside stacks of old movie reels at the back of the room. It became apparent that it was a room just for Hunter, a unique sanctuary where he could immerse himself in cherished memories and feel connected to his family.

After the tour, we settled in the lounge, cuddling on the sofa as we watched Lola and Dominic flirting. Within minutes, the comfort of Hunter's embrace and the day's activities took their toll, and my eyes slowly fluttered closed.

It wasn't long until I was jolted awake by the shift of Hunter's body beneath me. He sat upright as Dominic handed him his phone.

"What is it?" I yawned.

Hunter frowned. "Hannah's messaged again."

"Saying what?"

"The same thing," Hunter answered.

"Has anyone replied?" I asked.

Dominic shrugged sheepishly as he glanced at Lola, his distraction. "I meant to," he said. "I just forgot."

Spirit Born

"I'll do it," Hunter nodded.

Hunter sent a speedy reply, his agile fingers skipping across the screen. But before he'd even set his phone down, there was another reply.

Hunter typed aloud. "We... are... home," he said, and set his phone on the mahogany coffee table.

"She's still missing, right?" Dominic said. "What if Beau's got her, and he's using her phone?"

"I don't think kidnapping's his style," Hunter answered.

"But murder is?" I said, raising one eyebrow.

"Fair point, but he loved her; he probably still does. He wouldn't do that to her," Hunter dismissed. "Besides, Sadie said she's taking a leave of absence."

"Like we can trust anything The Handlers say anymore," Lola said indignantly.

Hunter's phone chimed again, and after reading it, a low growl rumbled in his throat, his jaw tightening at the repetitive responses.

"Look, whatever this is, she's insistent," Lola nodded. "So, me, Harper and Dominic should just go home."

Dominic shrugged, trying to appear nonchalant, but his disappointment at being separated from Lola was evident in his expression. "It's not like we can relax when she's sending texts like that every five minutes anyway," he remarked.

"True," Hunter grumbled. "But let's stay in touch. And girls, you're in the same building; at least you can stick together."

We trudged wearily into the hall. Lola and I perched on the stairs, and Dominic leaned against the unfinished walls as we pulled on our shoes and prepared to leave.

However, as I laced my combat boots, Hunter paused. His tall frame stiffened, and his once relaxed features became taut as his gaze fixated on an invisible point in the distance.

"What is it?" I asked.

Hunter's breathing quickened, growing ragged as his jaw tightened and every muscle in his upper body quivered with tension.

"Hunter, what is it?" I repeated, trying to catch his gaze.

His hand drifted to his mouth, his fingertips trembling against his lips as he finally spoke, his tone low and filled with dread. "I... I think we're in the wrong home."

Chapter Twenty-five

Lola and I quickly sprang into action, grabbing the jackets and bags we had left scattered in the lounge. Meanwhile, the boys struggled to lace their shoes, tying their trembling fingers in knots as Dominic rambled in a voice several octaves higher than usual.

Despite his composed expression, every light within Hunter's expansive townhouse exuded a shimmering glow.

"But...Captain was watching," Dominic stuttered, desperately tugging Hunter's collar. "Nobody returned. Beau, he...he wouldn't do this, not to us. Would he?"

"I don't know," Hunter said, swallowing hard. "We've just got to move and hope Hannah's given us a decent head start."

"Why couldn't she just tell us straight?" Dominic snapped.

"You know she doesn't see things clearly," Hunter answered. "Especially with matters involving Beau."

"So, what's the plan?" Dominic asked, his eyes flitting restlessly. "Where do we go first?"

My eyes shifted between Hunter and Dominic. "Well, unless you boys fancy drawing straws," I said. "We have to split up."

"But, Harper," Dominic stammered. "You can... fight him."

"With lights?" I shrugged. "That's all I managed around him."

"The Handlers, then," Dominic said, fumbling his phone from his pocket and sending it clattering to the floor.

Hunter shook his head. "Beau despises them. If we bring them and he's there, it'll only aggravate him," he said. "Harper's right, we split up. Lola, get us to the cinema, then you and Dom head for his family's pub."

"I've only seen that cinema once," Lola said, biting her lip. "I'll never remember..."

"Then just get us as close as you can," Hunter interrupted. "We'll regroup later."

"What if he shows up?" Lola asked. "Dom and I could end up stuck in Ireland."

"Then escape on foot, and we'll find another way to get you home," I said. "And if he turns up at the cinema, we'll do the same."

We placed our hands on Lola's shoulder and reappeared in a narrow alleyway flanked by rows of quaint houses. Tangled bushes of thorns overflowed into the thin dirt path, penetrating our skin.

Hunter and Dominic exchanged a heartfelt embrace, each wishing the other luck. Moments later, Lola laid her hand on Dominic's shoulder, and they vanished.

"This way," Hunter said, grabbing my hand and pushing through the thorny underbrush. The adrenaline left him invulnerable to pain as thin trickles of blood ran down Hunter's arms, flashes of crimson between the snags of his shirt.

Once out of the alley, Hunter's head swivelled back and forth, scanning the surroundings. He pointed ahead and surged forward. Despite the challenge of keeping up with his long strides, I pushed myself to the limit, my lungs straining and my muscles burning.

We came upon a quaint high street bustling with pedestrians who seemed to regard suspiciously as Hunter impatiently shouted at them to clear a path. However, as the sidewalks became more crowded, he gave up. He bypassed the crowds by running down a bicycle lane, which offered a clear path except for the occasional cyclist gesturing angrily as we passed.

We had run a mile or so when Hunter stopped. His eyes flicked to each side of the street, then back the way we had come. As he ran both hands through his hair, his face paled. It had been years since he had broken the rules and visited his grounding, and his panicked expression hinted at a fear that we had made a wrong turn.

In the distance, I saw an old marquee extending over the street, which Hunter had overlooked.

I tapped him on the shoulder and pointed towards it. His frown disappeared, and his eyes widened as he started running again. The blaring of car horns served as a soundtrack to our mad dash across the bustling road. Finally, as we closed in on the building, we stumbled onto the pavement, manoeuvring through the sea of people once again.

The building was in an advanced state of disrepair, looming over the street like a crumbling sentry, forgotten by the scores of people passing it.

Chapter Twenty-five

It appeared faded, as if it were cast in black and white in a world that had moved on in Technicolor.

The presence of the building reassured me that we had beaten Beau there, but my mind grew foggy with possibilities of what we would do if he turned up. As we battled the crowds, edging closer to the old cinema, I abruptly collided with Hunter's back as he stopped dead in his tracks.

"What is it?" I asked.

Hunter remained silent, staring ahead, his face set like a stone into a look of torturous despair that I couldn't understand. We had almost reached the cinema, but his unblinking eyes had filled with tears as his body crumpled inwards, his height cowering several inches.

I had never seen him look so beaten down, and it terrified me. Despite my insistent questions, he didn't seem to hear me or even register that I was present.

I tried to pull his face towards mine, but his thick neck remained rigid, staring ahead in a trance. "Hunter, *talk to me*," I pleaded.

Slowly, Hunter raised a trembling hand toward the throngs of people passing around us as if we were rocks in a stream.

As my eyes followed his arm forward, he finally spoke. "It's my dad."

My eyes fell on a tall, middle-aged man wandering aimlessly. He had the same shade of sandy blonde hair as Hunter and hollow, darkened eyes. Instantly, my heart felt like it had been replaced with a brick.

He cut a striking figure in his impeccably tailored dark plaid suit and tie. He possessed the same ruggedly muscular build as his son but stood even taller.

Despite his imposing physical presence, his cautious and bird-like movements overshadowed his strapping appearance. He kept his hands buried in his pockets, and his shoulders appeared tense, drawn up around his neck. His eyes darted back and forth, flinching at things only he could see as he shuffled down the street.

Feeling the eyes of every passing stranger weighing on me, it was an awful place to be confronted with such a tragedy. Even though his father wouldn't understand, at least I could convey some sort of goodbye to alleviate Hunter's grief.

I looked around for a more secluded area and spotted an alley running alongside and behind the cinema. I approached Hunter's father, praying he would follow us.

Hunter raised his hand, sniffing. "Please... don't touch him. Not yet."

"I won't."

I turned to Hunter's father, ignoring the judgemental looks of members of the public, baffled by the strange couple talking into space. "Sir?" I said.

The eyes of several males passing by shot towards me.

"Sorry, not you," I said as they stared confusedly.

Hunter's voice trembled. "James. His name is James."

"James?" I said.

His eyes met mine, blinking as he swallowed and nodded.

"Yes, James," I nodded. "We need to talk to you. Will you come with us? It's a little loud here."

James frowned; the confusion evident on his face. "Is it?" he asked. "I've only seen you two. What's happening?"

"Come with us," I said. "We'll explain everything."

As I kept my gaze fixed on James, I stepped backwards through the bustling crowd, gently beckoning him to follow while Hunter lagged behind, struggling to steady his breathing.

As we entered the alley, the cinema's marquee flickered to life for the first time in almost a hundred years while the lights from neighbouring businesses dimmed.

With persistent encouragement, he followed my voice until we reached a quieter area away from the sounds of traffic and pedestrians. Ignoring the musty smells hanging in the air and the faint echoes of dripping water, we walked past graffiti-covered walls and overflowing bins until we arrived at the cinema's damp, dimly lit storage area.

As Hunter took a seat on the steps of a boarded-up back door, holding his head in his hands, we noticed that a small excavator or other heavy-duty vehicle had ravaged the rear corner of the cinema.

A thick crack extended from the pavement to the roof, severing the precious foundations, and piles of sodden, crumbling bricks were scattered around us.

Hunter cleared his throat as he nodded to the damage. "Beau emptied Captain's barracks the same way," he said. "He does that for buildings he... *appreciates.*"

I had no clue how Beau had found out we'd stayed at Ettington. We hadn't encountered any of his miscreants inside, and Captain had diligently guarded the property. However, those questions would be answered later. Right now, my focus had to remain solely on easing Hunter and his father's pain.

Chapter Twenty-five

"I want to be the one to do it, okay?" Hunter said.

I nodded, holding up my hands. "Of course. I'll just translate."

Hunter stood, swiping away tears and leaving streaks of shimmering black on his cheeks as he carefully edged toward his father. James eyed us cautiously, his behaviour childlike.

"Dad, it's me, Hunter. Your son, remember?"

"He's come to visit you," I added, squeezing Hunter's shoulder.

James frowned. "You're not my father."

"He's confused," I said, shaking my head. "He said you're not his father."

Hunter sighed, his bottom lip trembling. "This is pointless."

"He followed us down here, didn't he?" I said, turning back to James. "*This* is your son. See...he looks just like you."

"No, my boy's... dead. But... then he wasn't," James mumbled.

As I echoed his father's words, I observed a faint flicker of optimism illuminating Hunter's fatigued and burdened eyes.

"It's hard to explain, but we were sort of... in heaven," Hunter said.

James hung his head. "And I ruined it?"

"You could never ruin it. Someone else did," I answered. "And your son left to help people. You'd be so proud."

James sighed. "I went looking for an Angel. But she left me."

"There aren't any angels here, just us," I said, smiling sympathetically.

"Wait... he said that word? He said, 'Angel'?" Hunter frowned, focusing intensely on James. "That's what he used to call my mother."

"He said she left him," I said.

Hunter shook his head vehemently. "She'd never leave you," he said. "She's just... lost too."

"Why can I only see you two?" James asked.

I smiled. "We're special."

James chewed his lip, glancing down the alley. "I should get back. My parents will have dinner waiting," he said.

"Your parents died a long time ago," I said softly.

"Then, if you're not the police to bring me home, who are you?" James said, pacing erratically.

"He thinks we're the police," I repeated.

"I shouldn't have run away," James sobbed.

Seeing James's stress rising, I knew we didn't have long. "Hunter, he's confused," I said. "I don't know how long we can keep him here."

Hunter stepped forward, trying to catch James' flitting gaze. "Dad, listen. We can send you to The Infinite if that's what you want," he said.

"I can't. I must look after the... the..." James closed his eyes, clicking his fingers.

"The cinema?" I asked.

"No, the little girl," James answered.

"Hazel?" I frowned.

"But I can't find her. I can't find anyone," James said, tears pooling in his eyes. "I'm lost."

He reminded me of an exhausted Alzheimer's patient, trying to grasp onto fading memories like smoke slipping through his fingers. When I recounted James' words to Hunter, it stirred a powerful emotional response in him, manifesting in his demeanour and expression.

"You're not alone, Dad, I'm here." Hunter's trembling, clammy hand squeezed mine. "We're here."

James started pacing and wringing his hands. "I... I don't...have it," he stuttered. "Please, don't hurt them."

"He says he doesn't have it." I leaned towards Hunter and whispered in his ear. "Do you think he's remembering his death?"

"I've no idea. He was my guardian. When I left, he knew everything." Hunter shrugged, turning back to his father. "Dad, where's Mum and Hazel? Have you seen them?"

The evening had crept in, painting the alley with eerie shadows cast by the warm glow of the orange streetlights. Despite our efforts to keep James on track and uncover the whereabouts of Hunter's mother and sister, his disorientation grew with each passing question.

We knew gaining any actionable intelligence from him was highly improbable, but beside me, as the embers of James' soul died out, Hunter's composure began to crumble.

"Angel? Are you the angel sent to collect me?" James stuttered. "An Angel of death?"

"No, James," I sighed. "We're..."

"I knew a James once," he interrupted, stepping dangerously close to us as his pacing grew more unpredictable. "I should go home."

"James, wait. Please," I begged.

"I knew a James once," he repeated, shifting his weight from foot to foot.

I stepped before Hunter, my fingers tracing delicate paths along his jaw. "Hunter, I'm so sorry," I soothed. "But it's time."

Chapter Twenty-five

Hunter nodded, sniffing loudly. His tears parted the smudges on his face, resembling rivers, as his usually relaxed stance shook violently.

Hunter approached his father, and I could hear his laboured breathing. The alley's lights, cut off from the electrical grid decades ago, flooded the small space with light. As aged, tired circuits struggled, bulbs exploded, showering us with sparks as the tips of Hunter's fingers started to glow.

"Dad, look at the light," Hunter said firmly. "Imagine it filling your body and making you whole again."

James obeyed his request, staring at the lights, then Hunter's hands.

"Now look at me," Hunter directed, but James' eyes were still fixed on the lights, mesmerised.

"Dad, please," Hunter said, his voice breaking. *"Look at me."*

James finally found his son's eyes and remained focused on them.

"Don't feel guilty about what happened," Hunter said. "You were an incredible husband and an even better father."

I gazed upward, tears blurring my vision as I struggled to maintain composure, biting down hard on my quivering lip. When I returned my focus to James, his restlessness had settled, almost as if his soul had found a safe harbour amidst the chaotic tempest.

His shuffling had ceased, and his back had straightened, increasing his height several inches. The creases of tension on his face gradually faded, giving way to a subtle smile that played on his lips as a spark of life returned to his eyes. The vibrant green hue that resonated in Hunter's eyes seemed to unfold and flourish within James'.

James smiled down at Hunter. "I'm ready, son," he said, his voice even, confident.

"He... he knows you," I said, cupping my mouth with both hands. "He says he's ready."

"It happens sometimes with new or powerful Ungroundeds," Hunter said. "At their last moment, they remember."

James cocking his head, his penetrative gaze fixed on his son. "Do me a favour, though," he said. "Find the girls and send them my way."

"He can't hear you," I said, almost sheepishly.

"But you can?" James' eyes narrowed. "Could you pass on the message then, Miss...?"

"Reynolds-Woodbury, Harper Reynolds-Woodbury. I'm Hunter's..."

I hesitated. The word "boyfriend" seemed adolescent. It didn't seem significant enough for the bond we shared. "I'm just... Hunter's."

A warm smile creased James' eyes. "And he's yours, I presume, Miss Reynolds-Woodbury?"

"I hope so." I sighed, glancing towards him. "Because honestly, I don't know where I'd be without him."

"That sounds like Hunter," James said. "Even as a boy, he always carried the weight of the world on his shoulders. But it brings me peace knowing you'll be around to share the load. Forgive me for not shaking your hand, Harper, but I'd like my last moment to be with my son."

James approached Hunter, locking eyes with him. Slowly and deliberately, he mouthed the words "I love you".

James grasped him by the elbows, leaned forward and pressed his forehead against Hunter's. At that moment, I realised that the gesture had never been solely ours but something that Hunter had opened his heart and shared with me. As Hunter struggled to contain his emotions, James enveloped him in an embrace.

The lights in the alley drained like someone was turning a dimmer switch, and James' body filled with the light that had flooded the small space.

As I shielded my eyes from the glare, echoes of James' voice resonated through the air. Among them, I caught fragments of what seemed to be his final moments as he pleaded for his family's safety. Yet, amidst the sadness, there was overwhelming joy, laughter and the excited squeals of children, interspersed with declarations of love.

As the brilliant light waned, James's ethereal form gradually dissipated into nothingness. Hunter found himself cradling empty air as he crumpled to his knees and wept.

I knelt down, feeling the damp tarmac instantly soak through my jeans as I cradled him in my arms.

Despite his height and mass, he was as limp as a rag doll. I guided him onto his feet, then to the steps at the back of the cinema. I could've been leading him through the seven circles of hell, and he wouldn't have noticed or even looked up. He was lost in a maelstrom of sorrow, and I hadn't a hope of reaching him until he'd expelled some of it from his system.

I sat him down, and he folded his arms across his chest, drawing his knees up and burying his face in them. As he sobbed, I rested my head on his shoulder, my arm wrapped around him, patiently waiting until he had found the strength to speak or move.

Chapter Twenty-five

I remained silent, but inside, my heart was ablaze with a hatred so all-encompassing that its embers scorched every inch of me. I had endured conflicts with people in my new life before, but this was unlike anything I had felt before.

It felt dark and insidious. I knew that if I let it in, even for just a moment, it would take me over entirely. But despite its malevolence, it also ignited a sense of strength and empowerment, fuelling my desire for vengeance against Beau for his unforgivable deeds.

As Hunter wept, brilliant forks of lightning split the starry sky, momentarily illuminating the shadowy alley. The rapid succession of thunder suggested the storm was close, but not a single drop of rain fell. Despite Hunter's strange, innate fear of lighting he still didn't look up or even flinch.

I was unsure how long we were sat there, but it was long enough for the cloudless electrical storm to pass. Eventually, Hunter's rocking ceased, but he remained silent and eerily still, staring at a spot on the ground that his eyes refused to shift from. He was utterly unreachable.

When my phone started to ring, and Lola's name illuminated the screen, I let out a relieved sigh, hoping that she could help me get him home safely.

"It's Lola," I said softly. I squeezed Hunter's hand before stepping away and answering. "Hey, are you guys alright?"

"Hey," Lola answered, but her voice was uncharacteristically flat. "Did you make it?"

"No. You?"

Lola sighed. "Same. How's Hunter?"

"He's so still it's scaring me," I whispered. "We found his father wandering the streets."

"Jesus," Lola breathed softly. "Poor Hunter."

"How's Dom?"

"Devastated. His family's pub was on fire, so the street was cordoned off." Lola said. "I tried getting us closer, but with police everywhere, we didn't get far."

"Where's Dom now?" I asked.

"He's here," Lola replied. "I'm taking him back to my place. He shouldn't be alone right now in the state he's in. He'll only end up going after Beau and getting himself killed."

"I'll bring Hunter home as well. They'll need each other," I said. "Have you tried Hannah?"

"No answer. I left a voicemail."

"I don't understand. We were so careful," I said, my brows furrowing. "Do you think Beau's infiltrated The Spirit Borns or something?"

"You didn't get a note?"

"A note?" I said. "No."

Hunter overheard my reply and stirred, staring at me disconcertedly.

"There were these flyers scattered everywhere in the street," Lola said. "You didn't see any?"

"I'm not sure. We were sort of preoccupied with Hunter's dad," I answered.

"Look, we're on our way, but it'll take us a little while to find the cinema," Lola said. "So, while you're waiting, look."

Before I could ask what was on the flyers, Lola abruptly ended the call.

I turned to Hunter and gingerly outstretched my hand. "Lola's coming, but they found a note," I explained, searching his vacant eyes. "I'm going to have a look around. Do you want to come?"

He stood in silence as he took my hand, his grip feeble and almost lifeless in mine. I guided him towards the street, the sound of his shuffling feet reverberating against the alley's walls strewn with rubbish.

As Hunter remained eerily still, I gingerly sifted through the soggy sheets of paper clinging to the damp concrete, remnants of countless businesses and advertisers. However, the only sign of Beau's visit was the colossal crack that had left a jagged scar on the back of the building.

Having rubbed all manner of muck onto my jeans, we reached the front of the cinema and found the entrance barred by thick, rusting chains looped around the door handles, rendering entry impossible.

I wiped a small square of glass on the grimy front doors clean, and peered inside. The place was in ruins. The ceilings were collapsing, peppering the once-decorative counter with splintered wood and chunks of grey plaster. Even the floor was surrendering to decay, with the faded red carpet bearing deep tears resembling wounds.

Among the disarray, I could just about identify the shattered glass box that had once held popcorn, standing beside a bronze mechanical till. Against the counter leaned the large, black letters that had previously spelt out picture titles on the marquee, but there was no message from Beau anywhere.

My only comfort came when Lola arrived, with Dominic trailing behind her, clutching an enormous bottle of Irish whiskey.

Chapter Twenty-five

Upon seeing their arrival, Hunter released my hand and stormed towards Dominic, enveloping him in an emotional embrace as the whiskey sloshed over them both. They offered no words of consolation but merely clung to one another as if they were saving themselves from drowning.

Lola let out a weary sigh as she wrapped her arms around me. "So, you got one too," she said.

"No, I looked everywhere."

"What?" she frowned. "No, look, you're just too close to see it."

Lola dragged me towards the curb and guided my gaze back towards the cinema.

Written on the marquee, as if it were the latest movie title, was Beau's message. Scrawled in thick black paint, dribbling downwards in places, were the words, "Who did you think was in room 102?"

Chapter Twenty-Six

Back home, the boys sat on the sofa, passing Dominic's whiskey bottle back and forth in silence, their gazes fixed on the floor. As Lola gathered their overnight essentials, I struggled with a sense of helplessness. I busied myself preparing cups of tea that went cold and sandwiches that remained untouched, the bread slowly crisping on my new plates.

Lola, however, having endured it all before, was well-practised in the art of nursing grief. She knew exactly what to do in a routine that had become, tragically, routine, her quiet efficiency a stark contrast to the tense stillness surrounding her.

Lola fetched glasses for the boys' drinks and pulled out a bottle of sleeping pills. Gently, she overturned their hands and rattled the medication into their palms before handing them their glasses of whiskey to wash them down with. But the quietness of it all felt unnatural. Our foursome had quickly grown close, and for half of our little group to be rendered incapacitated felt traumatising.

Once the whisky bottle was almost empty, Lola and I helped them both to bed. First, we draped Dominic's heavily inebriated arms around our shoulders and transported him to Lola's flat. After helping him change into a fresh T-shirt and tracksuit bottoms, we tucked him into bed.

I lingered in the doorway while Lola knelt by his bedside, gently stroking his tousled hair, and the gesture seemed to stir something within him.

He finally looked directly at her, catching her coffee-coloured eyes with his. A sympathetic smile graced her face as she leaned forward, kissing him softly on the lips. It was no more than a peck, but it felt as intimate as any moment I had shared with Hunter, leaving the faintest smile on Dominic's face as Lola quietly closed the door.

We repeated the process with Hunter before I, too, kissed him goodnight. However, Hunter seemed consumed by his grief, and no amount of endearment could rouse his senses.

Chapter Twenty-Six

He rolled over slowly, curling his body into a foetal position, his back turned away from me. I struggled to maintain my composure but couldn't contain the overwhelming flood of emotions. I sniffled loudly, desperately trying to stifle my sobs while the lighting struggled.

Lola's arm enveloped me, drawing me away gently as she closed my bedroom door behind us. She guided me to the sofa, a deep sigh escaping her as she refilled the glasses with the remaining whiskey and passed one to me.

"Should they have taken those pills after drinking?" I asked.

"Probably not," Lola shrugged. "It just kind of became the procedure when everyone else's families were ungrounded. Besides, they need the rest."

I grimaced as I sipped my whiskey. "So, what now?"

"They can't work tomorrow, and we shouldn't leave them alone," Lola said. "When their tears are spent, the rage will kick in, and they'll only get themselves hurt going after Beau before we're ready."

"Sasha and Lucie are on annual leave tomorrow. I can't call in sick; they'd kill me."

Lola squeezed my hand. "It's fine. I'm working from home tomorrow. I'll watch them," she said.

"Thanks." I rested my head on her shoulder. "I just feel so helpless. Hunter wouldn't even look at me."

"It's nothing you've done," Lola soothed. "I just think he's got it worse than Dominic."

"Why was Dom not close to his family?"

"No, he was. Incredibly so," Lola said, nodding. "But knowing Hunter, he'll be feeling guilty, too. Dominic didn't want to risk it, but Hunter still made the call to stay and finish the assignment. We should've known better."

"What'll happen with Beau now?" I asked.

"He'll probably return to trying to overwhelm us by creating more assignments. But now he's got nothing to bribe us with anymore, so how do you stop a man with nothing to lose?" Lola said, resting her chin in her hands.

As I turned toward my bedroom, I could almost visualise Hunter's pain seeping through the walls, thickening the air with an almost tangible sorrow. Beau had hurt people I loved in some mindless, bitter vendetta, leaving me feeling adrift and unsure how to help. At that moment, I could feel the very foundation of my beliefs tremble as something inside me snapped.

I knew if we left Beau to slither off into the shadows, we would never be free of him. He would always linger in the back of our minds, leaving us continually looking over our shoulders, fearing the inevitable return of the man we could never see coming.

Beau had to go. As rage blossomed within me, I accepted the fact it had to be me who would deliver him his fate. Nobody else had a hope of confronting him and getting out of it alive.

"We kill him," I said, each syllable resonating with the unwavering strength of my conviction.

"I know, right," Lola said, throttling an imaginary victim. "If I ever got my hands on him, I'd..."

"No," I interrupted flatly. "I mean it."

"You can't be serious?"

"I'm deadly serious," I nodded. "Beau has to die."

By the time I left for work, Hunter was still asleep, and when my knock on Lola's door went unanswered, I assumed she and Dominic were too. That or she was avoiding me, praying I'd called for Beau's death in a fit of anger.

As I headed for the train, my head reeled with all the atrocities I longed to enact on Beau. Witnessing firsthand how his reign of terror had affected the people I cared about had bent a part of my morality that would not be unbent.

My helplessness became fuel for the merciless retribution I longed to rain down upon him, my desolation evolving into anger and from anger into empowerment.

Finally, I believed Hunter's declaration that dealing with Beau was what I'd been brought back to do. It was the reason my talents were so extreme. So that I, The Thirteenth, would be strong enough to eliminate the abomination that had come before me.

As my train sped and suddenly slowed, the brakes squeezed the rail and sprayed sparks across the tracks, jolting startled passengers back and forth. I imagined the frantic driver at the helm, trying to keep control as the splintered scarring on my arms glowed beneath my leather jacket.

Chapter Twenty-Six

My talent felt potent yet controlled. My resilience had unlocked a higher level of my skill set, letting me toy with the train as if it had come from a box on Christmas morning.

I glanced at the lights overhead and dabbled with them, flicking them on and off while opening interior doors. Only when I saw the passengers' mounting unease over the functionality of their defective train did I relax and let it be.

I was still grappling with the concept of generating energy from nothing rather than tapping into existing sources, but it was my responsibility to discover that myself. I had to find my core and unlock my true potential alone, but for now, I hoped I was strong enough to eradicate Beau.

I would fight on behalf of every Spirit Born, avenging the loss of their families. I would become their arrow, their hangman, the tip of their spear.

Jumping onto the platform at my stop, I was met with an intense heat radiating from the train's glowing axles, a result of my self-administered test of strength. Although I felt a slight pang of guilt for the driver, leaning out of his cab and scratching his head, I couldn't help but feel a sense of accomplishment at my growing aptitude.

I approached Red Rock and pulled the keys from my pocket. Alfie was nowhere to be seen, and I couldn't feel his eyes on me anymore, leaving me with a niggling sense of unease.

With no reservations or guests to attend to, I saw an opportunity to delve into Alfie's violent outbursts. I lifted the leather-bound accident log onto the polished front desk, the heavy thud resonating through the empty house.

The first few were nothing out of the ordinary, just bumps and bruises. However, once I had started working at Red Rock, accidents and near misses quickly became a regular occurrence, but only for Holly.

The incidents escalated until her final fall on the servant's stairs that landed her in hospital, all because, in Alfie's unhinged state, he had thought she was me.

Having seen reports of what he had been doing to her, I had to see it for myself. I stormed to Alfie's room to view the CCTV of the accidents on Lucie's computer.

I pulled up the footage of Holly's accidents. The first few had potential explanations; she could've been overbalanced or overloaded with cleaning supplies. However, every accident was preceded by her sudden apprehension as she scanned empty rooms and halls as if she'd seen or heard something.

As the number of accidents grew and their severity escalated, the fear etched on her face, and the palpable tension in her body intensified. Wherever she went, she seemed to be followed by light anomalies or wisps of pale smoke similar to those I had witnessed at Ettington.

The later accidents, however, became entirely inexplicable. Holly was pushed or pulled from steps and shoved from chairs as she sat quietly, taking a break.

In one clip, as she dusted bookshelves in the library, her French braid was seen floating freely as if lifted by an invisible string before her head was jarred violently backwards, and she was pulled off balance.

After several weeks, the incidents had become a nightly occurrence, each more incomprehensible than the last, until her final fall.

Holly had paused at the top of the servants' stairs, which ran the height of the house, with small landings on each floor. She was catching her breath, wiping her brow as she heaved a large vacuum cleaner to the top floor when her mood shifted.

Her body became rigid, gripping the hose tightly as she glanced down the empty corridor. She dropped the vacuum cleaner on the top landing and raised her hands to protect her face.

It was over in an instant. Holly was on the landing one second, and the next, she'd been launched several feet into the air, tumbling down the stairs with a piercing scream that made the hairs on my arms stand erect.

Any ordinary person may have attempted to convince themselves that it was just a bizarre accident. However, the presence of the vacuum cleaner, resting securely on the landing far from the edge, made that implausible.

Within moments, it was catapulted into the air, making a series of clattering noises as it careened down the stairs before striking Holly with a resounding thud that made me flinch.

A large orb of light streaked away from the scene, disappearing into the shadows. Meanwhile, Holly lay there, contorting in agony, virtually immobilised until she was found the following morning.

With Sasha or Lucie on leave and the house empty, I had the freedom to search for Alfie and question him myself. But my search upstairs remained fruitless, my markers only appearing outside my family's and Annabelle's bedrooms and near the centuries-old sleeping spirits I'd yet to meet.

As I turned my attention downstairs, I felt desperation bloom within me. "Alfie," I begged. "Alfie, get out here."

Chapter Twenty-Six

As I searched every inch of the ground floor, my aggravation evolved into concern. I feared that if Alfie wasn't in the house, he'd wandered off again or that the Handlers had finally had enough of the brutality he'd wrought upon defenceless Holly and had exiled him to The Infinite before I could say goodbye.

As I got home, the aroma of a simmering Bolognese sauce filled the air. Standing in the kitchen, Hunter swayed slightly as he stirred the sauce with a wooden spoon, his movements almost rhythmic.

Without turning to look at me, he handed me a glass of wine. Meanwhile, Dominic sat at the breakfast bar, swigging a bottle of beer.

While Hunter didn't speak or make eye contact with me, seeing him on his feet and not curled up in a ball helped me overlook the abundance of empty bottles littering my flat and the strong smell of alcohol emanating from him and Dominic.

By the tone of the room, Lola had clearly kept my dark intentions about Beau to herself. Not that I had any semblance of a plan or even knew whether I was strong enough yet to punch a hole in his considerable armour.

Regardless, it wasn't the time yet for suggestions of vengeance. Lola was resolute in her belief that Beau was too dangerous to be confronted and doing so behind her back and without Hunter and Dominic's involvement seemed underhanded.

At dinner, Lola nagged Hunter to stop poking food around his plate, swearing that we wouldn't allow him any more alcohol unless he ate something like a parent refusing a child dessert. However, Hunter remained silent, his body rigid and unmoving, even as the conversation inevitably shifted to Alfie.

"It explains a lot," Dominic nodded, his voice lacking its usual vibrancy. "He can't touch you, so he's attacked the closest thing."

I shrugged, absentmindedly twirling spaghetti onto my fork. "But Alfie's never been violent before."

"He's unstable, though," Lola said. "If he hadn't left Red Rock, none of this would've happened."

Beside me, Hunter's jaw tightened as he squeezed his eyes closed. He was already burdened with enough self-inflicted guilt to be reminded that Alfie had only drunkenly left Red Rock because of Hunter's developing relationship with me.

"I just don't understand how he's gotten so powerful so fast," Dominic said. "I thought it took centuries for Informeds to be able to see and interact with the living like that."

"Duh," Lola replied, nodding towards me. "He's got a paranormal battery."

"Fair point," Dominic said. "So where is he then?"

The room fell into a hush, accentuating the weight of Lola and Dominic's expectant gazes as they awaited my response. Meanwhile, Hunter's unwavering focus on his plate continued, his vacant stare fixated on the food in front of him, almost as if he were purposefully tuning out the conversation swirling around him.

I had no answer to their questions. I had scoured the entire house, but the gnawing ache in my gut that told me that something had happened to Alfie was only growing.

Whenever I grappled with unanswerable questions or doubts about myself that kept me up at night, Hunter was the person I turned to. However, his own inner torment, consumed by guilt and grief, left him unable to offer me the guidance I needed.

"I've no idea," I replied shakily. "Alfie's... gone."

Chapter Twenty-seven

After a few days off work, most of which they spent in various states of drunkenness, the boys gradually returned to their old routines.

Hunter had overdue contracts that needed to be completed, and Dominic's music students had a string of exams imminent, so returning to work was crucial, for their own benefit too.

While the reclusive sanctuary Lola and I had created offered them support, it also afforded them ample time to dwell on the events that had transpired, to replay the scenarios in their minds, and to envision alternative outcomes, none of which did them any good.

After they returned to work, the atmosphere slowly began to feel normal again. Although subdued, Hunter's attentiveness and warmth gradually returned, as did Dominic and Lola's playful flirting.

At work, I would search for Alfie whenever I had the chance, often rummaging through attics and cellars on my breaks. I'd return frustrated, picking cobwebs from my hair or scrubbing the cellar's red stains from my boots.

At home, nightly discussions continued about his whereabouts and how someone so supposedly crucial to our cause could be allowed to just disappear.

I found myself completely absorbed in helping Hunter and searching for Alfie, and before I knew it, the weekend had snuck up on me once again.

As I dumped my bag on my bed at the Fort, my stomach churned with unease. Now that the dust had settled, we had no idea how The Handlers would treat us after we had raided their archives.

The uncertainty hung thick in the air, and we grappled with the uncomfortable truth that, despite our animosity towards them, we needed them.

We had little hope of compiling all the evidence required for each case while juggling the demands of our personal lives. And not a single Spirit Born envied the Handler's lifestyle, living out of suitcases with nowhere to call home. Some sort of middle ground had to be found.

Spirit Born

However, now that the remaining Spirit Born families had fallen, we were no longer under Beau's knife. We were free to develop a new approach at our own pace. However, we were uncertain how the Spirit Borns would wield their newfound authority or if The Handlers would be willing to relinquish any of their own.

The ambient lighting in the hall remained constant, casting a soft, reassuring glow. At that moment, a profound sense of pride and accomplishment washed over me.

The only unexpected flare threatening to break my equilibrium occurred when Hunter's eyes met mine in the briefing room. He beckoned me to the seat sandwiched between him and Lola while Dominic took his place beside her.

The others had followed suit, ignoring the Handler's previous segregation of the sexes. Amy sat between Sawyer and Beck, Theon chatted quietly with Aida, and Captain sat uneasily with the remaining girls. However, when Hunter cleared his throat, the Handlers' frowns and wrinkled noses made it clear that they despised the new seating arrangement.

"Before we start, let's get something out of the way, something most of you already know," Hunter said, his tone informative as he reached for my hand. "Harper and I are together. And we propose..."

"Proposing already?" Beck teased gently, winking.

"We *propose*," Hunter repeated flatly, "that the rules regarding relationships between Spirit Borns be abolished. Harper and I are going to be together, rules be damned, and I think The Handlers know that. But if others wish to do the same, they shouldn't fear reprisal."

Lola and Dominic locked eyes, a gentle warmth spreading across their faces as a subtle smile formed at the edges of their lips. It was a private exchange, a wordless acknowledgement of their unspoken bond, visible only to those who were attentively watching.

"In that case, Amy?" Sawyer pointed at her, winking and clicking his tongue. Amy, however, merely gagged.

"And I know a few of you have already heard." I sensed Hunter's unease as he looked down and brushed the ash from his fingertips, knowing what I was about to say. "But the Spirit Born families Beau threatened have fallen."

Gia's frown was immediate. "How?"

"The people in room 102 were with Beau," I replied. "Beau left them notes saying so. As soon as we went to that room, it was all over."

Chapter Twenty-seven

Beck slowly shook his head, his eyes filling with compassion. "Sorry, man. I wouldn't wish that on my worst enemy."

"Hannah's text meant their groundings, their original homes," Lola said.

Aida glanced at the only empty seat in the room. "So where is she?"

"When she received Lola's voicemail, she went straight to her grounding in the south of France," Sadie said.

"Hannah's family is gone too?" I asked.

Sadie nodded. "She's taking some time to visit the area before she returns," she said.

"And we're to believe anything you say?" Sawyer snarled, his lip curling.

I rolled my eyes. "Don't start already. We need to work together somehow. That being said, we'll need some things from The Handlers if you want our trust again."

"I suggest if anyone has any reasonable requests for how we run future assignments, ask now," Hunter added. "You might never get another chance."

Captain raised his hand. "I recommend we choose our own teams," he said. "We know our strengths and weaknesses and who works well together."

Kay exhaled sharply, pursing her lips, her voice flat. "Fine. Anything else?"

"Complete transparency regarding research," Amy said.

"And the right to refuse assignments if we...," I paused. "..*disagree* with your judgement."

"But where do we stand on The Ungrounded?" Kay asked, her eyes unsettled as she cast her gaze around the circle.

"We've no reason to pander to Beau's blackmail anymore, but it's clear that most of The Ungrounded are innocent. Needlessly sending them *all* to The Infinite should still end," I stated, staring Kay down.

"But the living still need protecting," Kay protested.

My brows drew together as I leaned into the table towards my unbearable Handler. "Like the girl lying in a hospital bed with a fractured spine?" I snapped. "You did a bang-up job of protecting her."

"You mean Alfie?" Gia asked. "He's hurt someone else?"

Without taking my unflinching gaze from Kay, I answered. "No, he's been targeting the same girl repeatedly. Why are you protecting him? Or have you already dealt with him behind my back?"

"I can't explain right now," Kay said. "But he *must* stay."

"Then where the hell is he?" I snapped.

Her frown grew severe, confused. "What... I... he was..." she stuttered.

"Alfie's no longer at Red Rock, Kay. I've looked everywhere."

"If he's gone," Sawyer shrugged, "then problem solved?"

"No, it just makes him someone else's problem," Lola said. "A spirit that powerful is too dangerous to leave roaming freely."

"Look, I think everyone agrees Alfie needs to be at the top of our "to-do" list," Hunter said, squeezing my hand. "Can The Handlers start building Alfie's file so we can search the local area next weekend if he's still not found by then?"

"You're okay with this, H?" Amy asked.

"I have to be. It's only a matter of time before Alfie ends up killing someone," I said, turning to The Handlers. "So, compile Alfie's damned file."

Stone-faced and unmoving, The Handlers met our inquiries with silence. Their inscrutable expressions gave nothing away, keeping a tight hold on the secrets they knew about Alfie.

I only hoped that with all the changes being made within our faction, The Handlers would finally divulge what was so remarkable about him that had prompted them to forsake their core beliefs.

"Regarding this weekend's assignments, I think it's too soon for The Spirit Borns to work with The Handlers like this," Captain said. "What you did is still too raw in our minds. I suggest that on this occasion, you leave the assignments with us, and we'll ensure they're handled. If we need your guidance, we'll call you."

Captain's Handler's jaw slackened, her eyes filled with a mixture of shock and disappointment. "You want us to *leave?*" she said. "But you'll only argue."

"I believe we've turned a corner," Captain answered. "Last weekend, we worked well together when left to our own devices. I'm certain we can replicate that success."

The handlers shot us a look of utter disdain, their furrowed brows and downturned mouths conveying an unmistakable sense of hostility. In a swift, almost violent motion, Kay propelled herself out of her seat, the screech of the chair reverberating across the room as she straightened her clothing.

"Then, before we leave," she said, "may I suggest that Harper stay behind and train?"

Chapter Twenty-seven

I stood, turning my eyes to the lighting fixtures one at a time, casting them into darkness and leaving one light directly overhead burning, enveloping me in a pool of light as the scars on my arms glowed.

The lone bulb struggled against the sudden surge of power, vibrating before shattering into a cascade of twinkling glass around me.

I glared at Kay unflinchingly. "No," I answered through gritted teeth.

"I'm going on assignment with the others."

Kay nodded disgustedly at the glass littering the table. "You need to master more than these... parlour tricks," she snapped. "I'm only trying to help. We're running out of..."

"I've all the help I need," I interrupted. "I don't need you or your patronising orders anymore."

Hunter pulled me back into my seat, his arms around me rigid as I restored the lighting to normal, save for the blown bulb overhead. "That's enough," he said. "You're both behaving like children."

"Look, we'll handle the assignments," Lola said. "The only people we're arguing with are you guys."

"Fine," Kay snarled as she pulled a stack of files from her bag and tossed them onto the table. "Have it your way."

The Handlers shuffled into the hall, their expressions a mix of shock and disbelief. Kay paused at the entrance, her eyes locked on me before forcefully closing the door behind her.

An uncomfortable hush descended upon the Spirit Borns as they exchanged uneasy glances, unsure how to proceed, while Lola carefully circulated the files.

"Uh, so two assignments this weekend," Hunter began awkwardly. "But they both look pretty straightforward. So, does anyone need some time off?"

"Damn, we're being allowed a break?" Beck chortled. "We should work alone more often."

Hunter half smiled. "Call it compassionate leave after last weekend."

"Actually, a patient of mine is having surgery," Amy said, raising her hand. "If I could be there, I'd be grateful."

Noticing the shadows beneath Amy's eyes, I imagined that if her patients had seen the level of exhaustion permanently ingrained on their doctor's face, they'd have had reservations about going under her knife. Yet, despite her visible weariness, her capacity for healing, both in body and spirit, exceeded that of even the most distinguished surgeons in London.

I nodded. "Sure."

Beck nodded to Hunter and Dominic, an empathetic smile curling his lips. "What about you guys?" he asked. "Do you need time off after...?"

"Thanks, man, but we're good," Hunter answered, smiling feebly.

"Yeah, I think we'd rather stay busy," Dominic added.

"Okay, so the first assignment is in Pluckley," Lola read.

Immediately, groans erupted around the circle as Beck repeatedly banged his head against the table.

"What's wrong with Pluckley?" I asked.

"It's supposedly England's most haunted village," Dominic chuckled.

"It'll be a nightmare, just like last time," Sawyer huffed, leaning back in his chair. "Ghost hunters and wannabe YouTube stars everywhere."

"I thought we'd pretty much cleared it out," Gia said. "Are there even any spirits left there?"

"At least one," Lola shrugged. "It's The Highwayman. Final warning. In all our dealings with him, he's never responded, so maybe Harper's a good choice for that team to finally get him talking?"

"What do we know about him?" I asked.

"Not much," Lola answered. "He's sometimes seen on the crossroads, though that's just residual. He's grounded to the church where he was hung. Supposedly, he was a real Robin Hood character. Typical highwayman, tri-corn hat, frock coat, handsome as hell, you know the type."

"Sounds lovely," I said.

"He's shoved someone into an open grave, and the victim broke their hip," Lola added.

My eyes widened slightly as I shifted my gaze. "Okay, not so lovely."

"Before his first and second warnings, he hid in the church during a service to evade us," Lola said. "So, The Handlers have suggested packing our "Sunday best" in case he does it again."

I fixed my gaze on Lola. "Can't you help? You could sneak us into the church before the service starts?"

"I wish I could, but it looks like I'll have my hands full on the other assignment." Her eyebrows rose as she reviewed the second file. "So, are you up for Pluckley H? If you could get a response, I'm sure it'd go a long way to appease The Handlers."

"I'd love to," I nodded.

"Me too," Hunter said.

"Shocker," Beck teased.

Chapter Twenty-seven

"Hey, you were just being so nice," Hunter smirked. "Don't ruin it already."

Beck grinned, half shrugging as he winked knowingly. "I am what I am."

"Stick me and Aida down for Pluckley, too," Gia nodded. "I've been before, I know the location well."

"I wouldn't mind Pluckley. I'm kind of interested in seeing H in action. Lols, are you sure you can't come?" Dominic said, smiling hopefully.

"I'll be stuck on the second assignment. A first warning at Dunrobin Castle in Scotland," Lola said. "The location's pretty spread out, and they don't welcome investigators, so we're essentially breaking and entering."

Sawyer nodded excitedly as he elbowed Beck, "Say no more," he said. "We're in. What's the assignment?"

"The castle was a hospital in World War One, and a Grounded has been attacking guides. One received a nasty head injury. The Handlers have commented that it's typical behaviour for a newly Informed Grounded acting out, and I'm inclined to agree," Lola nodded. "The only description is that he's in uniform, so it might require some leg work."

"I'll go," Theon nodded. "If he's recently informed, getting a read on his thoughts might help us relieve his anxiety."

"If he's a fellow serviceman," Captain nodded, "I'll go, too."

"I'll try and split my time between assignments, but if the Scotland team doesn't fancy being arrested for trespassing, I'll be needed there more," Lola said.

Hunter sighed. "Okay, this wasn't too hard, was it? We're all in agreement and not tearing each other's hair out."

I smirked mischievously. "Not yet."

Hunter met my eyes, the golden shards within them glowing. "Try me."

"Enough flirting," Dominic said. "So, the Pluckley team will be me, H, Hunter, Aida, and Gia, and the Dunrobin team will be Sawyer, Beck, Captain, Theon and Lola."

"Rooms have been booked at a pub in Pluckley," Lola said. "And for the Dunrobin assignment, you'll be staying in Golspie, just down the road from the castle."

Aida chewed her bottom lip. "Is... Beau likely to turn up again?" she stuttered quietly.

The mere mention of his name immediately unsettled the Spirit Borns, evident in their tensed bodies and rapidly flickering eyes.

Sawyer leaned across the table, his expression unexpectedly gentle as he reached out to Aida. "No, sweetheart, he's only interested in The Ungrounded," he said softly. "You're safe."

"Yeah, we've got your back, Aida," Beck added.

"If everyone's good, I'll start pickups in ten," Lola said, nodding sharply.

As I searched through the leather jeans and band T-shirts I had packed, hoping to find something suitable to wear to church, Hunter appeared in my doorway.

Leaning casually against the doorframe, he tucked one foot behind the other and slung his bag over his shoulder. The fading sunlight enveloped him in a golden sheen, casting a warm halo around his figure.

His relaxed posture and easy smile radiated the effortless charm I had fallen head over heels for.

He tilted his head. "Are you ready, gorgeous?"

"I don't have anything to wear in church," I sighed. "I'm going to have Lola nip me home first to raid her wardrobe."

"You might not need it."

"I'd rather be prepared," I answered. "With Lola in Scotland, I don't want to add more to her plate by going last minute."

"With all the shopping you two do, you seriously don't have a church-appropriate outfit?" Hunter teased.

I paused, glancing down at my Rolling Stones T-shirt, ripped jeans, and scuffed combat boots. A playful smirk crept across my face as I nonchalantly pointed down at my shirt and shrugged.

Hunter's deep, rich, caramel voice reverberated through the room as he let out a chuckle, the first I had heard since he lost his family. It felt like a ray of hope cutting through the darkness, bringing with it a sense of comfort and the promise of healing.

He nodded towards my feet. "And those combat boots?" he asked. "Are they church-appropriate?"

"I'll wear a dress if I have to," I said, flashing a mischievous smile. But the boots are non-negotiable. They're staying put."

Hunter dropped his bag on the floor, a devilish smile playing on his lips as he closed the distance between us, his eyes never leaving mine. With a swift movement, he encircled my waist and drew me close as if to kiss me.

Just as our lips were about to meet, he slyly changed course, playfully trailing his nose along my neck. The light brush of his touch sent a cascade

Chapter Twenty-seven

of shivers down my spine as he drew slow breaths of my perfume with an unmistakable hunger.

His voice rumbled low, almost a growl, as he softly grazed his lips against my jawline. "Do you know how much trouble you're in tonight?" he said.

"Why? What did I..." I paused, grinning as I realised what he meant. "...Oh."

"No Handlers, no hiding," he said, "We can just... be."

He slid his hand around my neck, his thumb tracing the curve of my spine. Leaning closer, he pressed his forehead to mine, the warmth of his breath mingling with mine, before he pulled away.

"I'll check us in at the hotel," he said, winking as he picked up his bag. "Don't take too long."

Lola left me at my flat while she finished drop-offs and arranged to collect me once I had found an outfit. Despite emptying my wardrobe first and dumping its contents onto my bed as I searched, I couldn't find anything suitable. Raiding Lola's wardrobe, with her permission, became my only choice.

I grabbed her spare key from the kitchen and entered the interior hall, enveloped by shadows. As I turned to lock my door, a fleeting movement caught my eye. Something light fluttered past my face, like a strange butterfly, flying horizontally past my eyes.

Instinctively, I reached out, my fingers grazing emptiness, swiping blindly as my other hand groped the wall, searching for the light switch.

I finally found the light switch, and the hall flooded with light. I searched for the culprit, suspecting that a moth or some other insect had startled me.

Yet, as my eyes settled on the door, a shiver coursed down my spine. My entire body tensed as I held my breath, my feet anchored to the floor.

One hand reached forward while the other instinctively covered my mouth, stifling a gasp.

I tugged down the piece of paper pinned to my door and held it in my trembling hands. Written in the same ornate cursive script as the letters I'd seen in every Spirit Borns' file was a message.

"Thirteenth,
I did say every Spirit Born family would fall. Come now, come alone.
Tell nobody.
Kindest Regards, Beau."

Chapter Twenty-eight

Even in the windowless hall, I could feel Beau's pale blue eyes boring into me. Beads of sweat began to form on my temple, glistening in the low light as they trickled down my face.

I had anticipated feeling fierce and impassioned when I faced him, but the weight of my family's afterlives hanging in the balance left me feeling utterly defenceless. The sense of tenacity I had so strongly felt on the train now seemed like a faded memory. Beau had the upper hand, and reclaiming it felt like an insurmountable task.

I scrambled downstairs, tripping over every other step like I was drunk, my hand grasping the handrail was the only thing preventing me from tumbling downward.

As I slammed the garden gate and prepared to sprint to the station, I was met by two well-built, emotionless men dressed in black.

Without so much as a glance in my direction, one of them extended his hand impatiently. "Phone," he ordered.

I obliged at once, my hand trembling as I handed it over. The other man pointed me towards the same black SUV I'd seen at Ettington, waiting in the street.

"You're... with Beau?" I asked.

He nodded and took me by the elbow, walking me to the car and directing me into the backseat. The men piled in beside me, and the driver sped off, jolting my body back into my seat.

The only sound I heard during the journey was my heart hammering in my ears. I closed my eyes, attempting to draw on the same inner strength I had displayed on the train, sourcing power from the car and streetlights.

My talent remained almost entirely dormant. All I could manage was turning the radio on, which the aggravated driver promptly turned off.

It dawned on me that if Beau could render even me redundant from afar, my aspirations of ending him had been nothing short of reckless and

Chapter Twenty-eight

overconfident. My only relief was that I was alone and hadn't dragged Hunter and my friends into this fight, a fight that felt impossible to win.

As we approached, the lawns of Red Rocks were bathed in a comforting, golden glow as each room on every floor illuminated the entire estate. However, knowing Beau's twisted mentality, he wanted the house virtually vibrating with energy to make a statement.

He wouldn't make the mistake of underestimating me twice, making it categorically clear that no matter how much energy was on hand, he wouldn't grant me a single amp of it.

The only thing that would have helped me was reaching my core and praying that unlocking my true potential would be enough to defeat him.

But I had ignored Kay's guidance, leaving me woefully unequipped against this monster. Beau and I were opposites, but the crucial difference between us was that he had reached his core, and I had not. And unbelievably, I found myself wishing I'd obeyed my Handler more.

From what I could see, the house was intact, save for a smashed window panel in the library where they had made entry, unlocking the doors from within. With such minimal damage, I tried to cling to hope that my family were still safe upstairs, blissfully unaware of the intruder who had invaded their home.

As Beau's henchmen escorted me down the halls, I tried to absorb some of the bounteous energy surrounding me, imagining drinking it like a thick soup. However, despite the occasional glimmer of the chandeliers, my efforts were in vain. While I had been preoccupied supporting Hunter and hunting Alfie, Beau had grown even stronger.

In the library, Beau sat by the fire, the contours of his face illuminated by the crackling embers in the hearth as he warmed his hands. Dressed in a smart yet relaxed attire of sleek black jeans and a navy shirt rolled up to his elbows, he exuded an air of understated confidence.

Like a jungle cat, his head barely moved, but his discerning eyes noticed everything and everyone in the room. His gaze fixed fiercely on me with alluring intensity as he accepted my phone. A grin spread across his face as he tossed it into the flames.

"Thank you everyone. Y'all can leave now," Beau directed, his Southern American drawl making him sound like the perfect gentleman. "Gentlemen... and lady..."

His eyes sparkled as he winked at the one other female in the room as she maintained watch at the door. Her cheeks flushed as she glanced downwards, fighting a smile, appearing simultaneously flattered and flustered by Beau's attention.

"Go wait in the car at the end of the drive. Whatever y'all see, whatever y'all hear, don't move. I'll call you when I'm ready," Beau instructed. Then, turning towards me with a welcoming smile, he guided me towards the chair opposite him. "Welcome home, Harper. Please, sit down."

"If you only had a stiff drink and an oversized cat," I remarked stiffly, taking a seat. "You'd make the perfect villain."

"Why? Y'all got a bar hidden in here?" he chuckled, looking around the room. "So, how was the drive?"

"Enforced," I scowled, my jaw tightening. "If you're here to start a fight, Beau, you better ensure your first shot's a good one because..."

"There's no need for violence, Miss Reynolds-Woodbury."

"Where are my family?" I demanded. "I want to see them."

He glanced upward, his pitch rising as he reclined in his chair, rubbing his chin. "They're asleep," he said. "We can cause a ruckus and wake them if you'd like, but is that really a clever idea? With them being Uninformed and all? From what I hear, it's been quite a spell since they last saw you. They'd only want to embrace their prodigal child returned, don't you agree?"

"And Alfie?"

He shook his head as he smacked his hands on his knees. "Ah, the man *everyone's* talking about, but *nobody* can find?" he teased.

I released a noise that was half chuckle, half huff. "You can't find him either?" I smirked. "Good."

"I didn't say that did I?" he grinned. "He is one slippery lil' son'bitch though."

"Agreed."

"Well, what do you know? We *agree* on something," he said. "Well, H, do you mind if I call you H? Everyone else does."

"Yes," I replied through gritted teeth. "Only my friends call me H."

"Fine. Thirteenth."

My glower was instantaneous.

He raised his hands. "Harper it is then," he chuckled. "Well, you know the saying "the enemy of my enemy is my friend."?"

"Alfie's not my enemy."

"Well, y'all were together eighty years," Beau said. "Yet nobody seems that fond of him anymore, yourself included."

Chapter Twenty-eight

"He's made mistakes. But I don't need to tell you that. It seems like you know everything about him already."

"Maybe even more than you," Beau said, leaning back in his chair and examining his nails. "Seeing as he's your core an' all."

I crossed my arms. "Bullshit."

"You still think your little fling will get you the power you need?" he scoffed. "If that were true and he really was the centre of it all, then why on *earth* haven't you figured it out yet, child? Maybe your little tryst isn't as passionate as you'd hoped?"

My cheeks burned, and my teeth ground together as my blood boiled at his politely worded torments and gentlemanly insults. Unable to muster any power whatsoever in his presence, I lunged forward without thinking. I'd never hit anyone in my life, but still, I clenched my fist and drew it back.

In one smooth movement, Beau pulled a hunting knife from between the cushions beside him and pointed its tip at me.

I froze, raising my hands in surrender as he wagged his finger with the same hand that held the weapon. I saw my own stunned reflection in the blade, around five inches long, with an expertly crafted leather pommel.

"Uh, uh, uh," he tutted.

I staggered back into my seat as Beau began picking his nails with the knife, his eyes fixed on me.

"Is that what we're resorting to, physical altercations? And there was me thinking you were a lady? You *must* be struggling," he raised his brows, nodding.

"I've not seen Alfie in weeks," I said. "He has nothing to do with me anymore. He's disappeared."

"But not at night, right?" his seductive accent purred as half his mouth smiled. "And not for poor little Holly?" Beau paused, licking his lips as his eyes narrowed. "Didn't you ever question why he isn't already serving time in The Infinite?"

"Yes, but..."

"Or wonder why The Handlers are letting him attack innocent girls and are refusing to pass him on?" he interrupted.

"They..."

"Because they've no choice, little girl," he said, shaking his head. "They can't go losing their star player now."

"Regardless of who or what he is, he's dangerous," I said. "The Handlers have agreed that he goes next week."

"That's if y'all can find him," Beau sniggered.

"There are twelve of us. We'll manage."

"And The Handlers agreed, did they?" he probed.

"Not exactly, but…"

"I'm telling you now, they won't ever pass him on," Beau interrupted. "Not till he gives you what you *need*."

"Alfie's a mess," I scoffed. "He can't give me anything."

"You're wrong," Beau said slowly. "Whether you want to believe it or not, your core's entangled with that poor boy, and he'll be going nowhere until you figure out how to use him."

"Then why haven't The Handlers told me?" I asked.

"Because even Hannah has her limits. She knows just the same as I do. Alfie's touch is involved, but as to *how* or *why*? She's as clueless as anyone else. That's why The Handlers have hidden him until you know what to do. That's if he'll even help you."

"Is that why he's losing it?" I asked, feeling the heat of the fire on my cheeks as I unconsciously leaned forward. "Because The Handlers keep taking him away from Red Rock?"

"You're just too close to the problem, sweetheart," Beau winked.

"Then you know where he is?"

He grinned, twirling the blade's tip against the arm of his chair. "I have a pretty good guess," he said.

"Beau, please. *Tell me*."

"Don't worry," Beau said, checking his watch. "He'll probably be along soon enough."

"If he can help me, why's he being hidden?"

"Because you're not ready," Beau answered. For the first time, he wore a gentle, empathetic smile, his once intense eyes softening with understanding." But more importantly, it's to keep you both safe."

I frowned. "Alfie's dead. What's he got to be afraid of?"

"*You* darlin'. Ever since he laid hands on Holly, y'all have just been itching to end him." His pitch crept higher. "But The Handlers can't be having that. The reality is, that bitch Kay is doing you a service. Putting it bluntly, she's hidden him to save your life."

"Alfie can't hurt me. If he lays a finger on me, and he's gone," I laughed, savouring the opportunity to taunt Beau back. "Or have you been away from The Fort so long that you've forgotten how things work?"

Chapter Twenty-eight

"That's true. But there's something The Handlers aren't telling you, another... secret." Beau leaned closer, his knife gleaming in the firelight. "If you or anyone else passes him on, it would sign your death warrant."

"What?" My eyes narrowed. "How?"

"There are rules and secrets deeply entwined with our... *your* faction. Things no Spirit Born is ever told," he answered, emphasising each word. "If a Spirit Born fails to reach their core within their first year, the miracle that brought you back fades, and you'll return to your grave."

I couldn't tear my gaze away from him, afraid of betraying my vulnerability. Trying to maintain a stoic facade, I struggled to hold back the bitter tears welling in my eyes.

My heart pounded in my chest, and my bottom lip trembled with emotion. Beau's words resonated deeply, shedding light on why I was allowed to keep my job. It occurred to me that perhaps The Handlers hoped that being close to Alfie would expedite my journey to reach my core.

It explained why they had refused to pass him on and had hidden him when they'd feared I'd do it myself. And Kay's repetitive warnings that I was running out of time mirrored Beau's warning at Ettington.

I had assumed they had both meant the clock was running out until my inevitable confrontation with Beau. With so much hope being pinned on Alfie, I'd assumed Beau's comment of losing their star player was aimed at him, but he'd always meant me.

"You find yourself in an unenviable position where the man whose heart you've truly broken and whose afterlife you've shattered now holds your life in his immortal hands," Beau said gently, raising his free hand. "Now, I swear, I'm not sure how exactly you use him. I only know what Hannah once told me, but should you ignore what I've disclosed, your new life will be over before it begins."

"But... I controlled the train," I stuttered, running my hands through my hair. "I stopped the rollercoaster."

"Yes, I read about that incident in the paper and presumed you were involved. It was... impressive, but that's not your talent, is it, sugar? You've been dabbling with electricity to make life safer, but you're not even remotely close to reaching your core. Why do you think Kay pushes you so hard? Because she knows you're not ready. The others all had the luxury of time to master their talents, but you... girl, you're running on borrowed time. Poor old Alfie can't hold on much longer, whether he stays hidden or not. Soon, he'll be useless to anyone."

"I don't believe you," I lied, closing my eyes and swallowing.

"Y'all call me a monster..."

"No, calling you a monster would be an insult to monsters everywhere," I interrupted.

He let out a low chuckle. "You're feisty, I'll give you that. But regardless of what I've done or what they call me, even my fiercest enemies will agree I never lie."

"If we were in danger, The Handlers would've told us. They can't keep something that important a secret."

"Like they didn't keep my letters a secret?" Beau arched one eyebrow. "The Handlers keep it a secret because the truth would only affect performance, and because Spirit Borns rarely fail. Roughly one every century dies. This century, it was meant to be me. My talent was never meant to be unleashed on this world."

"So why are you telling me now?" I asked.

"I can see you're a wilful child, Harper. It's a trait I very much admire you for. I see how close y'all are to hunting Alfie down, but losing a Spirit Born with such progressive potential would be a waste." Slowly, he crossed his legs, leaning on one arm of his chair as his eyes found mine.

"I've high expectations for you. Only with your help can I relinquish The Handlers' stranglehold over The Spirit Borns. But you'll need to reach your core to do that."

"How did you even discover all this?" I asked. "I can't imagine The Handlers disclosed their secrets willingly."

"They didn't. You see, my core wasn't as pretty or easily attainable as everyone else's. Mine was pain, torment. It was understanding death," Beau answered, his voice turning gravelly. "During training, we assumed that meant making peace with my own death, but we were wrong. It wasn't until I *saw* death played out in front of me that I reached my core."

"You mean Laura?"

He nodded and returned to picking his nails with his knife. "I'd been back almost a year when I started fading, physically and mentally."

"Hunter said you were sick," I said.

"Incredibly so. And all the progress I'd made evaporated," Beau said. "I'd already distanced myself from The Spirit Borns, but I couldn't understand my diminishing abilities, so I visited Laura one last time."

Chapter Twenty-eight

Beau stood tall, his piercing eyes fixed on the floor as he began to pace back and forth in front of the fireplace. Each step seemed calculated, designed to block any chance of escape.

"I begged for answers, but all Laura said was that it would be over soon, never once looking me in the eyes. It was only when I laid my hands on her that she whimpered the truth. She knew I'd only reach my core through extreme violence. As I'd weakened, Hannah saw what would be required of me to reach it and ran to Laura like the little Handler's whore she is," Beau snarled. "The Handlers couldn't abide me taking a life, even if it meant saving my own. My talent was meant to be one of protection, and they knew defiling it with murder would've potentially created a monster."

I frowned, my nose wrinkling in disgust. *"Potentially?"*

He swung around, pointing the tip of the knife in my face as his voice roared. "Don't look down your nose at me, Harper Reynolds-Woodbury!"

Taking a deep breath to steady himself, he ran a hand through his hair before continuing in a composed and unwavering tone. The stark contrast in his manner reminded me of the classic tale of Dr. Jekyll and Mr. Hyde.

"Being faced with death does peculiar things to a man," he said.

It didn't surprise me that a man as hateful as Beau had a core choked by vines of hatred. If the dark act of murder had unleashed his talent, I imagined years of developing his dark gift would've only desecrated his soul even further.

Having heard his confession to Laura's murder, the knife in his hand underwent a sinister evolution, morphing from an instrument of control into a deadly weapon, ready to eliminate anyone obstructing his path.

"What do you want in exchange for sharing the truth?" I asked. "You don't strike me as a man who reveals information for free."

He grinned, his white teeth shining in the firelight. "As I've said, I admire you," he said. "Despite all the arguments that I suppose are happening at The Fort lately, you're the only one who has completely severed ties with their Handler."

"So, you *are* watching us. And there I was, thinking that was just a bedtime story."

He smiled innocently. "Of course. Do you really think I wouldn't look in on you occasionally? The Spirit Borns interest me, you especially. You go to work, which, by the way..." He glanced around the room, nodding. "...bold choice. *Dumb,* but bold. And you see your friends, but you never see Kay."

"And?"

"Well, barely back six months, and you're already living independently, free of your Handler? It's commendable," he said. "I thought that might mean we understand each other. I wanted free of mine, too."

"Being free of and murdering are two extremely different paths, Beau," I answered sternly.

"I had no choice. I'd like to see you make "the right" choice in that situation," Beau said, making air quotes with his fingers.

"Well, I am... kind of," I shrugged. "You're saying if I pass on Alfie before I reach my core, then I'll die. But if I don't, he'll only end up killing someone, and I don't want that on my conscience or his."

Beau crouched at my feet, his intense gaze meeting mine as he gently placed his hand over mine. His other hand stealthily concealed the knife behind his back as if he wanted me to forget it was there.

"I agree, sugar, Alfie's got to go. I'm just saying, wait," he said, a hint of desperation in his voice. "The Handlers are watching him to ensure he doesn't hurt anyone else. Don't sacrifice yourself needlessly."

The room fell silent as I locked eyes with him, taking in his intoxicating scent. Despite his handsome features, a wave of repulsion washed over me. I couldn't fathom or forgive what he had inflicted upon Hunter and the other Spirit Borns. I yanked my hands from beneath his as if his touch had seared my skin.

"Why are you helping me?" I asked.

"You're immensely powerful, Harper. I can feel it radiating off you," he said. "I need your help to free The Spirit Borns from The Handlers. But you'll need to reach your core to do that."

I frowned. "Surely me reaching my full strength would be detrimental to you?"

He shrugged nonchalantly as he approached the fire, staring into the flames. "I don't care what you do to me, Harper," he said. "Roast me over an open spit when our business is through if you like, so long as The Handlers are gone."

"And what makes you think I'd help you?" I glared. "After what you did to Hunter, Dominic and Hannah? Or all of them, for that matter?"

"Well, the enemy of my enemy is my friend," he repeated, winking.

When he had said that before, I had assumed Beau's objection to Holly's attacks meant that our enemy was Alfie. However, it was now evident that

Chapter Twenty-eight

his true adversary had always been The Handlers, the common enemy that bound Beau and me together.

"Since you arrived, there's been unembellished hope for change, where Spirit Borns rule themselves. Furthermore, I believe you'll help me because your family is resting soundly upstairs, and you wish for them to *remain* so." He raised his eyebrows, his accent curling his Rs seductively. "Bring the Fort under Spirit Born control, and you can keep your family. My word is my bond." Beau bowed his head and placed a hand on his chest. "But should you kill me and go against yours, I have a small army that will demolish Red Rock brick by brick."

"What if the others won't follow me?" I asked, shifting.

As he placed his hand on the back of my seat and leaned in, he scoffed, "They already fear you. Do you really think they won't follow you? They've been crying out for a torch bearer for years. So, light the match and *lead* them."

"You know The Handlers won't go without a fight, and I won't hurt them, Beau. I'm not like you," I stated firmly, shaking my head and leaning back in my chair to create some space between us.

"They're just paper pushers, nothing more," he said dismissively. "*You* hold all the power."

"But you've burned all your bridges with us. Now you've ungrounded the last families they'll never bend to your will again, whether it's to save mine or not."

"You'll keep my involvement and the threat to your family secret," Beau said. "You'll lead the charge. Just keep me informed of your progress."

"And if I refuse?"

He straightened his posture, and I felt the tension leave my body as I slowly exhaled the breath I had been unconsciously holding.

"Then you can kiss goodbye to your family here and now. And y'all will be looking over your shoulders until my dying breath." A slow smirk crept across his face. "I'm growing stronger every day; I can render y'all *useless*. And without you after your little suicide mission passing on Alfie, what hope will they have of ever stopping me?"

"I get the feeling that's what you've always wanted anyway," I remarked. "To be the only one wielding any power. Laying waste to everything that makes us special and torturing those who cast you aside."

His response was straightforward, delivered with a hint of a growl in his voice. "You'd be wrong," he said. "The living need Spirit Born protection, but as long as you're under The Handlers' rule, your cause is not your own."

"With The Handlers gone, we'd be left more vulnerable. Our normal lives would be over, consumed by research," I said, glaring. "And if I never figure out how to use Alfie and reach my core, or just follow my instincts and send him to The Infinite anyway, what's to stop you from taking over?"

My jaw tightened, and my fists clenched as my anger reached its crescendo, rage flooding my veins. I knew that Beau's oppressive and tyrannical nature meant my family would always be in danger.

They'd be a hand he'd play to subjugate me with, in a game that likely would result in me losing them anyway, whether it be due to my rebellious nature grating on him or a future command I'd refuse to obey.

Whatever the risk to my family, there was no way I'd make a deal with this devil. And knowing what my following words would be, and what they meant, a single tear dampened my cheek.

My eyes found his, the blues and greens of my irises sparkling in the firelight as my tone remained fierce. "I refuse," I growled. "You're a *cancer*, Beau. Nothing... more."

His face contorted with aggression, and as his pale eyes darkened and gave way to vehemence, I tried to sprint towards the door.

Before I had time to react, Beau hurled himself towards me, and we toppled into a heap by the fireplace in a tangled mess of arms and legs.

He twisted his fingers into my sandy blonde curls and wrenched my head back as my limbs flailed helplessly. "I swear to God, Harper Reynolds-Woodbury, you *will* obey me," he spat, his breath hot in my ear as he pulled his knife towards me.

"I don't care what you do me, Beau. Roast me over a hot spit when our business is through," I smirked, repeating his words and looking directly into his eyes. "But I will *never* obey you. It seems you've bitten off more than you can chew with me."

I writhed violently, attempting to free his hands out of my hair, but his strength was overwhelming. The only thing within my reach was the fireplace.

I reached into the hearth, ignoring the blistering pain as I grabbed a handful of glowing embers and hurled them directly at Beau's face.

With an almighty growl, he jerked away, dropping the knife as he brushed away the ashes smouldering on his cheeks.

Chapter Twenty-eight

He struggled to his feet, his other hand still tangled in my hair, pulling my body upwards. I reached for the blade, but my fingers were just inches short of its smooth leather handle.

Despite my struggling, Beau's reached the knife easily. He pulled me up onto my feet by my hair, and even with both of my arms clawing deep scratches into his forearms, he was able to pull the knife towards me as I felt its cool steel pricking my throat.

Frantic to gain some distance from the knife's glinting edge, I dropped to my knees, and with all the strength I could muster, I simultaneously wrenched my head to one side, ripping huge chunks of hair from my head and leaving Beau clutching a hand full of blood-soaked curls.

I bolted toward the door, the jarring noise of chairs and side tables crashing to the ground reverberating through the room as I frantically manoeuvred over them. Beau threw the tangled handful of hair on the floor and gave chase. Within seconds, as I struggled over an overturned armchair, I felt his fingers closing around my ankles, swiftly pulling me to the ground.

My face cracked onto the floor, and the sharp scent of copper overwhelmed my senses as blood poured from my nose.

As he dragged me backwards, my nails clawing at the polished wood floor, I managed to wriggle one foot free. I aimed my heel directly at his jaw and kicked repeatedly. As he shook his head, dazed and fighting to keep conscious, he dropped my other leg, and I crawled away.

I knew he was too fast, too strong, to escape from without a weapon of my own. In a split-second decision, I dashed towards the fire axe, its red handle encased in glass by the door.

I clambered to my feet, my heart racing as if it wanted to break free from my chest. Suddenly, I felt that familiar tingle shooting through my forearms, where the inky tendrils of my markers had begun spreading. When I turned to Beau, a wicked grin spread across his face as he glanced downwards and noticed the streaks of black marring his own skin.

I couldn't bear for my family to see me like that: beaten and bloodied, desperately trying to outrun a stranger, and I couldn't escape the house and leave them to suffer Beau's fury alone. I had to draw him away somehow until I could get help.

But my hesitation had given Beau time to block my route to the axe. As my eyes frantically darted the room like a cornered animal, the blood from my head trickled into my eye, washing my vision with scarlet as the metallic tang of the blood from my nose reached my mouth.

As I wiped my nose, streaking my leather jacket with claret, I spotted the hole in the window. Seeing the feral look in Beau's eyes, I knew he would chase after me rather than whichever member of my family had awoken early.

With Beau at my heels, vehemently intent on conquering the woman who had spat in the face of his guidance, I sprinted towards the window.

I pulled off my remaining boot, thrashing it against the glass until a piece broke off that was big enough for me to wield as a weapon. I carefully slid one leg through the hole, wary of the loose shards of glass both above and below me.

The glass at the bottom of the hole tore into my jeans and sliced into my skin as I ducked my head to avoid the glass looming over it. As the cool night air hit me, spots developed behind my eyes, my knees weak, and I had to pause and steady myself.

But despite nearly being out of the building, my markers had only darkened, yet I'd heard none of the REM pods I had hidden in the halls sounding as they should have.

I gasped for air, my entire body quivering with adrenaline. I focused all my energy on not losing consciousness, silently praying for the endurance I needed to lead Beau away. But as I took a deep breath and prepared to run, I felt Beau's hand grip my leg and press down as he dragged me back through the window.

I cried out as glass tore deeper into my thigh and dropped the shard I'd been brandishing, smashing it to fragments at my feet. Beau tucked his knife into the waistband of his jeans and pulled his phone from his back pocket, rapidly dialling and bringing it to his ear.

"Ram it!" he screamed, his face flushing red. "Destroy the boundary! I'll take care of the house!"

My face snapped towards the drive, but I couldn't discern the black SUV's movements in the darkness. I struggled to free myself, but every movement inflicted deeper cuts into my leg. As desolate tears ran down my face to the symphony of Beau's maniacal laughter, I looked outside helplessly.

Walking out of the shadows appeared a figure on the lawn, and despite knowing there was nothing he could physically do to help me, my heart still fluttered in recognition of his familiar form.

Chapter Twenty-eight

Alfie lurched forward, his hands outstretched in an automatic response of endeavouring to help. I recoiled, edging towards Beau.

When Alfie stepped into the light, I couldn't help but notice his remarkable transformation.

His once sunken cheeks now exuded youthfulness, and his striking features seemed restored. His tailored clothing no longer hung loosely but appeared to embrace his revived form.

Alfie frowned, opening his mouth to speak, but whilst his arrival had taken me aback, Beau had dropped his phone and pulled his knife from his belt. I felt its keen edge crushing my windpipe as he dropped my leg painfully onto the broken window.

Beau wormed his fingers back into the bloodied, tangled remains of my hair, pulling my head around and forcing the blade harder onto my skin. In response, Alfie raised his hands as if Beau was holding him at gunpoint.

"I win, Thirteenth," Beau cackled. "You've nowhere to run."

Alfie's voice resonated with unwavering resolve as he demanded, "Don't hurt her."

Alfie's chest swelled as he took a deep breath. The oceanic blue of his eyes, the unique colour I hadn't seen in months, glistened with tears.

"This must be it," Alfie said, nodding. "One last time."

"What?" I croaked.

"Time for you to go, boy." Beau spat. "Your boundary's coming down, and the house is next. Better say your goodbyes while you can."

"I'm not leaving her," Alfie said defiantly, his back straightening. "Let her go, Beau."

Alfie's eyes found mine as he stepped forward, his pace and stance confident as he reached toward me. Whilst I was ready to die to protect the living from his instability, I didn't want to send him to The Infinite in such a traumatic manner. And without me to defend the rest of my family from Beau's lunacy, he would raze Red Rock to the ground, and they'd all suffer the fate of The Ungrounded.

"Look at me, Harper. It's time," Alfie smiled, blocking out all the violence surrounding us and pinning his eyes on mine as if we were the only people there. "I'll get to touch you one last time."

Beau grinned with wide, untamed eyes. "Then touch her," he snarled. "Reach out and take her hand. Save me the job of gutting the bitch myself."

The blade pinched my throat, slicing the top layers of my skin, but I ignored the pain and drew back from Alfie, even though it meant inching further into Beau's grip. I tried to speak, to explain that his touch would end us both, but the knife pushed so hard against my windpipe that only a few words could escape.

"Alfie, *run!*" I pleaded.

But he didn't run. He inched closer until he stood within reaching distance as Beau started wrenching my leg back through the window. I felt my jeans growing sticky as the sickly scent of blood permeated the air.

Alfie's soft smile was overshadowed by the glisten of tears in his eyes, reflecting the depth of his sympathy. "I was promised I'd get to hold you one last time," he said. "And I'm tired, Harper. I *want* this. I don't care what's waiting for me in The Infinite. I can't stand being here anymore, confused and out of control."

"Whatever happens, I'll get my way," Beau said, the warmth of his breath tickling my ear. "You touch her, she dies. You run; she dies."

Ignoring Beau's reproach, Alfie's eyes remained fixed solely on mine. "I love you, Harper," he purred. "No matter where I end up, I'll love you."

"No," I struggled. "Not like this."

Alfie ducked beneath the broken glass, enveloping me with one arm around my neck and the other around my waist, drawing me close as his lips gently met mine in a tender embrace. Beau's grip on me slightly loosened as he watched, waiting for the end of us both.

Alfie's pure and virtuous touch offered a fleeting respite from the searing pain that consumed me. In those moments, I yearned to savour the sensation of his lips on mine, the tender embrace of his arms, and the way his presence briefly dulled my agony. But amidst it all, a haunting realisation loomed large: embracing him would seal my family's fate.

A crack of thunder shattered the night sky, followed swiftly by another and another, reverberating through the air and rattling the house to its core. The chandeliers in the library swung violently, casting erratic patterns of light and shadow as pockets of dust floated down from the ornate ceiling.

A look of unsettled intimidation clouded Beau's features as he glanced into the room, but my focus remained on Alfie as echoes of his voice saturated the air.

I heard his gentle chuckle, which had once sent shivers down my spine, and his promise that I'd do amazing things, interwoven with admissions of love.

He pulled away, glancing at the sky and smiling as if he could see the explosive lightning that disrupted the sky with its fierce beauty in his world,

Chapter Twenty-eight

too. As his figure became enveloped in a radiant, golden light, his voice transcended the ether one final time, carrying with it a sense of finality and peace.

Alfie nodded, his cheeks glowing with a beaming smile. "You'll know what to do," he said. "And I'm *so* goddamn proud of you for it."

"Alfie, no," I sobbed. "Not yet."

As his glow and the echoes of his voice slowly faded, I reached for him, unleashing a guttural scream as my heart shattered, not for my own fate, but for Alfie's and for abandoning Red Rock without a guardian. I squeezed my eyes closed, forcing tears down my face as my fingers crackled with bolts of energy brighter than I'd ever seen them.

Beau released my leg, his eyes cautious and edgy as he backed away toward his only exit in the library, never once turning his back on me. The lightning crackled overhead, growing more aggressive with each strike, illuminating the trees that bordered the property and causing heavy, glowing branches to collapse onto the grass.

I didn't pay much attention to the thunder or how the ground trembled as the strikes grew nearer, but as Alfie faded from sight with a proud smile fixed on his face, I noticed the flash.

I clambered through the window, ignoring the pain as my leg raked over the broken glass, and dropped to my knees, wailing as grief enveloped me, running through me in painful stabs. I instinctively stretched my hands, clutched into trembling claws, into the air.

Forks of lightning grew nearer, progressing across the lawns towards me until they were mere feet away, leaving scorched craters in the earth that turned Red Rock's lawns into what looked like a battlefield.

I couldn't think or hear anything but the hollering of my own cries as vivid light surrounded me, momentarily illuminating everything in vista. A deafening crack vibrated through the air, and the ground shuddered as the light passed through my outstretched arms and into my body.

As my lungs felt ready to burst, I glanced downwards, turning my hands over. My eyes widened as my jaw dropped at the smoke curling around me, its acrid tendrils stinging my nostrils. Forks of energy danced over every inch of my skin and sparkled across my eyes.

I stood still, allowing the moment to wash over me as I closed my eyes and tilted my head towards the sky in a silent prayer of gratitude. As I reopened my eyes, in my peripheral vision, I noticed the car that had brought me here speeding into the distance, abandoning its master.

My attention snapped towards Beau. He stared straight back, his pale blue eyes wide as his jaw quivered like a fish out of water. Facing his palms towards me submissively, he shook his head.

Watching him inching towards the door like the coward he was incensed me with a rage I'd not thought possible for my body to conjure.

I knew what I was going to do. I even paused to take pleasure in it, souring Beau's blood with the same fear he had inflicted upon the Spirit Borns. With a slight tilt of my head, I observed his frantic movements as he stumbled over the furniture, clearly afraid to turn his back on me.

I wished I could have heard his desperate pleas for mercy or his ranting apologies, but the resounding crack of the second burst of lightning that emanated from within me was of an entirely different calibre, its raw power eclipsing all other sounds.

However, in the split-second before the beam of energy struck Beau, amid the cacophony of the windows shattering and the walls trembling, I thought I heard him scream, "No." This haunting singular moment and word would repeatedly replay in my mind in the weeks and months.

I threw my hands, clutched into rigid claws, in front of me, projecting a beam of raw power directly towards Beau's cowering body as he covered his face with his hands. There was the briefest of screams, the kind of agonised scream that turned your blood cold and sent shivers racing up your spine, the type of scream that haunted your dreams and kept you up at night.

The shock killed him instantly, illuminating the entire house as Beau's lifeless body crumpled onto the floor. But I didn't stop. I couldn't stop. I continued holding my hands twisted in front of me in a continual stream of energy.

Even when I noticed wisps of blue flame streaking from his body, my thirst for vengeance and retribution kept me locked in place.

It didn't bother me that charred, blackened skin was progressing from my fingertips up my arms or that my legs had been consumed by ash, scorching the spot was rooted to.

I released all my rage onto him, screaming into the night like a wild animal, demanding that my self-declared justice be sated. I craved more power to lengthen the moment and continue my gratification until, finally, my body reached its limit, and the force projected backwards.

As I tumbled through the air, everything moved in slow motion. I could see the fire taking root from Beau's blazing body. Flames had engulfed

Chapter Twenty-eight

the area he had been standing in, spreading towards the bookshelves and threatening to destroy Alfie's legacy.

Panic coursed through me like an uncontrollable wildfire, the weight of responsibility to save Red Rock and my family pressing down on me. Every muscle in my body twisted and turned as I helplessly fought against the unyielding force of gravity.

Finally, I landed in a crumpled heap on the lawn, the impact sending a sharp jolt up my spine. A dull thud echoed in my ears as my head struck the ground, and darkness engulfed me as I slipped into unconsciousness.

Chapter Twenty-nine

I was eighteen years old when I was reborn, thrust into an unfamiliar world and embroiled in a conflict whose origins eluded me. Even when the dust had settled, I still struggled to understand what was the truth and what had been the artful fabrications spun by a corrupted narcissist.

The Spirit Borns were aware of the acute threat Beau posed. He had been a stain on our eccentric faction for years, the proverbial bogeyman that had haunted every one of our stories, his malevolent energy casting a continual sense of unease amongst us.

Despite our best efforts, he had always remained one step ahead, a master of deception who lurked around every corner and disguised himself in the murky depths of each twisted shadow.

The hopes for an end to our war with him had rested on my shoulders for some time, relying solely on my fledgling skills as a Spirit Born. Yet internally, I was fighting an unforgiving battle within myself, trying to repel the malevolence living quietly inside me, a formidable demon that I found impossible to exorcise. It was like a tinder box waiting for a single spark to ignite an inferno, and my boundary between control and chaos seemed to blur more and more each day.

As I slowly came to my senses, my eyes stung with tears, and the acrid taste of ash filled my mouth, a tangible reminder of the destruction around me. While I had proven myself a potential asset to the bizarre band of individuals I had fought alongside against The Ungrounded, all that remained in front of me was the bitter taste of defeat, lingering in the air like a palpable presence.

My bloodshot eyes reflected the desolation I felt inside. Each ambitious dream I had nurtured had crumbled into dust, replaced by a profound sense of loss. It was hard to believe that our confrontation would spiral so disastrously out of control or that the price we would have to pay would be so steep, exacting a heavy toll on both sides.

Chapter Twenty-nine

As my vision grew sharper, the smoke billowing from the sprawling property ahead stretched towards me, its coarse tendrils attacking my nose and lungs. The once-clear night sky was now obscured by a dense cloud of black, and the oppressive heat made my skin prickle with discomfort.

As I surveyed the scene, the gravity of the devastation I had wrought upon those I loved registered. Not only had I become everything I despised about Beau, chasing the monster until I became one myself, but I had also failed the war heroes and healers trapped inside Red Rock's towering walls. The sandstone masonry glowed orange and red as flames licked in and out of every blown-out window, painting the night sky with an eerie glow.

In my ambitious fantasies, I had envisioned myself as the fearless leader of The Spirit Borns, the vanguard in our battle to maintain the fragile balance between the living and the dead.

However, my rise to that position had come at a steep price. I was the one person able to defend those I loved, but instead, virtually swaggering with pride, I had led the wolves to their door.

I closed my eyes, muttering in a delirious mantra. "Please, please, please," I whispered. "You can't be gone. You must have made it out."

But as I lay on the dampened grass, feeling the dew soak through my clothes and cool my skin, a howling emptiness resonated from my gut, telling me they were gone.

The daylight had yielded to the darkness, turning the sky into an inky canvas on which the fire could paint its destruction. Its voracious appetite devoured everything in its path, its thunderous roar like a freight train.

As I struggled to expel the smoke from my lungs in hacking throes, I had no desire to escape the flames. My sole impulse was to find my family, no matter how futile or suicidal the endeavour seemed.

I tightened my jaw, my teeth grinding as I growled to myself, forcing my body and mind past its physical limitations. "Move, Harper Reynolds-Woodbury. *Move.*"

I rolled onto all fours, a groan escaping my lips as what remained of my sandy curls fell around my face in bloodied clumps, but it wasn't being half-scalped that hurt.

As the adrenaline in my bloodstream dwindled, every movement sent pain radiating from the ravine-like gash in my thigh, leaving me reeling with nausea as my jeans became sticky with claret.

I tore a strip from my T-shirt and bit my lip to stifle my screams. As I wrapped it around the wound and tied it in place, the property's adjoining structures set alight, and the bare bones of the house were revealed, sticking up out of the flames like disjointed limbs trying to claw their way free of the inferno.

The once bright masonry succumbed to an ominous hue, rendering it unrecognisable. The intricate stone carvings of the aces of hearts, diamonds, clubs, and spades that had lined the gutters like curious gargoyles came tumbling down like children's building blocks, fracturing into jagged pieces at my feet.

A sharp crack cut through the cacophony of sounds as the final shards of the roof gave way. The floors collapsed under the weight like dominoes, one onto another, projecting fragments of burning rubble skywards. Against the backdrop of billowing smoke, the fiery debris glimmered like a swarm of fireflies, creating a breathtaking yet haunting effect.

I gritted my teeth, suppressing the pain and forcing myself onward. I had already lost one of my loved ones to Beau's lunacy, and I couldn't bear the thought of losing any others due to my own.

Feeling soil clogging my nails, I plunged my fingers deep into the lawn. Clenching my trembling hands, slick with blood, around fistfuls of grass, I dragged myself forward, clawing and thrashing like a dying animal as toxic fumes swirled around me.

As I reached the driveway encircling the house, my crawl slowed, and each agonising push felt like a herculean task. The world around me seemed to ripple and distort as I shook my head, struggling to fight off the encroaching unconsciousness.

Physically, I couldn't edge any closer to the flames, but I couldn't summon the strength to turn back, either. I had devoured the last of the adrenaline that had been fuelling my body, pushing through the ordeal, leaving me depleted and suffering in its absence.

Every jarring stab of pain was a reminder of the limitations my injuries had imposed on me as my muscles seized, feeling like iron against my bones.

As I lay dying, I turned onto my back, my anguished cries carrying the names of my loved ones into the boundless sky. Tears cascaded down my face, washing away the soot on my cheeks as my voice grew hoarse. My ash-mottled eyelashes fluttered weakly as my mind fought against my battered body, willing it to survive.

In the distance, the comforting wail of sirens echoed through the valley. However, we were in the middle of nowhere, and the grim reality set in that no rescuer would arrive in time to save me, the house, or those dear to me.

Chapter Twenty-nine

But as I faded in and out of awareness, I found myself grasping onto the sound of a voice, its fraught and anxious tone barely discernible amidst the chaos of the blaze and my own ragged coughing.

The billowing smoke enveloped my surroundings, making it difficult to see through the haze. My raw, stinging eyes strained to make out any signs of life amidst the chaotic scene, but the twisted remains of the house stood unchanged, with no one miraculously emerging from the debris. And with the emergency services miles away, nobody had yet come to my aid.

However, I still heard it, the voice growing progressively louder, calling my name.

"This is it," I slurred, my words barely coherent. "It's all over. I'm going home."

The battles I fought, both triumphant and tragic, had led me to the inevitable embrace of death. It was as if it beckoned me back to the beginning of my journey, to a time of innocence and purity when the mistakes I would later make had not yet wrought their trail of utter destruction.

Through the haze of smoke, a figure emerged, her tiny body convulsing with violent coughs as she stumbled closer. Standing over me, her muscles taut with tension, she swiftly threw her jacket over her head, seeking refuge from the relentless advance of the flames.

Despite the heat, her complexion was as pale as the flakes of ash that peppered her ebony hair like snow. Her trembling voice called my name as her unblinking eyes danced across my body. Her gaze lingered on each injury before settling on the telltale charring on my limbs that she had seen firsthand once before.

Her hazel eyes narrowed, blazing with palpable fury. Her jaw tightened, and the veins in her neck stood out like cords, visibly pulsing with each frenzied beat of her heart.

She stood frozen, her hands trembling as she brought them to her mouth, her chest heaving. "Christ, he... he did this to you?" she asked, her voice wavering between shock and rage.

An explosion erupted deep within the bowels of the property, the shockwave rippling through the earth and stunning her into action. She grabbed my ankles, throwing all the weight her diminutive frame granted her into tugging me to safety.

I struggled against her grip like a rabid animal, clawing desperately at her hands. "No, Lola!" I shouted. "They're in there!"

Once we reached a safe enough distance where the flames no longer posed an immediate threat, Lola carefully lowered my legs to the ground. She kneeled, pulled my head onto her lap, and gently rocked me, providing a soothing rhythm that helped counteract the devastation surrounding us.

Her face was a portrait of empathy as her fingers delicately traced a path along the contours of my face, gently brushing away the tears cascading down my cheeks with her thumbs.

Lola's gaze held mine with a gentle intensity. "I know, honey. And I'm so sorry," she soothed. "But Red Rock's boundary's been broken, and the house's foundations will be wrecked. We need to get out of here."

"But they're still inside."

Lola gestured towards the ruins of Red Rock. "Look at this place," she said. "They can't be. Deep down, you know that."

"But... ambulances are coming," I argued, my voice hoarse and unconvincing.

"Yes, but the *police* will be on their way as well, and what would we tell them?" Lola reasoned, her eyes widening. "We can't be here when they arrive."

My bottom lip trembled as the weight of Lola's words sank in. "I can't just leave them," I said.

"I promise we'll come back, but right now, we need to get you to a hospital," she said, concern etched onto her face as her eyes twitched towards the bloodied dressing on my thigh. "Your leg, how bad is it?"

I bit my lip, my entire body tensing in anticipation of the pain as Lola gently pulled the makeshift bandage free. The jagged six-inch-long cut had soaked my jeans, turning them a vivid shade of crimson that infused the smoky air with the sickeningly sweet smell of arterial blood.

Lola recoiled, swallowing hard as her eyes widened. The concern on her face mounted, teetering on the brink of panic. "There's so much blood," she said. "How long has it been like this?"

Her words sounded muffled and indistinct as if I were submerged underwater. The world around me took on a surreal quality, with colours and sounds blending together in a disorienting kaleidoscope.

Lola tore off her studded belt and used it as a makeshift tourniquet. As she wrapped it tightly above the wound to stem the flow of blood, she noticed my eyes shifting in and out of focus, alternating between moments of clarity and haziness.

Chapter Twenty-nine

Her voice grew louder as she tapped my cheeks roughly, her face inches from mine. "Harper, stay with me!" she yelled. "Come on. Let's get you up, okay? We need to leave."

I howled as Lola dragged me to my feet, wrapping my arm over her shoulder and gripping my waist to stabilise me. Pulling her phone from her back pocket, her fingers trembled as she dialled.

Lola spoke into her phone, her voice clipped with panic. "I've got her, but it's bad. I don't know how she's even alive right now..." she stammered. "No, she was alone. He's still out there... Yes, hospital...now."

As Lola finished the call, my vision swirled, mimicking the smoke encircling us. My head slumped backwards as my body folded into Lola's like a marionette abandoned by its puppeteer and freed from its strings.

Lola begged me to stay awake, her voice low and urgent, as if she was trying to keep me tethered to life. As her pleas faded into the distance, I wanted to fight it, but it was like trying to hold back the tide. The darkness crept in, tugging at the edges of my awareness, eroding the boundaries of the world around me until they gave way.

There was peace only in the sweet relief of unconsciousness, a blissful nothingness that was a welcome respite to the pain and sorrow as Lola's voice faded into a whisper. "Just hold on."

Chapter Thirty

The sharp, artificial scent of antiseptic assaulted my nostrils, jolting me awake. As I slowly opened my eyes, the sterile hospital environment came into focus. The distant, tinny echoes of a PA system crackled in the hall as the rhythmic beeping of the heart monitor at my bedside provided an almost hypnotic soundtrack to my awakening.

Turning towards the machines pumping medications into my arm, I winced as dried blood from my raw scalp stuck to my pillow, leaving spots of crimson on the crisp, white linen.

On the windowsill were two dozen cards, with small bouquets of wilting flowers that offered the small room its only colour, and boxes of half-eaten chocolates.

Each breath I took under the oxygen mask was accompanied by a faint wheeze, and though my limbs hurt, it was bearable. The morphine drip had enveloped my mind in a fog, dulling my senses and easing the pain in my thigh to a distant throb.

I slowly extended my limbs, wincing at the ache in my muscles. My left arm was encased in a bulky cast adorned with names and whimsical doodles from twelve Spirit Borns, restraining my range of motion.

As I retraced the events in my mind, I envisioned the injury occurring when I was flung across the lawn. However, the fact that I didn't sense the break at the time left me pondering what other hidden injuries I might have sustained during the incident.

I gingerly tugged down my overly starched blankets. My hospital gown exposed one leg, appearing mostly healthy, save for some blackish discolouration towards my feet and branch-like burns like the ones I had suffered after the rollercoaster incident. The other leg was bound with thick surgical bandaging that extended from my knee to my upper thigh.

Under the haze of pain relief, it took me a moment to notice Hunter fast asleep in a chair. Slouched over the end of my bed, his head rested peacefully on his folded arms as if standing guard over my slumber.

Chapter Thirty

His eyes seemed swollen, with bruise-like shadows hanging heavily beneath them. His hair was unkempt, and his well-groomed stubble had been replaced by a virtually full-grown beard.

Glancing at the side table, I noticed Hunter's laptop nestled among a stack of invoices and a collection of crumpled receipts. The sight painted a vivid picture of him managing his business from my bedside. Considering the extent of his makeshift workspace, I couldn't help but wonder just how long I had been there.

As I laid back and tried to make myself comfortable, I noticed Kay, also asleep, in a stiff-looking armchair in the corner, her head leaning uncomfortably against the wall.

She bore no resemblance to the Handler I knew. Her face was devoid of makeup, her complexion pallid. Despite her natural beauty, she looked as exhausted as Hunter.

Her unwashed hair cascaded around her shoulders in dishevelled tangles, and she was dressed in the same outfit I had seen her wear on the night of Beau's attack, now wrinkled with coffee stains on the front of her blouse.

Surrounded by a mass of empty paper cups and vending machine wrappers, she had a cheesy-looking romance novel lying open on her lap.

I coughed, tugging off my oxygen mask, but my hoarse voice was no more than a whisper. "Hunter," I said.

Kay's soft and gentle voice caught me off guard as she whispered, "Let him sleep."

My gaze locked with Kay's, and I saw a profound vulnerability in her eyes that I had never seen in her before.

"He doesn't sleep at home," she whispered. "He only rests here when he's with you and knows you're safe."

She silently lifted her chair and carried it to my bedside, fluffing up my pillows and readjusting my oxygen mask, ensuring it sat comfortably on my face.

"You need to keep this on for a few more days," she said gently. "You took in a lot of smoke."

"How long have I been here?" I asked.

She glanced upwards thoughtfully. "I think this is... day six, maybe seven? The days have sort of blended into one long nightmare, honestly." Tenderly, she smoothed the hair out of my eyes and continued. "They had to keep you sedated after surgery so the nicked artery in your thigh could heal, and they were concerned about a bleed on the brain."

"Couldn't Amy just fix me?" I asked.

"When Lola brought you in, she was in surgery, and treating you couldn't wait," Kay explained. "And once you'd been seen by other doctors, if you suddenly made a miraculous recovery, people would notice. But she's been coming by regularly to help get you home faster."

I held up my cast. "And my arm?"

"You don't remember breaking it?" Kay frowned.

I shook my head, shrugging.

"Well, you did a proper job on it."

"You know I don't do things by halves," I smirked.

"It's broken in four places and needed a pin put in during your second operation. But it'll heal," Kay nodded.

Kay delicately cradled the fingers poking out of the end of my cast, and her expression softened with surprise and relief as I didn't recoil from her touch.

"Harper, I'm so sorry about your family," she said, her features softened by a compassionate smile. "And about Red Rock."

"How did Lola even know I was there?" I asked.

"When you weren't there when she came back for you, and your phone kept going to voicemail, she was worried," she explained. "Lola searched the house and found Beau's note crumpled in the hall. She thought you'd left it as a clue."

I shook my head again.

"Then it's lucky she found it. The doctors said she got you to the hospital just in time. Do you... want to talk about it?" she asked slowly. "If not, then..."

"No," I interrupted. "It's okay."

"So, Beau destroyed Red Rock?"

I shifted, my teeth grinding as I looked down and picked at the rough edges of my cast, my eyes swelling with tears.

Kay sighed, bowing her head. "I see," she said. "But in Beau's presence? How?"

I half-shrugged, my voice barely audible as I struggled to speak. "I reached my core," I whispered, my words filled with shame.

"Alfie?"

Chapter Thirty

I nodded sullenly, my eyes cast downwards. "Beau wanted me to get rid of The Handlers in exchange for my family's afterlives, but I refused."

Kay squeezed my fingers. "Good girl," she beamed. "You brave, brave thing."

"He attacked me, but I managed to get away, losing half my hair in the process," I said, wincing as I ran a hand over the enormous bald patch. "I got pinned escaping through a window. Beau was on one side with this knife, and Alfie was on the other. I'd no way out. I swear, I didn't mean for it to happen."

"Shh, I know," she soothed.

"Beau told me about my first year. He knew Alfie was involved because Hannah told him years ago, so he thought I'd die either way, either under his knife or if Alfie touched me and was passed on before I reached my core. But if I had died and left my family unprotected, Beau would've destroyed the rest of the family."

Kay's brow furrowed as a wave of guilt washed over her. "He told you?" she said. "I'm *so* sorry we weren't honest. We were just so desperate to save you. It's why we kept Alfie hidden."

"Where, though?"

"He was always with you," Kay smiled, nodding. "I told him we knew his touch was involved in helping you reach your core, meaning whatever happened, he'd have to go to The Infinite for you to live. But, of course, that was an easy choice for him. He returned every day to spend his last days with your family, but he moved into your cottage to give you space until you were truly ready to... let him go."

I shuddered involuntarily as the sound of Beau's twisted voice seemed to echo in the depths of my mind. *"You're just too close to the problem, sweetheart."*

"When I saw Alfie disappearing," I continued, "I lost it. But I didn't want to kill him, not initially."

"But Harper, he was already dead. And there was nothing you could've done to save him. He'd already hurt Holly too much. He was always going to end up in The Infinite eventually."

"Not Alfie," I whispered, shame enveloping me as the weight of my words settled heavily on me. "Beau."

I felt shame enveloping me as the weight of my words settled heavily on my conscience. "Not Alfie," I whispered. "Beau."

Kay's eyes widened as she gasped, cupping her mouth. "Beau's dead?"

"When Alfie touched me, I felt... enraged," I confessed. "Everything around me crackled like the air was on fire. I just cried, reaching into the sky, and it was like..."

"Lightning?" Kay interrupted.

"How did you know?"

"When Lola brought you in, we spun the doctors a story about a bonfire gone wrong, but one of them said that if he didn't know any better, he'd assume you'd been struck by lightning."

"If Hannah saw it, why couldn't you tell me?"

"Because it was so entrenched with Beau that nothing was clear. We only knew that Alfie's touch would help you, but it was obviously something you'd only have one shot at, so until you were ready, we couldn't risk Alfie getting close to you. We only planned to hide him until you were stronger," Kay explained, her voice breaking. "It was an impossible situation, but I couldn't have lived with myself if we'd lost you."

"It's okay," I nodded. "Once Beau told me the truth, things made sense. But if I'd have just known the risks..."

"You'd have passed him on anyway," Kay interrupted. "You'd have rather died than risk Alfie killing anyone. It's just who you are. But I understand if you hate me for keeping it from you."

"I don't hate you, Kay," I whispered, slowly shaking my head as I squeezed her hand, dulled pain shooting up my broken arm under the strain. "Now I've seen how violent, how evil Beau is... I understand more than you know."

Kay sniffed loudly, pulling a crumbling tissue from her pocket and dabbing her eyes.

I frowned, a slight smirk on my face. "Kay, are you *crying?*"

She let out a strained chuckle. "If you ever tell anyone, I'll kill you."

Seeing her display genuine emotion was refreshing, and her relief that our hostility had been resolved was evident. Kay had made some undoubtedly questionable choices, but after Beau's revelations, I knew she had made them for legitimate reasons.

"So, Beau's really gone?" Kay asked, a clear hint of disbelief in her voice. "We figured you'd tried to stop him, but with Red Rock in ruins and you on death's door, we assumed you'd failed. We've had people stationed with you around the clock in case he showed up to finish you off."

"He's gone. I watched him burn," I nodded. "But I promise I didn't want to kill him, not until Alfie disappeared into The Infinite. I just wanted

Chapter Thirty

to escape and lead him away from Red Rock. I told Lola I'd kill him for what he did to Hunter, Dominic, and Hannah, but when he described Laura's murder, I knew I could never do that. At least I *thought* I could never do that."

My bottom lip quivered as my vision blurred with tears.

Kay squeezed my hand, her eyes fierce. "He was trying to kill you," she said. "Even in the eyes of the law, it's self-defence."

"The law?" I chewed my nails, still tasting like dried blood and soil. "They'll know I was there."

"Shh, you're fine. The CCTV was destroyed, and the house is gone, there's nothing left," Kay said. "A garage full of gas tanks exploded and destroyed the remains of Red Rock. And Lola's been checking the police's evidence lockers to ensure there's nothing on you. You're safe; there's been no mention of a body in the house."

"Has anyone searched for my family yet?" I asked.

"Not yet. We thought that would be an assignment you'd want to run yourself when you're back on your feet." Kay smiled, cocking her head. "We can help ensure they're sent to The Infinite peacefully."

My answer was immediate as my brows drew together. "I'm not sending them to a place I don't understand," I said. "Red Rock's in the National Trust, so with any luck, it'll be rebuilt. And when it is, I want to try and get my family home."

"But sweetheart, they've been ungrounded," Kay answered.

"So was Alfie, and he managed to hang on."

"That was a unique situation. Hannah had a vision of his ungrounding happening, and The Handlers intervened, dragging him home before much damage was done. That's how he made it back to Red Rock," Kay explained. "But being ungrounded for a few hours pales in comparison to being ungrounded for days... or even weeks."

"I know it's a long shot, and I understand it's not been done before, but if Beau succeeded in leading all those Ungroundeds to Ettington, there's no reason to suggest we couldn't return my family to Red Rock in the same way."

"And then what? How will you keep them there?" Kay asked.

"I don't know," I sighed. "Maybe The Ungrounded just need to be reminded of who they are?"

Her eyes narrowed, but her tone carried a hint of genuine curiosity. "You really think that'd work?"

"I've no idea," I shrugged. "But I'm responsible for this mess. I have to at least try and fix it. I just think there's something we're missing here. Every Ungrounded I've encountered has held onto a fragment of their identity."

"But the house is gone," Kay said. "And it'll be months before it's rebuilt."

"The gamekeeper's cottage must still be standing, right? If we create a new boundary, we can keep them there until Red Rock is finished," I said.

Kay nodded slowly, rubbing her chin. "It's an interesting plan. With your talent, your family would undoubtedly follow you," she said. "Especially now you've reached your core. But how will you ensure they stay? It's unhealthy for you to remain at Red Rock alone to keep them there."

"I don't know. EM pumps, maybe?" I shrugged. "We'll figure something out."

Hunter stirred at the foot of my bed, stretching his arms and swatting receipts and papers over the floor. As He worked out the kinks in his shoulders, he leaned over me and kissed my blanketed feet, half asleep and oblivious to the fact that I was awake and smiling down at him.

As he wearily rubbed his eyes, he crumpled a discarded receipt into a tight ball and casually tossed it into the area Kay had been sleeping in. As the paper landed, the rubbish littering the floor surrounding her corner suddenly made sense.

He stretched his arms above his head, arching his back as a long yawn escaped his lips. "Coffee?" he asked.

Kay and I remained silent, watching his adorable sleepiness.

"Oi, Kay... coffee?" he repeated louder.

He finally opened his eyes and focused on Kay's corner. Noticing her absence, a sudden alertness overtook him. Panic etched across his face as his body tensed and his back straightened. With a sharp breath, his chest expanded as his face immediately shifted towards me.

His emerald eyes, the amber fragments within them sparkling, locked onto mine. A relieved smile softened the tension in his cheeks, and his shoulders visibly relaxed as he moved towards me, his arms outstretched. However, he hesitated.

He dropped his arms, gently biting his lower lip. His gaze wandered over each of my injuries, the crease on his brow conveying his concern about causing me more pain by drawing me into his embrace. There wasn't an inch of me that hadn't been bruised, broken or burnt.

Chapter Thirty

He leaned over the tangled tubes and wires surrounding me like a dishevelled spider's web and sighed shakily as he tenderly pressed his forehead to mine.

His voice was hoarse as his hand carefully caressed my neck. "Where have you been, H? You've been hiding somewhere I couldn't reach," he purred, his breath warm on my skin. He pulled away, his face inches from mine as he stared into my eyes. "Don't you *ever* do that to me again."

He stepped back and flew into a frenzied whirl of fussing, adjusting my pillows and blankets. With trembling hands, he poured water into a beaker as the room's lighting flickered erratically. But in my depleted state, it was glaringly obvious that Hunter was to blame.

"Are you thirsty or in pain? Should I get a nurse?" Hunter rambled, holding the beaker towards me, its contents sloshing up the sides. "Or a doctor's better, right? I'll find a doctor.

"Calm down. Look, I'm okay," I smiled, patting my bed and shifting my aching body to make room for him. "Relax, you look exhausted."

"I'm not the one that's refused to leave," Hunter said, nodding to Kay. "They've tried kicking her out every night, but you can imagine how that went. So, if anyone asks, she's your mother."

"I'm not the one who's been refusing to eat," Kay remarked, nodding back at Hunter.

I chuckled. "I see you two are finally getting along."

"We've a... mutual interest," Kay smirked. "That said, now you're awake, I'm going home to take a very long shower."

"Finally," Hunter teased. "I told her two days ago that she reeked, but she still hasn't budged. I've been spraying her with deodorant in her sleep."

"Uh, thanks for that," Kay said slowly, frowning at Hunter. Their wry smiles hinted at a sense of camaraderie that had developed while I was unconscious, as if they had finally found common ground.

Kay slipped on her heels and lingered in the doorway. "I'm *unbelievably* proud of you. Everything you went through," she said, shaking her head. "I didn't realise people could be that strong."

As I recounted my ordeal to Hunter, he begged forgiveness for not being there, his guilt building and receding like the tide.

However, Hunter's presence gave me the courage to share intricate details I hadn't disclosed to Kay.

I vividly described Alfie's serene expression when he disappeared into The Infinite and the stark contrast of the fear ingrained on Beau's face. And I confessed that I was already finding it impossible to shake both haunting images from my mind.

In the few hours I'd been awake, Beau's eyes already haunted me. His gaze resembled that of a lost little boy, frightened and alone. That imagery seared into my memory forced me to question the morality of my actions and how they would inevitably change me.

Despite Hunter's reassurances, I couldn't fight the overwhelming regret that consumed me. If I hadn't sought such destructive vengeance, Red Rock would still be standing, my family would be safe, and I wouldn't be crushed by the weight of the guilt stemming from taking a life.

As the evening progressed and darkness settled outside, I was drawn into Hunter's protective embrace. The undamaged but tangled side of my hair, still carrying the potent aroma of smoke, cascaded gently over his broad shoulder. Meanwhile, his sturdy work boots were casually crossed on the edge of the bed.

Eventually, the nurses reached the end of their patience with Hunter's persistent pleas for "just five more minutes." Despite his considerable charm, they ultimately insisted that he leave and go home.

Since I had been admitted, even with Kay never leaving my side, Hunter had been convinced that Beau would descend on the hospital when we least expected it.

Every day, he would arrive long before he was allowed onto the ward, eyeing his watch impatiently as he waited to be let in and stayed long after visiting hours ended.

Every Spirit Born had taken turns guarding me, spending hours at my bedside with Kay whenever Hunter needed a break. Even Sawyer and Beck had helped, which was probably where the adolescent cartoon penis on my cast had come from.

But now that Hunter knew I was out of danger and that Beau was no longer a threat, he could finally rest peacefully.

Chapter Thirty-one

In the hushed stillness of the sleeping hospital, I found myself standing alone in my small ensuite, unable to sleep. In my hands were the clippers I had requested from the nurses to confront the tangled mess left of my hair.

Before a fleeting rise of uncertainty could take over, I turned them on, feeling the vibrations course through my hand as their hum filled the air.

As I took a deep breath and steadied my hand, I slowly guided the buzzing clippers over my head, fully embracing the imminent change. The sharp, metallic sound of the blades meeting my hair reverberated through the room, each pass marking not only a physical alteration but also a profound shift in my mindset.

Despite being tainted with specks of blood and dirt, the hair on my left side remained resilient and healthy, and it seemed a shame to waste it. With careful precision, I meticulously trimmed the stray strands sticking up from the bald patch and refined the edges.

Stepping back, I turned my head from side to side, examining my work. It still looked and felt painful, but the section of my hair I had removed formed a neat, moon-shaped pattern around my right ear, encompassing about a third of my head.

If it weren't for the tender spots, it could have easily passed for a deliberate and edgy haircut. As I set the clippers down, I pictured myself embracing the bold look once the healing process was complete.

As I drifted off to sleep, a sense of satisfaction washed over me. However, as soon as I closed my eyes, my mind was flooded with memories I wished I could erase.

Throughout the night, I tossed and turned restlessly, feeling as though Beau's lingering presence permeated the room. It was as if his spectral figure was whispering into my ear, taunting me for becoming the new and improved monster who had destroyed her own family.

The following morning, I was exhausted, roused by Hunter desperately trying not to wake me as he juggled his laptop and my weekend bag.

His imposing figure in the relatively cramped space caused everything he touched to shift out of place. He cursed under his breath, reprimanding the inanimate objects around him, much like a partner returning home drunk after a night out.

After watching him awkwardly rearranging cards on the windowsill for a few moments, I cleared my throat. Startled, he turned towards me, inadvertently knocking the cards down once again.

"Careful, you'll wake the dead," I teased.

"Sorry, H," he purred. He stooped down to kiss my forehead and gently ran his hands over my hair. "What happened? You get halfway and chicken out?"

"It was actually intentional."

"I love it," he grinned. "Very G.I. Jane."

"I thought you'd hate it," I said, picking my cast.

"Stop that," he said, gently swatting my hand. "It's off in a couple of months. And sweetheart, you could wear burlap sacks for the rest of your life, and I'd still find you attractive."

"Did you get much sleep?" I asked.

"Knowing you were okay and that... *he* was gone, I ate a probably unhealthy amount of Chinese food and slept like a baby."

Hunter was very careful not to mention Beau's name aloud or delve into the specifics of the fire. Instead, he always chose to refer to it as "that night" or "you know".

I sincerely appreciated his wariness. Even hearing Beau's name in my head made my stomach twist into knots. My guilt already enveloped me like a heavy blanket, and hearing his name only added weight to it.

"More importantly, how did *you* sleep?" Hunter asked, popping a pillow under my cast.

"Not bad."

Hunter arched one brow as he popped a pillow under my cast and perched on the edge of the bed. "Now, let's try the truth," he said.

"Just bad dreams," I sighed. "I heard *his* voice whispering like he was in the room."

"That's understandable."

Hunter cradled my face in his hands as I closed my eyes and leaned into his touch. I didn't want to talk about Beau or my vivid dream surrounding him, so I was grateful when I heard the rhythmic clicking of Kay's heels cutting through the air.

Chapter Thirty-one

She swept into the room looking fresh and polished, but she'd left her glossy, auburn hair tumbling in bouncy waves around her bust.

Despite her familiar appearance, her demeanour had a newfound softness. Her eyes, usually guarded, now sparkled with a sense of peace. With the absence of fear from Beau's retribution, her open posture and warm expression exuded an aura of hope.

"I've just met with the other Handlers," she announced, smiling eagerly. "Now, we'll have a bit of mopping up to do after Beau's antics..."

My body reacted involuntarily as I flinched and swallowed the bile rising in my throat at the mere mention of his name. Hunter, noticing my discomfort, gently squeezed my hand, offering silent support.

"...but without him creating more Ungroundeds," Kay continued, "we've agreed that the entire team can be devoted solely to finding your family and getting them home."

I blinked repeatedly. "That's incredibly generous, Kay. I'm sure we'll..."

"There's more." Kay interrupted, waving her hand excitedly, ushering silence. "The National Trust just received a sizable donation to rebuild Red Rock as quickly as possible. We've already contacted Harrison Reynolds-Woodbury, who rebuilt the house after the bombing in the forties, and he has complete blueprints and detailed photographs of each room. Work starts as soon as the land is cleared."

"Damn, Kay, you work fast," I chuckled.

"And Hunter, your company is hired to complete the rebuild....," Kay added. ...fFor which you'll be paid handsomely."

"How did you..." I stuttered, my mouth agape.

"That's Handler's business," Kay winked. "But whatever happens, you'll eventually have the house and your job back."

"Are you sure you can dedicate the entire team to finding my family?" I asked. "Without a job for a while, I could probably just do it myself."

"There's no way I'm letting you do this alone," Hunter said. "And if I'm helping, Lola and Dominic will want to be involved, too."

"You'll need *everyone's* help," Kay said. "We've approved that except for emergency cases and last warnings, this will be what you'll be dedicated to. And there's another thing." Kay paused, smiling as she took a deep breath and squeezed my shoulder. "There'll be no more blanket passing on of The Ungrounded."

I smiled back, reaching upwards and patting her hand. "Thank you, Kay. It's the right call. But I can't expect..."

"The Handlers have a vested interest in this," Kay interrupted. "If you succeed in re-grounding them, it'll change everything. I won't lie; we've no idea how this will turn out, and you need to prepare yourself for what must be done if you fail and they become a problem."

"I understand," I nodded.

"But equally, you need to be prepared if it works. It'll make your jobs infinitely more challenging. But this is what you were brought back to do, Harper...*H*..." she smiled, "...to bring peace to the afterlife."

"So even succeeding could make The Spirit Borns hate me even more," I chuckled. "Great."

Hunter's brow furrowed. "Stop saying they hate you," he said. "After what you did, you're their hero. So now you'll have to learn how to lead them."

"You're kidding. I'm the newbie; I'm no leader." I shook my head, running my hand through the remains of my hair.

Hunter arched one brow, his lips curling into a half-smile. "The newbie who took down the biggest threat we've ever had, single-handled."

"No," I said. "This is too big. I..."

"The assignment is finding your family, right?" Hunter interrupted. "Well, nobody knows them better than you do. It *has* to be you to lead us in this."

"Hunter's right," Kay added. "We'll be relying on you for advice about your family's habits, likes, and dislikes—things that even as an Ungrounded, they could be drawn to or fear."

An image of me standing in front of a whiteboard like the one we'd had at Ettington popped into my head.

In my mind's eye, I could see myself pointing a long stick to various traits listed under photos of my family members while a class of eager Spirit Borns sat attentively, taking notes.

The mere thought of the scene made me start to chastise and berate myself, especially as I looked at my broken body. It all seemed so utterly ridiculous.

I felt like an ancient teddy bear, my stuffing held in place by a few careful stitches, with my worn fur barely intact. The fear of falling apart consumed me, as if just one stitch coming loose would lead to my complete unravelling.

I didn't feel like a leader, and the teary-eyed looks of gratitude that suggested that I was for killing Beau only made me feel unworthy.

Chapter Thirty-one

I had barely gotten out of the confrontation at Red Rock alive. My body felt utterly derelict, and my mind felt ready to fracture. Yet, Hunter and Kay looked at me with all the hope in their eyes of a child on Christmas morning that I could somehow lead our temperamental group.

It was clear that the burden of the emotional and physical pain I was enduring was self-inflicted, yet their faith in me remained unwavering.

Even if I managed to achieve my goal, our methods of working would be permanently altered, and change isn't always easy. It's often exhausting and met with resistance. However, the thought of not helping my family after I had led Beau to their doorstep was inconceivable.

I knew that working alone would greatly diminish my odds of success, so if Kay needed me to become a leader to have a decent shot at bringing my family home, then that was what I would have to become.

For the second time in my short new life, I would reshape myself into something new and persevere, as all the while, the unsettling memories of the man I had murdered and the family I had scattered to the winds tormented me.

Slowly, I drew a deep breath, my chest still wheezing from smoke inhalation. Before considering the consequences or developing any semblance of a plan, I gathered my courage, steeling myself for what lay ahead.

I opened my mouth, forcing confidence into my voice as I gave my response. "What do I need to do?"

NICOLA HODGES

Born in Hampshire, Nicola's journey to becoming a writer has been anything but ordinary. After a brief career in the police, Nicola faced numerous health problems, resulting in a coma and lasting brain damage. With family called to her bedside, she wasn't expected to survive. Yet Nicola not only defied those bleak odds but continued to battle the obstacles that her health limitations presented to her. With an indomitable spirit, she turned her struggles into a powerful narrative from which the Spirit Born series was formed.

Always driven by creativity, after boring her family to death with the seed of an idea, she finally put pen to paper in 2021, pouring her thoughts onto the page and completing every draft in her (infamous) red notebooks. Despite the difficulty of writing with brain damage, she finished Spirit Born in 2022, marking the beginning of an entire series.

Nicola currently lives in Kent and is passionate about inspiring and empowering writers with disabilities. When she's not writing, she can usually be found with her cocker spaniel, H, hiding at her sister's houses or playing endless games with her six nieces and nephews.